# AND THE SUN GOETH DOWN

## Book Two of
## THE VIM HOOD CHRONICLES

THANKS for reading!

T.M.

# AND THE SUN GOETH DOWN

### Book Two of
## THE VIM HOOD CHRONICLES

## TERRY MARK

ISBN: 9781706520337

*To my wife Alisa.*

# INTERLUDE 1
Sunday, March 18, 1917, 8:22 am
Near Fort Wingate, New Mexico

The young soldier dragged himself slowly across the sand on his stomach, scraping his hands on the limestone, his skin blistering in the heat. *Just a few more inches.*

His hand dipped into clear water. He sipped, threw a handful across his face and turned over, staring up at the two-hundred-foot limestone walls surrounding him.

The Liberty Truck broke down west of the Continental Divide just after breakfast. *Got stuck in cactus and sand. Which is funny, because that's all there is out here.*

Orders were to pick up a load of ordnance for destruction back in Albuquerque. Heading back along the Defiance military road to Fort Wingate the truck swerved out of control. He would have to explain to the sergeant about how his truck ran off an otherwise empty road, and then his primary job would be latrine duty forevermore.

At first, he waited a couple of hours for another vehicle to drive by. But then a band of young Navajo appeared off to the north, and a couple of them carried rifles. *Nobody really worries*

1

*about the Navajo anymore. They're drunkards and thieves mostly.*

The years of troubles with the tribes had long passed. But there he sat, alone, in the middle of all that damn empty desert staring at armed Indians. So he ran, thinking he could circle back around to the highway a few miles out. *So much for following the road. Turns out, one plateau appears just like any other.*

He headed west, following the afternoon sun, which beat down on him relentlessly. For the first couple of hours, it beat down on him and he thought he could deal with it. He'd suffered New Mexico for a year and a half walking perimeter, digging latrines and standing in the damnable heat. *I'm going to be okay, right?*

He couldn't handle it. Too soft. No telling how far south or east he wandered, how far still to go. The hundred-plus degree heat and the sunstroke caused him near delirium. *Trail markings.* He staggered forward toward a sandstone bluff. *So thirsty.*

But his luck held, and he ended up here. Rolling onto his stomach he reached for another handful of water. Wanting more, he pulled himself forward. After drinking deeply, he inhaled, filling his lungs with fresh air, water dripping from his face. Licking his cracked lips, he plunged his face into the water. *And here I am.*

He dipped his cupped hands into the water and poured it over his scalding head. He let out a short moan. But the sound continued even as it no longer came out of his throat. He glanced up.

An Aztec warrior wearing the skull of an eagle on his head, festooned with the feathers of a dozen macaws, parrots, and toucamets, stood over him. The warrior lifted the massive club in his hand and brought it down. The soldier rolled aside as it struck down on the rocks. The impossible figure leaned forward and the soldier saw the muscles and veins move beneath its yellowish, translucent skin. *Rotter!*

# INTERLUDE 2
March 18, 1917, 3:44 pm
El Morro National Monument

Theodore Roosevelt, the twenty-sixth President of the United States, stood next to his great bellowing, humped animal, as he wrote in the notebook he kept next to his chest. He preferred to be called T.R. by his friends and Colonel Roosevelt by his men. He had gotten much thinner in his late fifties, after braving most of the Upper Amazon and losing fifty pounds from malaria. The camel hollered again and the ex-president patted it soothingly.

*I have been, I believe, emphatically right, emphatically the servant of the best interests of the American people. In the days when this Republic prized manhood, the motto was "Millions for defense and not a cent for tribute." Now it seems our motto is "Millions for tribute, not a cent for defense." The Great War in Europe is upon us. The only question is whether we make war nobly or ignobly. I shall be profoundly unhappy unless I get into the firing line.*

*Making all attempts at preparation. Spent the last four days training the 1st United States Volunteer Cavalry Regiment. Since appropriate cavalry or training grounds exercises are long-delayed, I*

> *brought the first two battalions of the formation*
> *to the National Monument I founded in El Morro,*
> *though they are not yet full strength. The terrain*
> *is ideal for open trench warfare and we com-*
> *mandeered a herd of a hundred and fifty Camelus*
> *dromedarius.*

T.R. glanced up as two soldiers approached on camelback. Captains John Groome, of Pennsylvania, and Seth Bullock of South Dakota, both saluted. They wore the same khaki desert fatigues as the ex-president, with USVC patches on their collars and lapels. Each carried a British SMLE slung over his shoulder. Every soldier in the USVC divisions carried the exceptional British Lee-Enfield rifle that not even the U.S.Army possessed, given the ex-president's relationship with the Royal Family.

"Colonel Roosevelt, the men return from their march." Captain Groome lowered his salute.

"Excellent, Captain. Instruct your men to extend the latrine another ten yards and the fence posts another hundred yards in every direction. Captain Bullock, rotate your men up to the oasis by the squad and bring back water for the evening meal while they finish constructing the second barracks."

"Any word from Washington?" Captain Bullock asked flatly.

"Nothing yet from the red-tape and pipe-clay school, who are hidebound in the pedantry of wooden militarism. They are short to understand we need a flag on the firing line as soon as possible," T.R. said as he pulled out a USVC bandana and wiped his forehead. He checked the dampness, watching for heatstroke. "We owe it to humanity."

Sounds of gunfire came from the base of the sandstone bluffs, near the water hole. T.R. rose to his feet. More gunshots and shouts. Captains Groome and Bullock urged their camels into action with riding crops. The ex-president climbed on his camel as it raised on its hind legs. He swayed in the saddle as it got to all fours and took off at a gallop to follow the others.

# INTERLUDE 3
March 18, 1917, 4:05 pm
Two miles from Shakespeare, New Mexico

Ernest Hemingway rode the Santa Fe Trail line all the way to El Paso. Once he'd arrived he'd found a caravan of pilgrims. They were on their way to St Patrick's Church on the other side of the Arizona border. Just outside of Hachita, they said goodbye with a sack of hardtack and jerky and a skin of water. He stuck them into his duffel bag with a smile. They promised to look for him on their way back in a few hours. *Sure were generous.*

Ernie waved at the pilgrims as they moved on. *Hello, Shakespeare, New Mexico. My first big assignment as a beat reporter for the Star!*

The railroad missed the lost little town by about three miles on its way to Lordsburg, but it's silver mine kept the hardy souls who stuck it out alive. Rumors started a diamond rush in the 1870s and nearly killed the town once. When the dust settled and no diamonds were found, people not shot or arrested had fled.

*A wagonload of supplies made its last regular route up to Shakespeare over a week ago. No one has seen it since. And no one has heard from anyone in town in over a month.*

He followed the signs from the main highway for over two miles before he saw signs of civilization. A water pumping windmill stood high above the town as a marker, dead calm in the afternoon air. *When I grow up I want to write and travel.* He laughed to himself. *I wrote that at the age of nine. No wonder I'm in this mess. I want to be a hunting guide or a forest ranger.*

As he got closer, he saw the town stood still. Nothing moved. He stopped in the middle of a four-way crossing. A railroad pole with the x-shape "railroad crossing" stood at one corner, but Ernest could not see any remnants that railroad tracks were ever laid.

On the main street, he peered into the window of a building with a sign marked "bar" hanging in front. He didn't see anything inside. No movement. Further down, the JP Holland General Store resembled a mausoleum. He walked in. The bell at the top of the door announced his entrance. Not another sound. He walked up to the counter, looked over the candy, picked a handful of horehound hard candies and stuffed them in his pocket.

"Hello?" he called out. "Customer!" he yelled louder.

At that moment, he heard movement outside. He rushed to the door. Flinging it open, he stepped outside with a huge welcoming grin.

An Aztec Warrior stood in full battle gear in the dusty street, a jade lip plug and a headdress made from the skull of a jaguar. Jagged scars across the warrior's chest and one arm looked completely out of place.

The warrior raised a blowgun up and gave a sharp huff.

Ernest jerked his head aside just as a dart sang past and embedded in the doorframe behind him. He ran. *Grandmother's shoes, don't fail me now.*

# INTERLUDE 4
March 18, 1917, 5:15 pm
El Morro National Monument

The USVC soldiers approached the base of the sandstone bluffs in screen formation, with riflemen on camelback providing cover as foot soldiers leapfrogged forward. The surrounding dune led down into the oasis. As the soldiers came to the edge of the rocky drift they heard a scream.

The Aztec warrior wearing a giant eagle headdress pulled a soldier in green fatigues away by the collar. Several USVC soldiers fired down, striking the warrior. The Aztec dropped the man, turned an and let out an inhuman howl. The captive conscript on the ground tried to crawl away. The eagle warrior raised his club and brought it down on the soldier's back, lifted him with one arm and carried him away.

T.R. came up behind the soldiers, to the edge of the bluff. He saw the intricately dressed Aztec warrior drag the screaming soldier into a limestone passage. He shouted, "Forward men!"

Urging his camel into action with his riding crop, he rode down the side of the bluff into the oasis, bouncing up and down in the saddle. "Do not shoot if it can be avoided, but never miss!"

At the south side of the escarpment, the ex-president and his Volunteer Camelback Brigade came upon several Aztec warriors in different headdresses waving bows and clubs. They seemed odd, an opaque yellow hue to their skin, their limbs misshapen.

7

The loosed arrows couldn't scale the cliff walls, fishtailing before they could reach their targets. The USVC fired their SMLEs back. Several warriors dropped.

"Captain Groome, take your brigade around the crags to the right." T.R. proclaimed as he moved to the left and down the slope leading them to the oasis.

Groome and his squad moved off. They made their way to the entrance to the carnage where they found several strange bodies. One wore a wooden helmet, and featherwork adorned the head and arms of another.

The ex-president stopped five yards from the first body. Sergeant Hamilton Fish rode past him and dropped down off his camel to inspect one of the Aztecs with two gaping chest wounds. As he knelt down, the Aztec sprung to life, gripping the USVC by the neck with one hand and bringing an obsidian blade up into his neck with the other.

Sergeant Fish stood up, staggered, and collapsed. Three USVC soldiers brought up their weapons, The warrior sat upright and stared at them, getting to his feet. Shots rang out. The amber-skinned warrior staggered but continued to rise.

T.R. shouted "Sergeant!", jumped down off the camel, pulled out his sword with the Navy sharkskin hilt and with one furious swipe removed the Aztec's head from its shoulders.

Slowly, the other Aztecs on the ground rose. One opened his mouth and let out a low, hungry moan.

"My god, it's a rotter!" TR exclaimed.

The soldiers around him fired. They struck the Aztecs directly, but they did not drop.

"Killing them is like nailing jelly to the wall!" The ex-president exclaimed. "Fire!"

The soldiers around him fired another salvo.

# INTERLUDE 5
### March 18, 1917, 5:29 pm
### El Morro National Monument

The terrified soldier on the ground screamed again. The foul-smelling figure dragging him would not let go. A hand gripped his neck like a vise. He kicked, he twisted, but he could not get free. The huge nightmare dragged him through a dark passage and Sgt.out into the sunlight again. To his horror, several more of the warriors stood at the entrance, two with fierce eagle headdresses and powerful wooden clubs with jade blades jutting out of their edges. He yelled and struck out frantically.

They made sounds—moans and grunts. The ancient warrior automatons moved in some uniform fashion, in the same direction, blind to their surroundings. They shuffled and bumped into one another. They trudged forward, schlepping the soldier along as an afterthought. He dug his heels into the dirt, hoping to leave a trail to follow.

The afternoon sun fell behind the cliffs and it grew cool in the small enclosed ravine.

As they rounded the bluffs, a commanding "Halt!" descended from the edge of the ravine, where the hill rose and the wall dropped. The moans from the Aztecs turned into growls and hungry snarls. They raised their jade axes and moved quickly toward the source of the sound.

9

The soldier on the ground twisted his neck, trying to see when a burst of gunfire and a cloud of smoke erupted. He squeezed his eyes shut as fragments of rocks and bodies ricocheted around him.

He lay there for long moments, huddling and shivering. He observed a body lying next to him now. Slowly, he tried to move. But the hand clamped around his throat tightened! He tried to open his mouth but the pain became excruciating and only lessened when he closed his mouth. He laid still. *I'm a basketcase!*

He could hear footsteps approaching. He could make out they were speaking English.

*No! Stay back!* He opened one eye and watched the boots and khaki trousers of a soldier. One boot reached out and kicked at the prone Aztec. His shout came out as a muffled mumble. *Too late anyway.*

The other arm of the Aztec holding him shot out, grabbed his leg and lifted him into the air. The other 'dead" warriors moved at the same time. A couple of shots rang out, a blood-curdling scream, a gurgle, and Sgt.several of the soldiers fired their weapons again.

The rotter holding onto his neck yanked him up, got its forearm around his neck and lifted him into the air, carrying him at a faster pace. He watched as two of the warriors still standing approached the soldiers, swinging their clubs.

The soldiers fired another volley and one Aztec's arm blew clean off. It didn't even slow him down. The arm around his neck tightened and the soldier slowly blacked out.

# INTERLUDE 6
March 18, 1917, 5:55 pm
Shakespeare, New Mexico

E rnie ran back up the street in the direction he first entered the town. *I don't know what the hell is going on, but the Sheriff or the Marshall belongs here. Not me!* He skidded to a stop. Two more Aztec warriors stood at the end of town. One wore a simple wooden helmet. The other warrior wore a Jaguar headdress just like the one behind him. A window in the General Store across the street sat open. Just as he moved, he heard another "Huff!" and a dart embedded itself in the storefront in front of him as he ran. He ran faster, glancing back. One of the warriors raised his bow and readied as if to fire, but he dived through the window before an arrow flew.

Once inside, Ernie went through a door farthest from the window, into a back room, and ascended the stairs. He stayed toward the rear of the building, threw open a window and glanced up. Able to reach the galvanized iron roofing, he stepped on the sill and boosted himself onto the roof.

As his head came fully over the edge, he nearly screamed and let go. A bloody, bloated dead body sat twenty feet away, facing him. The middle-aged corpse wore a smock that said JP Holland, *The proprietor.* The corpse sat with its back against the sign that read JP Holland General Store to those on the street and jutted several feet above the rooftop. A pistol sat next to the dead man, with two shotguns propped next to him and his brains all over the sign behind him.

Slowly, Ernie climbed. Satisfied the deceased would not move again, he raised one of the shotguns. As he glanced at it he shifted his feet so as not to touch the dead guy's leg and he kicked something that rattled. He stared down at a box of shotgun slug shells between the man's legs.

In the street below, two Aztec warriors still shuffled about. *Shooting whitetail in northern Michigan is easy. But these are men...*

He raised the shotgun, picked the nearest staggering warrior and fired. The blast took a chunk out of the Aztecs' left thigh. The warrior didn't flinch and now moved in his direction. *No, not real men. Where is the other one?*

He fired again, aiming higher. This time the slug caught the Aztec rotter in the face and blew off his nose and the upper part of his mouth. It shook its head and kept walking. *Walking dead men...*

Ernie loaded two more slugs and fired again. This time both shots in the same spot. First, he blew off the creature's right knee, then he blew off its left foot. *Not walking so good now.* He heard something and glanced around—scrabbling toward the back of the building.

Sure enough, he found the other Aztec clawing and growling, trying to get onto the roof. The sickly yellowish creature hissed and reached out for him. He reloaded the shotgun, approached the inhuman thing, stuck the shotgun through the maw of the Jaguar headpiece, and blew a hole through the back. The rotter's head sagged and its body flopped off the roof.

# INTERLUDE 7
March 18, 1917, 6:09 pm
El Morro National Monument

T.R. stood over a ghoulish figure on the ground whose right leg kept moving, even though blood and bone were missing below the knee. The right arm, missing below the elbow, oozed greenish sediment—not blood exactly—onto the limestone, as the rotter struggled to stand. It stared at the ex-president with milky dead eyes and let out a long groan. He raised his sword again as the Aztec thing reached out its left hand toward him. He stopped.

The Aztec's left forearm exhibited a tattoo. T.R. peered closer. The design resembled a faded King George V dragon tattoo. He brought the sword across, separating the head and headdress from the shoulders. The torso flopped over and continued to twitch. "This man is a sailor!"

T.R. looked about the carnage in the open square, tall rock formations on three sides. USVC soldiers marched two by two through the passages in the formations with torches. Gunfire could be heard inside intermittently. Desiccated bodies lay strewn about as he stepped around hacked limbs.

Cadaver stitching crisscrossed the torso of one poor creature. The left arm possessed a scar that completely encircled the clavicle and across the chest to include the first and possibly the second true rib, before going under the arm and around the back. The skin tone of the limb resembled a parchment yellowed in the sun. *This arm does not belong...to this man.*

T.R. took his foot and moved the head of the Aztec rotter to make out the face. The mouth sat agape in a final attempt to reach a victim. *The upper left canine. It has gold foil filling.*

The ex-president walked over to another Aztec, wearing a massive eagle headdress and elaborate plumage. Two of his men rolled the body over while two more held rifles at the ready. They pulled the headpiece from the body to find the top of the rotter's skull a pulpy mass. T.R. looked the body over. He pulled back the knitted fabric to find a roadmap of stitching ran across the chest.

"What the hell?" one of the soldiers muttered.

The words HOLD FAST were tattooed across the dead figure's right hand.

Several soldiers wandered out of the caverns, dazed. Others looked quite shaken. Two Volunteers helped another who, on shaky legs, stopped every few steps to vomit.

"Men, there are very strange things afoot. We need to be very clear. We are not facing Aztecs here. These are not some forgotten savages from the primordial." One of the creatures twitched and T.R. kicked the rotter in the head. "These are—or rather were, modern men. Sailors, mostly, from the looks of it, with tattoos and gold fillings. Whatever they did to themselves or what evil and foul practices have fallen upon them, they were men once."

Another series of shots sounded from the other side of the oasis and T.R. moved toward his camel. "Captain Groome's men! To arms, brothers. To arms!" He leaped on the camel, tilting back in his saddle gracefully as the animal reared up in its awkward stance and took off.

# INTERLUDE 8
March 18, 1917, 6:12 pm
Shakespeare, New Mexico

Ernie sat still, afraid he might vomit again if he moved. He ran his tongue around in his mouth and spat out the acid bile. *What the hell were those things? I've got to think clearly. Their hollow sounds, their yellowed dead eyes, worse than watching a suffering buck. At least there's a way out for the creature in pain. The rotter just maintains his misery. Can't get the images out of my head.* He swayed for a moment.

Walking slowly to the edge of the building, he hesitated for several moments, then looked down. Nothing in the street. Streaks of green gore trailed back up the road. *I could just stay here.* He shook his head. *No. The pilgrims are coming back this way. I can't have them looking for me.* He smiled to himself. *Pete Wellington is going to love this story!*

Slowly he made his way down from the rooftop and into the window he had come through.

On the second floor, he found a sink. He stripped off his shirt and threw water over his upper body, scrubbing his face and arms with a bar of soap for several minutes.

If he found a smear of blood on his hands or arms he scrubbed again, vigorously. *I don't know what to do. I'm just a kid. I should be back home with Mother making my dinner. I should*

15

*be hanging with the boys, chasing girls and drinking beers, I need to be anywhere but here!*

He got his shirt and went to put it on. Covered in gore from the exploding head, he couldn't bring himself to wear it. He wadded it up and tossed it in a corner. *This is a Dry Goods Store. I guess I should look around.*

He went into the main store, to the clothes in the corner, and got several white shirts with starched collars. When he found one that fit, he searched for a sack coat that fit him. Visions of the Aztec creature hanging on the side of the building filled his mind. He shuddered. *But there's something about him.*

Ernie went to the back door, cracked it open and looked around furtively. Hearing nothing for several moments he stepped out. There, ten yards away, lay the body of the Aztec rotter whose head he blew off with the shotgun. The creature lay flat on its back, arms and legs splayed out like a snow angel.

He stepped over to the body and gave the helmet a kick like a football back at Oak Park, sending the fanged headgear spinning into the air. Brain matter toppled from the skull. Nothing but fleshy pulp above the Aztec rotter's nose and mouth. *Like momma's jelly back home.*

His stomach heaved, but he held on, studying the rest of the body. On the palm of the brown skin, two branded S's were visible. Slave Stealer. Slave owners branded escaped slaves with the double S, so they could be identified in the future. *This Aztec warrior demon used to be an American slave?*

# INTERLUDE 9
March 18, 1917, 6:23 pm
El Morro National Monument

T.R. led his men on camelback, thundering around the base of the monument, drawing closer to the sounds of gunfire, the smell of blood and the smoke of cordite.

When the detachment broke around the final bend and spotted Captain Groome's brigade, they faced a horrible scene. More than a hundred Aztec warriors charged up the southern hill, bellowing, and growling. Most wore wooden helmet caps, while others were festooned with Jaguar helmets or Eagle regalia. They overran Groome's ranks and several soldiers lay strewn across the center. While the Aztec rotters converged on both flank positions, the ex-president watched the undead move up over the rocky ascent leading south and away from the oasis. Worse, the Aztecs dragged several of his Volunteers away screaming.

The USVC shot constantly into the horde, but the creatures would not drop. Some of the soldiers engaged in hand to hand combat. A Lieutenant managed to decapitate a yellow-tinged warrior with one arm and it—stopped moving.

"Forward!" T.R. shouted, and raised his steel blade in front of him. As he came up behind the first Aztec rotter, he swung and hacked the eagle headdress clean off the shoulders. Three freaks turned from the herd and made their way toward T.R. He buried his blade in the skull of one of them while the other two managed to grab hold of the huge beast under him. The camel cried out, toppling over.

"Colonel Roosevelt!" Captain Groome shouted. "Pull your swords, men!"

The soldiers dropped their rifles and pulled their army swords, charging into the Aztec swarm. One by one, the rotters dropped as the soldiers hacked their way through. Men behind the ex-president descended on the two fiends scrambling over the camel as it kicked wildly on its side. The soldiers hacked until the rotters stopped moving.

T.R. stood up, and Captain Groome's men appeared at his side while the remainder of the Aztec force moved up out of sight to the south. A faint scream for help could be heard. "Let's go!" he shouted as he charged up the rocky hill, Captain Groome and his men right at his side.

They got to the top and looked over. A shot rang out and the Volunteer next to Captain Groome collapsed.

If the Aztec demons were not enough to make the ex-president speechless, this truly did it. He and his men stared as soldiers in two-hundred-year-old Cavalry uniforms rode past.

Indeed, elite Uhlan cavalry, wearing double-breasted jackets with colored panels, armed with lances and pistols, and riding majestic Arabian horses galloped by. The cavalrymen raised their pistols and fired, and the USVC returned fire. One Uhlan cavalryman fell, his lancing hat flying off.

As gunfire drove the ex-president and his men back down behind the hill, the cavalry turned south and followed the Aztec horde. When the ex-president got over to the fallen Uhlan cavalry soldier, he turned him over. Dressed in traditional feldgrau gray wool uniform, he wore a unique symbol on his brightly colored shoulder tabs.

T.R. studied it. *What does a double-headed eagle crest with an F in the shield represent?*

# INTERLUDE 10
April 9, 1241, 4:43 am
Legnica, Silesia

The Mongol army rampaged east for five thousand miles, subduing Russia, Poland and the rest of Eastern Europe. The horde now numbered 60,000 mounted archers on horseback ready to ravage the rest of Europe. On Christmas Day, 1240, Batu Khan, grandson of Genghis Khan, sacked Pest, the largest city in Hungary.

A few months later, his forces converged in a pincer movement, coming north from Hungary, south through Bohemia and west from Russia. Crossing the River Don, they passed into a depression formed between the Carpathian Mountains and the Sudetes which funnels into the heart of Christian Europe and had earned the name "The Moravian Gate." Silesia sits at the western end of the Gate.

The Mongol General Kaidu had initiated his attack several days earlier, burning small villages in his path. The royalty of Europe fielded their entire assembly of Teutonic Knights against the horde. Ten thousand experienced Crusaders from a dozen wars across Europe, Russia, and the Middle East gathered in the valley of the Gate to bring the Mongols to bear at the point of God's sword.

The first morning rays emerged across the sky, though sunrise would not come for another hour. Knights of the Keep stood watch from atop Great Owl, the tallest mountain in the range, the lowlands valley spreading east from their vantage point. The Keep consisted of three concentric walls with flying buttresses running between them and Sudeten cliffs on three sides that encircled three cathedral citadels each five hundred feet tall.

Keep Knights wore thinner, more fitting armor than the Teutonic templars of Europe, with flexible protection on the shoulders and chest, the Silesian crest of a double-headed eagle and an elegant F in the center of a shield stamped on it. A thick woven fabric interlaced with tight chain metal protected the rest of the upper body. More shielding covered the legs across the thighs, flexed at the knees, with woven fabric down to the boots. Each Knight wore an arming sword on his hip and several gun-powder bombs draped across the chest. Assigned in pairs across the breadth of the outer wall, eight-foot-long ordnance leaned against the stone barricade between each team.

One Knight manning the forward most wall position, and a foot taller than the other spoke. "They'll be here soon."

"Yes, can't keep death waiting," the shorter Knight said as spat over the wall and watched it drop a hundred feet.

The Keep Knights observed the Christian templars, adorned all in white with the cross of Christ on their shields, bringing the fight to the Khan's men. But the black mass of the horde contin-ued to push steadily west, ever deeper into the valley, and the Crusaders continued to lose ground. Ever closer to the cliffs of the Keep. As if in response, the temperature dropped and snow fell across the valley..

The stampeding fury of Mongol warriors on horseback, black fur draped over their shoulders, left Teutonic white bodies in their wake. The Mongol army broke through the lines, closing on the Sudeten Range, the Teutonic Knights army split in two. The shorter Knight leaned down and picked up two semaphore flags split in black and yellow and started signaling the Keep.

# INTERLUDE 11
April 9, 1241, 6:17 am
Legnica, Silesia

The Mongol horde collected at the base of Great Owl. In the valley behind them, a few scant pockets of white armor could be seen fighting to their end. Unable to scale the peak on horseback, the Mongol warriors moved in on foot within five hundred yards of the first wall.

The two Knights at the forward position watched with fierce anticipation. A shadow fell over them. They turned and immediately stiffened and made a Roman salute, fist over heart.

There, a Knight well over six feet tall sat astride a magnificent black and white shire steed twenty hands high. Thick protective fabric interwoven with steel mesh covered the rider from neck to boot. A yellow and black double-headed eagle standard with the F shield draped the Knight's chest. The same fabric and mesh adorned the horse down to its haunches.

The rider wore a shining golden helmet that covered the entire head, with a raised ridge running from the top of the crown down the middle of the flat face, telescopic eye lenses and protruding vent-tails at the sides of the mouth.

A volley of arrows darkened the morning sky. They flew over the heads of the Knights on the outer wall and against the second rampart. After the assault ceased, the Golden Knight raised his arming sword. The Knights in front of him picked up the

21

eight-foot-long gunpowder lance between them, synchronous with the other teams across the wall. The shorter Knight placed the weapon on his left shoulder, while the taller soldier stood behind off to the side, prepared to light the fuse.

The Golden Knight looked up and down the wall seeing all the Keep Knights manning their positions, then checked over his shoulder. Black Knights rolled trebuchets into place at every battlement along the second fortification. He stared down the mountain from atop his steed. The Mongols readied another fusillade and closed within three hundred yards, scrambling across boulders and loose shale. The Golden Knight dropped his sword and the valley exploded.

Five pounds of iron grapeshot belched forth from the eight-foot culverins from over 200 positions along the outer wall. The hollow cast iron balls were themselves filled with gunpowder and exploded on impact. The blitz left hundreds of Mongols disemboweled, beheaded, with arms and legs ripped apart. Many of the Mongols caught in the midst of explosions disintegrated into red mist.

Then the trebuchets fired and launched massive metal barrels into the air. The Mongols, shaken from the first barrage, but still pushing forward from the oncoming force behind them, saw metal objects sailing down and tried to move out of the way. The projectiles struck the mountainside, bounced once or twice, and exploded with pressurized fury. The bouncing mines literally vaporized anything within a hundred yards. Even half-ton boulders turned to powder.

So much damage occurred two hundred yards from the first wall, that it started a rock slide further up the mountain where the Keep concentrated its largest boulders. Dozens of them, most weighing several tonnes, had been transported close to the top of the hill and precariously braced into place. As the Knights watched, they broke loose and tumbled down the mountain into the swarm of Mongol raiders with little room to maneuver.

The boulders laid waste to two hundred yards of soldiers in their paths, crushing everything in their wake until gravity slowed their momentum. The horde paused, long enough for the rest of the Mongol army to arrive, and nearly all of it lay in sight of the Keep.

The Golden Knight raised his arming sword again. This time, a hundred yards behind him, huge ballista appeared through massive slits about halfway up the face of the third and final fortification. An arrowhead twice as big as a man's skull poked through. The Golden Knight dropped his sword and loud striking noises rang out over the valley as the ballista launched.

At first, the Mongols sought cover as the giant arrows shot into the sky. But as the weapons flew over their heads, they shouted victory and quickened their pace.

The ballista struck the ground well to the rear of the center of the Mongol advance, cutting off a few thousand Mongol riders still approaching. They spread out every fifty feet or so across the valley floor and went several hundred feet up the sides of the surrounding mountains. Their thick wooden stalks stuck deep into the ground. Then the fuses in them burned down, and they exploded.

The black Knights readied their gunpowder lances again. The Golden Knight raised his sword, dropped it, and thousands more of the horde were obliterated with hollow iron grapeshot. The onslaught paused the invaders long enough for them to notice the blaze behind them.

A searing blue fire burned across the valley. Mongol riders that charged through were draped in agonizing blue flame, while others tried to put the fire out with blankets and water. The flames only spread, and soon men ran about screaming "Greek Fire!" Panic seized the horde.

The sword went up and fell, and the trebuchets launched again. This time, the Mongols retreated. The metallic canisters landed a hundred yards further than before, bounced and exploded.

The Knights on the outer wall could not see any movement down the hill beyond the first hundred yards. The debris, burnt gunpowder, and dirt in the air shrouded everything.

The Golden Knight raised his sword once again. The black Knights readied their gunpowder lances. The horde came charging through the smoke screaming with fury, desperate and rabid.

Ballista struck across the mountainside this time, crisscrossing the swarming mass of Mongols. The missiles exploded, and Greek fire blossomed across the ridge.

The Knights on the front wall fired their gunpowder lances, striking down swaths of the stampede. But still, the mass of frightening humanity came. Mongols, many on fire, reached the base of the outer wall, carrying ropes and ladders, and climbed.

The Golden Knight drew a second arming sword in his other hand and dropped down from his majestic steed. He walked to the edge of the wall and peered down. A ladder appeared. A Mongol appeared over the top of the wall nearby. The Golden Knight struck out, removing the man's head from his shoulders. Then, kicking the ladder aside and holding his swords out, he leaped feet first over the edge.

# INTERLUDE 12
April 9, 1241, 1:04 pm
Legnica, Silesia

The Golden Knight towered above the Mongol warriors around him. Covered in blood spatter and gore, the arming sword in each hand struck out at warriors as they approached. Mongol bodies littered the battlefield amid black Knights of the Keep.

Three Mongol archers stood shoulder to shoulder ten yards away, pulled arrows from their sheaths and fired as one. With his left sword, the Golden Knight sliced through the arrows in the air before they reached him. With his right sword, the Golden Knight hacked the arm off a Mongol prepared to plunge his ceremonial ild into his back. As the three prepared their next volley, the Golden Knight took six steps, beheaded each archer on the left and right, then plunged both swords into the chest of the center man.

The Golden Knight stood still for several moments. Licks of blue flame continued to burn across the mountainside on dead bodies and the sparse foliage that remained. Then, the master of the Keep, the benefactor of his people, and the prince of Silesia removed his helmet. He possessed strikingly handsome aristocratic features, with well-groomed, dark curly hair he wore long, Victor Frankenstein appeared to be no older than thirty. He wore a thin bead of sweat on his brow as he surveyed the mountainside.

25

Frankenstein stepped forward three paces to a dead Knight of the Keep. He knelt and turned the man over to find massive trauma to the chest and arms. Victor looked over his shoulder to several black Knights behind him, pointed at the dead body, and moved on. Black Knights dragged the body back toward the wall.

Further down the mountain, he came across a Mongol warrior moving slowly across the shale rock on his stomach, leaving a trail of blood and gore from his wounds, making his way back down the mountain. Frankenstein plunged his sword into the man's back and he gurgled and stopped moving. Frankenstein found eight more bodies of Knights on the mountainside, indicating three should be returned to the Keep.

To the east, he watched his black Knights pursuing fleeing Mongol warriors through the lowlands valley. One black Knight stepped up to him on his right, watching the receding battle.

"Beg pardon, sire. But some of the men are wondering."

"Wondering..." Frankenstein stated flatly.

"Yes, sire. If the barbarians are routed, why are we pursuing? With the losses inflicted, the horde are fleeing Europe, not to return in our lifetimes."

"If the princes fail, the battle will fall to the King of France," Frankenstein sighed. He put his helmet back on and turned to the soldier next to him. The Golden Knight noticed the man for the first time, missing his right arm below the elbow. "Aders, your arm is missing."

The man looked down at the stump and shrugged. "Yes, sire."

"Let us get back, Aders. There is much work to be done."

"Yes, sire."

"I'll make you good as new before long."

"Thank you, sire."

# INTERLUDE 13
May 1, 1813, 7:17 am
Silesia

The disastrous Russian campaign in the winter of 1812 devastated Napoleon's Grand Army. Following the eastern humiliation, the French retreated west fighting rearguard actions the whole way. In late November, Napoleon left the exhausted remnants of his forces on the west bank of the Oder River to hold together his Confederation of the Rhine and returned to Paris to reconstitute his forces.

By March of 1813, Napoleon raised another three hundred fifty thousand soldiers and marched his new forces to hook up with the remnants of his Grand Army. But the Emperor's new soldiers were inexperienced and he feared a rapid march would be too much for the new recruits. Thus, reaching his destination took longer than expected and the forces allied against Napoleon were about to cross the Oder and reach Berlin first. His Rhine Confederation would be broken and he would be driven back into France.

Eighty thousand Prussians, a hundred thousand Russians, and twenty-four thousand Swedes were on the march trying to link up with the Army of Silesia in Breslau. While Napoleon now fielded a larger army, he ended up slogging through the fields of Saxony trying to reach the Oder on time, fighting running battles with Silesian liberation forces.

On the day after Napoleon reached Brno, Austria, he determined the remnants of his Grand Army should abandon their positions on the west bank. Reports reached headquarters the Russians were crossing the Oder further north and moving on Berlin. Napoleon nearly ordered his new army north to meet the Allies and the remnants of his Grand Army in Leipzig. Then fortune turned for Napoleon.

Marshal Kutuzov, the hero of the Russian campaign and overall commander of the Allied forces, fell ill and died with his troops in Silesia on April 28th. The overall command of the troops fell between the Prussian General and Tsar Alexander, so utter confusion reigned at what orders to follow. Napoleon stood on the same battlefields of his greatest victory, Austerlitz in 1805, with a sense of destiny.

The Allies dithered and Napoleon, hearing of the death of Kutuzov, made a dramatic move. With most of his horses lost in the Russian campaign, he could maneuver on foot. He would pivot east over the Sudeten range and come down right on top of the confused and leaderless Allied forces.

Knocking one or more of his enemies off the field of battle would secure victory for eastern Europe for twenty years. He would retain the lands taken from Prussia and Russia, maintain Germany and the Confederation of the Rhine, and hold his realm in Italy. Then he could turn toward his campaign in Spain. He would cross over the Owl Mountains and into the lowlands valley where the disorganized Allies awaited.

Napoleon moved east and on May 1st reached the outskirts of the Owl Mountains. There, the Emperor encountered an imposing fortress. It literally towered over the entire valley and its three concentric walls were *incroyable*. Marching forward in diamond formations Napoleon created known as *Bataillon Carré*, the French split into four Corps, each with two dozen teams of six valuable horses pulling their twelve-pound Gribeauval cannons.

Speed being of the essence, Napoleon cautioned his field commanders against siege tactics. His failed siege of the Ottoman city of Acre in 1799 impressed upon him the difficulty of taking a determined fortress. They breached the defenses of Acre, after heavy casualties, only to find a second inner wall and resigned from the field. Three walls protected this fortress, each taller and heavier than the preceding one. He needed to get through the valley and he needed to be on the eastern slope of the Sudetes as quickly as possible. This meant instead of taking the castle, a breach merely needed to be made so his forces could navigate through the valley.

Napoleon halted his troops half a mile from the castle. The locals referred to the place as *le garder* with awe and reverence. They also kept their distance. Perhaps a peaceful resolution might be more suitable as long as it came from a position of strength. And so the Emperor went forth on horseback with a small group of his advisors, that they might parlay passage east.

The group advanced to within twenty yards of the wall, but no one appeared. Then they saw a pig being lowered in a basket from the top of the first wall. The basket reached the ground and the pig sprang out and ran directly toward Napoleon and his men.

At that moment, a single soldier in black appeared on the wall. The Knight of the Keep wore thick black fabric interwoven with extremely fine mesh metal over most of the body, with a gray beret. The soldier raised a weapon and several of his adjutants moved toward Napoleon to shield him but he held his hand up. The pig continued to run. The Emperor kept his eyes on the soldier. A brief flash, no smoke or gunshot could be heard or seen, and the pig squealed and skidded to a halt, a bullet through its brain. Then the soldier disappeared. Napoleon returned to his troops, message received.

# INTERLUDE 14
May 1, 1813, 10:22 am
The Western Wall of The Keep, Silesia

T he French configurations operated as autonomous units, each choosing the best approach to reach their final destination when they would be brought together for the final battle.

Once the format ions reached within sixteen hundred yards of the outer wall, the Corps moved their artillery into place, each six to nine hundred paces apart. From his vantage at the center of his forces, Napoleon directed the French round shot toward the western wall.

High upon a tower on the innermost concentric wall, three giant apertures of thick enameled glass watched out over the valley. The panels on each end, divided into five hexagonal sections, were filled with blue, purple, green, yellow or red glass. A single band of white glass rotated horizontally, then vertically in the center. With a Knight holding a flame behind the glass in different positions and the center light aligned horizontally or vertically, the castle possessed a semaphore system of over 8500 words. The lights blinked in rapid succession the coordinates of the French troops approaching.

Three-quarters of a mile up over the Owl Mountains hovered a manned balloon, the torch firing at its center. The Golden Knight adjusted the telescopic lens in his right eyepiece and turned to the semaphore hanging from the side of the balloon, a small version of the Keep communication system. Opening an aperture behind each colored glass panel activated the lens, lit from the flame at the center of the balloon, to send a signal to other forces awaiting his command.

As the first Gribeauval shots slammed into the western wall, the Golden Knight swiveled the semaphore to face the castle. Then, communicating the message to the Keep, he watched.

The second salvo of twelve pounders blew a hole in the western wall. A hundred square feet of masonry collapsed. Shouting "Long live the Emperor!" Napoleon's advance elements rushed forward into the gap.

Revolving portcullis opened up across the second wall and cannon moved into place. The French grenadiers paused when they saw the odd-looking double-barrelled cannon. The Fusiliers leaders barked orders, urging the regiment forward.

When the cannon fired, the result created carnage unlike anything the French had ever seen. A chain connected the cannonballs coming out of each barrel. The barrels were naturally asymmetric in their firing times. Even off a fraction of a second created one ball pulling the other behind it, which then created a dramatic whipping effect. They didn't function as long-range weapons but proved devastating and unpredictable. The cannonballs whipped out and tore up an acre of ground before flying off and slamming into the cliffside. Or they bounced and plowed through hundreds of men before the chain broke and they went in different directions. It created absolute pandemonium.

The cannon exchange between the French forces and the Keep went on for more than an hour and the French Emperor shouted orders, reading the landscape, trying to get enough troops through the breach in the wall to create a passage to the other side. Reports came in of hundreds of casualties. Then the wild, spinning cannonades stopped. Napoleon signaled for his cannons to cease firing also.

Glancing about for a way to maneuver against the imposing walls and the devastating double cannons, the Emperor saw new life on the battlefield. From the ten-foot-wide fissure in the wall poured first dozens, then hundreds of black-cloaked riflemen. Napoleon breathed deeply and smiled. He quickly scribbled several orders and passed them to couriers.

# INTERLUDE 15

May 1, 1813, 12:07 pm
The Western Wall of The Keep, Silesia

The Keep Knights moved forward in close-order formations, in squads of ten or more men, organized around a two-man team. One soldier carried a Congreve rocket launcher and another carried extra rockets. The rockets were not especially devastating or even dangerous, but they were psychologically effective. The other soldiers came equipped with what Napoleon's men discovered to be a superior version of the Austrian air rifle, after retrieving several from the battlefield. The repeating rifles didn't use gunpowder but compressed air. Keep Knights advanced on Napoleon's right flank and the French soldiers pulled back beyond the village of Sokolec.

As the black-clad soldiers advanced, Napoleon signaled his reserve regiments to begin moving up behind him. As at Austerlitz, Napoleon initiated his favorite gambit. Retreat your position, allow the enemy to roll up on your weak side, only to charge up the center and split the opposing forces. This time, Napoleon even sweetened the plan. Ten thousand men hid beyond the cliffs in the Jugów pocket, behind his forces moving back through Sokolec. When his men moved far enough back to draw in the Keep soldiers, the reserve troops would move out quickly and counter-attack. Then the Emperor would spring the trap.

Two miles south of Napoleon's gathering forces on Kalenica Peak—a mere four-hundred-feet shorter than Great Owl—four steam-powered platforms sat, each brandishing a giant gun barrel more than twenty feet long. With the message relayed, the Keep Knights in position on the platforms got to work. They slowly swiveled from their easterly bearing, turned north and settled on a northwesterly alignment into the Jugów pocket before them. The western wall lay north and slightly to the east, with Napoleon in between.

Known as "The Thunder of Archimedes" and based on drawings of DaVinci himself, the steam guns could fire fifteen to twenty-pound projectiles over two miles away. Beneath the iron and copper muzzle breaches an enormous drum revolved. As the steam power pushed through the barrel and another shell fell into place, the guns could fire over fifty times a minute.

Napoleon's flank retreated beyond Sokolec as the Keep soldiers continued to advance. They also started moving more troops into the opening and pushed against Napoleon's flank. The ten thousand men in the Jugów pocket readied themselves for the march.

Then the steam guns fired. They didn't go off with the explosiveness of a gunpowder weapon but their sheer velocity made the valley floor shudder and the French forces staggered with the vicious onslaught. Over five hundred iron projectiles struck the valley floor with incredible force, tearing up the ground and breaking apart bodies.

From his strategic vantage a half-mile from the battle, Napoleon watched as his few remaining organized heavy cavalry units suffered an incredible barrage from the mountain top. His soldiers looked about for a source of the assault but saw nothing. Then they ran for cover. A counter-attack, perfectly timed, turned into a rout.

The Emperor faced increasing pressure on his flank, his men pushed forward into a situation they might not extricate themselves from, and the men behind him were being obliterated.

Napoleon glanced about and realized the situation of his offensive. The Emperor turned and galloped to the scene of the new action, regrouping his regiments for a decisive move. In twenty minutes, the French army turned and started a running march. Napoleon would no longer march east over the Owls and into the flank of the Allied forces. He would take the battle to the Allies in Lützen, over three hundred miles to the north.

As his forces moved off, Napoleon crossed close to the Keep wall. The Emperor never distanced himself from the damage war inflicted. He would often tread the battlefields, Glancing over the bodies of dead loyalists and remark about their families, and the lives they lived. As he rode through he observed hundreds, no, thousands, of Frenchmen dead and dying.

Napoleon stopped his horse, staring out for several moments, silent. He grew ashen. Then the Emperor let out a slow scream, through gritted teeth, one hand tearing at his hair, and put his horse into a gallop.

Keep soldiers with ghastly wounds, missing limbs, torn and shattered bodies, rose and turned back toward the opening in the castle wall. Across the entire battlefield, not a single black-uniformed soldier lay still.

# INTERLUDE 16
November 10, 1914, 11:22 pm
The Great War, Eastern Front

The Russian Silesian Offensive marked the opening of the war on the Eastern Front, launched in September of 1914 against the Austro-Hungarian Empire at Przemy l (sheh-mih-shuhl) and against the Germans at Tannenberg. After initial successes, the Russians pressed on toward Silesia as winter settled in along the five hundred mile front from the Baltic Sea in the north to the Black Sea in the south.

At the start of hostilities, the Ninth German Army under General von Hindenburg moved north from Budapest to attack the Russian flank. Hindenburg pressed into the Fifth Siberian Corps from the south, trying to force a gap between the First and Second Armies. But the heralded German rail transportation lines were several days behind moving troops north and forcing a gap all the way to Warsaw.

In response to Hindenburg's advance, the Russians increased First Army's pace to advance on Łódz, Silesia. On November 10th two hundred thousand men marched to cut Silesia off from the rest of Germany and begin cutting Prussia off from the rest of Europe. The Russians advanced along the natural barrier of the Carpathians, west into the Owl Mountains, which brought them into the path of the Keep.

While Russian forces were normally ill-equipped, the First Army consisted of seasoned troops with plenty of weapons, ammunition, and horse transportation. The First Army also included a battalion of FT-17 light tanks and, even more valuable, a pair of Sikorsky Mourometz bombers.

High up in the center citadel of the Keep, in a room with vaulted windows facing East, a black-clad soldier sat at a desk in front of a telephone condenser and a wall of inductor coils, magnetic detectors and multiple tuners powerful enough for sending and receiving signals from England to Moscow.

The equipment buzzed as the soldier scribbled notes. "Ja, mein Herr. The Russians are not very bright," The Keep soldier shook his head in disbelief. "They are transmitting their troop movements in the open without encryption."

The Golden Knight paced back and forth in the room with anticipation. He stopped at the window as the message continued. A flurry began, with thick and heavy flakes. "Yes, the Russian High Command thinks Europeans are asleep in bed instead of listening."

The room remained quiet, save for the buzzing and humming, for several more minutes. The Golden Knight stared down into the massive courtyard, behind the innermost rampart, soldiers in black uniforms at attention in long rows, silent and unmoving. Hundreds of them waited in perfect formation. The snow fell upon them and not one hand moved to brush it from their faces. Not a single man shifted. Soon a sheet of white powder covered the courtyard. Still, nobody moved.

"Almost perfect soldiers," the Golden Knight muttered to himself.

The radio operator glanced up from his equipment. "They are coming."

# INTERLUDE 17
November 11, 1914, 5:07 am
The Keep

The Russian 76mm guns bombarded the mountain and the outer wall of the Keep for more than an hour before the barrage let up and the Second Army moved in. As thousands of Cossacks, Muslim Turks, Buddhist Kalmyks, and ethnic Russians pushed through the lowlands valley, they stared up the mountain at the fortress that lay before them. The staggering size of the Keep dwarfed the surrounding mountains themselves. Three rings of walls encircled three towering citadels, their massive flying buttresses reaching out into the cliff walls. The Russians to a man were silent as they strode forward in the new-fallen snow. They were confident, assured of an inevitable outcome. There were simply too many of them. Each man looked around himself and found thousands and thousands of other ethnic Russians marching beside him. Then the valley exploded with thundering noise and volleys of gunfire from all directions.

Fifty miles behind the front lines, on a makeshift field outside Warsaw, the pair of Muromets bombers took to the skies with half a ton of bombs per plane.

The Keep soldiers lay behind rows of thick razor wire, minefields, and hundreds of reinforced bunkers, manning Lewis Machine Guns and creating a two square mile killing zone of overlapping machine gunfire. Knowing the timing of the approaching enemy, they were ready.

The light tanks rolled up between the advance units, trampled the razor wire and belched fire with their cannons. Heavy gunfire erupted from the concrete bunkers dotting the mountainsides and cut down dozens of Cossacks every minute. But the .303's bounced off the armor. One of the tanks crushed the barbed fencing in its path, barrelled up the hillside, pummelled one bunker and drove atop another. The concrete box broke apart, crushing the soldiers inside.

Kapitan Lopukhov, of the 4th Don Cossack Division, led his squad of troops up behind the tank atop the crushed bunker, keeping low under the cacophony of cannon fire. The ear-splitting staccatos of machine-gun fire from three sides made hearing anything else virtually impossible.

The ricochets of multiple shots from all directions made him drop to his stomach. The men of his squad did the same. The tank atop the bunker moved forward, it's metal tracks crushing the cement sections into rubble. The Kapitan and his men scurried forward on their bellies behind it, keeping as close to the tank as possible for safety, but not wanting to be squashed flat if it moved quickly.

The tank's cannon blasted away at a fortification about ten yards away on their right. This brought more gunfire from all directions. In response, Kapitan Lopukhov and his men moved back and took shelter amid the shattered concrete and smashed bodies of the destroyed bunker.

They couldn't see anything, hear anything, or fire at anything. Their boots waded and skidded in the human gore at the center of the entrenchment. The stench made several men in the squad vomit. The Kapitan searched the hill for signs more troops would follow them up and proceed in numbers, but every group of soldiers that rushed the mountain were torn to pieces by the triangulated machine gunfire. Only soldiers following the light tanks through the barricades moved anywhere in the tangled ground and thick snow cover.

From atop the first fortification, the Golden Knight observed the machine gun nests, the barbed wire, and the minefields slow the Imperial Russians down. But it didn't stop them. The tanks seemed impervious to everything he threw at them.

# INTERLUDE 18
November 11, 1914, 6:12 am
The Keep

Making his way to the base of the outer wall, the Golden Knight led a small group of his black-clad soldiers through a concealed and fortified passage and out a secret gate hidden in the rocky terrain. Every man carried a satchel on his chest. One by one, the Golden Knight stood before each Keep soldier, pointed to a different Russian tank pounding the hillside, and sent them running down the mountain. He watched his soldiers disappear into the white debris cloud without fear or hesitation. Then a rumble in the sky drew his attention upward.

The light tank silenced the bunker ten yards away then turned left, moving eight or ten feet forward for a better angle on its next target. Kapitan Lopukhova signaled to his men to get ready to advance and turned to watch a running figure, clad from head to foot in black, leap from the side of the hill above them, land at the front of the tank and scramble underneath. Lopukhova only hesitated a moment, in total amazement at what he saw, then the Kapitan waved his arms. The Russian soldiers went to their bellies as a powerful explosion blew the turret off the tank, sending

41

it ten feet in the air. The explosion sent shrapnel a hundred yards in every direction, knocking the entire squad out cold from the percussion of the blast.

Russia named the world's first four-engine bomber, based on a design by Igor Sikorsky, the Muromet. Originally conceived as a luxury aircraft, they were built with insulated passenger booths, comfortable chairs, and even a toilet. Reconfigured for long-range bombing, the planes carried eleven hundred pounds of payload and came equipped with nine machine gun placements.

When the first tank exploded, the two bombers started their dive from five thousand feet.

Major Nomokonov led his Siberian Rifle Division into the shadow of the great Silesian castle before them, trailing the company of FT-17's attached to his units. The three tanks deployed forward destroyed a hundred yards of concrete bunkers in front of them, greatly reducing the deadliness of the route ahead.

The Major paused, ready to lead his men en masse through the gap in the mountain defenses when the first tank blew up to the left. He hesitated only a moment before signaling his men on a route still covered by the two remaining light tanks ten yards ahead. His men took position behind a slight dip in the mountain, the only place they could keep the tanks in view through the heavy snowfall.

Another explosion on the other side of the valley caused the Major to turn and he slipped in the slick, frozen ground, cursing. Lying there he stared up the mountain, studying the terrain. Then he saw something—black-cloaked figures running toward the Russian soldiers through the thick flurry.

"Fire," the Major shouted, pointing up the hill.

Two of the black-clad figures hurtled themselves down the rocky shale through the barrage. As the Russians watched, helpless, the two figures ran directly under the FT-17s and exploded.

The hulls of both tanks cracked like eggshells. The turret of the first tank collapsed forward and dug into the ground. The second tank split down the middle and both halves came to rest on their sides. The explosions drew machine gun fire from bunkers from both directions, and Nomokonov and his men were pinned down. Then the Major heard the sounds of engines overhead. The bombers came into the valley at five hundred feet, zeroing in on the smoking hulls of the tanks, and released their half-ton payloads on the surrounding area.

The payload dropped across the eastern slope of Owl Mountain flattened most of the boulders and foliage remaining. First, the ignition and chemical reaction pushed out a wall of gas and air faster than the speed of sound. A bubble of static pressure enveloped everything the shock wave encountered. The pressure dropped, creating a vacuum. The secondary shockwave threw the debris into the air, ripped apart dozens of bunkers and soldiers and set the surface on fire. The fire burned, dust asphyxiated and everything died.

# INTERLUDE 19
November 11, 1914, 6:43 am
The Keep

When Major Nomokonov and his men glanced up from the dirt, they were blanketed in several inches of snow. Silence loomed in the thick haze that blanketed the valley. No machine guns. No tank cannons. No one called out. Just the distant sounds of plane engines. The Major sat up and gave a short laugh in triumph.

With a hundred yards between his men and the wall, he motioned his men forward, got to his feet and ran. "Head for the wall!"

The Major ran past two bunkers that were collapsed and burning. He felt his men behind him and his legs were carrying him halfway to the wall…until the screaming started.

Kapitan Lopukhov awoke to utter silence. He clapped his hands together to see if he still had his hearing. A thick dust cloud mixed with the snowfall covering the valley and bunkers burned across the landscape, turning everything a soupy brown. His Cossacks sat up one by one and Lopukhov touched each one as they awoke to keep silent. Signaling the men, he pointed to the blown-out bunker at ten yards. Lopukhov led the men across the open hillside, waiting for a machine gun to open fire.

He leaped into the bunker pit, surrounded by broken concrete and rebar, his gun swinging around at the frost-covered bodies at his feet. Keep soldiers in black uniforms lay splayed out with ghastly wounds and shattered bodies. Arms were missing. Legs were missing. Russians came in behind him, crouching low and glancing up the hillside for more suicidal attackers.

From somewhere up the hill, the Kapitan heard screaming start. Then brief reports of gunfire. The sounds drew his attention from the corpses at his feet as he tried to peer up the hillside into the darkness.

A hand closed around his ankle and he slipped. Lopukhov turned to berate the soldier who tripped him. He blinked his eyes and gaped in shock as a set of teeth clamped down on his face. Lopukhov screamed, brought his pistol up under the head chewing on his face and pulled the trigger repeatedly. The head exploded and the pain subsided, replaced with an aching throb.

Major Nomokonov stopped running and spun around, instinctively acting to assist his fellow soldiers. What he saw froze him. Imperial Russian soldiers in and around the blown bunkers were grappling with Keep soldiers he walked over only seconds ago. Entrails fell out of the massive wound in a rotter's stomach as it shoved a bayonet into the chest of one of his men.

Keep soldiers rose against his men from everywhere. Dead men in black uniforms rose from the smoking pits and fell upon young Cossacks. The figures were missing an arm or a leg, with blown torsos and strips of hanging flesh.

Young Russian soldiers looked on in horror as monstrosities reached out and dragged them down, tearing at their flesh. The young soldiers tried to fight back but their attackers moved with inhuman strength, impervious to pain or damage.

The Major glanced about the hill as Keep soldiers rose from bunkers. Some bunkers were collapsed and smoldering, but black-clad soldiers were climbing out of the untouched bunkers now. They were all hollow-eyed husks of men, their skin yellow and translucent. Some were still burning. Most carried a rifle and opened fire.

Russians fired back, striking the ambulating soldiers who took bullets to arms, chests, and torsos but still kept coming. When they opened their mouths, their throats only produced inhuman groans.

Nomokonov pulled his father's White Russian Colt and started shooting. He struck one of the horrors in the throat and blood as black and thick as tar flowed from the mouth. The Major fired again, striking another black-clad rotter in the head. Green dripped from the hole, eyes rolled back, and the figure dropped. Around him, Cossacks fought hand to hand and died horribly.

# INTERLUDE 20
November 11, 1914, 7:27 am
The Keep

From atop the outer wall, the Golden Knight watched his ancient entourage emerge from the bunkers and begin to fight hand to hand with the Russians. The colors of beige and green swarmed the hillside. The mines did their damage. The razor wire slowed them down, but they kept coming. Bullets rang out against the wall, a chip flew up and struck him in the chest. Above, the sounds of engines approached.

The Golden Knight raised his right arm, and on the second rampart, the row of arbalists aimed high toward the sky. His arm fell and the weapons took flight. Three seconds later their short fuses lit the charges and the mighty projectiles exploded in midair.

Gases of the Greek Fire hung in the frosty, chilled morning air and lit the sky over the valley. The sounds of engines got closer. The Golden Knight raised his arm, and the second set of arbalists were loaded and now pointed down into the valley. The arm dropped and the projectiles fired directly at the base of Owl Mountain. The six-foot thick stalks plunged into the ground, exploded instantly, and set everything afire.

The two Muromets bombers broke through the snowy, dusty haze, passing into the blanket of Greek Fire hanging below. One of the bombers lit on fire and it faltered. A second later the rest

47

of the payload exploded, sending shards into the inferno and knocking the second bomber off position.

Smoking, but not catching fire, the second bomber released its payload in order to try to pull out of the dive it found itself in. The bombs fell on the valley floor, amidst the hysteria. Hundreds of burning bodies and several tanks were obliterated. Absolute chaos reigned on the ground, breaking the back of the Russian horde. The second bomber tried to pull out of its dive and struck the center citadel about halfway up.

Victor Frankenstein removed his helmet and watched as his magnificent tower cracked and buckled. Its huge granite stones, carved centuries ago, broke apart and collapsed into the center of the castle and the Prince of Silesia screamed in fury.

Kapitan Lopukhov and the remains of his men were being driven across the shale and snow. Keep soldiers who were already dead were coming from every direction. Lopukhov picked up a rifle from the ground and fired as he moved. He hit three of the walking dead in the head. They collapsed as he continued to move through the haze, motioning his men to follow.

Major Nomokonov and his men were forced back from proximity to the wall. He fired at a Keep soldier who took the bullet to the cheek and grabbed him with inhuman strength. He pulled the battle knife from the sheath along his back and plunged it into the hideous things skull. It went slack.

Nomokonov swung the pistol up at a figure in the snowy mist and found himself face to face with a fellow soldier—a Kapitan. Then a hollow, unearthly moan drifted across the snowstorm. The two Russians stared at each other, and at their men, then out into the storm, up the mountain.

A horde of Keep soldiers in black uniform appeared through the snowy haze. Three or four would set on every Russian soldier they encountered. The Major and the Kapitan and his men fired headshots as fast as they could. Much of the horde sprinted past, bloodlust in their dead eyes. A calm peace fell for the space of a breath before a tall figure in a golden uniform and golden helmet came out of the flurry, a sword in each hand. The end came quickly to them all.

# INTERLUDE 21
November 11, 1914, 11:07 pm
Beneath The Keep

Two Keep soldiers stood, rifles ready, in near-total darkness in the tunnel. They stood at attention next to a massive steel door. A lone torch a hundred feet away threw the only light in the tunnel, casting their features into shadows.

A metal latch clicked on the far side of the huge entryway. The soldiers both turned toward the sound. Then the barricade bar across the door slid open—agonizingly slowly. It stopped halfway and silence lingered for long moments before it moved again. Then the lever snapped into the fully unlocked position and the door opened. The massive gateway of ancient European oak nearly a foot thick creaked and groaned as it swung inward.

Frankenstein stood in the doorway, hair matted to his blood-covered face, some of his golden armor damaged in battle. He stepped forward, limping and in pain, using a longsword for support, but keeping his shoulders square. Victor's eyes were bright with the victory but tired. They darted side to side at the soldiers and he took another slow step forward. "The day is ours," he said.

The two soldiers emitted long hollow moans. As Victor moved past them, they stepped away from the wall and watched him go, throwing their visages into the lamplight. Their sunken faces and milky eyes watched their master proceed down the tunnel.

Victor did not look back. He got to the end of the tunnel, turned left down a long hall, stopped at a white door and opened it.

At the far end of the room, a wide staircase extended out the other end of the castle. A heavy gate came down with a shudder. Keep soldiers with medical armbands descended, carrying or assisting injured Keep soldiers down the stairs. Lining both sides of the room were beds holding damaged bodies. A few of the soldiers moaned, the ones missing a limb or more. Several soldiers had chest cavities blown open or suffered severe torso damage. These soldiers looked at Victor as he entered the room and gave the Roman chest salute with whatever functioning limb still moved.

An older man in a doctor's uniform came up to Frankenstein, a worried look on his face. "My Prince. We may not have enough oxygenated fluids for full immersions." He glanced around worriedly. "Many of these men may have to suffer for some time."

Victor put a hand on the man's shoulder. "Doctor Kowalski, I increased production several days ago when we expected this attack to occur. They will have to hang on a little longer, but you should see supplies keeping pace shortly." The man looked visibly relieved. "Any progress with the overall program, Doctor?"

Doctor Kowalski glanced down at the floor, ashamed. "The planarian stem cells still break down over time, my Prince. Six months, sixty years, every man is different. But eventually, the process is irreversible." He glanced at Victor. "For everyone except you, of course."

Frankenstein furrowed his brow. "If I hadn't strayed off course in my pilgrimage to England and gotten my cog swamped, I would have never found the elders to give us the gift."

"If only we knew how they initiated the process."

"We will continue to endeavor, Doctor. Silesia just needs more time."

51

Victor entered a narrow room made of polished marble no more than six feet wide and lit with a single bulb. The chamber ran about twenty feet long with a round pool in the center filled with water and ice, stairs on either end. Another door waited at the far end of the chamber. Victor slowly unshackled the pieces of his armor, pulled off his boots, then looked down at himself. The blood of men soaked into his mesh outfit beneath the armor.

"Probably ruined," he muttered, as he shed the bodysuit. Bruises marked his naked body from his thighs to his shoulders, and he stepped forward into the icy pool. Round stones were embedded into the inner surface of the pool, each about the size of a baseball. Set several inches apart they covered the circumference and lit up a bright neon green as Victor immersed himself in icy water up to his neck. The Silesian prince closed his eyes and sighed.

# INTERLUDE 22
November 12, 1914, 12:21 am
Beneath The Keep

Viktor blinked his eyes as the door in front of him opened. A healthy, young Silesian soldier with dark hair and sharp features stood at attention, staring straight ahead, with a towel and black and yellow robe in his arms. The green lights within the pool dimmed and went out.

Invigorated, Victor climbed the stairs without a flinch of pain or physical exhaustion, bruising on his body gone. He donned the robe with the double-headed eagle crest emblazoned over the *F* across his back and dried his hair with the towel. He walked into the inner chamber, opened another smaller door, and closed it behind him.

He stood inside his palatial bedroom chamber. A superb extended dining table of English mahogany, made from the finest Central American timbers, sat as the centerpiece of the huge room. Victor ran his hand along the top of the table as if savoring the feel of it. A long copper tray of fruits and cheeses sat in the center of the table. Frankenstein went over, stabbed a large piece of melon and shoved it into his mouth, chewing with obvious delight. His eyes half-closed with bliss.

*"Comment était votre dernière Victoire grand prince?"* The voice came from across the room, dripping with sarcasm.

Still chewing the melon, Victor circled around the massive table, past a wall-size portrait of Emperor Ferdinand III, approaching a set of French curtains. He got six feet away and the curtains parted.

Allefra stood dressed in a replica of Princess Charlotte's wedding dress from 1816. The room beyond the curtains glowed in the same neon green as the bathing pool. The woman smiled and cocked her head. "Hello, darling. How did the war go?"

Victor did not approach the curtain, but stepped back, threw the robe over one of the Rococo chairs and opened a Louis XV mirrored wardrobe. He pulled a shirt and woolen trousers out and got dressed, glancing over at Allefra. "The Russians are retreating. They will not be returning."

"So sure are we," she said dryly.

"Yes, my dear. The Russian Emperor has neither the experienced men nor the material for a prolonged fight." Frankenstein tightened the belt around his woolen trousers, moving on to buttoning his viceroy dress shirt. "What he did have, we destroyed in the valley."

Allefra smiled with apparent pride and honor. "Then we have done a great thing."

She stepped through the French curtains, the green glow falling from her face and shoulders, toward Victor. She took two steps and her pallor changed, her eyes grew cataracts and her gait wilted. The smile of pride turned into an evil grin. "Kiss me to celebrate," the creature rasped.

Victor lifted his chin and his face struggled to maintain a look of pleasure and comfort, but it cracked for a second and horror crossed his eyes. He put his hands on Allefra's shoulders and pushed her back behind the curtain barrier. Instantly, her beauty returned. She gave a little pout. "No kiss?"

"The central citadel has been destroyed. The outside world is becoming more violent. I have much to do to protect the castle."

Allefra laughed softly.

Victor stared at her, annoyed. "That amuses you?"

"You're a prisoner here, just as I am. You can't leave or it would all fall apart. I can't leave or I will fall apart."

Victor waved a hand. "You are not a prisoner. Anything you wish can be provided. Anything you care for can be brought in."

"Within this room! Within this prison!"

"You have eternal life." Victor insisted.

"A life of nothing! You are not even around to help me enjoy it. And…" she stuck her hand through the curtain, beyond the green glow, and it immediately shriveled and decayed. "You would not touch me, even if you were here." She drew her arm back in and turned away, nearly closing the curtains.

Victor watched her walk away, the sound of her soft sobbing barely audible. His eyes softened and he took a step toward her.

With a loud screech, Allefra poked her head and shoulders through, beyond the green glow. The desiccated flesh, sunken cheeks, milky eyes, and teeth snapped at him behind thinned lips. "I'll chew your face off if you step through these curtains!" the creature shouted. "I can't even remember who I am!"

Victor finished the last button on his collar and gave the creature a look up and down its torso. The Allefra thing snapped its teeth again.

"I will learn how to restore your humanity permanently. Then you will appreciate me for the savior that I am."

She cackled with a voice like swamp gas rasping through dry leaves.

"Savior? You cannot save yourself!" The creature laughed its dead, dry laugh, drew inside the curtain, giggling endlessly as Victor left the room.

# INTERLUDE 23
March 18, 1917, 9:04 pm
Outside Shakespeare, New Mexico

Ernie sat shivering beneath the rock outcropping, rubbing his hands together and blowing into them for warmth. He stared up at the stars and heard a wolf howl in the distance.

"Well, I'd better get moving," he mumbled to himself, reaching into his small duffle. He pulled out a small Altoids tin, a piece of flint, a metal striker, a small plastic vial and a thin blanket. Unscrewing the vial, he rubbed citronella around his neck and over his face as he glanced around. In the dark, he made out a patch of cherrystone juniper and another patch of red elderberry. He went over, pulled some of the branches apart, and started peeling the bark for kindling.

Ernie opened the small tin, pulled out a thin piece of char cloth and laid it in the kindling. Then he struck the piece of flint, and sparks flew. In a few moments, the low burning fabric lit and the kindling started burning. Another few minutes and enough cherrystone and elderberry branches were gathered so the blaze roared with heat and life. He sat watching the fire burn. *Gather twice as much as fuel as you think you will need.* Sighing, he gathered more wood for the fire. *Good to know all those nights camping stuck with me.* He broke branches, stacked them in his arms, and walked back toward the fire.

"A frying pan is a most necessary thing to any trip, but you also need the old stew kettle," he said aloud with mock seriousness. *I don't have to worry about that. No food anyway.*

While the fire burned, he stared at the single thin blanket. "It's always twice as cold as you think it's going to be," he said sadly. The wolf howled again.

Ernie climbed into a small debris-filled ditch next to the fire. He matted the debris down and pulled the small blanket over his body, his breath coming out in icy clouds as the temperature continued to drop.

"Rustic camps can fit in the basket and provide trainloads of benefit," he muttered. "Too bad I didn't bring a basket." Sleep came quickly.

# INTERLUDE 24
March 18, 1917, 9:17 pm
Ramah Navajo Reservation

T.R. and three hundred Volunteers in the USVC Battalion under Captain Bullock rode south in pursuit of the Polish cavalry. Captain Groome and a hundred or so went on to Fort Wingate with the wounded to report what they encountered. The battalion followed the horse tracks and rode camelback for several hours until they came upon an offshoot of the Rio Grande river. Low conical hills ran along the banks, covered by groves of cottonwood. In places, they observed small herds of goats and wild horses drinking from the river. Waterfowl were plentiful. Large flocks of Muscovy ducks soared the skies.

T.R. pulled his camel to a stop as an extraordinary creature strolled out of some shrubbery up ahead. About the size of a small black bear, it had a long toothless snout, a bushy tail and powerful claws on its forefeet. "Ant bear!" he exclaimed. "I hunted these in Paraguay. They are fine bush meat."

One soldier raised his rifle but the ex-president waved him off. The soldiers sat in silence, watching as the huge creature lumbered across their path and disappeared into the tall grass.

They rode for another hour until the sun fell behind the horizon and they were navigating by starlight. They came upon an open field and T.R. paused, glancing about.

The ex-president squared his shoulders and turned to his men. "I think we should decamp here gentlemen. It's a good flat space with open approaches. We shall set a fire and tell stories." When he saw the dubious looks of his men, anxious to continue the chase, he nodded. "Men can restore their spirits and remake their bodies by camping in the woods. We will stay here tonight and continue the pursuit at dawn."

The men broke out supplies, got fires going and the lean-tos up. Several soldiers returned from the river with beautiful large cutthroat trout and they were thrown on skillets while pears from a local grove were sliced up and distributed among them. One man yelped and swatted at his arm.

T.R. pointed to the tree next to him. "Watch for fire ants men. You'll find them on a species of small trees or sapling on the outskirts of the camp, with greenish bark. They bend their whole body as they bite, thrusting downward. The poison causes considerable pain and for a little while you'll get a festering sore."

# INTERLUDE 25
March 19, 1917, 6:17 am
Outside Shakespeare, New Mexico

Ernie awoke with a start, cheeks blue. He glanced around, lost for a moment, then let out a long sigh. *The call of the wild may be all right, but it's a dog's life.*

He stood up and stretched his stiff body, then relieved himself next to a cottonwood. *Someone will be expecting me in Albuquerque before the day is out. But it could take several more days before anyone comes looking. I need water. I want to go home. I don't want this.*

He put his fire-starting supplies back into the duffel, along with the rolled-up thin blanket. He took a small wooden box out with "first aid" engraved on the lid. He examined the gauze, adhesive plasters, dressing, bandages, and sutures inside. *Well, if I get hurt I'm probably dead anyway.*

He stared up at the sky, getting his bearings. *It's about twenty miles northeast to Silver City if I recall. No turning back towards Shakespeare. Going to keep moving away from the Aztec rotters. Any man who questions my manhood or intelligence will have my fist in his face.*

He climbed to the top of a large boulder and stood atop it, aligning himself in a northeasterly direction searching for landmarks. Then he rubbed his eyes and sighed. *Going to walk as far as I can today. Keep an eye for water sources and any place that would be a better place to lie at night. If I am tired, I am more likely to make a mistake or react out of emotion.*

He summoned his courage, picked up the shotgun, jumped down with the duffel over his shoulder, and moved on.

# INTERLUDE 26
March 19, 1917, 6:36 am
Ramah Navajo Reservation

When T.R. awoke with the first light of dawn he sat up and glanced about, then let out a small harumph of surprise. An encampment of Navajo tipis sat on either side of the field where they had pitched camp. They had stumbled into the midst of a native village in the night without realizing it. Women and children seemed to have left in the intervening hours. Only braves stood among the tipis watchfully. From this distance, not even a shout would have been discerned.

Captain Bullock came over to the ex-president. "Sir, prudence may dictate we move, in an orderly fashion."

T.R. smiled. "Not to worry, Captain. My time with the Indian Affairs Office has put me in good stead. Geronimo once said of me 'no man has a more practical sympathy with the Indian' and it remains a proud moment in my life."

Captain Bullock looked confused. "He is Apache sir. These are Navajo."

"Their languages are very similar, Captain. In fact, there are dialects of Navajo closer to Apache than they are to other dialects of Navajo." He walked across the field toward the largest gathering of Navajo braves with a bag of supplies. While his men watched, he shook the hand of each warrior, handed over some of the bacon and flapjacks the men were cooking and pointed south animatedly.

Several long minutes later the ex-president came strolling back across the field, a bounce in his step. He stopped about halfway to observe a huge swarm of colorful butterflies swirling above the field. He laughed, pointed at the air, and took out his journal. After a few moments of writing, he continued his walk and came over to Captain Bullock. "We are in luck. These Ramah Navajo were part of a tribe that had some land parcels swindled from them in a land swap and bribery scheme. I put 146 men in jail for that fiasco my second year in office. Fired the Land Commissioner. And the next year set aside the first land for Native American heritage sites."

"Did they see the Polish cavalry?" a Volunteer asked.

"And the Aztecs too," T.R. added. "That's why the women and children are gone into hiding. "Not from us. They were already spooked. They can take us to the edge of their reservation and lead us to where the monsters disappear."

"Monsters?" asked Captain Bullock.

"Yes, Captain. The Navajo tell quite a story. There's a place called Black Mountain. It's in the Gila Forest Reserve. I founded the Reserve in 1905, so I know the area quite well. Hunters have been observing soldiers and the "nayee" or monsters, heading into Black Mountain for over a year. And when the Diné follows them, there are no signs of camps or fires or hunting." He spread his hands slowly, palms open. "They 'disappear'. And so do others. We have to find the Alamo people. Their reservation is right at the foot of Black Mountain. The Ramah are fearful. They have not heard from their brothers and sisters in some time."

# INTERLUDE 27
March 19, 1917, 10:36 am
South of Black Mountain

E rnie stood on the crest of a small hill overlooking a grav-
elly sandbank in an ancient riverbed. Two dilapidated sluice
boxes sat in tall weeds. *If there's gold-panning going on, there's
water close by.* He picked among the broken pieces of a sluice.
Finding the remnants of a firepit,, he crouched down on his
knees and searched among the bordering overgrowth. He discovered an old canteen and tucked it into his duffle. Not finding
anything else of use, he moved on.

He followed the dry riverbed for several miles until he saw
signs of cultivation. Wheatfields were followed by wheat stacks
and the distant sound of running water. He came to the small
stream and did a little jig. He waded into the water, stuck the
canteen into the flow. He poured the water from it once to clean
it. He sniffed it, refilled it, then poured the water over his face
and into his open mouth, laughing.

Hunting rabbits and picking squash occupied the rest of the
afternoon. When he had enough food he started a fire. He took
some of the wood he'd appropriated from the broken sluices
and some nearby cottonwood and stoked until he had glowing
flames.

From the stream, he took a large flat rock and slid it into the
center of the fire. He set his wet socks and shoes off to the side

to dry. While the fire burned, he went to the stream and bathed. *I feel almost human again.*

Returning to the fire, the flames had subsided, leaving hot coals and the flat rock. Ernie slid the stone out with two sticks, poured water over it to clear it of ash and used the sticks to slide it back onto the hot coals. Within moments he had rabbit frying atop the flat stone, along with chunks of Calabacitas. As the flames spit and his meal cooked, he took out his small notebook and nub pencil and scribbled.

*To Pete Wellington, Editor, Kansas City Star*

*Greetings, you old abysmalite. If this note finds you without me anywhere in earshot, I shall have succumbed to the desert. I believe one can still read my unsteady script. Poor handwriting has not crippled me yet.*

*How is it that I have found myself wandering the Black Mountains without supplies or preparation? Well, sit back and let me give you an earful. I took the ticket from the front office and caught the train to El Paso. I found a caravan of pilgrims on their way to Arizona and borrowed a seat. A nice lady gave me some hardtack and meats. She is a real peach. They were on their way to St Patrick's Church so if you find her, give her my thanks.*

*After a small hike to Shakespeare. I found the town deserted. And not from the pox. Well, now I can hold up my hand to God and say I have been attacked by rotters. That's right. All dressed up as Aztecs. I've never had a blow dart shot at me, but now one came rather close. They chased me about with hatchets and bows, and I managed to take them out with a shotgun like hunting deer back in Michigan. A*

65

*Negro slave had dressed himself like an Aztec war-*
*rior so there is much more to find out here.*

*If someone mentions stuff missing at the General*
*Store, it weren't for emoluments and I will reim-*
*burse the new owner. I'm afraid the old one is rather*
*dead.*

*Love from the Great Hemingstein to you all.*

Ernie re-read his letter while his dinner cooked. A loud grunt made him look up. A brown bear sat nibbling on a juniper bush, studying him with interest. He didn't move and slowly the bear stood on his hind legs and his upper lip pulled back in a sneer. He glanced around as his heart sank. He had laid the shotgun down while he prepared his meal. Now the bear stood nearly on top of it. He scrambled to his feet, shouting. "Do you know you're nothing but a miserable, common bear?" He picked up a rock from around the firepit and threw it at the bear. "You're cocky and you stand there, threatening to eat my dinner, or eat me. You're nothing but a miserable bear."

The bear stared at Ernie, then hung its head. It dropped down on all four and turned away. It stopped, nibbled at some juniper berries on the ground and glanced back.

"And you're not a polar bear or a grizzly bear. Just a plain ol' bear. What do you think of that?"

Slowly, the bear slunk off behind a hill.

Ernie went over and picked up the gun and let out a loud breath, then shouted, "If you come back I'll shoot you for dinner!"

# INTERLUDE 28
March 19, 1917, 4:22 pm
North of Black Mountain

The ex-president and his USVC Battalion rode their camels all day along the edge of the Gila National Forest. They reached the edge of a high bluff and peered out over the canyon.

After observing the scenery for several minutes, T.R. turned to Captain Bullock. Pointing ahead of them and towards Black Mountain in the distance, he said, "Between here and the mountain we'll see yellow pine and alders. If we're lucky we'll find wild cherries along the way for some campfire cherry pies."

The ex-president climbed down off his camel. "Let us make camp here for the evening." He stopped as a strange call came from a nearby grove of Nut Pines. "Is that bird or beast?" he asked.

"I think it's an owl," said Sergeant McBryar.

Presently, the sound came from another part of the grove.

T.R. squinted up at the sun. "Not an owl, but it certainly has wings." He glanced at Captain Bullock and winked. "After we set up, we'll go run that bird down." As the men made camp, he walked among them. "There are plenty of yellow pine amongst us men. The best place for a night's sleep is a bed of their brown needles. But watch the flames, they catch quite quickly. Keep the fires well away from your bedrolls. Set the lean-to's back an extra six feet. They'll still catch the warmth opened wide and can be made low and tight if the wind or rain picks up. It will keep you dry. No asthmatic or consumptive patient ever regained health in a damp tent. And no man ever kept his health in one."

While the men broke down their packs for camp, T.R. jumped back on his camel and headed for the grove. He beckoned for two soldiers to follow. Captain Bullock soon took off after them.

After a few minutes, it became clear that the object of the ex-president's chase could not be whatever bird or creature had made the sounds. Instead, he followed what appeared to be a game trail.

Occasionally, T.R. would look back and, seeing his accompaniment making slow progress, waved his entourage on impatiently. As they came over a hill, the object of the President's quarry became evident. A wildcat stalked a small family of pronghorns from a nearby rocky perch, and he kicked his camel into a tearing pace after the fleeing deer. He chased the small herd to a rocky outcropping where they could run no further and the President stopped, laughing like a schoolboy.

The wildcat, standing on the edge of a nearby cliff, upon seeing the soldiers between it and its quarry, let out a loud screech and stalked off. The deer, quivering and their tongues lolling out in exhaustion, stood huddled together begging for mercy. With no more movement from any apparent predator the deer bounced onto an outcropping and fled.

The scouting party followed a winding path that led to an elevated plateau with a spectacular view of open landscape three or four miles across. From here, herds upon herds of pronghorns scattered over the slopes and valleys.

"I estimate there are three or four thousand deer before us. What a spectacle!" the President said cheerily. He climbed down from his camel and stretched himself upon a large flat rock. Squirrels chattered among the pine boughs as the men relaxed for long minutes, enjoying the scenery.

After a half-hour or so an erratic series of trills and chitters erupted from the nearby brush. The President jumped to his feet and stomped amongst the tall grass. "Lawrence's Goldfinch. Let's go flush him out."

The next few minutes found the ex-president and several of his men in the woods, climbing over logs and boulders. They stood under a locust tree and peered into the branches, searching for the handsome and uncommon finch. They all heard the sounds of the bird.

T.R. smiled at his men, eager as a small boy showing visitors a special view. "There is a delight in the hardy life of the open. There are no words that can truly tell the hidden spirit of the wilderness, its melancholy and its charm. The nation behaves well if it treats the natural resources as assets which it must turn over to future generations increased and not impaired in value."

# INTERLUDE 29

March 20, 1917, 5:06 am
South of Black Mountain

The morning found Ernie sleeping soundly on a bed of pine needles and fans of cliff ferns. He awoke and poked at the embers. He took handfuls of dried leaves, twigs, and sticks and fed them into the heart of the campfire. Then he used a long branch to stoke the fire. In a few moments, flames licked to life and he held up his hands, warming them. A whip-poor-will called out and several answered from every direction. A turkey gobbled nearby.

Ernie stood up and crossed over to nearby spruce, and brought down a rabbit killed the night before he had hung in the tree. When he turned back to the campfire, a shadow crossed over his frame. The young brown bear walked lazily, sniffing amongst the remains of rabbit and squash next to the fire.

He didn't move for several moments until he slowly squatted down reaching for the shotgun on the ground next to his bedding. He stood facing the bear, still busy licking the flat rock for leftovers. He nestled the stock of the gun under his armpit and fished out a slug cartridge. "The gun should be held at all times with your non-firing hand on the stock, roughly in the middle of the grip. Cradle it firmly, using the v created by your thumb and forefinger," he whispered softly, remembering his hunting lessons. He loaded the gun. The sound caused the bear to look up. It growled and raised up all five feet on its hind legs.

Ernie brought the barrel up off the ground, aiming at the bear's midsection. "Failing to keep the shotgun tight in your shoulder will make the kick more painful when you shoot the gun," he said louder.

The bear roared.

"Pull the trigger smoothly!" He yelled and fired

After he got dressed and cleaned up the campsite, Ernie drank his fill from the stream. Bear steak chunks popped and sizzled on the fire as he sat, scribbling thoughts into his notebook, turning the meat. Smiling in satisfaction, he grabbed a bloody piece and popped it in his mouth. "Tastes like juniper berries," he said, chewing loudly, trying to keep it from burning his mouth.

# INTERLUDE 30
March 20, 1917, 6:12 am
North of Black Mountain

T.R. woke early and sprang into action, wanting to enjoy the local hot springs before the day started. The best springs lay on the Gila River at the north end of Grant's County. The Gila Forest takes in all of the Mogollon and Black Mountain ranges. A thousand square miles of scrub oak, pinon, juniper and mahogany. "This evergreen forest is a haven of wild animals, men," he pointed into the forest. "If we weren't on an active expedition you'd find me stalking the bear, the fox, and the cougar!"

Then they came to it. Situated in a steep canyon and flowing from the base of a hill into a fork of the Gila River, the water pulsed from the ground in one-minute increments. Deep pools dug out of solid rock held water that bubbled up at about a hundred degrees.

"I found these Springs when I established the Gila National Forest in 1905 as the nation's first Forest Reserve," T.R. said as he immersed himself in the therapeutic *Aqua Pura*, his notebook in hand. "It is said that the early Spaniards knew about these springs. But that isn't the case. The Apache held these grounds for two and a half centuries against the white man. They knew about the health restorative properties of these waters, curing their sick of pneumonia and other fevers."

That afternoon, the ex-president wrote in his journal as his men bathed and relaxed around him.

> *Awoke to a beautiful sunrise and birds singing. My hunger for the aboriginal is returning with fierce abundance. On most hunting trips we are accompanied by a large retinue of camp laborers, an orderly or two and a guide. But none of these are available or of use to us now. We might have passed a trading outpost for something other than rabbits and squash but United States greenbacks are of no use in this part of the country. I had not been on a saddle for this many miles since Yellowstone.*
>
> *Over breakfast, I told the men of the story of a Rough Rider who had written me with troubles. Hopefully to draw their minds away from our current state. He wrote to me "Dear Colonel Roosevelt, I am in trouble. I shot a lady in the eye, but I did not intend to hit the lady; I tried to shoot my wife." The camp roared with laughter and broke into reverie the rest of the meal.*

# INTERLUDE 31
March 20, 1917, 9:33 am
South of Black Mountain

Ernie moved up across the hilly terrain with only a general idea of where Silver City should be in his path. He knew he needed to basically go north. *Simple right? Figured I would come across a road or something that would lead me to it. Sweating to make the jack and it's still morning.*

Only once atop a particularly tall ridge did he look out around him and realized that he had missed the mark by quite a few miles. He had traveled several miles to the west and north of Silver City. He now knew he'd strayed much further than he expected. *In the name of all things just and unjust!*

The ridges became more impassable the further he proceeded. Ernie had to choose whether to work his way back several miles the way he came or keep going and move even further north into the forest and further up before he might find a way down. He reached into his bag, pulled out a strip of bear meat, tore a piece of with his teeth and chewed thoughtfully, glancing around, before moving on.

He reached the edge of the Gila Wilderness and stopped, searching for another way down the mountain to reach Silver City. He only saw steep rocky terrain in his path. Further up were narrow canyons and caves. *Might be of use if I don't find a hibernating bear. They don't tend to wake until late March.*

*Which happens to be right about now.* He shook his head in frustration. He took another tear at the hunk of bear meat.

He traversed a steep ledge and came down on the other side to another narrow canyon and collapsed alcoves only to stop in astonishment. There, carved into the side of the cliffs themselves were human dwellings. Small homes, two or three stories high, with windows and multiple rooms. *Heard something about these. Cliff People lived here hundreds of years ago.*

Ernie made his way along the cliff edge, looking at the amazing stonework. Several of the homes were collapsed. *No sense in taking a chance of wandering about and causing a rock slide.* He caught sight of pottery shards. *Think I'll look further in.* He made his way through the canyon and came across a small valley in the narrows. A stream ran through its center and tall junipers grew on one side and wild corn grew on the other. *This is where the Cliff People grew their food!*

He had nearly burst with excitement before he saw three figures step out of the juniper shadows and move toward the far end of the valley, through another narrows. Their backs were to him so he couldn't see their faces but he knew who, or what, they were. Their headdress, the clothes on their bodies, the weapons they carried, their shuffling movement were also indicative. *The Aztec rotters!*

He dropped to his knees then realized that would be useless. *Nothing to hide behind up here.*

The Aztec rotters shuffled out of sight. *Maybe I'll follow them. Yeah...that's a smart idea.*

A thrumming, pounding noise filled the air, coming from the ground below. They sounds were like driving railroad spikes into the ground. *Never heard anything like it. No, that isn't true. I watched them lay railroad tile in Kansas City at the tender age of fourteen with my father.*

Then something moved into his view. At first, he couldn't believe his eyes. *I'm seeing a steam tractor.* Except it didn't have wheels. And the metal monstrosity didn't stretch long enough to be a tractor or anything.

75

Standing at least seven feet tall and walking at a healthy pace, the ground shuddered with every step as the Thing moved across the valley. The Thing appeared to be a man, from the shoulders up. One arm appeared human also. But the other upper append- age stretched out into some inhuman metal claw from the shoul- der down.

There might have been some stomach or back present but mid-chest the impossible thing became metal again, with a strange green glowing light at the center of its back. The legs moved with that steady hiss-thump of steam engines, but each one moved independently. Enormous boots sat at the end of each "leg" which settled squarely on the ground each time they lifted and settled. Hiss-thump, lift, settle. Hiss-thump, lift, settle.

The Thing machine moved its head slightly and Ernie caught glimpses of eye movement. Intelligence. *So they aren't just mak- ing rotters from men. They are putting men back together with machines. I've read some priceless yarns, but Jules Verne...eat your heart out.*

Slowly, the rotters and the monstrosity moved through the valley and into the narrows. Only then did Ernie make his way down to follow, adjusting the pack over his shoulder. *We're hav- ing a whangleberry of a time now.*

# INTERLUDE 32
March 20, 1917, 10:15 am
Alamo Navajo Reservation

About halfway through the morning, the USVC soldiers came upon a small tributary of the Rio San Jose without a bridge in sight.

T.R. paused his camel. "These flea-infested filthy beasts." He studied his men. "I would not forego the blessings of long trousers for all the gold in the desert." He urged his dromedary camel forward onto the near bank and into the water.

"Colonel Roosevelt," Captain Bullock said slowly, "Camels can't swim."

"Nonsense!" replied the ex-president. "The camels of Gujarat swim miles to reach their feeding grounds. It's not that they can't. They just don't—usually." Slowly the camel moved across the tributary. "The riverbed can have treacherous patches of quicksand. Move quickly and surely." About two-thirds of the way across the camel let out an angry bellow and paused. Finally, its large leathery two-toed pad reached hardpan and continued up the far bank. Its feet were covered in mud from the mid-leg down.

Seeing the ex-president standing on the other side of the river watching expectantly, the rest of the USVC soldiers moved in straight away.

Only one camel lost its footing. T.R. jumped down with a rope and together with several soldiers they pulled the errant howling beast and rider to shore.

Then they were on the march again.

After about half an hour later the riders passed a small grove of Ponderosa Pines, and they rode about fifty yards past when the ex-president stopped. "I saw turkeys in the Pines back there." He said to Sergeant McBryar. "Have a couple of your best marksmen go back and shoot a few. We'll have turkey stew tonight."

McBryar looked back at the grove of Ponderosa. "Turkeys in trees, sir?"

"Turkeys don't nest in trees son, but they fly high enough to hide. Now, who's going to bring us back some dinner?" The ex-president looked among the riders and three men volunteered.

After a quarter of an hour, gunshots rang out and the men all came back with a couple of large wild turkeys each.

"Merriam's turkeys," T.R. said, smiling. "Delicious. Let's keep going."

The camel riders continued southeast. The land stretched out flat, and Black Mountain rose directly south. Far to the east, another mountain range could be seen just in front of the horizon.

"Blanca Peak, the sacred mountain of the east for the Navajo, gentlemen." T.R. pointed. "It is said, the Creator placed the People on the land between the four sacred mountains representing the four cardinal directions. They never travel much outside their holy land."

The terrain rose up in front of them and the caravan moved around the small plateau. The USVC troops came abreast of the tall limestone cliffs and finally glimpsed the Alamo reservation in the distance.

# INTERLUDE 33
March 20, 1917, 11:34 pm
Black Mountain

Ernie slowly worked his way down the mountain. He stopped once, hearing the hiss-thump of the Thing's movement. But the sound grew fainter until it disappeared completely. At the base, he found where the stream water emerged from an underground tributary.

He followed the current, watching the shadows among the juniper trees and listening to the bubbling of the water. The buzzing of dragonflies and the skittering of water bugs on the surface were the only things that moved. When he pushed through the last stalks of wild corn he came face to face with an Aztec in full dress uniform, seated and holding a jade club. He leaped back and fell on his butt with a yelp. When he scrambled to his feet and ran, he looked over his shoulder. The Aztec hadn't budged.

Ernie slowly made his way back towards the motionless figure. The Aztec rested in a sitting position on a large boulder at the bank of the stream. The head hung down as if it had fallen asleep, with its Jaguar headpiece slightly askew and a club resting loosely in its hands.

He placed a hand on the thick wooden club, wrapped in ornate leather strips. The weapon had a deep groove at one end and a sharpened piece of jade embedded in it. He counted his breaths, watching, but the figure didn't move. Slowly, he removed the club from the horror's hands.

*I want to see what's underneath but, Jesus! Did it move? No, you're freaking yourself out here Hemingstein.* He carefully gripped the Jaguar headpiece and readied himself to jump if the figure sprang to life. But nothing moved, so he slid the headdress off. The slack-jawed visage that looked back opened its mouth and a hollow hiss emerged as the face sunk in on itself. The milky motionless eyes dropped back into their sockets and disappeared into the empty shell.

Ernie stepped back as the head sunk between the shoulders as if there were no bones to support it. The head lolled, slumped forward, one arm slid out of its socket and the form collapsed into a heap. He stood looking at the sunken horror for several moments, his mouth agape. *Whatever I must do, men have always done.*

The other edge of the passage opened into a larger gorge than the fertile valley behind him. *Nothing but rocks, sand and steep cliffs here.*

He had moved off to the side and back up the hill about ten feet, worried that some rotter might wander up behind him and eat him. *Wait. Do they eat people?*

The remnants of a prospector camp lay scattered—a broken down shack with junk strewn around and several dead pack mules that looked tied together. A large sluice lay broken down near the widest part of the stream.

A huge iron cauldron sat near the far edge of the valley, below the mine entrance, propped up by a massive wooden gantry. The boiler glowed with heat and it had a strange green luminescence coming from its base. On the outcropping above, Aztec rotters watched as Navajos in ankle chains shuffled in and out of the mine tunnel. The fettered Indians hauled the unrefined ore aboveground, dropped it into the cauldron, turned and moved back into the tunnel.

Two Aztec rotters stood on either side of the cauldron, each holding a metal chain wrapped in rope and leather. One Aztec pulled on the chain. This opened an aperture and allowed molten ore to flow down a channel and into a shallow pit. Then the rotter on the other side pulled his chain and the door closed back up. More ore dropped into the boiler from shackled Indians wearing broken and despondent looks.

*About twelve altogether,* he counted. Aztec rotters standing around and three of those scary Thing machines. The metal monsters moved around the perimeter of the circular pit paved with stones, using their giant metal claws to crush and mix the ore. A silvery slag rose to the top. The metal claws collected it and Aztecs carried it in flat Indian baskets to strange-looking vehicles.

The transports resembled sailboats, except that they sat high on wooden struts and had large solid wooden wheels. A thick mast jutted from the center of and a canvas sail sat atop it, shaped like a windsock.

*Strangest thing. A boat with wheels. And that looks like... like a windsock on top. I've seen them at the Milwaukee Mile. It's like a sand boat.*

# INTERLUDE 34
March 20, 1917, 12:47 pm
Black Mountain

When the five hundred strong USVC caravan entered the Alamo Navajo Reservation, there were no Indian children running about, no one coming to greet them or sell their trinkets.

T.R. pulled back on the rein and brought his dromedary to a halt. He stared silently at the empty village for several moments. "Something is indeed very wrong," the ex-president muttered.

The USVC Battalion rode slowly amongst the stucco buildings nestled in the shadow of Black Mountain. A small flock of chickens scattered as the camels walked through, snorting and spitting. The soldiers moved into the center of the reservation.

"The Diné, or People, live a lively communal lifestyle amongst their stucco Hogans and wooden pergolas." T.R. got down off his camel and walked around in a wide arc taking the silence in. He stopped when his eyes fell upon four Navajo on horseback, motionless on the outskirts of the village. They slowly moved into the village and he walked toward them.

The USVC soldiers sat and looked around nervously for several minutes. Sergeant Berry's camel hacked a glob towards a wandering sheep. The animal bayed and disappeared through a doorway.

T.R. came striding back. A couple of his men were poking their heads into the homes and he waved them off. "We wouldn't find any bodies here in the village. The Navajo feel its bad medicine to keep the dead nearby. They would have moved them into burial grounds."

Colonel Bullock looked around. "So where are the burial grounds, Colonel Roosevelt?"

The ex-president shook his head. "It wouldn't make any difference. There would still be someone in the village. Everyone wouldn't leave."

"Beg pardon sir, but how do we know they're not all out hunting or something?" Bullock asked.

T.R. took off his glasses and wiped them with his bandana. After he put them back on he studied the Sergeant. "The Navajos teach a story about a Coyote that decides to take a long walk. Coyote meets the Old Woman out walking. The Old Woman warns Coyote not to go too far or he'll come across a Giant. The Coyote tells Old Woman to mind her business and keeps going. After walking a long time, Coyote goes into a cave when he gets tired. He picks up a big stick to defend himself inside the cave, but, to his surprise, comes across Old Woman again. She tells him he doesn't need the stick. It's too late. Coyote already walked into the belly of a Giant when he thought he entered the cave."

The ex-president looked around sadly. "It means the People never go too far." He realized his men were no longer looking at him. They were looking over his shoulder, several were reaching for their weapons. He turned and instead of four Navajo warriors on horseback, they now numbered fifty or more. Each of the Navajo warriors held rifles in one hand and pointed up with their other hand towards the peak of Black Mountain, behind the soldiers.

T.R. turned back to face his soldiers and pointed up the mountain the same as the Navajo. "Black Mountain is where we have to start. That's where the Skinwalkers are. The mountain is where we'll find what we're looking for."

# INTERLUDE 35
March 20, 1917, 1:22 pm
Black Mountain

Ernie watched the scene play out over and over for what seemed like an hour: Indians coming out of the mine, dropping ore into the cauldron, then loping back inside. The Thing machines worked the amalgam as it cooled, producing a layer of silver slag on top. They scraped it off with their metal claws and the rotters collected it and carried it to three waiting sand boats.

Without any apparent signal, the Thing machines stopped their work and moved toward the vehicles. The huge mechanical creatures stepped agilely on the small fold-out steps on the sides and into the boats full of baskets of silver ore. A couple of Aztec rotters removed the tire chocks from two of the vehicles, the windsocks opened and the boats surged forward. A green glow came from the base of the windsock pole of each of the sand boats, and they picked up speed. The vehicles left a cloud of sand in their wake as they went out of sight.

At the mine entrance, an Indian stumbled with the ore and fell to his side. An Aztec standing nearby walked over, raised a club like the one in his hands, and brought it down on the cowering Indian, driving the jade blade into his head. Two Indians behind the one that fell put down their loads, picked the body up, threw it down the hill, and went back to carrying their ore. An Aztec

84

came and fetched the dead Indian after a few minutes, dragging him into an open tent. *Jesus, did they just get a new recruit?*

He watched for several moments. Two rotters each carrying a basket full of silver ore placed them in the remaining transport, two more walking rotters watched the Indian slaves moving the ore out of the mine. Then two Aztecs at the cauldron moved to the slag pit and used shovels to mix the molten ore.

Ernie observed the Indian prisoners march in and out of the mine. *Can I get over there? Oh really, what are you going to do when you get over there? I could do something! You're just going to go over there and maybe get yourself killed. I should do something. But what if I don't want to do anything? I could get out of here. Never mistake motion for action, that's what Grandfather said.*

Making sure that the rotters moving around had their backs to him or didn't have him in their line of sight, he carefully made his way around the edge of the valley. He lay hiding behind some Fern Bush, about twenty feet from the smelt bin. He watched the Indian prisoners about ten feet up, dropping the ore into the cauldron.

*I can feel the heat from here. Now what?* Ernie sighed. Four Aztec rotters down on the hardpan, scraping silver ore. Two above and behind him, in front of the mine. Again, he made sure the rotters all either had their backs turned or were moving on a line that left him out of their sight. He got up and moved toward the cauldron.

When he got next to the smelting vat, he saw a long chain hung on the front. He grabbed it, stepped back and pulled. The bin tilted downward and poured forth. Pretty soon it overran the small channel.

With one final tug standing behind the bin, he upended it and ran for the rocks as the molten ore ran everywhere. Rotters looked down to find themselves standing in molten ore. The smelt burnt their feet off at the ankles. With a moan and a sizzle they toppled over into the igneous rock and melted into the sliding mass.

85

# INTERLUDE 36
March 20, 1917, 2:37 pm
Black Mountain

The USVC Battalion led by T.R. and Captain Bullock made their way up the north side of Black Mountain along Snow Creek, guiding their camels along the marked pathway. The caravan stretched back down the mountain over a mile along the narrow track full of switchbacks.

The ex-president rode his camel slowly around a couple of boulders wedged in the cliffs above. "Snow can be found on the summit until early June up here. Right now, in this high altitude, the snow can get seven or eight feet deep, men. The Black Range can have drifts that have been known to measure as much as thirty feet." He stopped and looked over his shoulder. "That means don't stray from the trails."

Captain Bullock and the forward soldiers looked to their left. Navajo on spotted ponies rode in the same direction as the Volunteers. But they proceeded along no discernible path, across snowdrifts, without impediment. One of the warriors looked over at the soldiers and gave a sad grin.

T.R. saw the men looking and smiled before guiding his camel to traverse a muddy patch that might catch his mounts foot. "I've been around the Indians a good bit in my day." He pointed to a small pile of rocks between the soldiers and the Navajo. "See those rocks? The shape, the size, the number of stones, all have different meanings for the Indian." The ex-president turned and pointed in the other direction, toward the face of the granite mountain. "And all the pictures you see scratched on boulders and cliffsides, they all have a meaning to the Indian. It tells them where to go, what to avoid, what's ahead."

One of the camels stumbled in a drift, fell forward on its belly and bellowed with annoyance. The USVC soldier shouted an obscenity as both camel and rider sank up to their necks in the snow. The Navajo warriors snickered as they moved their horses through the cover effortlessly.

The ex-president said nothing and pressed his camel forward. Two riders threw the stranded soldier a rope and the rest of his men followed. The procession bore to the left. What seemed to be hundreds of feet of snow-capped mountain behind ridge after ridge before them finally led to a narrow gorge.

The soldiers paused at the mouth of the narrows, mutters of complaints up and down the line.

"Colonel Roosevelt," Sergeant Berry said softly, "the Navajo are gone."

Soldiers stopped and peered through the live oak, walnut and junipers for movement but saw nothing. They looked up and down the mountain, then at each other, and fell silent.

T.R. climbed down from his camel to lead it through. Only man or beast in a single file could proceed. "The Indian uses a number of tricks to coordinate and evade enemy activity," he chuckled. "They've got advance scouts, flanking scouts and rear-guards. They've got eyes on us, they've got eyes on the mountain behind us, and chances are they already have eyes on what we're looking for."

Water streamed through a crevice at the mouth of narrows. The ex-president stuck his hand in the water, dabbed his tongue with a wet finger, and spat. "Rich with alkali. Unfit for man or beast. Keep away."

The soldiers at the front of the line dismounted and led their camels in line behind their leader. As they proceeded, the rest of the battalion behind them did so in quiet unison as they reached

87

the entrance. Within the narrows, they passed several springs of fresh water that both camel and man stopped at to drink their fill. Huge impressive rocks sat wedged between the cliffs above them, with bushes and trees clinging to the walls.

The ex-president pointed to a scraggly trail heading up the rocks to the right. "Ignore the goat path, and the ground might be loose so take care." Another hundred yards and he stepped through a widening gap in the narrows and onto a field of wildflowers.

The soldiers stood at the top of a steep hill that led into a small open valley ringed with cottonwood and aspen. USVC soldiers led their camels through and filed out to stand side by side next to the ex-president, looking out. Granite and Limestone loomed all around them as they took in the valley.

Half a dozen USVC soldiers dropped the reins on their camels and stepped in front of their Colonel, guns raised, as a Thing machine came over the hill. It stomped the wildflowers with an eerie hiss-thump, metal claw raised up, a green glow with silver trim in the center of its chest.

# INTERLUDE 37
March 20, 1917, 3:05 pm
Black Mountain

Ernie sat huddled behind the Pine Fern and rock, waiting for the two Aztec rotters on the ledge above him to make a move. *Did they see me?*

After a minute, he heard scraping, then footsteps. Soft moans and groans drifted over the air until the sounds receded across the small gorge. He peeked out and saw the two Aztecs had moved to the other side. One of the rotters led five chained Navajo towards the remaining sand boat. The second loaded baskets of silver ore.

Ernie crawled out from behind the rocks and moved low towards the toppled cauldron. He crept slowly towards the green light in the ground until he knelt on his hands and knees above it. Green can be mossy or garden-like, but the crystal set in the silver base cast a deeper green than any found in nature, without inclusions or flaws.

He reached out to the green crystal and held his palms out to it. *Nothing. No heat.* He put his hands on the glowing medallion about six inches across, set deep into about two inches of jagged and uneven silver around its periphery. *How the hell did it melt the ore?* The encrusted crystal had simply been laid into the dirt and he lifted it out and held it in his hands. *About the weight of my sister's cat Manx.*

Ernie looked up, searching for the rotters, making sure he knew where they were. He found them in time to see the last of the silver ore baskets being loaded into the remaining vessel and gasped as the second Aztec raised his jade club. The rotter beat one Navajo over the head, knocking him to the ground, then proceeded to strike him repeatedly until the bound Indian lay still. The Aztec broke the manacle around the foot of the dead Indian and kicked him aside as the other four cowered in terror.

The Aztec rotter swung his club and struck the second Navajo—a young woman—across the head. She had instinctively raised her hands up and the first strike dealt a glancing blow, knocking her off her feet. Crying, she held her hands up defensively to ward off the second blow.

The three others stared over the rotter's shoulder as Ernie, his satchel over his shoulder, ran up behind the Aztec and swung his club hard. The jade blade sunk into the back of the rotter's neck, nearly severing its head. He couldn't pull the blade out as the undead warrior turned on him and the two came nearly face to face. That's when the three Indians jumped on the rotter. He never let go of the shaft and the blade pulled free as the Navajo pulled the Aztec to the ground.

The Aztec aboard the sand boat had not reacted to the scuffle. He still kept stacking the last of the ore baskets and stepped on the foot lever at the bow. The hull of the boat hummed and the rotter turned around.

Ernie leaped into the boat and swung the jade club, striking the rotter across the face, separating the rotter's jaw from its head completely. The mandible flew off in grisly bits and disappeared over the side. The rotter staggered, then lurched. He jumped aside and around the mainmast as the Aztec fell past him and crashed into the piles of stacked silver ore. He took a couple of steps back to put more space between them and glanced over at the Indians on the ground. "Get back!" he shouted.

The Indians were crushing the skull of the rotter on the ground with their leather-clad feet. Ernie took another step back and his foot fell on a pedal recessed into the floor of the boat. He looked down where he had stepped as the sand boat shuddered. "Mother…." he moaned.

The Aztec knocked several baskets of ore aside as he rose to his feet, rasping with half a face. Ernie had his jade club held up over his shoulder, prepped for a fastball when two Navajo leaped into the craft and knocked the Aztec off the side. The Indians were still chained together, and so two of the Indians were clinging to the side of the vessel. The rotter hit the rocks below and broke apart. Arms and legs separated from the torso and tumbled among the boulders as the rest of the skull shattered and the form lay still.

# INTERLUDE 38
March 20, 1917, 3:44 pm
Black Mountain

The USVC soldiers poured through the narrows gap into the gorge. They led their camels by the reins, moving the patient, graceful creatures at a fast trot into single line formation. T.R. took off his spectacles, wiped his face with his blue polka-dotted handkerchief and guided his men through a shallow crossing.

On the right flank, several squads were focused on beating down the impossible man-machine that had attacked them as soon as they came through the narrows. The monstrosity plowed into the brave Volunteers as bullets bounced off its metal hide.

Sergeant Berry rallied his unit and charged the hideous creature, firing his weapon. "Formation men, keep your formation!" The creature's huge metal claw swung and knocked the Sergeant off his camel.

Four soldiers jumped on top of the creature. They had their guns aimed into its body and were firing furiously. One of its legs blew off, its knees buckled, and it struggled to move. The man-machine fell down but not out. It twisted and knocked one soldier off. One Volunteer put a bayonet on his rifle and jammed it into the metal chassis. Sparks flew and the monstrosity screamed in pain. A second soldier fired a three-round burst from his SMLE up into the fleshy chest. The Thing let out a final roar that ended in a bloody gurgle. As the machine man-thing collapsed, the USVC soldiers fell on top of him in exhaustion.

The soldiers studied the thing, grotesque beyond the explanation of Lovecraft or Shelley. It had a bizarrely plain-looking visage of a man who could have been a midwestern farmer or a bricklayer, but not an Aztec. Thick metallic cables ran through its neck and into its chest which rested in a steel-plated chassis.

On the open grassy plain sat a square metal structure that measured thirty feet per side. It had a dozen interlocking metal arches and resembled something like a dead spider on its back. At its center, several man-machines were adding silver blocks. Four of the metal monsters moved around the periphery.

Two more of them stood around what appeared to be a rotary steam motor. But it had no boiler. Steam went into a cylinder which caused a piston to move a large drum, emitting steam in the air. A lone Thing machine stood behind the mechanism, the other stood to its side, and tilted a crate of silver balls over its head. Four-pound silver shot poured out of the box into a channel that fed into the rotating drum. With soft thumps, the four-pound shot erupted from the cylinders and slammed into the mountainside.

On the hillside, USVC soldiers yelled in panic as the ground exploded around them. Bodies were ripped apart as projectiles fell out of the sky. Trees splintered. A single shot slammed through both a USVC Sergeant named Ousler and the camel he sat on. They toppled over, nearly ripped in half.

Men called out in pain, twisted and broken bodies lay behind them, as the troops moved forward into the valley. With a roar, a couple of hundred rotter warriors erupted from tree cover, adorned with eagle and jaguar headdresses, their loincloths flapping in the full run, battle armor glinting in the afternoon sun, pounding up the hill in leather sandals and waving their jade clubs and axes.

Aztec undead rushed up the hill toward them. The USVC soldiers laid down a wall of .303 fire with their SMLE's cutting through the undead horde. The volley of bullets struck a warrior in a Jaguar head mask repeatedly. It staggered and kept running. Two Volunteer soldiers took aim and the headpiece exploded. A rotter in an eagle mask with a huge plume got within ten feet of the USVC formation and four men directed their fire at it. Its torso disintegrated in a hail of steel.

T.R. ran back to his camel and jumped on. He tied the blue polka-dotted kerchief around his head, put his hat back on and charged down the mountain ahead of his men, his sword held high.

Sergeant Berry stood next to Captain Bullock, laying .303 fire into the swarm of Aztec horrors running toward. He jabbed the Captain with his elbow and pointed to the ex-president heading down the hill. "What the hell is he doing sir?"

The Captain turned and ran for his camel. "He wore that bandana on San Juan Hill. I think he's still got a touch of malaria!"

At that moment, on the far cliffs, a bugle broke out in a rendition of "assembly" as Navajo warriors on horseback came galloping out of a break in the rocky cliffs above. The Indians leaped from the cliffside astride their ponies. As they landed the riders pulled their bows and began shooting at the rotter horde as they fanned out across the open field.

# INTERLUDE 39
March 20, 1917, 4:17 pm
Black Mountain

Ernie stared at the horrors before him. The Indians on the craft were being pulled over the edge by their two companions hanging off the side. "Hold on!" He shouted to the Indians, who studied him with incomprehension. Both strained against the rail as their companions threatened to pull them over. He turned and pressed the lever on the floor of the vessel as the boat picked up speed.

He leaped across the boat and gripped the hand of the closest Indian hanging off the side. The woman with a bleeding head had lost her grip on the railing as she ran alongside. She tried to maintain her footing as the vessel picked up speed, knowing one fall would pull them all over.

"Grab my hand!" Ernie shouted, holding his hand out. *They don't understand.* He reached down, grabbed the wrist of the Indian who still clutched the railing and pulled him in. Once the man had two arms over the railing, he reached out towards the woman.

"You can do it!" he called out. The girl studied him. She nearly stumbled, cried out, and jumped. He caught her right arm above the elbow, her left arm gripped his shoulder and in another moment all four Indians were in the sand boat, panting and gasping. His face changed as the base of the mast emitted a green glow he knew quite well. The windsock sail overhead opened up, and the trail before them loomed.

"How the hell do you steer this thing?" he muttered. He knelt on the deck of the sand boat, gripping the handrail with one hand as wind hummed through the windsock sail. With the other hand, he searched around near the pedal on the floor, looking for another lever or way to reverse the action. The vessel continued to pick up speed.

Ahead, two large boulders loomed directly in the path of the fast-moving craft. Ernie looked back at the Navajo as they braced for a collision. His legs tensed as he prepared to leap aside before the impending collision when the vessel shifted slightly to the left and sailed past the rubble. *The thing is steering itself! What's that sound?*

Gunshots resonated in the distance and above the din rang a tinny tune. *A bugle.*

The cliffs and trees raced by and sounds of gunshots grew louder. The sand boat took a hard left turn into a small valley filled with screams, smoke, and violence. Ahead and slightly to Ernie's left coming into the valley, the hillside exploded. American soldiers were racing downhill—on camels! Dirt and bodies scattered on the hill, debris browned into the air. Just to his right, Navajo on spotted ponies came pouring out of a gap in the cliff, firing arrows.

And before them all, a mass of horrific Aztecs came racing up the hillside, wielding jade axes and inhuman visages. Soldiers and rotters collided as Indians circled the periphery slinging arrows into the undead. *I'm in the middle of a war!*

The craft took a right turn, swinging past the fighting. Several dozen chained Navajos cowered behind six Thing machines. One of the monstrosities worked a steam weapon that shot projectiles into the air.

The sand boat closed on the Navajo and the hideous man machines. Ernie shifted his satchel around his shoulder and the green crystal slid out. He pushed it back into his bag and pounded on the deck of the vessel in frustration. *Stop, dammit, stop!*

The Thing machine swiveled the steam cannon around and pointed it in his direction. He turned and pushed the first Navajo in front of him over the railing.

The Indian dragged the other three overboard and they fell and rolled into sumac and sage. A soft thump, an expulsion of steam, and the bow of the boat shattered in splinters.

Ernie staggered and leaped off the back of the vessel as another four-pound shot struck the sand boat. He hit the ground hard. *Like falling off a horse.*

When he opened his eyes, the young Navajo woman with blood running down her head kneeled over him. Three Indian braves approached at a gallop, their arrows drawn. The young Navajo woman turned and held up her arms. "Shik'is," she shouted. The riders slowed, lowered their weapons slightly, then turned as a Thing machine came striding their direction. The warriors charged the monstrosity, firing arrow after arrow. Three of the Navajo helped Ernie to his feet and they ran.

Behind them, the Thing machine batted a horse and rider aside with a single swipe. It staggered under the brunt of a dozen arrows in its face and chest but kept moving. The two remaining Navajo on horseback circled behind it, firing more arrows into its flesh. The metal monster roared, turned and gave chase.

# INTERLUDE 40
March 20, 1917, 4:33 pm
Black Mountain

"No man is allowed to drop out to help the wounded!" the ex-president shouted. He dismounted his dromedary and fired his Mauser to the left, swinging his sword to the right. Leaving one Aztec rotter flat on its back, a hole in its forehead. A second Aztec crawled around on the ground for its missing arm holding a long thin sword studded with obsidian blades.

Three soldiers fought side by side with T.R., firing their SMLE's into the moaning, howling swarm. A corporal went down with a bullet through his hip. He fell without a sound. The ex-president dragged him to a tree and propped him up with his gun.

"Can I have my canteen please?" the corporal asked, without a hint of pain.

The ex-president grabbed it out of his pack and left him there.

More men had joined the line moving against the Aztecs. One of the men cursed.

"Don't swear—shoot!" T.R. yelled, joining the line.

Three USVC soldiers at the extreme front were overwhelmed by rampaging Aztecs. The corporal next to the ex-president stepped forward with brave coolness into the undead who were tearing his comrades apart. He fired his SMLE until a tide of rotters carried him away.

Captain Bullock grabbed the ex-president's arm and pulled him back behind the line.

The attack stopped, and the men paused, sitting or leaning on trees, panting and out of breath. Sergeant Berry came over to give the ex-president a quick count of the dead.

"Sergeants Wood, Dame, McIlhenny and Dimick are down. First Platoon seven dead and eight wounded. Tenth Platoon one dead, ten wounded. Third Platoon is nearly wiped out. Altogether, fifty-two dead and another sixty-odd wounded. Fifteen camels are dead, another thirty have run off."

Then the ground exploded.

"It's that damnable artillery again! We've got to stop it!" T.R. said.

The USVC scrambled to maintain position and stay organized as the ordnance slammed into the ground. A squad of men gathered around some trees or brush, preparing to advance. The next moment they were gone, replaced by a crater in the ground.

The artillery stopped and sounds of alarm erupted along the line.

"Here they come again!" someone shouted.

Another swarm of Aztec rotters came stampeding through the trees and brush.

T.R. turned to Captain Bullock. "Lead your men down the mountain and take out those guns!"

The troops started moving in disciplined formation with the Captain's direction, keeping at intervals from one another, firing slowly and taking careful aim. The Aztec bodies piled up.

The ex-president ran down the hill, sliding into a small depression. An Aztec spear sank into the ground in front of him. To his right, USVC soldiers were holding off a swarm of rotters with suppression fire. To his left, four Navajo lay huddled with their ankles bound in chains, cowering next to a young man in a sack coat, a duffel over his shoulder and holding an Aztec jade club.

# INTERLUDE 41
March 20, 1917, 5:06 pm
Black Mountain

The ex-president and the remainder of his USVC battalion took up position along the tree line. Navajo riders were moving the last of their survivors up into the cliffs to safety. Rotter attacks continued sporadically. Roving groups of Jaguar and Eagle warriors were still roaming behind them and the occasional Volunteer would disappear. Men were glancing over their shoulders and firing into the trees and bushes wildly.

T.R. moved closer to the cowering Navajos as two Volunteers removed their manacles. The young man next to them stood up as a Jaguar warrior with a bullet-ridden chest and wielding a six-foot ebony-tipped spear ran up to them. Ernie swung the club in his hands like a baseball bat. The warrior's head flew off his shoulders along with the Jaguar headpiece.

"Who are you, son?" The ex-president asked, putting a hand on the man's shoulder.

The young man spun around bat at the ready. "Ernest Hemingway, sir. You're...you're President Roosevelt!"

"How did you get here, boy?" Nearby, several USVC soldiers opened fire on a group of charging rotters.

"Long story sir, President sir! I'm a writer. The Kansas City Star assigned me to investigate the cause of some disappearances. That led me to these rotters!"

"Bully for you, son! Do what you can, with what you have, where you are. That's what I say!"

The ground shook. The rotters stopped charging and the soldiers looked around. Dirt and gunsmoke enveloped them like fog in the gorge.

The bizarre structure in the center of the valley shaped like a dead spider stirred. Its legs uncurled, revealing thickly studded tires as tall as a man. The legs unfolder completely and settled on the ground. Three remaining Thing machines climbed aboard the craft as the large wheels settled into the dirt. The metal body lifted, groaning under the weight of the silver ore it carried. A green glow emanated from its belly as it lifted off the ground and a pipe emerged belching steam. Aztec undead turned in unison and marched for the pass.

Cheering broke out on the left.

"The men are charging!" T.R. exclaimed. He stepped in front of Captain Bullock and shouted, "Forward!"

The USVC raced across the wildflowers firing their SMLE's. Several camels made the charge. Aztec rotters turned, firing blow darts. More Volunteers fell.

Sergeant Cash spotted the ex-president from the side of his eye and called out, taking him for one of his men. "Keep your interval! Keep your interval and go forward!" A spear struck him down a moment later.

The massive vehicle moved past the cliffs, through the arroyo and into the clearing beyond the valley. Aztec warriors were falling now. Only a few dozen rotters remained as the Volunteers advanced, confident and disciplined.

That's when the nightmares appeared.

# INTERLUDE 42
March 20, 1917, 5:34 pm
Black Mountain

The forms broke out of the early evening haze making a terrible high-pitched racket. The pace started slow, with the figures in loose formation as they entered the arroyo. As they came through the open end of the gorge, they had closed ranks and moved at incredible speed.

Giant dark horses with metal soldiers atop them snorted heat and flames rippled in the air, their hooves pounding the earth as they approached. These beasts reached out and plucked USVC soldiers off the ground from twenty feet away, lifted them into the air and flung their broken bodies aside. Most impossibly, each horse displayed a pair of white wings eight feet tall unfurled across their backs giving them nightmarish height and size, and they made a terrible racket.

The USVC soldiers were frozen, paralyzed in astonishment as the figures charged. They ran through the center of the line and the two hundred or so battle-exhausted khaki-clad soldiers scattered.

Captain Bullock shouted to his men. "Maintain the line! Maintain the line!" But chaos reigned.

USVC soldiers broke and ran, and the terrifying winged figures before him broke through the brown haze when a hand grabbed his lapel. "What are they?" he rasped.

The ex-president leaned around the trunk and stared with rapt pleasure. "Winged Hussars. Magnificent. They haven't seen battle for more than two hundred years." He pointed. "Look, they're not monsters."

Ernie turned slowly to peer around the yellow pine and saw the figures. He could now see that they were in fact, soldiers on horseback. Armored riders atop large black stallions, wielding twenty-foot lances, turned after breaking through the USVC ranks and headed back out of the canyon. He spotted beautiful, enormous wings displayed from wooden frames on the soldiers' backs, making a tremendous banging noise while the feathers rippled in the air. The flames were red and yellow banners that waved atop the wooden frame.

"First Uhlan cavalry, now seventeenth-century Winged Hussars—in New Mexico." T.R. shook his head. "Astonishing."

After breaking the American lines, the Hussars broke into two separate columns. Each spearhead made wide flanking turns to the outside, clashing again with retreating soldiers. In moments they had turned completely around and were charging out of the gorge. No one pursued the winged nightmares as they moved through the arroyo and were soon out on the open desert. The trail of the horsemen followed the dust and tracks from the spider-like vehicle.

The ex-president and Ernie ran to the edge of the valley and looked west from Black Mountain as the sun set. The spider vehicle maintained a faint green glow as it disappeared over a hill.

Captain Bullock and a small squad on camelback rode up behind them, towing a spare camel.

T.R. studied Captain Bullock with a frown. "Al Shamlal?"

Bullock shook his head. "Your camel is dead, Colonel Roosevelt."

The green glow faded, and the winged soldiers grew smaller as the ex-president watched with frustration. Then something caught his eye and he turned up and to the left. Three Navajo were on a rocky perch high on the cliffside, watching. One of the warriors looked down, paused a moment, and held his arms up slightly in front of himself, palms out. Then he thrust them outward in a zigzag motion.

*They are going to follow them.* T.R. turned to Captain Bullock. "The camels are too shook to be ridden. The Navajo will show us their trail."

Ernie looked angry. "So, they're just going to get away?"

The ex-president stopped and put a hand on the young man's shoulder. He motioned his head up toward the cliffs. The Navajo waited a moment more before turning and disappearing into the mountain. "Native Americans invented what we know as hit-and-run tactics. They will not leave them alone. We will follow them in the morning."

# INTERLUDE 43
March 21, 1917, 5:04 am
Black Mountain

*It is the morning of March twenty-first and most of the camp is still getting well-needed rest. We have some rations that amount to a handful of beans, coffee and sugar, and some hardtack and bacon. What started on the afternoon of the eighteenth has turned into a trek of over a hundred miles through New Mexico badlands. Contrary to President Wilson's notion that America is impartial in thought as well as in action, we encountered hostile Uhlan cavalry at El Morro where we were training. Our brigade lost a dozen men and suffered two dozen more wounded. I directed Captain Groome to take his half strength brigade and accompany those needing attention back to Fort Wingate. Captain Bullock rallied the second brigade in proper form for the unexpected efforts and we pursued the renegades south for nearly two days, arriving within sight of Black Mountain.*

*We encountered a nearby tribe expressing great concern for the general welfare of a missing village, including women and papoose. Darkness came on and we set camp, sleeping under our rain-coats on top of saddle blankets. That night, I made the rounds of the sentries and worked to calm the uneasy excitement. It is almost simpler the night before battle because it is known what is expected. But these soldiers did not know what the following day would bring. Neither did I.*

*It struck me, the quiet soldierly way the men set about their duties. Later that morning we arrived at the abandoned Navajo settlement. Accompanied by a small force of Indians on horseback, we proceeded up the north side of Black Mountain. Hundreds of square miles of immense wilderness broken only by the trails of animals and indigenous tribes. Not without a certain thrill of the naturalist or explorer, our surroundings brought us to a narrow gorge where we encountered a horde of unspeakable horrors.*

*Men of imaginary Gods of some primitive tribe whose ancestors had perished before Piltdown. They were adorned as Mesoamerican warriors but were blasphemous abnormalities. Once dead they now walked again. Grotesque beyond the description of a Poe or a Radcliffe, they were damnable human in form. We made a frantic descent into the small valley, battling man and automaton alike. A steam cannon shattered the narrows as we met. Had I not faced an undead in combat, I might have cause to consider it all a phantasm and seek St Vincent's for more malarial rehabilitation.*

*The Indian joined the fray and we drove the horrors into retreat along with their strange vehicle. The Volunteers sought to give chase but a cadre of*

*Winged Hussars gave cover. They were glorious warriors with twenty-foot lances and magnificent plumage. The tumult became more than desperate men's minds could take and the enemy escaped. We will begin pursuit at first light when the nearly one hundred dead are buried and we have eaten the last of our rations. I can hardly describe the mood I am left in by this harrowing episode.*

*Dear Father, Mother, and Children,*

*If this letter finds you, I am writing to you somewhere in New Mexico. My boss sent me here on assignment and I have found nothing but hardship and bad omens. Entire towns and villages are missing and it looks like the campaign slander against the Spaniard is true, he is a cowardly cruel bastard. I beheld a gladiator contest with Spanish warriors in Aztec costume on one side and President Roosevelt and his Rough Riders on the other. He is as bold an adventurer in real life as you, Father. As you said, Generals rarely die except in bed.*

*It's ok, I know it won't make much sense for now. I am healthy on this writing, and I am glad for it. The last time I laid in hospital, doctors nearly removed my Adam's apple, taken for a cyst. Mother, when a parent brings a son into the world, she knows someday that son is going to die. The mother of a son who has died for his country should be the proudest. How much better to die in the happy period of undisillusioned youth than to die old and disillusioned.*

*I would like to come home and see you all but I can't until this is finished.*

*As ever, Ernie*

# INTERLUDE 44
## March 21, 1917, 11:22 am
## Outside Hillsboro, New Mexico

Nearly four hundred USVC soldiers made their way from Black Mountain south on this dry, temperate day. Two-thirds of the men moved on foot, as most of the camels had died or ran off. Ernie walked next to T.R., astride his camel.

"Cliff dwellings you say. How extraordinary! I'll make a note to survey the mountain after we return." the ex-president brushed dirt from his eyes with his signature bandana.

Ernie reached into his ruck and pulled out a cloth covering several chunks of bloody meat and handed one up to the ex-president

T.R. tore a hunk of bear meat off, chewing loudly. "Cooked middling rare, lots of fat. A bit rank and a little stringy but otherwise excellent. Did you shoot it yourself, son?"

"I did, President Roosevelt, sir. With a shotgun, I picked up back in Shakespeare."

"Montana is where you should go if you want to hunt bear. You can hunt elk, deer, bighorn sheep, but your best bear hunting is there. I used to have a ranch in the Dakotas and the hunting there is the best in the world. You take an old horse, put it down, and use it as bait. Wait for the big fellas to show up."

Sergeant Berry came riding back from the forward positions. "Stagecoach approaching, sir."

The Concord stagecoach that came into view moved east across a faint trail.

The ex-president smiled. "Mark Twain wrote, 'Our coach—a great swinging and swaying stage, of the most sumptuous description.' "

It slowed as it came upon the soldiers on camelback and stopped in front of T.R. A small woman sat alone in the driver's box. She looked to be no more than five feet tall and a hundred pounds, wearing a high fashion dress and smoking a cigar.

The woman stood up, pulled the cigar from her mouth and spat. Even at a distance, the woman cut a shapely figure, with long black hair and blue eyes. "What in the wide blue world of fuck are you doing out here?"

The ex-president raised his eyebrows. Captain Bullock studied him sideways and cleared his throat.

"Madam," Captain Bullock said dryly, "We are the First Volunteer Regiment. I am Captain Seth Bullock. This is Colonel Theodore Roosevelt. We are short of rations and have wounded among us. Can you assist us or lead us to someone who can?"

"Roosevelt? As in President Roosevelt? Colonel is a bit of a step down isn't it?" She sat down. "My name is Sadie Orchard, and I run an establishment in Hillsboro. We can tend to your wounded and feed you. I've got the best table in town."

"Very good, madam."

"I voted for you, Mr. President," she said, nodding, "I think you did fine."

T.R. looked over at Ernie, next to him astride his own camel. "What do you think, young Hemingway?"

Ernie chewed on a piece of bear meat and tilted his head. "Well, Mr. Roosevelt, Mr. President—the best way to find out if you can trust someone is to trust them, my mother always said."

# INTERLUDE 45
March 21, 1917, 3:36 pm
Ocean Grove Hotel, Hillsboro, New Mexico

With Sadie leading the way, the caravan of tired and wounded strolled into the small mining town of Hillsboro.

The ex-president came bouncing up on camelback and got up next to Sadie. "Where can my men get fresh provisions, madam?"

"We got a General Store that services every prospector, gun runner, rancher and settler for a hundred miles. More than enough for your men to stock up if you can pay."

The coach stopped in front of the one-story hotel that stretched about a block long, with bars on the windows and doors.

Ernie dropped onto the porch, exhausted. T.R. climbed down from his camel and studied the area, moving in a full circle.

"Captain Bullock, have your men set up observations in that tower," he said, pointing to the church at the end of the north block, "and another on top of the general store at the other end of town. Then I want roving patrols in all directions, at half a mile and a mile out. Use fresh runners every thirty minutes. I want up to the hour reports."

Captain Bullock saluted. "Permission to speak, Colonel Roosevelt."

The ex-president motioned for him to continue. Captain Bullock's eyes glanced toward the hotel and back. The ex-president turned and saw Sadie in the doorway, two young women in bright dresses standing behind her.

"We've got pozole, green chili stew, and whiskey." Sadie winked over her shoulder. "And a dozen girls to entertain nightly."

T.R. stepped into the brick building and looked around. The restaurant had a dozen tables placed randomly about the room. Only two locals sat in the far corner. He looked back out the door to Bullock. "Captain, rotate your men in by company."

A whoop went up from the USVC soldiers. A middle-aged Asian man in a dark shirt and an apron came out of a door that led to a kitchen.

"This is Tom Ying. He runs the restaurant." Sadie said, placing a hand on the man's shoulder. "He'll get you anything we have to eat. Mr. Ying, this is President Roosevelt At least he used to be President." The man stiffened. "Now he's a Colonel, and these are his men. They've been traveling across New Mexico for some days and need food and rest."

Mr. Ying nodded and motioned to the tables. Soldiers came in and sat and several women mingled among them.

Ernie awoke and opened his eyes, finding himself lying flat on the wooden slats of the porch. A young woman with short dark hair and brown eyes stood over him. He braced himself on his elbows and raised up partly, blinking.

"Hello," the pretty woman said.

"Ma'am," Ernie said slowly. He sat up and looked around. "I fell asleep I guess."

The woman smiled. "My name is Mary."

"Nice to meet you, Mary. I'm Ernest Hemingway, you can call me Ernie." He slowly got to his feet.

"You look like you could use a bath and a rest, Mr. Hemingway."

Ernie smiled and blushed. "It's been a heck of a couple of days. We were chasing some...bandits. We've got them on the run I think."

Mary smiled and led him by the arm, "We'll get you something to eat. Come on in."

Ernie smiled, walking unsteadily. "Thank you, Mary."

Mary walked Ernie into the restaurant and sat him down at an empty table. Mr. Ying carried an armful of empty bowls and plates from soldier's meals. Mary placed a large mug and a pitcher of water in front of him. He sat at the table trying to keep his eyes open, reaching for the water. "I'll go get your food," Mary said softly.

# INTERLUDE 46
March 21, 1917, 5:11 pm
Ocean Grove Hotel, Hillsboro, New Mexico

Ernie had made his way halfway through another large bowl of green chili stew. An empty large bowl sat nearby, along with a nearly empty basket of cornbread and the pitcher of water. T.R. and Captain Bullock sat with him as he ate loudly.

"We've got another ninety miles to travel, Captain. There is a General Store in town. I've wired authorization for enough funds to be transferred to the store to make sure we are well supplied. Make a list, Captain."

Captain Bullock removed a notepad and a nub of pencil from his breast pocket.

"We must make sure the men get a good night of rest. We won't be taking accommodations here at the hotel," Bullock glanced up with disappointment but quickly kept writing, "so we are going to need plenty of coverage. We don't have the luxury of a Supply unit or a Corps of Engineers preparing more suitable environs. First, make sure we have plenty of Citronella."

Bullock nodded. "Citronella."

"If it weren't for the bugs we would all live in the bush. It's the natural impulse of the human being." T.R. said smoothly, looking at Ernie as he pulled the small capsule of citronella from his pants pocket and set it on the table.

The ex-president tilted his head thoughtfully. "Make sure every man has a can of Crisco, a pound of bacon, a pound of coffee and a Duck Tent. Every platoon will have a stew kettle and flour. Soldiers will learn soon enough the cook is the man who brags."

"Bacon, coffee, stew kettle...flour. Got it, Colonel Roosevelt."

"If they have a tent stove, buy that as well. Preferably one with a large firebox." The ex-president held up a hand and a single finger. "Now for the tents. Insist on quality. The proprietor may see government dollars coming and try to cheat you. Nothing over 5 pounds. One for every two men. Pull-outs should be sewn into the seams. Beckets over grommets because grommets cut the fabric when stressed—and they will pop out. Also, make sure all stress points are reinforced." He paused while Bullock continued to write. "Sod cloth should NOT be joined at the corners so they can be turned out. Lastly, plenty of rope. That'll be all."

Captain Bullock closed his notepad, saluted and left the restaurant. Ernie finished his second bowl and let out a long belch, then drank from the huge carafe of water, gulping as he swallowed.

"Sergeant Berry!" T.R. called out.

"Colonel Roosevelt, sir!" The Sergeant stood up from a table across the room and moved toward the ex-president.

"I saw some ideal spots just outside of town to set up camp. There were several groves of young trees. You need to send two companies out to start collecting wood." Sergeant Berry stood before him now. "Tell the men to collect twice as much as we need."

Sadie walked up to the table. "I know where you're talkin about. There's a small Protestant church on the outside of town. Some of the girls put money together to build the town a church." The ex-president smiled Sadie. "So I'm sayin that you can use the church to put some of your wounded up. If you need it."

"Thank you, Madam. Sergeant, see that some of the walking wounded are put up in the church."

Ernie set the carafe down empty, and exhaled, then let out a long yawn.

"Yes, sir!" Sergeant Berry saluted.

"Tell the men to be aware when they collect wood. The mere fact that there are downed trees does not mean there is good kindling. Maple and Oak are the best. If they find Arizona Sycamore, all the better."

The Sergeant stood, waiting for more.

"That's all, Sergeant. Get moving."

Ernie had his head on the table, snoring.

# INTERLUDE 47
March 22, 1917, 5:06 am
Ocean Grove Hotel, Hillsboro, New Mexico

The door burst open in the small room in the hotel. Mary sat up and cried out with embarrassment, covering her breasts. Ernie turned over slowly, sleepily, to find the ex-president standing at the foot of the bed, wearing his slouch hat, dark blue flannel shirt, khaki trousers, and white canvas suspenders.

"Let's go, boy! It's going to take most of the day for the supplies to get put together. My men are purchasing every burro from here to Kingston and we have important guests arriving this evening. So, we are going to explore. I want to find a Clark's nutcracker and maybe an Evening grosbeak."

With that, T.R. turned and left the room in a spirited jaunt.

Ernie looked at Mary, who sat in dumbfounded silence. Slowly he rose out of bed and put on his clothes. "I'm gonna go now, ma'am," he said, putting on his pants, "You were really nice."

Outside the entrance to the hotel, Sergeant Berry and Captain Bullock stood amid stacks of rations and supplies. He counted rolls of canvas, heaps of coffee, stacks of stew kettles and piles of tent stakes.

The ex-president stepped out on the porch. "The former governor is going to be visiting this afternoon. Bill McDonald put this state together amidst Pancho Villa. He'll know what we need to do."

"We're having trouble finding a decent tent stove, Colonel. We did find a couple of Montana stoves at the small General Store in Kingston." Captain Bullock pointed to a stack of small stoves with legs, with hot water tanks, pans and utensils fit inside them.

"That will do, Captain. Sergeant, please put me up a lunch." Ernie ran out the front door, one shoe on, his shirt half-buttoned. "The boy and I are going to go bird watching."

"Sir, I don't think that's a good idea."

"Could I get some breakfast?" Ernie asked from the porch. Mary brought out several biscuits wrapped in a cloth napkin and handed them to him, smiling.

T.R. smiled at Bullock. "Put us up a lunch. We'll be back this afternoon."

"Let me send a couple of corporals with you, sir."

"No need." The ex-president waved him off.

The Captain pressed. "Then let me send you with an orderly."

Ernie came stumbling down the stairs.

"That's enough, Captain," the ex-president said. "All set, young Hemingway?"

"For what, Mister President?"

"We're going for a hike, my boy! Have you ever been birdwatching?"

Ernie rubbed his eyes sleepily. "I shot a great blue heron once."

Sadie came out on the porch and handed T.R. a small ruck-sack and a canteen. "I packed you some ham and chicken salad sandwiches," she said and winked at Ernie. "And I threw in some Peppermint Life Savers for the boy."

# INTERLUDE 48
March 22, 1917, 3:17 pm
Hillsboro, New Mexico

The soldiers had put up their tents and gathered firewood. Several fires were going with spatchcocked quail roasting on a rotisserie. Some men were playing cards, others were staying warm with Cuba Libre in the forty-degree weather, singing war songs.

The ex-president came bounding out of the wilderness east from the camp. "Boys, I have had a remarkable day!" He appeared energized as if he had just awoken.

Ernie came stumbling behind him. He appeared exhausted and haggard. "Anybody have any water?" A soldier handed him a canteen and he drank deeply.

"Men, conservation is the chief question that confronts us, second only—and second always—to the fundamental questions of morality." T.R. went and stood in a group of singing soldiers who stopped to listen to him. "The vast wealth of lumber in our forests, the riches of our soils and mines, the discovery of gold and minerals, combined with the efficiency of transportation, have made conditions of life unparalleled in comfort and convenience."

Ernie stumbled and sank down on his butt. The soldiers around him were grinning at him knowingly. One soldier handed him a fried quail. "It's unbelievable," he said. "We were moving at an incredible pace. We did that for over two hours before he stopped to look at birds." He took a bite. "We skipped over logs and rocks. He would stop, crane his neck this way and that, then move again for no reason." One of the soldiers snorted.

The ex-president sat among the men. "So great and so rapid has been our material growth that there has been a tendency to lag behind in spiritual and moral growth." There is applause from the men at this. "It is safe to say that the prosperity of our people depends directly on the energy and intelligence with which our natural resources are used. We have to, as a nation, exercise foresight for this nation in the future; and if we do not exercise that foresight, dark will be the future!" More applause.

Ernie took the canteen and poured it over his head, swallowing the last of the bird. He looked both ways at the soldiers sitting around him. "We walked eighteen miles." One of the soldiers put a hand on his shoulder as he whispered softly, "He's part billy goat." More laughter.

"I'm proud of you men. No force is worth anything if its members are not intelligent and honest; but neither is it worth anything unless its members are brave, hardy and well disciplined. It has been my pleasure to recognize men over a thousand times for special mention because of some feat of heroism. Once this is done I will have several dozen more to add to that list."

# INTERLUDE 49
March 22, 1917, 4:43 pm
Ocean Grove Hotel, Hillsboro, New Mexico

Former territorial Governor George Curry arrived in a Case Touring Car decorated with the American flag, the flag of the State of New Mexico and a thick layer of gypsum sand. A tall man with a firm demeanor, a high forehead, and a chin strap beard, he is dressed in a morning suit with a stiff collar and gray and black striped pants. When the car stopped in front of the hotel, George Curry stood up and put on a light gray hat. A young man in the backseat emerged and opened the Governor's door. Curry stepped out and T.R. approached with a hearty handshake.

"Mister President, it's good to see you again."

"Welcome, welcome!" the ex-president said jovially. He turned and led the former Governor from the car. "Governor, the men of the United States Volunteer Cavalry Regiment, second battalion." The ex-president waved his arm across the small town, pockmarked with tents and campfires.

Ernie appeared behind them, notepad in hand, still wearing his white, stiff collar shirt which had developed a worn fade. But now he had a khaki Rough Rider jacket on, unbuttoned, and sported a pair of Rough Rider leather high boots with his trousers tucked in.

George Curry studied the men bivouacked throughout the town, camels tethered to trees. "Cavalry, Mister President? Where are the horses?" The men continued to walk.

"The military has been slow with resources for our training. We requisitioned these dromedaries from the wild to execute our exercises. They are descendants of the Civil War Camel Corps, and so disposed to being cooperative. We are preparing to enter the war in Europe."

Curry nodded. "I imagine Wilson is still not in any hurry to commit troops."

T.R. shook his head. "The Zimmermann telegram has shaken them up in Washington. But its still not enough. I fear it will get worse before saner heads prevail. We need your help."

They approached the small church at one end of town.

"You were responsible for nominating me for territorial governor, Mister President. You will find me unflagging in my support for my friends. What assistance can I provide?"

"There's been an incursion from Mexico."

"La División del Norte?" Curry inquired, his voice rising.

The ex-president shook his head. "No, we don't think so. It's worse than that. We think that the Axis have troops in Mexico and are crossing over. The Zimmermann telegram is only the first shot. The second front has already begun."

"My God!"

"Yes, we had a lengthy battle with soldiers near Black Mountain. I believe that's deeper than any incursion by Pancho Villa."

"Soldiers?" Ernie blurted out and immediately looked down.

Curry glanced at the young man, then at T.R. who gave the writer a piercing glare.

"This young man is Ernest Hemingway." The ex-president said, pulling his eyes from Ernie and smiling at Curry. "He's a writer for the *Kansas City Star*."

"You're a long way from home," Curry said, without looking back at Ernie.

"Yes, Governor. We have reports of missing folks. My editor sent me here on assignment."

George Curry stopped and turned, his brow furrowed. "Missing? How many? How long?"

"Not sure how many, sir. But they've been missing weeks. Grocery runs, dentist trips, the like."

"Where is this? There hasn't been anything in the papers." Curry's eyes narrowed.

Ernie glanced at his notebook then back up. "Shakespeare."

Curry studied him, eyes wide. "Shakespeare! You might as well tell me you're looking into a ghost town. I doubt anybody lives out there."

Ernie stepped forward. "I assure you, Governor, people lived there—recently."

T.R. cleared his throat. "Shakespeare is closer to the border. We believe it may have been a staging area. Remote, sparsely populated, relatively inaccessible." The ex-president opened the front door of the church and motioned Curry inside while waving Ernie off.

Inside the chapel, several dozen men lay about the room, with women tending their wounds. Some sat against walls, some laid flat. All had bandages around their heads or chests. Several men were missing arms below the elbows or legs below the knees. In one corner, two bodies were completely covered. Men laid or sat against the walls moaning or crying.

"We need an introduction to Cavalry Camp Columbus." The ex-president stood with his hands clasped behind his back, chest out, chin up. "Before Wilson moves to war, more men and women may die like the Lusitania. We need them to be ready to listen. I need local authority to let them know we are coming."

"I am certainly eager to see any threat to the democracy confronted, Mister President. I will be glad to notify them of your arrival. This is the Second Battalion," Governor Curry cocked his head. "Where are the rest of your men, sir?"

"I telegrammed Captain Groome and the First Battalion to make haste from Fort Wingate. While we move south, the First

Battalion will be taking the Pacific to Las Cruces and meet us the morning after our arrival."

# INTERLUDE 50
March 22, 1917, 9:22 pm
Ocean Grove Hotel, Hillsboro, New Mexico

The ex-president sat with a couple of dozen soldiers around a blazing campfire. Bottles of Cuba Libre were being circulated among the men, the rum providing warmth in the 19°F New Mexico night. "We were hunting this time of year off the Little Missouri. But a month of March in North Dakota has a far more bitter feel. The frozen river we ferried across produced no meat nor trophy. When we returned to where we had left our little ferry, bandits had made off with it."

There were grumbles around the fire, soldiers shaking their heads.

"We spent three days building a new boat and set off after the scoundrels. My companions wanted to go home, but I couldn't let the scofflaws escape. For another three miserably cold days we navigated the icy, winding river, enduring temperatures down to zero."

Ernie sat on a large log in the back of the crowd with a flask of rum, next to Mary. She had a blanket around her shoulders, but she shivered and leaned in to speak into Ernie's ear. His eyes widened and they both got up from the fire and moved toward the hotel.

T.R. waved Ernie over. The young man nodded to Mary and went over to lean close to Roosevelt.

"No other happiness in the world is so great or so enduring as that of two lovers," The ex-president said softly, then patted Ernie's cheek, before turning back to the fire.

Ernie left the campfire behind.

The ex-president continued. "We finally caught up with the thieves, led by a hard case named Finnigan. My hunting partners and I got the drop on them easy, as they had not expected anyone to follow." He took a heavy swig on his water flask and stuck his hands out towards the fire. "We tied them up, took their boots, and made our way back. Unfortunately, the river had developed an impassable ice dam we couldn't navigate. It held us up for more than eight days. Those boys suffered the cold something miserable!"

"Tell us what happened next, Colonel," a voice called out from the audience.

"I provided respite from the weather reading Anna Karenina to my fellow passengers." T.R. laughed uproariously, pumping his fists. "I think those poor boys were ready for hanging by the fifth day!"

"So did you hang them, sir? " Sergeant Berry asked. "They had it coming."

"On the contrary, son. After watching over the criminals for more than forty hours at a time, while my fellow hunters slept, I performed my duties as a Deputy Sheriff and arrested the men."

"You went easy on them, sir?" muttered a soldier from the darkness.

The ex-president studied the faces around the fire. His jovial nature turned somber. He pulled a cigar from his breast pocket and lit it. Billowing clouds of Cuban smoke wafted in the air before he spoke again.

"In 1902 the governor of Mississippi invited me on a hunting trip. After three days, I never managed to spot a bear. On the fourth day, one of the hunting guides tracked down an old bear we had chased off days before. The guide, Lieutenant Collier, happened to be a born slave and former Confederate Cavalryman. A tougher man you'll be pressed to find. He had staked the bear to a willow tree and waited for me to make my kill." The President paused, puffed on the cigar. Everyone around the fire stayed silent. "I couldn't do it. The bear looked mangy and starved, clearly on its way to dying. I told Holt to put it out of its misery. Over the next few weeks, the papers played it up. And you all know what came next."

"Last Christmas," said one soldier, "I bought my daughter a Teddy Bear." Laughter in the crowd.

"Hunting is not about the kill, men. Never forget that."

# INTERLUDE 51
March 23, 1917, 11:16 am
Sixty Miles From Mexico

The 1917 Case Motorized Car came to a halt at Pony Hills, its six-cylinder continental engine grinding and sputtering, as the cloud of sand around it spread into the air and settled into clothing, eyes, and hair. The convoy had turned east, crossing the sloping desert mesa to avoid a deep deflation hollow before they would turn again towards the Mexico border.

The ex-president stood up in the open car, hands on the windshield of the touring vehicle, and brushed the terrain from his clothing. Beside him, Captain Bullock stopped atop his camel, and four hundred and twenty soldiers of the Volunteer Regiment fell into line behind them riding new horses, burros and the remaining camels. Everyone watched the spectacle that travelled from north to south in front of them. No one budged. No one even coughed.

At the distance which the USVC caravan observed, over a mile away, the figures traversing the desert on foot might have been mistaken for a herd of antelope, except these beasts ran upright. Their heads had odd random shapes. Some seemed to have plumage. Every single one of them moved across the landscape at an untiring pace.

"Look at them run," Captain Bullock muttered.

"I'm counting thirty from here," T.R. responded.

A Private astride a pale little donkey on a nearby outcropping pointed further north. "Look, Captain!"

Five vehicles came over a high dune, kicking up a sandstorm as they crested the drift. Four heavy armored vehicles, with a smaller vehicle slightly behind, moved in pursuit of the runners. Shots rang out from the heavy vehicles and the ground exploded amidst the fleeing numbers.

"Thirty-seven-millimeter cannon," the ex-president exclaimed. He pumped a fist in the air. "Bully!"

Behind the armored vehicles, four smaller and faster vehicles appeared and moved around the main group of trucks.

T.R. peered through a pair of binoculars. "Harleys with sidecars!"

The sidecars had armor plating to protect the gunner manning an 8mm gun through the slit. The motorcycles moved around the oncoming melee, in pursuit of the rotter horde. At the periphery, the combination closed on the lumbering rotters and, within a hundred yards, opened fire. Aztec rotters were cut in half or their heads burst within their wooden facades. Others stumbled, then kept on their single-minded journey.

The Harleys bore down on the horde, cutting the lopers down. It looked as if the undead warriors did not even notice the deadly barrage bearing down on them. Then, as if they were a flock of pigeons, the formation changed course which spread through the pack like a wave as the Aztecs reversed direction. The armored car cannon drilled into the troop of rotters and the Harleys rushed through them like galloping lancers. Bodies blew apart and the last of the soulless militia fell under the wheels of v-twins.

The skirmish over, T.R. and the USVC soldiers remained at the crest of Pony Hills, observing the armored vehicles and motorcycles regrouping and moving in their direction. The transports kicked up a dust storm as they approached. Twenty yards from their position the convoy stopped and Apache scouts in U.S. uniforms on horseback rode out of the whirlwind. Beside them, a Dodge Brothers Model 30 appeared in the settling dust, a dead

Mexican bandit tied to the hood, dressed in a uniform reminiscent of Pancho Villa, popularized by the 1914 movie, *The Life of General Villa.*

The vehicle came to a stop, the driver door opened and a single soldier emerged. The man stood straight, his dress uniform impeccably crisp and smooth, with a serious and professional demeanor. He approached the Case Touring Car, stopped once he recognized the occupant, and saluted. "Lieutenant George Patton, President Roosevelt—Colonel—sir!"

"We are certainly gratified for the presence of your ironclads, Lieutenant. But I am unaware of military operating in this area," the ex-president said, smiling.

"Hunting Villistas, Colonel Roosevelt." Patton slapped the corpse. "We encountered some of Pancho's men on our way back to Camp Columbus and ran them down with our armor." He turned and studied the field of battle where the ghoulish figures lay. "Now, these Bandidos fight strangely, and they're dressing in ancient uniforms for shock effect. I'm teaching my boys everything there is to know about armored warfare. They want shock," Patton smiled. "We make it quick. The shorter the battle"—he paused as the three remaining armored Davidson Cadillacs pulled up just behind Patton's Model 30—"the fewer the casualties."

# INTERLUDE 52
March 23, 1917, 12:15 pm
Fifty-five Miles From Mexico

The ex-president sat in the passenger seat next to Lieutenant Patton as the car drove at a leisurely twenty miles an hour so the horses, mules, camels and the rest of the USVC could keep up. Ernie sat in the back seat, bouncing as the car moved along the rugged terrain. Now instead of a Mexican bandit, Patton had bound a bloody Aztec warrior to the hood, thick layers of cotton still covering parts of its yellowish misshapen body, with strands of plumage adhering to a broken eagle mask.

"I am very fortunate to have been put in charge of the armored forces in the Punitive Expedition, Mister President," Patton said as he moved the weighted vehicle around a thick patch of scrub and over a series of transverse dunes. "However, politics has long dictated our path, instead of allowing the soldier to attack. We need to grab the enemy by the nose and kick them in the pants."

"Americans learn from calamities, not experience, Lieutenant."

"Indeed, Mister President." The car bounced dramatically. Ernie upended in the backseat. "In the wintertime, Caesar so trained his legions and so habituated them that when in the Spring he committed them to battle no necessity existed to give them orders. They knew what to do and how to do it."

"I understand you've made the most of the experience, Lieutenant. Your writings on motorized warfare promise changes that will revolutionize the battlefield."

"We are ready and willing to fight whenever the country may need us. I have to say, I did not expect to see active battle until I reached the open plains of Western Europe. But given what you have told me, Mister President, we will be on the field much sooner. I wish we might have been able to put more emphasis on training to meet a specific enemy. But the Congress can't say we're at war with Mexico, with bandits, or with anyone at all."

"There is no more thoroughgoing international Mrs. Gummidge, and no more utterly useless and often utterly mischievous citizen, than the peace-at-any-price, universal-arbitration politician," T.R. opined. "It's the type who is always complaining either about war or else about the cost of the armaments which act as an insurance against war."

"My men are ready for action, Mister President. They may be a bit soft, but they have accuracy and confidence. The charge is the chief feature and they are experienced in that."

"You've not experienced battle with opponents like these, Lieutenant. They use tactics and strategies the modern soldier has not experienced."

"When we go into battle, by studying history from recorded time until today, when a situation occurs on the battlefield, somewhere in that knowledge there will be a similar example. All the leader has to do is retrieve the information from his memory and use the current means at hand to inflict the maximum amount of wounds, death, and destruction on the enemy in the minimum of time."

"You're confident, then, that we can convince General Pershing?"

"Mister President, we certainly have something to show on the hood of my car. It will get his attention. We will increase patrols. My soldiers will be sent in groups of ten and twenty for fifty miles along the border. I can conduct armored exercises as deep into Mexico as we are authorized. But whether or not

General Pershing is able to convince Washington that we have Aztec Warriors and seventeenth-century Austrian dragoons in the New Mexico desert...." Patton shrugged.

Ernie leaned back in the rear seat, clearly exhausted. "But we've seen them, fought them, killed them, chased them." He blinked his eyes rapidly.

"Yes, but what have they done?" Patton glanced over his shoulder. "Subsumed a village of Navajo? A ghost town? Engaged in a gun battle with men who—while brave—aren't even soldiers?"

"While we continued in peace in Cuba for three years, we suffered many times more casualties in the murderous oppression that the misguided Washington philanthropists wanted to call peace rather than the three months of war. Yet we laid back while watching her death agony," T.R. muttered somberly.

# INTERLUDE 53
March 23, 1917, 2:41 pm
Cavalry Camp Columbus

The Packard Model 30 came to a stop at a rail crossing immediately south of downtown Columbus, New Mexico, a sparse village on the Mexico border. Stephenson's Livery Stable sat on one side of the main thoroughfare, across from an establishment with a sign that simply said, "Hotel".

"A year ago, Cavalry Camp Columbus headquartered the Thirteenth Horse, which patrols the border from El Paso to Hachita along the EP & Southwestern Rail." Lieutenant Patton said, pointing in either direction. "The encampment spread from a small outpost of three hundred and fifty men to more than fifteen thousand, including five thousand soldiers of the New York National Guard and the First Aero Squadron."

Doughboy trucks and pyramid tents spread south for miles before them along both sides of the El Paso line winding into Mexico. A bi-wing SPAD XIII flew low overhead, sporting the blue circle centered white star, as it wobbled in for landing somewhere on the far side of the encampment.

"That's part of the First Aero Squadron," Patton pointed. "Nine SPAD XIII planes, nine officers and fifty enlisted pilots."

"Sent by Secretary of War Baker to provide General Pershing aerial reconnaissance," T.R. said with awe.

Patton snorted and rolled his eyes as the car moved forward. "Without replacements or reserve. One always returns from a scheduled flight with engine problems. Then we found that the ninety horsepower engines couldn't get the planes over the ten thousand foot mountains Villa took refuge in, or overcome the high winds in the passes. Dust storms ground the aircraft for weeks at a time, and the wooden propellers de-laminate in the heat!"

"Good American engineering then!" The ex-president laughed. The car moved through platoons of marching soldiers of the New York National Guard and the 13th Cavalry Regiment. A mile-long caravan of Liberty trucks loaded with crates of supplies went by in the opposite direction.

"But!"—Patton said, holding up a single finger—"Twelve Curtiss R-2's arrived three months ago. A hundred and sixty horsepower, long-range aircraft. Not one of them has been able to take off. The landing gear can't stand up to the rough terrain, and I've seen better material on Momma's curtains!"

"Many of these men could be seeing the inside of a trench in France before the year is out. They want to live in the harness, striving mightily." the ex-president said softly. He looked over his shoulder into the backseat and found Ernie passed out. He placed a hand on the boy's shoulder and shook him but he did not rouse. He studied Lieutenant Patton. "We need to get him to a hospital. The lad wandered in the desert for days."

# INTERLUDE 54
March 23, 1917, 3:07 pm
General Pershing's Headquarters

General John J. Pershing's command tent displayed three flags at its entrance: the Stars and Stripes, the New York "Excelsior" flag, and the flag of the First Aero Squadron. Two long tables sat on opposite sides of the interior. One table had papers, books, and maps spread out upon it. Another table had plates of bread and meat, bowls of fruit, and pitchers of water. Four men stood in the tent: Ex-president Roosevelt, Lieutenant Patton, General Pershing, and his adjutant Major Shaw.

General Pershing paced before the other three. "Mister President, while I appreciate the effort you have gone to for access to Cavalry Camp Columbus—a governor, three Congressmen and two Senators so far. But that does not mean you have a voice in our operations here."

"General Pershing, first I want to thank you," T.R. replied. "You have been of immense assistance in getting the Volunteer Division assigned to the European Theater."

General Pershing shook his head. "And Wilson and the Congress have shot me down, Mister President. Repeatedly."

The ex-president rapped his fist on the table. "Much has been given to us and much will rightly be expected of our patriotic service. I am confident they will see the rightness in time."

General Pershing stiffened slightly. "Fine, yes. Let us hope so. Mister President, can you please tell me why a bunch of over-aged irregulars are traipsing around my New Mexico desert, armed with British weapons riding desert camels and why my Lieutenant has a desiccated bandit wearing a costume strapped to the hood of his car?"

"General Pershing, we have seen such a manner of felony and mischief in our domain that it should be said of us we shirked our duties as soldiers, no, as men, if we had not sounded the alarm."

From behind the ex-president, four USVC soldiers appeared, carrying the dead Aztec. The men swept the bread and water off and laid the body on the table. General Pershing opened his mouth to say something and T.R. held up a hand, cutting him off.

"General, we are not intending to use your tent as an autopsy chamber or a charnel-house. You must look at this creature." The four soldiers stepped back.

Pershing stepped forward, standing at the head of the table, with T.R. on his right.

The ex-president reached down and peeled the eagle warrior facade from the dead figures head. The pale, sunken, yellowish skin had begun to peel back from the milky white orbs in the sockets. Only patches of hair hung in a few places. Fully a third of its head had cracked open and the brain still oozed out. "This soldier expired for the last time in the desert only hours ago."

Pershing's eyes widened and he studied him for a moment with disbelief. Then when he saw his former commander-in-chief's face he looked shocked. He stepped closer to the corpse.

T.R. pulled out a blade and sliced down the front of the cotton tunic, then separated it. "Looking at the body you would think perhaps that it had wasted away from consumption. Yet despite its debility, this one and dozens more like it were moving on foot over sixty miles away and headed for the south of the border."

Pershing stared. "It can't be. Look at the desiccation, the deterioration of the flesh. The marasmus alone had to have taken weeks after this poor figure could have even been walking."

The ex-president nodded. "And yet, the Volunteer regiment encountered dozens of the same. They died hard, suffering incredible wounds, the loss of limbs, yet still fought. And look here…" He pointed to the face and chest of the dead rotter. "This one has spots and pustules all over its upper body. This creature would have succumbed to typhoid long before it dropped in the desert."

Pershing took a step back at the mention of typhoid. "What are you telling me, Mister President?"

"I am telling you, General, that this poor sailor died from typhoid yet somehow reanimated and appeared here in New Mexico." T.R. lifted one of the dead figure's limbs and indicated a tattoo on the upper forearm of a skull with a rat atop it, and the words "rats get fat while brave men die". "This is the tattoo of a British sailor." He pulled the seam of the sleeve at the shoulder, to reveal ugly scarring. "These chirurgical scars indicate that this arm had once been removed from its shoulder," He studied the three men. "And this is not the original shoulder."

# INTERLUDE 55
March 23, 1917, 3:41 pm
Cavalry Camp Columbus

The four men strode across the camp. Mechanics stood working around a Doughboy truck; a platoon of soldiers in t-shirts jogged by, slowed to salute and moved on. A Lieutenant ran up to Major Shaw, and he stopped for a moment to sign the paperwork, before running to catch up next to General Pershing.

"Since General Funston died last month and I assumed command," General Pershing said, "these men have looked to me for leadership. I've led men over three hundred and fifty miles into Mexico in pursuit of the revolutionary known as Pancho Villa. Major Shaw has been seen in combat with me in every war of the last twenty years. I've seen soldiers maimed, crippled, on death's doorstep, who fight as men possessed. During the Battle of Bud Bagsak, we faced six thousand Moro rebels who were absolutely fearless, counting death as a mere incident, and engaged us in the fiercest combat I've ever seen."

They had walked to their perimeter of the Camp, near the airfield. The men passed by half a dozen camels and now the soldiers of the USVC could be seen settling in around the area.

General Pershing paused as they entered the perimeter, turning his back to the others and addressing Lieutenant Patton directly.

"Lieutenant, please let your sister know that I had planned on seeing her this month. But the death of General Funston has put everything on hold. And there is a good possibility that I will be called to lead these men in the American Expedition to Europe if war breaks out. You must speak to Nita for me."

Above, two more SPAD XIII circled in for a landing.

The Lieutenant looked somber. "As a woman, she believes that people make time for people they want to make time for. She won't believe you're too busy, General." General Pershing shook his head sadly and turned back to the others. "But, she also knows that there are different ways of making an effort, sir. If we all thought alike, nobody would be thinking. Have a little faith, sir."

T.R. looked up as the plane passed overhead. "General, the body you saw could have a dozen different scientific explanations. I understand that. If I had not seen the creatures in battle myself, if my men had not encountered the unspeakable and met it in hand-to-hand combat, I would say the man who told me such a tale must be mad."

The group stopped in front of a tent and the ex-president motioned to several of his men. "That's why we brought proof."

"Mister President, even if we could convince Washington to let us have maneuvers, the feelings between American and Mexican troops has grown so tense that war could break out at any moment." General Pershing said.

"So it would necessarily have to be convincing to take any action, General."

General Pershing nodded. "The Mexican government has grown more accepting of Villa and his men. There is agreement among the General Staff that it is better to rest content that the outlaw bands have been punished instead of defeated and that the peoples of northern Mexico have been taught a lesson. The men are also tired, they are sick of the Mexican desert and may not possess the spirit for more fruitless conflict."

T.R. stepped aside as USVC soldiers came up behind him and laid the top half of a Thing machine on the ground in front of

General Pershing. Ripped from the mechanical waist and legs, with the green power sphere at its center missing, it cut a ghastly scene. Ropes of bloody metal distended from its upper chest and neck and hung loosely within the shattered chassis.

General Pershing stared at the pile of flesh and metal for over a minute, saying nothing, before speaking. "We have engaged in a systematic scheme of training, with courses in musketry and battle tactics and principles of attack and defense." He looked up and fixed the ex-president with a hard stare. "Our men are probably better experienced and more highly trained than any similar force of size has ever been. Where is the war, Mister President?"

# INTERLUDE 56
### March 23, 1917, 4:07 pm
### Cavalry Camp Columbus, First Aero Squadron Field

T he group of men stepped away from the grotesque Thing machine and most of the temporary quarters. They were now standing at the edge of the landing grounds for the First Aero Squadron itself. In front of them, a handful of planes and a hundred miles of empty desert stretched south across into Mexico.

Sergeant Barry and three other USVC soldiers approached carrying pieces of gleaming copper equipment. Two more soldiers came behind them carrying a large crate with shoulder poles. They set them down and Sergeant Barry and one soldier worked to put it together.

The ex-president paced as he spoke. "General, you and I both know that greater numbers of men have not been sent to the border for want of supplies. That fact alone should have prompted immediate corrective action. But we wish to enjoy the incompatible luxuries of an unbridled tongue and an unready hand."

The ex-president stopped when he saw that most of the steam cannon parts were put into place. "What we have here, General is a marvel of engineering. I am certain that the mechanics and principles are based on the diagrams of Leonardo Da Vinci. It is known as The Thunder of Archimedes."

The soldiers opened the crate and removed the gleaming barrel with the dozen chambers in it, like a cylinder from an enormous revolver.

"A copper tube is inserted inside this iron furnace." T.R. pointed to a long cylinder attached to the center brass column that stands about four feet high, "Copper is used because of its thermal conductivity."

General Pershing broke in. "Excuse me, Mister President. Did you call that the furnace? It doesn't look large enough."

"I know. But if you'll follow along General, there's more. The heating mechanism is these two canisters just below the cylinder." He pointed. "This is the real miracle here." He looked at General Pershing. "This is the boiler."

General Pershing looked incredulous. "That's impossible. You could maybe make some kind of projectile system work, but for every eight pounds of steam, you need a pound of water. A battlefield steam weapon failed in the War To Make Men Free for just that reason."

Sergeant Barry settled the steam barrel into its cradle and aimed the device to the east.

"And yet, that is just what it is happening. One canister contains one gallon of a type of propane which is energy for the furnace. The other contains a gallon of water, mixed with some type of alcohol." The former dipped his head to Sergeant Barry, who turned a small nozzle at the base of the furnace. "You'll notice they sit side by side, feeding into the furnace. We know how a steam engine works, General. This has all the properties of a steam engine. It's even simpler than any steam engine we use. There's no piston to move. We just don't understand how such a small device is superheating the water and creating the pressure."

To the west, the two SPAD XIII came in one behind the other, for landing.

The ex-president stepped back as the device hummed. Heat could be felt emanating off the weapon and the others leaned back subconsciously. The upper end of the furnace angled

143

sharply at the top, fitting into the cylinder at a slightly askew angle at the three o'clock position. Wisps of steam emanated from the cylinder and it slowly turned. In less than a minute a high pitched vent of steam blew through it and the cylinder spun fast enough that one chamber made a rotation every two seconds.

"Observe the three Gymnocalycium, each one with a red signal flag planted in it," T.R. said, pointing to a row of saguaro cacti east of their position. "When each chamber reaches the furnace on the half-turn, the four-pounders erupt," He said softly. Sergeant Barry took three four-pound shot, placed them in the small pan that extended off the cylinder at the nine o'clock position, and released them. The iron balls slid into individual chambers and made a half revolution. The shots erupted from their chambers and they struck simultaneously, fracturing ten yards of open ground, obliterating cactus and stone for another ten. "The impact of the three-shot at over six hundred miles an hour causes an explosion equivalent to half a stick of dynamite...over three hundred yards away."

The two pilots climbed out of their planes and ran over to the new weapon, still wearing their flying helmets and goggles. When they got twenty yards away one of them stopped. Slowly, he took off his helmet and raised his goggles.

The ex-president turned and smiled at General Pershing as the cylinder slowed, the machine hum ebbed and all the men sat silent, stone-faced. "We are not prepared for this new war."

"Father?" the pilot asked enthusiastically.

The ex-president turned at the voice. "Quentin? Quentin, my boy!"

# INTERLUDE 57
March 23, 1917, 6:11 pm
Cavalry Camp Columbus

A dozen USVC soldiers were in a pyramid tent eating a light dinner. T.R. sat at a table with three other men. "The Spanish were defending the village of El Caney fiercely," the ex-president placed a hand on the shoulder of the handsome man seated beside him, "but John Campbell Greenaway charged the hail of gunfire and saved the lives of hundreds of Rough Riders when he led the black soldiers to take Kettle Hill," He said to John Parker and Captain Bullock. "That's why Greenaway is one of the few men I turn to when I need a man for a duty of particular hazard."

"Lucky me!" Greenaway replied loudly, to roars of laughter.

T.R. then studied the tall, thin dark-haired man sitting across from him with the thick handlebar mustache. "And Captain Bullock served under me for seven years as U.S.Marshall for South Dakota. He never killed a man, but could stare down a cobra, so determined is his demeanor."

Captain Bullock said nothing.

"Now he owns the hotel in Deadwood." The ex-president studied all three men, drawing out the last sentence. "And when he mans the front desk, all the tenants pay their bills!" More laughter.

At that moment, General Pershing stepped into the tent, followed by Major Shaw.

145

Sergeant Barry, standing at the periphery stiffened and called out, "Ten-shun!"

All eyes turned to General Pershing as he slowly walked in. The soldiers parted until General Pershing stood five feet away. "I had the Army Signal Corp arrange for a phone call to Washington." General Pershing paused and gave a half-smile. "I failed to reach President Wilson directly, but I reached his secretary, Mr. Tumulty. I informed him that I had sent an official telegraph for the Chief Executive's authorization to pursue elements of Pancho Villa's forces into southern Chihuahua." General Pershing handed a folded paper to T.R. who took it and slowly opened it.

The ex-president read the telegram for several moments. "It says we should be aware of the anti-American sentiment in northern Mexico, as well as reports of heavy movement of Mexican troops." The ex-president looked up. "You are ordered to avoid anything that would bring you into conflict with Mexican forces. You are instructed to act conservatively."

"I sent this twenty minutes ago." General Pershing opened a second telegram. "I shall, therefore, use my own discretion as to when and in what direction I shall move seeking bandits or information regarding bandits."

The ex-president shook his fist. "Bully!"

"Mister President, since you and your men have first-hand knowledge of this new enemy, and Lieutenant Patton and his men have familiarity with the Chihuahua territory, it seems our resources are best suited for cooperation. You will, of course, have operational command of your men in the field. Those orders will be held within the guidelines of orders issued by my command, through Major Shaw and Lieutenant Patton when in Mexico. You will not engage in altercations without instruction, and will not fire unless fired upon. Is that clear?"

"General, my men have always advocated preparation for war in order to avert war. It is our duty, even more from the standpoint of national honor than national interest, to prevent the

146

devastation and destruction that may be inflicted on Americans."
T.R. and the dozen USVC soldiers saluted crisply.

General Pershing and Major Shaw saluted, then turned and left the tent.

The ex-president followed them to the edge of the tent, then turned to face his men.

"Men, despite the President delaying our induction, I think we've just been brought into the coming campaign."

The tough and battle-hardened soldiers gave a wave of hurrahs.

# INTERLUDE 58
March 23, 1917, 7:23 pm
Cavalry Camp Columbus

Quentin sat quietly in the ex-president's tent as the ex-president washed his hands at a bowl, wiped his face, and looked over at his son who sat stoically watching his father.

"So when did you get out of Harvard?" The ex-president asked his son.

"I asked Flora to marry me and joined the First Aero Squadron last month. We've been training on Long Island for three weeks until they needed replacements here."

T.R. finished drying his hands, then adjusted the shaving mirror hanging on the side of the tent. "So you haven't told your mother you dropped out yet," he said, removing his necktie.

"Father, the war is coming. You and I are both eager to do our patriotic duty."

"And what about your chronic back problem?"

Quentin shrugged. "What back problem?"

T.R. shrugged. "And the eye exam?"

Quentin smiled. "I memorized the eye chart."

The ex-president smiled.

"They commissioned me a First Lieutenant last week, father."

"Well, at least I have that good news to tell your mother." He turned and held his arms out and the two men embraced.

"I've met the race car driver Eddie Rickenbacker. He and I are set to be transferred to England together at the end of the month. He had seventeen days of student training and they're already calling him one of the best pilots they've ever seen. I'm in good company, father. What news of Kermit?"

T.R. sighed, giving up. "Your brother took Belle and the kids to Spain to live with her father for the duration of the war so they could be nearer when he took leave. The British enlisted Kermit as a Captain and sent him to Mesopotamia to fight the Turks."

Quentin smiled. "Kermit always did have a flair for the dramatic."

The ex-president chuckled. "He wants to be in Constantinople when its taken from the Ottomans."

"How long are you here for, father?"

"Captain Groome and the second regiment will be here in the morning, with fresh horses and supplies. When we move into Mexico is up to General Pershing. But I am quite certain we will be the point of dress in the next three to four days."

"We don't have much time then. I'll be put on sorties for a fortnight by tomorrow."

"Then how about a few rounds with your old man. Unless those Harvard pugilists have made you soft?"

"Father, you already lost most of your vision in your left eye. It's reckless. How about sparring with some heavy pads?"

"Well, you can either fight me all the way all the time, and give no ground, or you can watch me fight Sergeant Greenaway. I warn you, standing by won't help endear you to the intimate living in an aviation camp. So come on, show them you are square in everything you do, including boxing with an ex-president of the United States."

"All right," Quentin finally agreed, grinning.

The senior Roosevelt put his arm around his son's shoulder as they left the tent. "Your mother and I will be happy you will get to render some service to your country and show the stuff you are made of. No man can ask for the opportunity for more."

# INTERLUDE 59
March 24, 1917, 7:05 am
Cavalry Camp Columbus

The ex-president and several USVC soldiers stood at the rail depot as the 2-8-2 from El Paso made a long and short burst, announcing its arrival. The long line of freight cars came to a stop a hundred yards later. The freight doors opened up simultaneously on the cars, ramps dropped and Volunteer Cavalry in pristine pressed uniforms astride fresh mustangs and quarter horses emerged. Captain Groome entered the throng, looked about for Roosevelt, spotted him, and saluted as he approached at a trot.

"Good to see you, Captain!" T.R. said, saluting back.

Captain Groome dropped from his horse at ten yards and closed the gap at a stroll, smiling and searching about. He paused as a motorcycle with an armored sidecar honked and passed in front of him.

"There's certainly a lot of activity, Colonel Roosevelt. Washington finally approved our military integration?"

"Not for the European theater, Captain. We have a situation here that necessitates our attention south."

"South into Mexico, Colonel?"

"There's a lot to cover, Captain. First, I need an update on the battalion strength."

Captain Groome and the ex-president turned to watch the half-mile long train dispense hundreds of rested soldiers, fresh mustangs with well-oiled saddles, supply platoons with boxes of canned meats, vegetables, and crates of ammunition.

"We have delivered five hundred and fifty-three soldiers, two and a half million rounds of ammunition, five hundred horses and fifty tons of supplies from Fort Wingate," Captain Groome said matter of factly.

"It's barely enough for the regiment at its half strength for two weeks," the ex-president said, shaking his head. "Nations like our own are so happily situated that the thought of war is never present to their minds. We must never forget that there are military ideals no less than peaceful ideals. One day I asked a commander what his plans for arming and drilling his men were." He smiled at Captain Groome. "He answered that he 'expected to give each man two revolvers and a lariat and set them loose'."

T.R. and the rest of his men strode slowly through the procession of new soldiers, many of who came up to the hero of San Juan Hill and greeted him with appreciation and warmth. Soldiers on horseback trotted by with salutes.

Captain Groome stopped and addressed the ex-president directly. "What is our scope of operation, Colonel Roosevelt? I've read the coded telegraph brief and there are a number of details left out."

"Captain, General Pershing is authorized to pursue bandits deep into Chihuahua territory. He has a directive to avoid interaction with a growing Mexican military presence and an unfriendly populace, and we have supplies for less than thirty days. In short, Captain, our scope is limited, our enemy dangerous, and the terrain is hostile."

T.R. and Captain Groome stepped into a pyramid tent past two USVC soldiers stationed at its threshold. It took a moment for their eyes to adjust to the diminished light. The broken and bloody half corpse of the Thing machine lay on a gurney. The Captain took an involuntary step back.

"This is what I left out from the coded briefing, Captain Groome. If we sent this out and it got back to Washington, there's no telling what their reaction might be. They might Section 8 the whole lot of us. They would definitely send me back to my ranch in the Dakotas."

"General Pershing has seen this, Colonel?" Captain Groom asked without taking his eyes from the sight.

"He has," nodded the ex-president. "Thus the direness of action has produced a rapidness of response. We are to provide support and intelligence in pursuit of these forces."

"The report mentioned conventional forces as well, sir," Groome added, finally looking up.

"If seventeenth-century Polish lancers with wings can be considered conventional, yes."

# INTERLUDE 60
March 24, 1917, 10:01 am
Cavalry Camp Columbus

Ernie, sitting up in the hospital bed, scooped another spoonful of jello into his mouth and set the bowl on the cart next to him.

A young nurse came up quickly to his bedside, wearing striped cotton twill and a white apron with a Red Cross insignia on it. She smiled at Ernie. "Would you like some more jello, Mister Hemingway?"

Ernie smiled and blushed. "Yes, ma'am."

The young woman left, glancing back over her shoulder once and smiling at Ernie again.

Then a middle-aged man in a crisp officer's uniform stepped into his line of sight.

"Young man, my name is Captain Boghardt. I am one of the doctors on shift here. They brought you in for exposure, dehydration, and malnutrition. But you've had a night's rest and you don't look any worse for wear, son."

"Ah, you've done a peach of a job, doc." The young nurse passed by and Ernie's eyes followed her smile before snapping back to the Captain.

"But, while you are getting up and moving about the floor quite easily it seems, we are going to want you to take it easy for another day or two."

"Well doc, sorry, Captain, I'm not going to argue with you. Truth is, I still can't get a shoe on my right foot. It swelled up quite a bit, either from the heat or the strain. Then there's a nice old woman who came round yesterday with cakes and books and a fine-looking daughter. I felt too tired to eat or read much of it, but I am feeling much restored today. My legs stay steady under me when I stand. So I am going to lay right here, enjoy the books and the rest."

"Very good then. I'll look in on you. Surgeon Hemingway in Chicago will be most mindful of the care you receive." The Captain winked and left.

The young nurse appeared with another bowl of jello.

"So what were you doing out in the desert?" the nurse asked in a low voice.

"I went out to this little mining town called Shakespeare, where everybody had disappeared.'

"Oh my," she said, holding a hand over her heart.

"Yes. And well…" He paused, "we saw bandits. And they chased me into the desert."

"Oh!"

"And I wandered in the desert for almost four days, surviving on my wits and my camping skills my Papa taught me. I hid in the mountains until I saw President Roosevelt and his Rough Riders. The bandits attacked again and I came out and saved the President from being struck down by a brigand with a sword!"

"You were so brave," the young nurse purred, laying a hand on his arm lovingly.

The sound of someone clearing their throat came from behind her. The young nurse jumped with a start and turned to see a young Lieutenant with a clipboard standing there impatiently. "Sorry, sir," the nurse said and moved away. She went out of the door without looking back.

The Lieutenant moved forward and looked down at his clipboard. "Your name is Ernest Hemingway, is that correct?"

"Yes, sir."

"Son, have you thought about what you want to do with your life?"

"Sir?"

"Living on your parent's money, wandering about the desert like an aimless drifter. That's no life for a man."

"Excuse me?"

"Why don't you consider joining the army. Give you some purpose, some direction in life."

Ernie sat fully upright, indignant. "Listen here, I didn't ask to visit this God damned dry arid, friendless part of the country. But I won't be insulted. I happen to be a reporter for a major city newspaper."

The Lieutenant just stared at him with his clipboard in his hands, saying nothing.

"Now look, you go and tell the President that the great Hemingstein is more than willing to go and fight in his trenches. You sign me up, sir!"

"Except he's only seventeen," said a flat voice from behind the Lieutenant flatly.

The Lieutenant turned to Captain Boghardt, then back to Ernest.

"Is that right, son? Are you seventeen? You tell me the truth, I'll believe you."

"Well look," Ernie said defensively, "Mama Hemingway didn't raise no coward."

The Lieutenant tucked the clipboard under his arm, looked with disappointment to Ernie then the Captain before turning to leave.

"You didn't have to do that," Ernest said softly. "I'm going to go to Europe. You can't stop me."

"Son, your eyesight is so bad you probably can't read the nametag on my chest."

Ernie turned away, glaring.

"What do you think the Army will do once they find out your vision problems?"

"There's got to be something I can do at the front lines!"

"You just worry about getting some rest young Hemingway. Let the war take care of itself." The Captain turned and went out.

Through the far window, Ernie watched a crew of soldiers stacking supplies into a horse-drawn wagon. They wore t-shirts, smoked cigarettes, laughed and wrestled as they worked in the sun.

Ernie sighed and laid back, looking at the ceiling.

# INTERLUDE 61
March 25, 1917, 12:34 pm
Cavalry Camp Columbus

The ex-president, Captain Groom, and Captain Bullock strode amongst the soldiers until midday, organizing their placements, seeing to the distribution of the quartermaster's supplies and answering the soldier's questions.

"We will not let this country go soft. A little war is a good thing, and we shall be seeing it very soon boys," T.R. told a platoon of young men awestruck at an ex-president going to war alongside them. They let out whoops of excitement. The ex-president saluted the men as he and Captain Bullock departed.

Without meeting at the ex-president's eyes, Bullock said: "You remember when we first met?"

"On the road to Medora, transporting the horse thief for hanging."

"You remember what Crazy Steve said when you asked him why he'd stolen a horse, something that he knew would get him hung if he got caught?"

"He said, I want to get killed in one hell-firin' minute of action. And he got his way."

"Sometimes, Theodore, you sound like Crazy Steve." Both men laughed.

"I'm not eager for war Seth, but I think this country has to grow up. Or it'll turn into a failed agricultural experiment."

"I'm not saying you aren't right, Teddy. And I'll be the first one to build a memorial to you on the day you meet the Almighty. I would just as soon that day be far into the future. I don't see the sense in making such a fuss in trying to speed it up. You already fought your war."

T.R. glared at his friend, then appeared more considered, before speaking. "We will fight this war for others. But we will primarily fight this war for ourselves. We will do it to safeguard civilizations that do justice to others. It is not our alien enemies who are responsible for our complete unpreparedness, but the foes of our own household."

A train blast resonated across the camp and both men turned. Five short bursts announced the train's arrival.

"That's a five chime whistle. That means its a Chicago Burlington train coming in." Seth noted.

The two men studied each other, eyebrows raised.

"That's a military transport coming from the east," T.R. said wonderingly.

"We should probably see what's going on."

They arrived at the rail depot just as the single steam engine pulling over two dozen flat cars slowly came to a halt. Each one had a Renault FT 17 chained down on it. Soldiers were lined up fifty deep to get a look at the amazing vehicles, with their powerful tread tracks, the fully rotating turret, and the deadly 37mm sticking out.

"Now that will change the battlefield," the ex-president said proudly.

Several soldiers on the platform blew whistles and motioned the men back several yards from the train. Still, no one moved far enough to let the tanks get out of sight.

Roosevelt, Groome, and Bullock watched as General Pershing and Lieutenant Patton came marching down the gangway. When they stopped at the first tank Patton motioned to several soldiers and together four of them pulled a steel ramp out underneath the flatbed and secured it in place. Then Patton walked up the ramp, opened the drivers' hatch in the front, climbed into the seat and, with his head out, proceeded to carefully turn the tank ninety degrees on the platform, down the ramp, turned ninety degrees on the gangway, and over a hundred yards away to an open field.

T.R. and the Captains made their way through the crowd toward General Pershing. When they saw the ex-president the soldiers moved aside immediately, but it still took several minutes. Long enough for Patton to come back, climb into the next tank and start it up again.

"General, why is Lieutenant Patton the only one driving the tanks?" the ex-president inquired.

General Pershing grinned sarcastically. "Because he's the only bloody soldier that has been trained to drive one, Mister President. The Army Corp sent Lieutenant Patton here straight from Gettysburg where a few soldiers are training on these machines."

Groome, Bullock, Roosevelt, and General Pershing watched as Patton carefully guided the six and a half-ton behemoth down the ramp. He made the turn down the gangway and parked it right next to the previous tank.

General Pershing turned to his former Commander-in-Chief "Rifles and bayonets after lunch mess."

T.R. spoke up. "General, If I could make a recommendation?"

General Pershing gave an imperceptible nod.

"Our Volunteers, those possessing previous experience on the battlefield, might best be utilized at the firing ranges and teaching men to clean and disassemble their weapons."

General Pershing considered this. "That's very good, Mister President. Most of these soldiers have received most or all of their four months of training. But of course, we have long been short on replacement levels. They have experience on the open battlefield, and I will be looking to these men and their experiences to break the stalemate of trench warfare should we be sent to Europe."

## INTERLUDE 62
March 25, 1917, 2:09 pm
Cavalry Camp Columbus

Ernie walked out of the hospital with a slight limp. The nurse stood at the door, waving to him. His clothes were cleaned and pressed, his buttons shined and his boots were polished. The air came in hot stale gusts across the flat terrain. He placed Roosevelt's slouch hat on his head and looked about.

A SPAD XIII soared in overhead and banked as it prepared its approach for the landing strip at the far edge of the encampment. Ernie smiled and started off in the direction of the plane's descent. Around him, Cavalry Camp Columbus buzzed with activity. To one side, soldiers dug latrine trenches and unloaded a dozen horse wagons full of supplies.

An officer reviewing a clipboard addressed the troops as they stood at attention, a large canvas bag at their feet. "Men, in your packs are your uniform jacket, needle, thread, and spare buttons. The jacket is to be folded neatly and specifically as you find it and can be inspected at any time. You will also find the following items: knife, fork and spoon, a razor and a shaving brush, toothbrush, and a half-pint mug. Each man also gets one spare shirt and one spare pair of socks. This is your kit. You may find the razor suitable only for cutting meat."

A snicker went over the men and the officer stopped sharply.

"Nevertheless," the officer continued, "it is your duty to remain clean-shaven. Also, it is a crime to have dirty buttons. The army does not furnish you with the means to clean your buttons." The officer paced again, his voice growing louder. "It is expected that a soldier will be enterprising enough to find a way to clean his buttons. You will be awakened by reveille with time to dress and shave and at half-past six you will have a half-hour of PT before breakfast. Dismissed!"

To the other side, young men lined up in platoon order as they received uniform replacements from the quartermaster. Orderlies were searching for their officers, officers searching for their orderlies, soldiers staggered along under bundles of pillows, blankets, and rugs, and everything had that opaque film of desert dust.

"These boots don't fit me," one soldier complained, trying to pull on his boots.

The sergeant overseeing the process barked at him. "No such thing as boots that don't fit in the Army. It's your feet that are too big."

Further on, a group of soldiers sat around a stack of pallets playing cards and gambling coffin nails.

Ernie crossed most of the camp without incident.

Two hundred yards from the planes, a priest stopped him in passing. "How old are you, son?"

"Seventeen, Father," Ernie answered.

"So young. Would you like me to pray for you?" The bald priest bowed his head slightly and laid a hand on Ernie's shoulder.

"Not for me, Father, Not yet. Pray for the protectors of our land, for the servants called to battle. Me, I'm just a reporter." He left the preacher standing in confusion.

As he neared the planes, he saw two pilots were inspecting their planes parked next to one another, laughing and conversing. The planes were two-seater aircraft, not the single-seat fighter he had seen earlier.

"Hello, chaps," Ernie said as he approached. The two pilots either didn't hear him or ignored him.

"I had quite a thriller today. Rolling and tossing like a ship on the high seas." The pilot gestured with his hands. "It's quite a sensation to fall fifty feet and feel like the floor fell out from under you!"

The other pilot stood on the lower wing of his plane and wiped at the windshield. "I went into an Immelmann and got a face full of oil. The strain of the maneuver broke a feed pipe in the motor. It completely blotted out the windshield and my goggles. I nearly fell out of the sky blind."

Both men laughed as Ernie stepped closer and spoke up again. "Hello, chaps."

The closer pilot, the one cleaning his windshield, turned to Ernie and gave him the once-over. Then he nodded to his pilot compatriot and slowly stepped down from the wing. "Does your Lieutenant know where you are, Private?"

"I'm sorry?" Ernie looked down at his clothes and realized he wore the clothes of an enlistee. "Oh, I'm not a soldier."

The flyer made a face and looked away. "So, you too good to serve your country then? "

"Listen, but what the hell. I'm seventeen, and I write for the Kansas City Star. I already had a Lieutenant try to enlist me this morning. If I could I would be on the first French line out of New York. And when I can enlist that's right where I'm going."

The pilot looked over his shoulder at his friend and smiled then looked at Ernie and spoke in a softer tone. "What can I do for you kid?"

"What's your name?"

"First Lieutenant John Richards, pilot. This is First Lieutenant Crawford. What's yours?"

"Ernest Hemingway. Tell me about becoming a pilot, John Richards," Ernie said, staring at the biplanes with wonder.

In a short time, Ernie found himself in the tail gunners seat, Lieutenant Richards seated in front of him, the plane parked on the desert sand. Lieutenant Crawford stood on the wing, leaning on the pilot's windshield. "What's it like flying up there?" Ernie asked.

Lieutenant Richards chuckled. "First of all, these machines are made from wood, wire, and doped fabric." The pilot chewed on a toothpick.

"What's doped fabric?"

Lieutenant Crawford took the toothpick out of his mouth. "Aircraft dope is a plastic lacquer sprayed overstretched fabric to supposedly keep it airtight and weatherproof."

"Does it work?" Ernie sat forward.

Lieutenant Richards laughed. "Sure. As long as it's on the ground. Once you are airborne it's a whole different experience. And the engines are appallingly unreliable. At two hundred feet, the motor doesn't sound very good. The first time I reached three hundred feet the motor stopped."

"Cripes," exclaimed Ernie. "Doesn't that scare you?"

Lieutenant Richards studied the sky. "I find that I do not ever think of the personal danger while flying, my chief idea being not to smash up the ship."

Lieutenant Crawford snorted. "Lieutenant Richards has a disregard for the ground."

Richards continued. "I had to find a field to put down. So you learn to take it up slow. Spent two hours and forty-five minutes in the air today. We're up for another patrol before dawn."

"Just to have a look around?" Ernie asked, wonderingly.

"Got to assess where there might be Mexican military."

"You've got space here for a civilian observer, Lieutenant Richards."

"Well, young Hemingway, that would take quite a bit of doing."

"Like what?" Ernie sat up, eyes eager.

"Like an Act of Congress," Lieutenant Crawford said sarcastically. The two pilots rolled their eyes at each other.

"How about the permission of an ex-president of the United States?" Ernie added.

# INTERLUDE 63

March 26, 1917, 6:21 am
Cavalry Camp Columbus

E rnie ran out across the runway where Captain Richard's
SPAD XI sat and the pilot and two servicemen performed
the last of the pre-flight checks.

As Ernie neared, the Captain stopped and looked with
annoyance. "Another two minutes and I'd have left you here."
Lieutenant Richards said dryly as he stepped to the rear of the
plane.

"Sorry, Captain, won't happen again."

They both paused as the engineer cranked the prop and the
blades whirred to life.

Lieutenant Richards spoke louder without glancing at him.
"We don't have a headset for you this hop, so there'll be no
communications. Just sit in the rear cockpit, and watch." The
Captain paused then looked directly at Ernie. "You have been
officially designated a war correspondent. General Pershing
and"—Lieutenant Richards paused with a slight smile—"your
good friend President Roosevelt think its a fine idea to have a
civilian documenting this expedition. But they wanted me to
stress that everything you see and hear must be run through
the chain of command before you report anything, write a letter
home, talk to your girlfriend, whatever."

"Understood," Ernie said flatly.

The Captain rapped on the fuselage of the plane, just in front of the tail section. "We'll be taking pictures with the Fairchild over the northern Chihuahuan desert for a couple of hours." He stopped and pointed to Ernie's rucksack. "You won't be needing that."

"Goes with me everywhere, sir," Ernie said.

The pilot shrugged, then motioned him to the rear cockpit. "Climb in."

Ernie got in, stuffed the slouch hat into the bag and tossed it in. A serviceman made sure he had properly secured his harness, then gave the pilot the all-clear wave and stepped back.

Ernie looked down into the sack at his feet. He made out the President's hat and just a glimpse of the green glow from the crystal. He shut the bag and looked up.

Slowly the plane proceeded across the desert scrub then banked up sharply and lifted into the air.

As the SPAD XI lifted above five thousand feet and headed south, the land became a series of indistinct markings, the wide-open nature of northern Mexico became apparent. The terrain below him stretching over the horizon had a bleached and dry appearance. At this elevation, any sign of green or vegetation became blurred with the sand.

The plane banked east. *The largest desert in North America.*

Yet amidst the arid, bleak landscape stood a line of towering mountain ranges to the east and west that created the sense of sky islands, secluded oases of jungle growth.

They continued east until Ernie thought he could glimpse the Gulf of Mexico on the horizon and he looked down to see a panorama of sand dunes. Then they banked northwest and headed for home, the reconnaissance mission apparently complete.

# INTERLUDE 64
March 26, 1917, 9:11 am
Cavalry Camp Columbus

The ex-president came out of his tent and paused. "Where the hell is my hat?" he grumbled, then looked up as a plane came in low for a landing. Groome and several USVC soldiers joined him as they walked. Soon the group came upon a patch of ricegrass where a dozen or so new enlistees were engaged in saber training. Lieutenant Patton wore an instructor's cap and stood without a weapon, before a private with a saber, stepping back and forth and giving orders.

T.R. turned to Captain Groome. "Lieutenant Patton is the only enlisted man to ever hold the title Master of the Sword." This earned a look of admiration from the Captain.

The private thrust forward. The blade came within a foot of Patton's chest.

"Too soon. You've lost the advantage of your alert position." Lieutenant Patton stepped back a pace, then took two steps forward to the right. The soldier paused, remaining in the lunge position. Patton glanced at the other men before studying the man holding his thrust. "Should he fail to touch in the first attempt, a man will often pause in that position, staring at his enemy. This will give your opponent time to stick you or escape."

The private stood up, then lunged again. This time, the private had not fully extended his reach before the point touched the Lieutenant's chest.

"Too late. I would have beaten you to the touch."

The two men repeated this routine several times with the soldier stationary and the Lieutenant walking or at double time, the soldier walking and the Lieutenant stationary, then both at double time.

After several practices, Lieutenant Patton moved from the center of training circle, retrieved a saber and stepped back into the middle. "Now you will respond to my attacks." Patton assumed his position and moved forward with a high point.

The soldier responded to the instructor's parry with cuts or lunges with his opponent's saber in mind.

"It is a serious error to look for the blade of the adversary," Lieutenant Patton said, as he made a series of upper and lower thrusts. "Do not worry where his blade is. This is a defensive frame of mind and contrary to the cavalry spirit. You must always retain the position of the charge, even on foot. A man who seeks the blade of his foe may remain uninjured, but so will his opponent. And the enemy can be out of reach before he can make another lunge."

Patton took steps back from the trainee and raised his saber. "Sergeant Barry, Sergeant Greenaway, please step in."

The two sergeants moved forward, to the left and right in front of the trainee. Patton stepped to the right rear, out of immediate eyesight, nodding to Sergeant Barry. Barry moved forward with a thrust, then Greenaway responded with a downward cut. The trainee responded to each action.

"Do not shorten your extension," Patton barked.

The Sergeant's thrust and cut for several moments in tandem, increasing with speed and accuracy.

After several minutes, Patton signaled to stop and stepped into the trainees' sight. "Sergeant Barry, bring the lance."

The Sergeant moved through the crowd.

Lieutenant Patton paced back and forth in front of the men. "In attacking a lancer, a rapid approach is even more important than against another swordsman."

Sergeant Barry stepped back into the open circle carrying a dummy lance, lined up against Lieutenant Patton and charged.

As the point of Barry's lance came within reach of his saber, Patton lunged forward, forcing the lance to the outside. His saber scraped the length of the lance and came into contact with the Sergeant's chest.

"Your only danger is the moment when the point of the lance is within reach of the extended saber."

Sergeant Barry turned and again charged with the dummy lance.

"A lancer has more control of his weapon to the left, so whenever possible get the charging lance on his right." Patton stepped to the right of Barry and once again, as the lance passed the limit of Patton's saber thrust, the Lieutenant stepped into the charge, forced the lance to the outside and made contact with the Sergeants chest.

The Sergeant turned and Patton waved him off, then turned to the other soldiers. "At all times, gentlemen, the sword is an offensive weapon. And in the speed of your attack, and your offensive spirit lies nine-tenths of your success."

A round of applause went up around the observers and men converged around Patton to examine his sword and offer him plaudits.

The ex-president moved past the crowd of soldiers. Quentin, Groome and several soldiers in his retinue continued with him. "Gentlemen, every soldier at one time or another sees fit to brag about his regiment. But it does seem to me that there has never been a finer example of a regiment worth bragging about than ours." A murmur of agreement, even a chuckle ran through the group. "Our rank and file are made of the most seasoned veterans who have ever carried a rifle or rode a horse. We also have young fellows from the east; from colleges like Harvard, Yale, and Princeton. But the majority are Southwesterners, from this part of the country. They are accustomed to taking care of themselves in the open, being self-reliant. Such men are practically soldiers, to begin with."

The men were about a dozen yards from the perimeter of camp activity, on the shore of Bear Creek. The ex-president turned and his voice dropped. "Our adversary may be hypnagogic, but even an apex predator like the jaguar has an enemy in the forest. The white-lipped peccary is such a beast. The wild pigs travel in large herds and usually make a nice meal for the jaguar when it can pick them off one at a time. But when the jaguar makes a mistake, and it can't move quickly, the jungle proves deadly."

"Tell the story, Father." Quentin urged.

T.R. nodded. "We had traveled for days across endless miles of the swampy marsh of the Pantanal. I had interesting moments, don't get me wrong. We found ourselves being observed by swamp-deer and howler monkeys, spotted the big red wolf, and I talked about the opportunity for further explorations with the other naturalists."

"What he would have given for a warm shower," Quentin chimed in.

The ex-president nodded. "We had to cross rivers of piranha where a man could lose a finger or a thumb just by washing his hands in the wrong water. But we were really on the hunt for the great cat—the jaguar. No one had ever shot one and successfully brought a good specimen back for an examination you see." He studied Quentin. "And your brother Kermit and I were going to be the first."

# INTERLUDE 65
Through The Brazilian Wilderness
December 23rd, 1913, 2:06 pm

Theodore Roosevelt stood on the bow of the hundred and fifty-foot river steamer *Adolfo Riquelino*, smoking a Cuban cigar, his son Kermit standing next to him.

"The President of Paraguay is a very generous man to loan his gunboat yacht, father."

The senior Roosevelt smiled without looking at his son. "The perks of executive privilege."

On the observation lounge one deck below and aft, Brazilian Army Colonel Rondon, Dr. Francis Moreno, Anthony Fiala, George Cherrie, Leo Miller, Jacob Sigg, and Father Zahm sat playing cards as the boat made its way up the Paraguay.

"Fertile valleys for cattle raising as far as the eye can see," Kermit remarked, glancing out over the vast plains and giant ranches of roaming cattle.

"The saline soils attract a rich variety of plants and animals. The Chaco is one of the most uninhabited regions in the world."

Kermit sat down with a wince. "Where is the next leg of our journey?"

"We'll travel up the unexplored Matto Grasso, and then attempt the descent of a river that goes"—he shrugged.—"no one knows where. If this ninety horsepower bucket of bolts holds together." T.R. met his sons' eyes with concern. "How are those ribs?"

Kermit frowned and tilted his head. "They healed better than I thought they would. It's the knee that really bothers me." He rubbed the left knee, keeping it straight. "Bridge building sounded like a good adventure at the time. But since we are on the subject of body pain, how are you holding up?"

The ex-president rubbed at his chest, then waved his hand dismissively. "That delusional assassin's bullet did more damage to my speech than it did to me."

The two men were silent for a moment, contemplating.

The boat proceeded through the waterway and slowed every few minutes like it might run aground in the marsh. The trees on the river held flocks of birds that darkened the skies as they randomly took flight, soared aimlessly, then returned to the safety of the banks.

"Beautiful flocks of scarlet-headed blackbirds," T.R. said wistfully.

"There's certainly a lot of them," Kermit said with awe.

"There is more avifauna in South America than any other continent. On the other hand, in terms of mammalian life it hardly even approaches elsewhere. It once possessed a variety of megafauna—saber-tooth tigers, huge lions, mastodons, camel-like pachyderms, mylodons the size of rhinoceros. All of which disappeared in some great catastrophe a few scores of thousands of years ago, so that only the weak mammalian fauna that exists today persevered practically unchanged. Yet in this environment, the world's strongest feline, pound for pound, flourishes."

The boat slowed and a river outstation appeared on the right bank. A group of a dozen or so impoverished gauchos in baggy bombachas and cowboy hats waited for the boat's arrival. The baggage went into an ox cart and one of the gauchos indicated for the men to climb on a string of small ranch horses.

"It's six miles to Las Palmeiras," said one of the older gauchos. He wore a shirt and trousers and a leather apron, with spurs on bare feet that had two or three toes in little iron stirrups as he rode.

Marsh surrounded the men as they traveled slowly, occasionally giving way to some higher ground. The waters in the marsh were drying up in the middle of the summer season, and fish were sloshing around helplessly in puddles or dead.

A great muster of prehistoric storks clustered around the dying pools, feeding on the fish. "The great Jabiru stork," T.R. muttered softly before wrinkling his nose and pulling a handkerchief over his face from the stench of the rotten fish.

# INTERLUDE 66
### Through The Brazilian Wilderness
December 23rd, 1913, 6:18 pm

After several hours of riding, at last, they reached an area where the agriculture looked well-tended. They passed several parties of peasant workers and groves of giant fig trees. Beyond them, the land opened into a giant vista of farmland where thousands of cattle roamed for dozens of miles.

The houses in the center of the farm were laid out in a square, with whitewashed walls and red-tiled roofs, surrounded by low fencing. Also within the stockade were massive stands of brilliantly flowered trees where noisy parakeets and flycatchers swarmed within its green foliage.

After a few minutes within the fencing, as they approached the main building, Kermit turned to his father. "The mosquitoes are gone."

The ex-president cocked his head, nodding. "Indeed you are right. It must be the birds," he said, glancing up into the trees shimmering with avian life.

As the men dismounted, the gauchos lit a roaring bonfire and the men of the traveling party set up their hammocks and gathered around for warmth. Several of the gauchos revealed they had gotten a makeshift band together along with a detachment of soldiers or state police who had come to patrol the area during the night. First, the Brazilian flag

173

then the American flag rose solemnly while the band played both national anthems.

At the conclusion, the Americans had thanked the band profusely, Colonel Rondon sat next to T.R. and Kermit went off with two hunting dogs to explore. "The ranch has a cattle killer. He's a big cat, roams over several dozens of miles in any direction." Rondon pointed to two gauchos wearing near rags, both carrying spears, "Those two are jaguar hunters. They just came in saying they found fresh tracks about nine miles distant. It's a female. If we follow the peccary tracks we should find it within a couple of days."

Excitedly, the ex-president sat forward. "Such an abundant country! There is fertile land, pleasant to live in, any settler willing to work can earn his living. The mines, the water power, the rich soil!"

Cherrie and Miller came around the fire at that time, carrying a small caged owl. They opened the cage and held the animal out. It easily slipped onto T.R.'s hand where he petted it softly.

"When we are hunting for the jaguar, we will hunt for the peccary," Colonel Rondon continued.

"Why is that?" T.R. asked.

"Because the jaguar hunts the peccary. And this particular female has proven very adept at hiding her tracks amongst the trampling of the herds of peccary she hunts."

"Is that normal?"

"No, indeed. It's very unusual in fact. You will not find jaguar tracks on the game trail. The jaguar usually hides in the trees, especially among the peccary."

"Why?"

Colonel Rondon looked into the fire for several moments, then gave the ex-president a piercing, knowing look. "When stalked by man, the peccary flee. When stalked by the puma, the peccary flee. But when hunted by the jaguar, the peccary does something unique. Instead of running, they circle for protection, because the jaguar prefers to pick off those bringing up the rear. So when the big cat chases the peccary, what does it do? First, it picks off the stragglers. But it doesn't kill like a lion or a tiger on the plains of Africa, where it gets a beast on its back and crushes its windpipe until it suffocates. That takes time. In the jungle, the jaguar uses its massive jaws to kill quickly. This is its weak point. If it cannot kill quickly, the peccary can turn on it. If it has no place to go it can be cornered." Colonel Rondon smiled. "A cornered jaguar is an endangered jaguar in the wild."

Colonel Rondon pointed to a jaguar hunter sitting with his legs crossed on the other side of the fire, his spear across his lap. "Dom Joao once found the carcass of a horse that a jaguar had carried for over a mile. The jaguar has to kill quickly or he gets no meal, or gets killed."

"So we look for peccary tomorrow," T.R. smiled.

"Indeed." Colonel Rondon nodded. "The dogs, the horses, the spears. We will have a fine hunt."

# INTERLUDE 67
Through The Brazilian Wilderness
December 25, 1914, 9:21 am

One of the jaguar hunters on foot strode past the ex-president and Kermit riding their horses, carrying his spear, guiding a hunting dog and hacking away at the jungle while stepping through the muck of the marsh. Three other hunters followed the leader bounding through the tangled vines, chasing the sounds of barking dogs.

At one point, when Kermit got down to lead his horse, it got stuck in the mud. He dismounted and leaned against a tall plant with brilliant yellow and orange flowers. He immediately jumped back and let out a cry of pain.

"Fire ants!" he shouted, shaking his hands and brushing away the small horde of biting insects that swarmed his shirt.

Riding along the banks of a small river, two of the gauchos leading the supply ponies got stuck in the deep mud and had to pull their horses out. One of the men fell to his knees and his arms fell elbows deep into the gunk. After he had extracted his mare, the man wearing a slew of rags stepped off the bank into the small stream and bent to wash his hands.

Colonel Rondon put his arm out and placed his hand on the ex-president's chest. T.R. studied the Colonel who indicated, with an inclination of his head, to observe the man in the stream. The senior Roosevelt turned and watched as the man yelled out in pain, pulling his hand from the water. A large fish with a bulldog-like face and a bulging lower jaw had attached itself to his thumb.

"Piranha," Rondon said. "He knew better than to make a splash."

The gaucho pulled a small bone knife from his pocket, sliced the fish just behind its eyes, and nearly split the head from the flapping body. The man smiled as he wrapped his bleeding hand and got back on his horse.

They rode for another hour before Colonel Rondon slowed his horse, looking down into the ground. "Tracks," he called out.

Two hunters appeared out of the jungle, hacking with their machetes as if they had just been hiding in the brush waiting for the signal and knelt down to look.

When they stood and nodded in agreement, the ex-president gave a triumphant "Bully!"

Kermit took the lead, three dogs baying in the chase, his horse bouncing through the walls of vines.

T.R. and Colonel Rondon followed closely behind for more than a mile before the Colonel pulled up short and directed the ex-president to the left where one hunter had moved off into dense growth. The jaguar hunter glanced at Rondon, making a motion with his hand and giving a gutteral "Fffft, pfft!"

Colonel Rondon nodded and turned to the -ex-president. "Red wasp nests ahead," he said. "Six stings will disable a man. We get off the main trail here."

The two men dismounted and followed the hunter, hacking and slashing through the brush, until the barking of Kermit's dogs could no longer be heard. T.R., sweat pouring down his face, slowed from the heat and exertion.

One of the trackers came charging back through the marsh. "Peccary," he called out and disappeared behind them.

Colonel Rondon directed the ex-president back onto his horse and they moved a dozen yards back towards the main trail. A moment later, two hunters ran by, followed a minute later by the herd of peccary charging by. The wild pigs moved through the brush squealing and grunting.

"Let's pursue!" T.R. said excitedly.

"No," Colonel Rondon said softly. "They are just running back up the trail they came through earlier. I have a better idea." He led the ex-president about a hundred yards upriver where they crossed through a patch of water stargrass stretching from bank to bank.

On the other side, the two men backtracked down the opposite side of the river. At one point, Colonel Rondon indicated to T.R. to get off his horse and handed him a P14 rifle. They tied the ponies behind some thick tree cover and made their way back towards the river at a low crouch. Coming to a stop behind a rise at the river's edge, hidden from animal and man on the opposite side, they settled into the grass.

The two men lay there for more than half an hour before the barking of Kermit's dogs could be heard in the distance. Slowly the barking grew louder. Then from somewhere over the rise, and to the south, the same "Fffft, pfft!" sound from a jaguar hunter floated over the river. The herd of peccary once again charged through, backtracking on the trail a second time.

Colonel Rondon motioned very slowly to edge over the top of the rise. The barking grew very close, coming in from the north. The ex-president peaked over the crest of the hill. Two jaguar hunters with spears came into view, about fifty yards downriver to his right, standing on the riverbank. He turned to his left, and Kermit stood a hundred yards upriver, holding the baying dogs with all his strength.

Colonel Rondon tapped T.R. on the shoulder ever so slightly and pointed down. There, in the wide part of the river, stood a huge spotted jaguar carefully stepping through the piranha-infested river, treading so as to not raise a ripple. With dogs to the north and hunters to the south and dangerous peccary charging behind her, the cattle killer had no place else to go.

The ex-president smiled, raised his rifle, and slid the bolt action back.

As the jaguar heard the click, it looked up and saw the two men. Its eyes locked onto the senior Roosevelt. Two more steps and it placed the first paw on the muddy shore and growled. Another step and the jaguar leapt into the air as T.R. pulled the trigger.

# INTERLUDE 68
March 27, 1917, 7:24 am
The Second Mexican Expedition

General Pershing paced in his command tent, studying a map of northern Mexico hanging on one wall. Major Shaw sat to one side, reading papers quickly before writing responses to a stream of fresh-faced privates acting as runners to regiment and battalion commanders. Major Tompkins, commander of the Cavalry Camp Columbus Garrison, Colonel Roosevelt and Captains Bullock and Groome all were in attendance.

"We've tapped the communication lines for the Carranza regime, and deciphered all the local command communications. We had few reliable maps prior to our first expedition but we are much better prepared this time around. Our cartographers worked overtime in the ensuing months to make sure we don't spend endless days chasing our damn tails," Pershing grumbled.

"What is the situation like in Mexico?" the ex-president asked.

"Carranza is finding it impossible to govern. Zapata is in control of Morelos, Villa is roaming somewhere in the Sierra Madres, the economy is in shambles and the locals no longer cooperate with our native intelligence."

"No one wants to say anything that will help the gringos." Major Shaw interpreted.

General Pershing continued. "So we are going to avoid all major civilian sectors. We've scouted east as far Nuevo Leon and seen no signs along that tract. We are following time-tested measures that indicate the Sierra Madres are our surest bet."

Major Shaw started handing out thin leather binders. "We have flights going out three times a day over the Occidentals. We know where the enemy likes to hide in those mountains."

General Pershing pointed to the map as he spoke. "The Seventh and Tenth Cavalry regiments, supported by elements of the Sixth Infantry and our Apache Scouts will be crossing into Mexico in the morning first, at dawn. Major Shaw will be leading those forces. The Eleventh and the Thirteenth Cavalry, led by Major Tompkins, will bring up the rear supported by the Sixth Field Artillery." General Pershing addressed T.R. directly. "Your Volunteer Battalion will be dispatched among the forces. With Captain Bullock's First Regiment leaving first, we will be crossing the Tierras Prietas Plateau, well to the west of Carrizal. Our "contact" with the Mexican military last year has still left a bad taste with the locals there. Captain Groome and the Second Regiment will accompany Major Tompkins. They will be guarding the flanks and be ready to bring up the artillery."

Major Shaw opened his thin binder and turned the first page, waiting for the others to do so. "We will continue southward, west of the Mesa Blanca, while staying well east of the major towns of Sonora. Our first major encampment will be at Batopilas, the gateway to Copper Canyon. The population is still very favorable to us there. Intelligence is good, Pancho Villa sightings are rare and Carranza has too many other trouble spots than to patrol goat farmers and Tarahumara."

"Pardon me, General. Tarahumara?" the ex-president inquired.

General Pershing and Shaw glanced at each other and Shaw shrugged. "The Tarahumara are an unknown." Major Shaw explained. "They are perhaps the lost tribe of the Apache. Or they are lost descendants of the Aztecs. Mexicans call them The Runners. We've never seen them, only heard about them. Pilots report seeing figures running at elevations of ten and twelve thousand feet, miles from the nearest civilization."

"Our concern is staying away from the Mexican military and population centers, and making as little noise as possible," General Pershing noted, ending the discussion. "In two hours, the Seventh, the Tenth and the Sixth Infantry are going to be on the move. An hour later, the Eleventh and the Thirteenth will move out. Lieutenant Patton is confident he has three teams capable of driving the new tanks. So three tanks are all we're going to have. In forty-eight hours we will be at Batopilas and our resupply from the quartermaster will start arriving from Colonia Dublan." General Pershing closed the thin binder in his hands with a snap.

# INTERLUDE 69
March 29, 1917, 5:16 am
Batopilas, Chihuahua, Mexico

The Renault tank rumbled along the right bank of the Batopilas river until it reached the capital of the Canton of Andres del Rio and parked along the side closest to the river. They were at the mouth of Copper Canyon. Behind them, the elevation dropped three thousand feet, and the Batopilas shrank to a dribble in the dry and empty desert. Before them an island of forest and wildlife.

Barefoot farmers came out to greet the American soldiers. Lieutenant Patton climbed out the front of the tank as several of the Apache scouts approached the locals and spoke to them.

Patton looked around at the homonymous gorge, the high cliff walls, the rushing river, exotic trees, and amazing flowers, and breathed in deeply with evident enjoyment.

The Chiricahua scout leader came back to Patton. *"Pronunciados."* The scout said simply and returned to his men.

Sergeant Barry arrived on a horse-drawn cart and jumped down next to Patton. "There isn't a road sign for anything for fifty miles," he grumbled.

"The locals already know where everything is," Patton said dryly.

As if he didn't hear the response, the Sergeant asked, "What's with the locals?"

183

"They're *pronunciados*," Patton said, nodding. When the Sergeant studied him quizzically, Patton added, "They're pronouncing against the constituted authority. They hate organized government of any kind. As long as we're here to disrupt the status quo and not sticking around, they're fine. They may not even be willing to put a fight to any authority, simply looking to take if the opportunity arises. Be sure we post guards on the supplies at all times." Barry saluted and Patton turned and started directing the first caravan of wagons and supplies up towards the hacienda. Cavalry he directed to the other side of the road.

The din of horse hooves, wagon wheels, and soldiers taking amongst themselves soon drowned out the pleasant sounds of the valley. Patton continued directing soldiers left and right until Sergeant Barry tapped the lieutenant on the shoulder.

Patton held up his arms and everything paused and he turned to the Sergeant with irritation. "What is it, Sergeant?"

Barry pointed down at the ground. "Have you seen what we're standing on, sir?"

"What's your point, Sergeant?"

"The sidewalk. It's made of silver ingots."

Patton looked down. Thick patches of dirt and moss covered most of the trampled ground but silver could be seen every couple of feet.

"It's called the Durango Walk, Sergeant. A hundred and fifty years ago, a wealthy Don built the sidewalk from the river dock all the way to the church out of silver from the local mines in preparation for the Bishop of Durango's visit. The Bishop became so appalled at the extravagant display that he consecrated the ground of the sidewalk and the Church." Patton looked directly at the Sergeant for emphasis. "It's holy ground. The locals will never touch it. And neither will anyone else. Go get your men ready. You'll be carrying your favorite rifle."

Sergeant Barry smiled, saluted again, turned with a snap and left.

# INTERLUDE 70
March 29, 1917, 7:24 am
Over the Sierra Madres

E rnie yawned, despite the fact that he found himself at the crack of dawn seated in an open-air cockpit at eleven thousand feet going ninety miles an hour. *I'm freezing and this flight jacket provides no warmth.* Static over his radio headset focused him.

"Today we're going to be scouting the Sierra Madre Occidental range, through most of southern Chihuahua, the largest state in Mexico. It forms the western edge of the Mexican plateau. Most of the volcanic formations you see are eight to ten thousand feet high and we would need a much stronger engine to get over them. We are going to run the edges, scout any bandit movement and report back."

"Got it," Ernie responded.

"Down below you can see a small village with a lot of activity," Lieutenant Richards noted. "That is the town of Batopilas. That'll be the first stop of the military convoy as it enters the Sierra Madres."

"Wow," Ernie said. "I hear you really well. Can we talk to the Camp with this headset?"

"No. The radio is good for about two thousand yards. Pilots only use it to talk to each other in formation. Besides, in a military exercise, the enemy could pick your transmission out of the air so it isn't secure. That's why the Executive Order banned civilian radio since the start of the Great War."

"It's still amazing technology."

"Getting better all the time," Lieutenant Richards agreed. "From this point, its a six thousand foot descent into Copper Canyon."

"It looks huge," Ernie noted.

"It's four times the size of the Grand Canyon."

"That's incredible! Why do we make such a big deal about the Grand Canyon?"

"It's all we've got," Lieutenant Richards quipped.

They flew on for several more minutes before a striking set of peaks loomed in the distance.

"What are those mountains that are glowing red in the sun?" Ernie pointed to the south.

Lieutenant Richards banked the biplane so the mountains came into clearer view.

"That's Batopilas Canyon. It's 5,900 feet deep with a small river running through at its base. You can see it way down there. That's one of the reasons why the bandits are so hard to find out here. They know ways of getting back into these deep, deep canyons that no one else does, or it's nearly impossible to get well-armed troops into them. So they can hide out for years."

"On some of these mountains, I can see desert scrub, on other peaks I see snow," Ernie noted.

"Because of Copper Canyons' wide range of altitudes, you can get hot summer-like temperatures in one area, and freezing winter conditions in another."

"What is that, that huge green expanse?"

"That's the Mochogueachi Valley." The plane banked to the east, crossed a mountain ridge and soared over a lush valley with rivers and a beautiful set of waterfalls. "And those are the Rukíraso waterfalls."

"Wow. What's beyond that? Those are amazing mountains and those rocks. I've never seen anything like them. They're elongated. It's like a fortress."

"It's called the Valley of the Monks. But we haven't really surveyed it. It's outside of our range. We've got to turn back or we won't have the fuel to get home."

As they banked eastward, a powerful force picked up the plane, flipped it upside down and dropped it five hundred feet.

*The air feels very warm. Almost like....* But Ernie's thoughts were interrupted as the plane rolled and plummeted. *I'm going to be sick.*

The pilot managed to right the plane, but it staggered for control as it continued to drop in altitude. Then the fuselage shook from stem to stern. "I've got it," Lieutenant Richards words came softly, in control, into Ernie's headset.

*My teeth are beginning to vibrate,* Ernie thought to himself.

The tree-covered landscape rushed up towards them and at the last moment, the pilot managed to adjust the planes angle so the aircraft came in across the treetops. A wing clipped a large pine.

The plane shuddered and Ernie could hear the pilot mutter "Just lost the landing gear."

Then the SPAD XI fell below the treeline and, for the great Hemingstein, everything went black.

# INTERLUDE 71
March 29, 1917, 10:16 am
Batopilas, Chihuahua

The ex-president arrived driving the Packard Model 30. He had pushed through most of the town and the car came to a halt at the southern end, just before the wagon trail pushed higher into the canyon and the roads became much steeper and more treacherous. He stepped out and stood admiring a ten foot mural of the Virgin of Guadalupe drawn on the flat mountain surface that watched over travelers. "Simply marvelous," he said, with deep appreciation.

The soldiers dispatched from the trucks and wagons and took a position. They laid a series of pontoons across the rushing river and the Sixth Infantry broke out into platoons and moved forward in box formations. One platoon consists of three squads. One squad on the once silver-laden left bank, another squad on the right bank, and the third squad of USVC on the right bank bringing up the rear.

Lieutenant Patton ordered the units forward in this manner, platoon by platoon until they stretched up beyond the curve of the canyon. The Seventh and Tenth Cavalry Regiments moved in behind them, platoon by platoon, in the same formation, bringing along a train of pack mules with supplies.

Colonel Roosevelt drove Major Shaw, Captain Bullock and the Apache Scout leader in the Packard slowly up the canyon wagon trail, following the military advance along the river below.

"The temperature begins to rise with the advance of the day," T.R. noted.

The Packard followed the soldiers for an hour, moving along an endless series of switchbacks, and hugging the canyon walls closely because one of the car's tires several times hung out over the edge of the cliff as it made a tight turn.

"I saw movement in the cliffs above!" Captain Bullock said hoarsely, pointing.

"Goats or deer?" Major Shaw asked sarcastically.

"The Tarahumara," the ex-president said in wonder.

Then a humming sound emanated throughout the canyon. Every soldier paused. Flocks of small black and yellow birds took flight from the trees and disappeared. The humming grew louder and the air vibrated.

From around the far end of the gorge, three shapes appeared.

"Are they flying?" Captain Bullock asked.

"They are indeed. About ten feet off the water I should imagine."

The three shapes kept coming. The soldiers on either side of the river didn't move.

"They look like fishing boats, sir," Shaw noted. "But what is that on the mast?"

"They do look like fishing boats," T.R. said softly. "And that is a windsock stretching from the mast. Somehow, impossibly, they are flying."

As the craft approached, the windsock form became clear, like the flag of colors flying above it. Yellow and black double-eagle crest with an F in the center. *I know where I've seen that before*, T.R. thought.

Now the figures aboard became visible. Very quickly the ex-president could make out the forms. Several standing fore and aft, who didn't look around or even move, wore traditional Aztec military tunics and animal headgear. There were also people moving about who were in a sense "flying" the boats and they all wore black uniforms.

T.R. drew in a breath as he also saw that, in each flying boat, the form standing in the center of each could not be anything else but a monstrous, hideous Thing machine.

The craft had passed the American forward units along the riverbanks a hundred yards back.

*I wonder if they're going to even see us*, he thought.

That thought, in the eerie canyon quiet, broke as gunfire erupted from both sides.

The Thing machines immediately let out inhuman bellows and their mechanized arms belched automatic fire at the tree lines on both sides of the river. Aztec soldiers toppled awkwardly from the boat decks, wielding their jade axes and landing directly on top of terrified American boys.

*The black-clad soldiers move like real men*, T.R. thought as the flying vessels slowed. The forward craft turned hard to port, the second turned hard to starboard. Gunfire from the American troops increased from all positions.

Someone threw a hand grenade from within the treeline directly below. It exploded on the forward vessel and the craft broke in two in the middle. The Aztecs, black-clad soldiers, and the Thing machine all tumbled into the river and were ripped to pieces by gunfire. Their remnants floated down the Rio Batopilas, bobbing up and down lazily like flotsam.

A grenade exploded on the third vessel but it had not gone high enough, as the explosion occurred below the deck line. Smoke billowed out its port side, but it stayed aloft. Along the far bank, the ex-president thought he spotted Sergeant Barry carrying a large weapon.

The second vessel, its bow aimed at the far bank, glowed brightly. I've seen that before. On the giant vehicle in the canyon.

Pandemonium aboard the boat ceased and the black-clad soldiers aboard no longer ducked and leaped for cover. Aztecs started moving about. The last vessel flared.

*The bullets aren't hitting the boat anymore*, T.R. thought.

As if the soldiers knew their gunfire no longer worked, they dived into the river. First, they went in a couple at a time and got washed downriver. But then they waded in a squad at a time, then two squads, one right after another. And when a soldier lost his footing, the others held him up, as the Americans reached the hull of the lead craft and scrambled up the sides.

"It's getting warmer," T.R. noted aloud. The ex-president watched as soldiers on both sides of the river waded in and tried to reach the damaged vessel. Several soldiers made it and were hoisted up by others where they could get handholds and boarded the ship. Then Americans started screaming.

# INTERLUDE 72
March 29, 1917, 11:28 am
Mochogueachi Valley

Ernie woke up in the sky. Well, in the air anyway. He hung fifty feet from the jungle floor, hooked in his safety harness amidst a tangle of branches in a Mexican Douglas fir. "Captain!" No answer. He stripped off his headgear and waited several long moments, swaying upside down. Slowly, he maneuvered his right arm and bent it slowly back and forth. *Seems fine.*

He pulled it out from under the strain of the harness then looped his arm back through it, twisting it around and clenching it tightly with his bent arm. Then he unlocked the strap. The belt snapped free and Ernie's legs came out from the compartment and he flipped upright. As his body came free, so did his duffel bag and T.R.s' hat and they fell out of sight. *Well, luckily I'm headed that way.*

In one quick smooth movement, he now dangled above a jungle floor holding nothing but the leather strap. There were many branches between himself and the ground. Ernie found footing on a thick limb nearby and managed to steady himself. From his high vantage, he looked about. Far to the east, bits and pieces of the stunning rock formations of the Valley of the Monks poked through the dense foliage.

*Too far to go tonight.* "Helloooo!" He waited as his voice echoed through the great span of the gorges. He peered out over the copper and green shades of the Pine and Oak that extended in every direction.

"Well, great Hemingstein, you may not have the chance to die from the curse after all," he said aloud.

"Helloooo!" His voice echoed again. He waited and heard nothing else. Carefully, he lowered himself to straddle the large branch. Peering down, he spotted the body of Captain Randolph tangled in the underbrush.

*Damn, son. You really do know how to get yourself in a pickle.*

With deliberate slowness, he lowered himself to the much smaller limb below until his feet touched it. Still using the first large branch for most support and holding himself up with his hands and elbows, he shifted himself around.

*Careful now, the branch is small. Just enough to turn my body so I can reach behind me.*

Ernie maneuvered his body and when the branch seemed within reach, he let go and stretched out with one arm. His fingers brushed the bark as he heard a resounding crack. His chin hit the branch supporting him and he fell. His legs hit the branch below, and he looked up through the tops of the trees around him. His back snapped another branch and he screamed. He flipped onto his stomach and he watched the ground rush towards him.

"Uhhh," he moaned as he hit the earth. He laid amongst the bed of pine needles and cones for a long time, slowly moving parts of his body.

*Arms are still working.* He moved his hands up around his face and head and they came back with only a streak of dried blood.

Ernie sat up. On shaky legs, he stood up, groaning in pain. He looked down and saw a deep gash through his trousers from his hip to halfway down his thigh. *It's bleeding quite a bit.* He ripped a couple of strips of cloth from a blanket in his bag and tied them around his thigh. Finished, he studied Lieutenant Richards and stood over him.

The pilot lay on his side, with his legs at an odd angle. Ernie kneeled down and moved Richard's shoulder and he rolled onto his back. The Captain had a huge gash across his face and his eyes were wide open, unblinking.

Ernie stared at the man for a long time before he slowly got to his feet, picked up his duffel, stuffed the slouch hat in, and tossed the strap over his shoulder. *I shall certainly have more regard for the ground in the future.*

## INTERLUDE 73
March 29, 1917, 12:15 pm
Batopilas, Chihuahua

The ex-president saw the soldiers breaking away from the damaged flying boat. There were Americans in hand to hand combat on the lead vessel, but men in the water were scrambling back.

My God, the heat! I can feel it from here. That close it must be—

A half dozen of the soldiers nearest the lead vessel burst into flames and their agonizing shouts filled the air. All the Americans were scattering now, diving under the water or swimming downstream. Another dozen or so appeared to have succumbed to the heat but hadn't caught fire and just drifted away. Only a squad of men remained on the damaged boat, engaged with the undead enemy and black-clad soldiers. The lead vessel turned its bow upstream, struck the damaged vessel aside and gained speed.

T.R. dropped down into the driver's seat and hit the gas. "We can't let it get away!"

The damaged vessel listed badly as more smoke billowed from it, seemingly from both ends, its stern nearly dipped into the water. Americans had subdued the last of the black-clad soldiers and Aztec warriors and were leaping off.

As the moving vessel started back upstream, squads of the Sixth and Tenth Cavalry took chase along the riverbank, trying to keep up.

The dangerous cliffside passage took a couple of switch-backs that wasted several minutes, but by the time T.R. pulled back and the river came into full view, the flying vessel remained in sight. U.S.and Volunteer Cavalry moved right along with him. Then a rolling wave of heat came from behind them. he paused and looked back as the damaged boat finally succumbed to the flames. *It's imploding.*

The center of the vessel's main mast became the vortex of the effect that sucked water and all elements of the vessel and the men alive or dead inward. Then a bright green flare as bright as the sun billowed out and a rumble shook the very canyon itself. Debris fell along the height of the canyon the length of the visible river. A second wave of heat moved across everything as silence fell.

The ex-president resumed pursuit of the final vessel which now had a lead of a quarter-mile. Then the flying ship banked hard to the right and disappeared. He drove faster, the jeep tires skidding off the side of the cliff a couple of times, leaving the Apache scout to start muttering religious chants.

The jeep slowed a moment and Captain Bullock called out. "The cavalry is still there!"

The dirt trail made a switchback at the right turn where the flying boat had disappeared. As they rounded the corner, they entered a massive crescent canyon. A magnificent waterfall came into view, spouting from the crest of a high peak. The water appeared to come from two separate river sources before combining at the mouth and pouring forth into a majestic pool of rock formations and pine.

But the ex-president slammed on the brakes once his vision rested on the sight hovering in the center of the canyon.

Two massive Spanish galleons hovered in place, high in the sky, above the waterfall line. The tall masts of each vessel supported two windsock sails apiece while serving as stanchion supports for the massive lines of cable running between each. A multitude of walkways ran between each craft at the upper and lower deck levels so that it became clear that substantial permanent infrastructure between the two bodies made it one ship that hovered there, not two. And the yellow and black pennants sported the now-familiar double-headed eagle.

The smaller vessels fluttered about below the boat. At least a dozen hovered above the treetops in the vicinity. One by one, they glided up to connect to a series of ramps that extended as they got close to the twin-galleon flagship. And as the smaller vessels rose up, new masts spread from the port and starboard. They were black and yellow and formed like butterfly wings

*Must help them get altitude*, T.R. thought.

"Look at them," Bullock said hoarsely.

"They're coming this way," Major Shaw said urgently.

"We can't stay here," the ex-president muttered.

Most of the flying smaller boats were dropping away from the main vessel, but they did not approach.

The ex-president watched the craft hover in place for a long minute, his eyes moving around the canyon. Then his whole body jerked with some sudden thought, and he twisted in his seat to look back. He threw the car into reverse and stepped on the gas pedal.

The jeep kicked up dirt and jumped twenty feet just as the canyon ridge below where it had sat erupted. The whistle of the steam cannon projectiles could be heard as more four-pounders whipped by and blew chunks of solid rock out of the mountain above them. The ex-president nearly drove the car off the cliff because the cloud of dust kicked by the onslaught made seeing more than a few feet impossible.

Explosions rocked both sides of the mouth of the crescent canyon where the Seventh and Tenth Cavalry and units of the Sixth Infantry were taking positions below. The American troops and Volunteers returned fire as more blasts rocked the valley floor.

The ex-president paused before rounding a switchback in reverse and another series of four-pounders ripped up a section of riverbank. He backed the car up into a break in the cliffside, snapping bushes and bouncing over rocks, executing a three-point turn. The nose of the car now pointed out into the valley, the three men in the car watched in horror as American bodies were tossed into the air. Then, as quickly as they had started, the blasts stopped.

"Watch for fliers," T.R. shouted as he disengaged the reverse gear, pointing the four-cylinder T-head back the dangerous winding trail as he accelerated. Gunfire continued to rage below.

# INTERLUDE 74
March 29, 1917, 12:37 pm
Batopilas, Chihuahua, Mexico

Lieutenant Patton had fallen back to his armaments caravan of horses and mules. *Can't let them lose sight of the action.*

He urged them and his men always forward, eager to stay in the fight. *Loved seeing the men take out those bandit ships. Who cares if they can fly? They can burn!*

The explosions that shook the valley roiled his insides and he burned with the desire to get into the fight. But as the blasts got closer he slowed and ordered his men into position to be ready to strike should the enemy approach. He didn't have to wait long.

Another series of blasts, this time at the head of the curve and Patton watched as American soldiers and Volunteer veterans scrambled in retreat across the rocks and sand and waded through the rapids. They were getting away as quickly as possible. Everything went too quiet, except for the yelling of his men as they ran.

Patton could hear a humming. *What the hell is that?*

His answer came with three more of the flying fishing boats rounding the corner out of the canyon and heading back downstream. But they were flying much higher this time and had automatic fire and that damned steam cannon on full throttle. Treelines were torn apart and squads of U.S. soldiers were shredded in a single pass.

But the Americans fought back. Gunfire broke out from both sides of the river, and Patton could hear Brownings shooting from all positions and a familiar rat-tat-tat told him that Sergeant Barry had put his "favorite rifle", a light machine-gun, to use.

The flying boats passed Patton's position and he paused for only a moment before turning to the lead horse and opening the side of the single large crate on its back. He took out a Vickers Breech Loading Rocket Gun, shoved a handful of the huge shells into his khaki pockets, cradled the gun in both arms and waded across the river.

Once, he had to place his hand on a dead soldier braced against a broken tree in the rushing water. Another moment he slipped but only slid back a few feet before coming to rest against a set of boulders. An explosion made him look back and he grimaced as he saw the enemy craft devastating his forces. Patton made it to the far bank and slowly edged around the corner.

When he saw the twin-galleon behemoth hovering there it took his breath away. The smaller flying fishing boats buzzed around beneath the large craft like angry wasps around a disturbed hive. But at the same time as he looked on in awe, he reached into his pocket for a shell and loaded one into the weapon. *They were originally going to use these to clear out enemy trenches at three hundred yards.*

Patton slapped the breach closed and gazed up, measuring. *About two hundred yards.*

The Lieutenant raised the light artillery weapon and fired. *Close enough.*

Patton watched as the smoke trail from the shell traveled in a nearly straight trajectory and missed the huge floating vessel by a good hundred feet. *Shit.*

After the first shot missed, two of the buzzing crafts broke off and came in his direction. Patton loaded another shell, closed the breach, aimed and fired again. This time the shot hit true, striking the nearest galleon midsection. He hardly had time to enjoy it, however, as the two craft were upon him.

Patton tossed out the spent shell and loaded another one. The nearest flying boat took shots with its steam cannon and everything exploded around him. Automatic weapon fire also whipped by his ears and he braced to be hit, fishing for another shell. Then another sound came in, but it came in from behind him. He looked up through the smoke and dirt and two Curtis R-2 long-range aircraft flew in, firing their own Vickers Rocket Guns. One of the flying boats blew apart and the second banked hard, narrowly avoided colliding with the canyon and disappeared above the ridge.

# INTERLUDE 75
March 29, 1917, 2:15 pm
Rukíraso Waterfalls

From his duffel, Ernie removed a canteen and a roll of tamales he'd packed for lunch. *Food, check. Flint, check. Citronella, check. Maybe if I just sit here, they'll come looking for us—for me.* Then he shook his head. *I can't even see through the canopy of trees. I need to get to a higher elevation where I can signal.*

Limping badly, he moved through the ceiba trees, figs and bamboo towards a ridge that went further up. This led to a brush-filled arroyo with an amazing view of pinnacles and scalloped walls.

He continued to climb the steep rim. Here and there he spotted engravings on exposed rock. *Wonder how long those have been there.*

At one point he explored a trail where humans had walked in the not too distant past. The path led him to a small stream. His mood improved after finding water, and he followed the trail upriver.

The sounds of falling water drove Ernie forward for what seemed like miles. Pine trees and dazzling rock formations ran in all directions and, as he moved through them, splashing grew louder.

He spotted several trails made by game or man that ran off into unknown directions. A natural stone bridge came up but he hesitated because the rock looked slick with rainbow moss.

*Pay attention to everything and go slow. No matter what, don't let fear paralyze you.*

Instead of crossing the stream, he continued following as best he could. But the banks got steeper and steeper. As he gained elevation, it got colder.

*Can't go too much higher. If I don't find anything I can always turn back after about an hour.*

He spent another long hour wading slowly through a thick patch of coniferous trees, snapping branches, getting his bag or his shirt caught, and pulling free before the forest gave way to patches of frost-covered meadows. He sat down on a fallen oak, tired and shaken, his leg throbbing.

*Definitely colder. I need to look for a way down. I might be above the waterfall at this point.*

After he got to his feet and went another hundred yards, Ernie found a faint game trail that led down from the top of the next ridge and into a canyon. A few hundred yards further he came across a cattle trail that cut across his descent and followed that back in the direction of the plane crash. Not too bad. *But I still can't find the waterfall. The elevation, old man. Step, breathe. Step, breathe.*

He couldn't tell if he had gotten any closer when he passed through a thick patch of oak and aspen and came upon a beach with crystal clear water and a beautiful waterfall at the far end.

*Surely the clearest, cleanest pool any man or woman has ever laid eyes on. So clear I can see trout six feet from the edge.*

Ernie laughed and pulled at his clothes. Shocked, he found that they were caked with mud, his arms covered with scratches, and his hair full of twigs. He spent long careful minutes naked waist-deep in the cool water, rubbing out as much of the dirt from his clothes as he could before laying them out on a rock. *Not too deep after all, but could turn nasty if I don't get it looked at*, he thought as he rinsed his wounds.

He turned to face the waterfall before him, spread his arms wide and fell face-first into the lake.

Ernie rolled in the water, laughing and gaining strength from the relief of the clean feeling. He rubbed his hands over his face, scrubbed them through his hair and stood up. He walked back towards his clothes, and as his feet hit the rocky sand he paused and tilted his head back, eyes closed. With a sigh of relief, he urinated freely.

As he finished, his head came back down. He opened his eyes and fell on his ass.

In front of him stood a half dozen Indians on horseback wearing white cotton tunics, buckskin breechcloths, and red headbands. Several of the Indians were hunters as they had rabbits and game bird hanging from their horses. One even had a small deer tied to the side of his horse. But Ernie didn't take his eyes off the rider in the middle: a huge white man, six feet six or more—deeply tanned with a magnificent yellow beard and long blonde hair. He wore a shirt with images of clouds and lightning woven into it and a simple leather sash across his chest that went over his left shoulder. An enormous harpy eagle perched there, staring down like it would consider a howler monkey or a sloth for lunch.

# INTERLUDE 76
March 29, 1917, 3:27 pm
Batopilas, Chihuahua

S tanding next to the Packard in the center of town, Major
Shaw and Captain Bullock ducked for cover as two flying
ships sailed overhead, spitting their steam cannons into the
small village and the American troops in it. Soldiers shot up into
the air with a Curtis R2 in pursuit a moment later. T.R. had stood
next to them and didn't move for cover, staring into the air with
anger and vengeance in his face.

"Teddy, you're a damn fool," Bullock announced.

The ex-president shook his fist in the air. "It takes more than
a bullet to kill a Bull Moose!"

Lieutenant Patton arrived leading a ragtag bunch of wounded
and shell-shocked men. With barely a nod to Roosevelt and the
Captain, he marched over and got into the tank.

"I don't think we can stay here," T.R. said gloomily. "They
have far more equipment than we estimated. "

The Renault took up a position at the high point of the village,
on a hill overlooking the river.

The ex-president turned to Captain Bullock and Major Shaw.
"Somebody needs to ride to Major Tompkins. They need to get
word back to Cavalry Camp Columbus that we need more air
support. We need that artillery brought up immediately."

Seth Bullock stiffened. "I'll go."

T.R. looked at Major Shaw. "We can't fight a rearguard action for more than a day. They'll pick us apart. Lead the men out in as tactical a retreat as possible." Shaw nodded.

On the high hill, the 37mm gun swiveled to aim upriver. Before the sound of the oncoming craft could be heard, it opened fire, moving as it tracked a flying boat. Fifty feet overhead, the vessel broke up and crashed into the side of the canyon.

"Look out," the ex-president said matter of factly as he turned his back on the crash and closed his eyes. Bullock turned away too, but Major Shaw became dumbstruck as the craft imploded and sucked in a large section of the cliffside in its vortex before a brilliant green flash overwhelmed everything.

Major Shaw lay on his back, his hands covering his eyes in pain. T.R. grabbed one of Shaw's hands and pulled the staggered man to his feet. He swayed for several moments, leaning against the car.

The ex-president marched over to the Renault where Lieutenant Patton swiveled his head upriver and down, watching for the enemy fly over. The air vibrated and he turned downriver and saw the twin Galleon vessel move out of its valley inlet and proceed toward the village. *The mother-ship?*

Gunfire erupted from both shores of the river as the Americans fought back against the flying vessel. The twin Galleons glowed that eerie green and rained their steam cannon four-pounders down on the banks. American soldiers and Volunteer bodies floated past the ex-president and the Renault opened fire. Two Curtis R2s came in low from behind and banked up as they approached the massive vessel, firing their 1.59-inch rocket guns.

A green beam of light stretched out from the main deck of the port Galleon and struck one of the R2s. The plane banked slightly and hung in the air for a long moment. The beam crossed T.R. and he held his hand before the glare as the plane spun, end over end, and the beam carried the R2 into the cliff where it exploded. The second Curtiss kept firing as it banked sharply, reached the crest of the canyon wall, and disappeared.

The 37mm barked repeatedly, firing as a flying boat came in low and hovered, rotter Aztecs wielding jade axes leaping from its deck into the treetops amid the gunfire and shouts of Americans. When the gun paused, the heat from the barrel caused the air around it to simmer, even in the daylight. That's when the eerie hiss-thump could be heard in the distance.

The ex-president held his breath as he took in the vision before him. The monstrous Thing machines were stomping through the jungle brush on both sides of the river at least a half-mile away. But they weren't attacking the soldiers unless they were directly in their path. Infantry and USVC alike poured hot lead into the behemoth nightmares as the terrors crashed through their positions. A few Thing machines were brought down, but most plowed right past, staggered and kept right on going with that hiss thump, hiss thump.

*Coming right this way*, he thought.

Lieutenant Patton had the same realization too, it seemed. The Renaults engine revved up and he shouted, "Colonel, get in!"

The ex-president climbed on the side of the armored vehicle and looked back. Several soldiers guided Major Shaw, still blind, into the Packard. It kicked up a storm of dust and rocks as it sped around the tank and out of the village. Around them, American soldiers piled into wagons, leapt onto horses and camels, and followed Major Shaw. A steam cannon shot split a tree next to it as it disappeared from sight.

Captain Bullock ran for a horse.

# INTERLUDE 77
March 29, 1917, 3:52 pm
The Flagship Cornelius Agrippa

Victor Frankenstein stood on the deck of the main fore-castle of his flagship, hovering five hundred feet above the valley floor, hands on the gold plated helm. Through the glass enclosure, he watched as his soldiers and mechanized crusaders rained bloody hell on the Americans in the valley, and he smiled.

"My Prince, we are coming upon the village of Batopilas." The middle-aged Silesian officer wore a black tunic and grey beret and the distinguished epaulets of a decorated soldier.

The Prince acknowledged the information with a slight turn of his head. "Continue the artillery assault, Captain Breslau. Hold back on releasing more Needlefish. The Yankees have an air support presence at the moment."

Breslau saluted and moved back toward an array of equipment. The Captain picked up a headset and spoke into it briefly before turning back to his monitors.

A pair of Needlefish flying boats came around from over the edge of the canyon wall, skirted the top of the Cornelius Agrippa, and unloaded on the Americans with four-pounders. A long stream of automatic fire spewed from the armored carriage sitting on a hill overlooking the town. One of the Needlefish blew apart and vanished into the event horizon.

Victor smiled and watched as the Americans, so new to war-fare but so garrulous about war, fled before his single flagship and detachment of Silesian troops. He watched as an American motor vehicle and an armored carriage took off out of town ahead of him, watched soldiers flee on horseback.

*What the hell are those other things they're riding? Are those camels?* He had to hold back a laugh.

"Signalman!" he barked. When a Silesian soldier appeared, wearing plain shoulder boards and a green medallion around his chest, Frankenstein paused in consideration for a moment. Then he spoke. "Send a transmission to the Third Order. Tell them the enemy is moving out of Copper Canyon and onto the plateau. They are to move north to the Sinaloa border and await my signal."

The young soldier saluted and Frankenstein noticed the ugly dark veins and grey flesh that spotted the side of his neck and disappeared under the collar. He placed a hand on one of the control arrays on the panel beside him. It glowed a moment, then dimmed.

Victor stepped back from the helm. "Continue north at current speed. Cleanse the valley of any enemy remnants. Once we are back on the Mexican plateau, notify me." The bridge of black-clad soldiers all saluted with their closed fists across their chests as the Prince of Silesia departed the battle bridge.

He proceeded down the short flight of stairs, passed the second set of stairs that descended on the left and the right, and marched straight ahead, through a pair of sentries. The double doors opened without touch and closed behind him as he entered the quarters lit mostly by candlelight.

In the middle of the room to one side sat a single large desk on an ornate oriental rug, papers and scrolls stacked high upon it. On one wall hung a large scale fresco of the Owl Mountains and a two-foot diameter globe set in a bronze casing sat in the far corner.

On the other wall hung a series of trophies. The head of a Pyrenean Ibex with its tall majestic horns preened proudly from

209

the center of the display, the skull of a massive Cave Lion and a stuffed Dodo on either side. In the corner opposite the globe stood the skeleton of a wolf, except that it stood upright and its forelegs ended in extended claws.

On the other side of the room, a curtain draped across the width of the chamber and a familiar green glow seeped out from behind the fabric. Victor paused at the globe, briefly running a finger across part of it, lingering there thoughtfully. Then he went over and slowly pulled back the screen.

Allefra and a young boy of about seven or eight sat on cushions that ran the length of the wall, looking out an ornate set of windows. Two tall bronze lamps, one on each side of the room, cast their green light on the chamber. Upon hearing Victor, the young boy jumped from the bench and ran to him.

"Tata!" the boy exclaimed and gripped Victor's leg. Allefra did not rise but regarded Victor with a detached inquiry. She appraised him up and down, then looked into his eyes. "Things are going well?"

The boy scrambled up Victor's leg and the Prince cradled the lad in one arm. "The Yankees will have a second front and be too busy to enter Europe. We have beaten the Czarists and we can beat the French and the English. I will give us enough time."

"What about these new Russians? Will they honor the treaty?"

"The People's Party," Victor spat out the words. "We will crush them at home and then crush them in the new territories. The worker's revolution will only lead to bloodshed and famine."

An explosion sounded a bit closer than the other battle noises outside and Allefra's glass of water on the windowsill slid a couple of inches.

"Maybe it's not as sure as you think?" She asked softly, with a smirk.

"How is the boy?" Victor asked, ignoring the taunt and setting the boy down to run to the window.

They both watched him. "He grows fast. He is learning more every day."

210

"Good. You have much to teach him. I want him to understand his place, his value to his people."

"I will teach him. He will come to know who he is."

Victor nodded. "Good. Is there anything else you need? When this is done, and we are returning to the homeland, is there any place you want to see?"

Allefra smiled and seemed to ponder the question a moment. "I should like to see China."

# INTERLUDE 78
March 29, 1917, 8:22 pm
The Chihuahua Desert, Mexico

The sun had set and the grays of dusk started to fully fade when the ex-president and the remnants of the Seventh and Tenth Cavalry, the wounded and tired of the Sixth Infantry, and the Volunteer regiments had finally begun to relax.

After Captain Bullock had reached them, the Sixth Field Artillery moved up and had driven the pursuing Silesian forces back into the canyon with 75mm howitzer fire. The smell of gunsmoke still hung in the air as night inevitably followed day.

T.R. sat on the edge of the tank and watched the tired and the wounded try to organize themselves. Medics were treating Major Shaw in an army ambulance, a bandage around his face. Lieutenant Patton filled his canteen repeatedly from a water wagon, alternating between pouring it over his head and gulping it down. A line of soldiers waited patiently for the Lieutenant to finish.

Finally, the ex-president jumped down. "Major Tompkins!" he shouted.

Torches were set at intervals around the camp and T.R. walked among them. He shouted again, and this time Major Tompkins appeared from a hospital tent.

"Yes, sir?"

"Major, how's that line of defense along our southern perimeter coming?"

"Three lines, a hundred yards apart, Colonel Roosevelt. We're pulling every wagon, every truck, every crate we can spare and getting the men of the Eleventh and the Thirteenth up on the line."

Lieutenant Patton finished slaking his thirst, then turned and marched back toward the front.

"Do our Apache Scouts have anything to report?" T.R. asked.

"Yes, sir. The foreign troops have pulled back into the valley—at least a couple of miles."

The ex-president nodded and turned back towards the front lines. He found the first line a few minutes later. Men had dug shallow pits and dragged horse carts to stagger in between them. They were acting pretty casual, smoking cigarettes and laughing. *They haven't seen what I saw.*

He walked on, but before he got to the second line, he felt it. A vibration in the air—and humming.

"They're coming!" he shouted and crouched next to a squad of cavalrymen who appeared utterly flabbergasted at the ex-president in their midst. "Steady boys," he said calmly.

The greenish glow that T.R. knew too well came over the whole area. Three flying boats came in low overhead and blasted the front line with four-pounders. Explosions went off under young men's feet like sticks of dynamite as the steam cannons fired down. The Americans, young and veteran, fired wildly into the air, those that actually shot back. *Most of these kids are just staring at them.*

More explosions and more men dying seemed to knock the temporary revery out of the soldiers and more of them fired back ferociously. One of the flying boats passed low overhead and the men in the hole next to him were tossed into the air by the pounding steam cannons.

But T.R. didn't watch it go. Instead, he turned and stared out over the men, towards the front line. "You feel that?" he said to no one.

213

A soldier wondered aloud, "What is that?"

The ex-president stared into the darkness until one of the flying boats swung back over the field of battle and, for a brief moment, illuminated the desert. Winged Hussars, side by side a hundred yards wide, came galloping over the agave, mesquite, and yucca, directly towards them. As the light crossed them, they broke into a charge.

"Bayonets!" shouted T.R.

Torches flared up and down the front as the men realized the battle approached. As the charging cavalry with their twenty-foot lances and enormous wings came into view with the fire-light, American soldiers paused to stare in wonder. The huge wooden braces covered in feathers on the backs of the Hussars made an otherworldly sound. One Knight towards the back carried the familiar banner of the double eagle crest with the F in the center.

*Mesmerizing*, T.R. thought.

Most of the soldiers who opened fire were Volunteers who had seen the winged Knights charge on Black Mountain. The gunfire brought several charging lancers or their horses down within twenty yards, too little too late. Far too late. The chargers broke through the American lines and broke into two separate arcs of stomping, clattering madness. Soldiers broke in all directions, running across other units lines of sight. Friendly fire broke out all across the line.

One group broke left and the second group swung right. Each spearhead crossed the hundred yards to the second line at a full gallop in mere seconds. Many of the soldiers barely lifted their weapons before the Hussars ran them down, ran them through or ran them off.

Absolute chaos reigned. Men were firing in all directions. A soldier fell from a gunshot, then another.

*We're killing our own.*

The Hussars circled back through the front line, coming at a different section from the rear, and shattered the American positions again. Men were firing constantly now, and T.R. saw several Hussars fall. But he saw far more Americans fall under the horse or at the point of a lance.

Then, as quickly as they appeared and just like before, the phantom cavalry disappeared into the night.

# INTERLUDE 79
March 29, 1917, 9:45 pm
Mochogueachi Valley

Ernie sat tied at the waist to an oak tree and watched the Indian camp prepare for the evening. He observed the women, blankets with intricately woven patterns around their shoulders, preparing fry bread on hot rocks next to the bonfire. He watched Indian men sitting or moving about, shirtless, most with headbands. Many laughed with one another as a chant broke out among the people.

Four male elders got up and stood separate from the others. Holding a single arrow in their hands they made soft chants, then inserted the arrows into their mouths and down their throats, turning in circles. They repeated this routine several times.

*Apache. I'm in an Indian camp in the middle of Copper Canyon. Goodbye, mother.*

Ernie looked around and saw many of the Indians eating and paying attention to their children. No one, it seemed, had any interest in him. Then his eyes fell upon the giant white man sitting cross-legged at the head of the circle, staring right at him. He glanced around, wondering where the Harpy went and found it quickly, perched on a large branch of a nearby tree. His rucksack hung nearby. The giant eagle watched him intently. *It's ok. It doesn't think I'm dinner.*

The big white man stared at him, his eyes boring into him. After a few moments, the man stood up and approached him. When he came within two steps, the yellow-bearded giant hesitated. Ernie looked up and realized he had stopped breathing. Then the giant man sat down next to him. Not in a friendly way, not in an authoritative way, but like a little boy. He sat down first with his legs out in front of him, then drew his knees up to his chest. Then he wrapped his enormous suntanned arms around his legs pulling them closer.

He rocked there for several minutes in silence. "Mmm...my... name...." the giant said.

Ernie cocked his head, eyes wide.

The huge yellow man looked impatient, closed his eyes. "My name...." he said.

"Your name," Ernie repeated.

"My name...Chief Bronco."

"Chief Bronco." Then Ernie pointed to himself. "Ernie."

The giant yellow man smiled. "Ernie." The huge man bobbed and spread his arms across the small group of Indians. "Chief of Ndee."

"Ndee?"

Bronco searched for the word. "People. Free people. Free Ndee."

"I thought you were Apache."

Chief Bronco scowled. "Apache means enemy."

"Sorry. But...you are a white man." He drew back, unsure of the reaction.

Chief Bronco watched the dancing and the singing, the arrow swallowing and the women making fry bread for several minutes without responding.

Then he turned. "When six, Ndee came to home. I became Ndee. Now, Chief Bronco."

"You speak good English."

"White name Charlie." Chief Bronco tapped his chest.

"Charlie," Ernie repeated.

The Chief smiled and pointed towards several tall lanky men by the bonfire. "Tarahumara trade with men hunting gold and silver. Learn speak, and I speak Tarahumara. White man keep coming."

"Tarahumara?" Ernie studied the men. Tall and lanky, they were passing a large jug of some kind of wine or alcohol back and forth, because they were very inebriated. They wore cloth togas and instead of moccasins like the other Indians they had open-toe sandals cut from some kind of animal. When they weren't drinking they were also passing a pipe back and forth and smoking heavily, producing great billowing clouds.

"Great runners," Bronco said.

"Them?" He pointed at the men who probably wouldn't be able to get up in the morning.

Chief Bronco smiled. "Tarahumara run where see El Paso. No stop."

"That's like five hundred miles! Nobody can do that."

"Tarahumara can." Chief Bronco gave him a serious stare. "You hunt gold?"

Ernie sat up. "No. There are very bad people in the mountains."

Chief Bronco looked up into the sky, saying nothing.

"They have machines that fly. They are making slaves of Indians and white men."

The Chief's eyes looked sad. "Not slave. Daaztsa. Dead."

"You've seen the dead," Ernie said flatly.

Chief Bronco nodded. "Ndee see. Ndee see chindi."

"Chindi? What is chindi?"

Chief Bronco thought for a moment then called out to one of the men lying about drunkenly.

"Inda Jani." The man on the ground stopped laughing and stared at the Apache Chief.

"Ha-atii Ooweyy chindi?" Chief Bronco asked.

Inda Jani glanced at the Chief somberly, then at Ernie. "Devils," he said, reaching for the bottle.

"Yes, they are. Are you scared of them?"

"Devil not fly sacred valley."

# INTERLUDE 80

March 30, 1917, 5:13 am
the Royal Yacht Johannes Trithemius

The large flying boat moved slowly, a hundred feet in the air above the rocky desert terrain just south of the New Mexico border. Twice as large as the other flying boats which hovered nearby, it also boasted another mast and flew the double-eagle banner. Victor Frankenstein stood on the flying bridge of his personal Needlefish yacht, staring through the eyepiece of his telescope He adjusted the refracting lens so that he might better view the field of battle in the dim light.

The mass of American troops travelling north on horseback and wagon came into gray focus.

*There they are.*

The Americans had maneuvered all night and now were within sight. He watched them march on, slowly, for several minutes.

Victor turned down his navigation lights and checked his master gyro. "Full stop."

Two co-pilots sitting in lowered seats in front of him touched several glowing dials.

The gunboat yacht slowed to hovering and he turned to his radioman. "Are the Yankees talking?"

The senior signalman, the one from his castle observatory, looked up and shook his head. "Americans are just bantering between each other in the air. There doesn't seem to be any air to ground coordination my prince."

*Of course not.* He stood over the Engineers station. "How much of the ore did we move?"

The young soldier dressed in black and a gray beret opened a notebook and scanned it. "Sire, brigade reports estimate eighty percent of retrievable ore successfully transferred before the Americans arrived."

"Current projections for processing? Are we ahead of schedule?"

"They are on time, sire. They had some shortages in man-power moving the loads. But, they have increased their transfer times and the kilns are at a hundred and ten percent capacity."

Frankenstein turned to Commander Aders, head of Third Order, standing at the duty station further to his left. *He looks fit for a man over two hundred years old.* The ornate sash over Commander Aders' chest had two glowing crystals embedded in the fabric. "What is the state of the cavalry, Aders?"

"Sire, the company masters reported minimal casualties. Few bodies were left on the battlefield and the rest are being rehabili-tated." The Commander's right arm trembled slightly.

"What are the reports of response to their initial incursion?"

"Disorganization, as expected. The first line became a com-plete rout, although troops encountered on Black Mountain put up a more immediate and organized defense."

Frankenstein nodded. "So, the Yankees learn quickly. We will have to keep them off balance."

"Sire, the company nobles are requesting another opportu-nity for a charge."

Victor contemplated this for a moment. "No, I prefer the Yanks to anticipate the charge in a defensive position. They're still on the move."

Aders raised his eyebrows in agreement.

"Aders, your grandfather and father served me, and you serve me well."

The senior commander put his fist to his chest. "Truth and virtue, Sire."

Frankenstein turned to his signalman. "How many Needlefish in the forward detachment?"

The signalman spoke into his connection, checking his notes. A squawk came back on his headpiece and he looked up. "Sire, four Needlefish returned to the flagship. Confirm five Needlefish ready for a sortie."

Victor peered out through the tall windows thoughtfully before turning. He exited the rear of the flight bridge and Commander Aders followed. The two men descended a staircase to the next level, passed through a long walkway to the rear of the boat and came out on the transom.

A glass and steel semaphore sat on a six-foot pole at the center. Slowly, Frankenstein opened and closed a series of colored glass shutters, sending out a series of commands. Five Needlefish rose from the desert, each with detachments of Aztec rotters and black-clad soldiers, and sped past.

Frankenstein turned to his Commander and stepped to the right. Both men moved slowly as they spoke. "Aders, what do you think the Yanks are expecting?"

Aders thought for a moment. "Continued harassment. Fly-overs. Hit and runs. But they have the mindset that the enemy is in the mountains to hide. That is what the aborigines do." He stepped onto the deck of a small craft, nothing more than a one-man platform with a single switch, clinging to the side of the yacht.

"So they'll regroup and expect us to wait until they find us again." Frankenstein smiled.

Aders nodded and pressed the glowing dial.

"Have the Crusaders move into advance position. I want them to pay a visit." Victor said.

Aders gave the Roman salute and the small vessel slowly descended.

# INTERLUDE 81
March 30, 1917, 5:13 am
The Chihuahuan Desert, Mexico

The first rays of dawn had just begun to cross the sky when T.R. snapped awake. He sat in the passenger seat of a buckboard wagon pulled by a team of horses. More than a dozen soldiers in the wagon remained asleep. He looked around to find what had awakened him. *We are completely disorganized and broken. Limping back to Cavalry Camp Columbus.*

Then he heard a shout from the front of the caravan. "They're coming back!"

Soldiers moved with alarm and urgency. "We've been pulling back all night and they still keep coming," one soldier muttered to another within earshot of T.R.

*It's true. We should have crossed the border into New Mexico some time ago.*

The ground shook and the soldiers in the wagon stirred, as did men up and down the caravan. Men piled out and detached the howitzers from their horse hitches. Sixth Infantry units rushed to the rear, fixed bayonets and prepared for what lies ahead.

Major Shaw pulled up next to him. "Colonel Roosevelt, we need to move you to a forward staging area."

"To hell with that, Major!" The ex-president grabbed the Vickers Breech Loader on the seat next to him, jumped down from the wagon, and started marching toward the rear, then he slowed. Major Shaw had turned around in his seat and squinted into the horizon. Then his eyes widened.

Between two small rolling hill ranges that lined the edges of T.R.'s peripheral vision, a dust cloud had emerged. And within the cloud the forms of the giant mechanical monstrosities could be seen.

*Dozens of them. "Thing machines" Hemingway had called them. I hope the boy is safe.*

A 4.5-inch howitzer went off nearby and he flinched at the cacophony.

"Major Shaw!" he shouted and turned. Major Shaw had long since departed.

All up and down the caravan, ordnance let loose on the oncoming behemoths. The artillery fired true and tore the valley floor asunder. Thing machines exploded or were knocked back, but still, they came.

The ex-president heard the thunder of the Renault engine as it blew past him, and Lieutenant Patton's head sank into the cockpit and the cover shut over him. The 37mm on the turret opened fire and American troops and cannon roared their approval as all three tanks charged the oncoming horror. When they closed within about a half-mile distance, the Thing machines raised their mechanical arms and opened fire. Bullets ripped up the cannon and the crew next to him and he flinched.

"Bully!" he shouted and fired the Breech Loader high into the air. With all the explosions and the smoke, he realized he had no idea where it went, reloaded, and marched forward again. More Thing machine gun fire tore up the wagon he rode in and killed both of the horses.

The tanks closed with the horrors and Patton, true to his motto, charged right through the enemy without regard for their weapons. He ran over three Thing machines and the 37mm tore apart a half dozen more before he had passed behind their position. All three tanks, in fact, caught up to the Thing machines. And the mechanized soldiers were not stopping.

That's when Captain Bullock came galloping by. He reached down underneath an arm and lifted the ex-President onto his horse.

"Confound you, Seth!"

"Mr. President, I will not have you die on my watch!" Together they raced for the front of the caravan.

The ex-president could make out the Renault tanks coming from behind the Thing machines, firing, bouncing over cactus and rocks. They caught up to the running monsters and one of the tanks came amidst the line of the enemy and opened fire.

The 37mm cannon poured dozens of rounds into the chest of one of the horrors. Metal shards flew off its chest and shoulders. The thick plate at the creature's center mass took a sustained barrage from the side as it spun off. The cannon continued to blast as the core of the creature exploded in a ball of green light.

"Oh God," T.R. whispered.

"Oh hell," Bullock said.

Six feet away, the gray Renault glowed. Then the vortex reversed and the tank disappeared behind the event horizon. So too did half a dozen other Thing machines. One had lumbered just beyond the pull of the swirling force. Its feet dragged in the sand, then it lifted into the air. As the vortex imploded, only half the Thing machine got sucked in beyond the limit and the evil machine became severed at the waist. What remained became vaporized instantly as a fireball of green energy burst forth and killed another Thing machine nearby.

"That's it!" the ex-president shouted. "Let me down!"

Seth slowed, and T.R. dropped and ran to the nearest pocket of soldiers. "Shoot their chests!" he shouted. "Pass it on!"

The word went up and down the caravan line. A second tank ripped a Thing machine apart from behind as it sped past. Soldiers all focused on shooting the metal giants center mass. One lumbering giant finally closed with the caravan and one started batting soldiers aside. The automatic fire from its mechanical arm tore a wagon apart.

The ex-president watched as one USVC soldier rushed the half-human Thing and leaped on it. USVC Sergeant Barry tossed a grenade into the body of the monster. The grenade went off and the whole area disappeared in a green inferno.

# INTERLUDE 82
March 30, 1917, 8:22 am
Cavalry Camp Columbus

When the military caravan pulled through the southern gates of Cavalry Camp Columbus, no celebrating and no congratulating occurred. Men did not head for their barracks or showers or talk about taking up a game of cards or dice later. Every horse-drawn wagon carried wounded or dead. Half the cavalry carried two soldiers to a horse, wounded or dead leaning forward in the saddle.

The ex-president rode in the passenger seat of the Packard, with Captain Bullock driving, and a body stretched across the backseat covered in military blankets. Blood had seeped through at several spots and a pale arm hung down.

As the twin-six came to a halt, T.R. stepped out, limping. He looked up as Major Shaw rode by on the back of a camel guided by a USVC soldier. The Major had a very shamed look on his face as he rode by.

The ex-president said nothing to the Major but waved over two USVC climbing out of a wagon nearby. He indicated the body in the back. "I am fond of the man who died, and I greatly prized his loyalty and faithfulness. See he is properly interred in a casket and put on a train back to Washington. I'll see he is buried in Arlington."

The two soldiers worked to lift the remains of Sergeant Barry out of the backseat and moved him toward the camp morgue. As T.R. followed, he stumbled and had to lean against a tent for a moment.

Captain Bullock ran to his side. "What happened?" Bullock asked. He saw the ex-president's injured leg

"It's nothing," he said, shrugging it off.

"It's not life-threatening Mr. President, but you need to get it looked at." Bullock motioned a USVC corporal over and together they helped the weak and woozy Rough Rider back to his tent.

Over the next hour, USVC soldiers, a couple of nurses and two doctors, a Captain John Oliver and a Sergeant Caulfield, moved an operating table and medical equipment into T.R.s tent. Captain Bullock stood watch, observing people come and go.

Captain Oliver came over to the bedside wearing a surgical mask and gloves.

"Captain, I see you are quite formal. You have your gloves on," the ex-president said jovially as he removed his left shoe and pants.

Captain Oliver inspected the leg. "Mr. President, it's not a serious wound but it is going to require a surgical procedure to prevent infection. Blood poisoning is a very serious threat. I'm going to apply a local anesthetic."

Doctor Caulfield reappeared with a mask and gloves. He had a scalpel in his hand.

Colonel Roosevelt waved him off. "I guess I can stand the pain."

Caulfield studied Oliver, who shrugged and tilted his head slightly. Caulfield took the scalpel and scraped at the infectious area on the ex-president's leg.

The ex-president hissed and looked at Seth. "Water!"

Captain Bullock smiled at one of the nurses. "Can someone get him a glass of water?"

That's when a stern middle-aged nurse approached him.

"This is Sister Stella," Doctor Oliver said, gesturing with deference to the nurse. "She has a long history of experience with

227

surgeries and is known for coolness and forethought in times of emergency."

"I didn't think he hurt his leg that bad," Bullock said, concern rising.

"Oh, he didn't," Captain Oliver spoke reassuringly as Doctor Caulfield continued to scrape the infection. "But we are on a wartime footing in this camp. And President Roosevelt is a man of significant stature." Dr. Oliver studied T.R.'s wounded leg. "It doesn't look too bad and the operation should be quick. But, we need to make sure of who comes and goes. The safety of our patients is paramount."

Bullock waited. Both the doctor and the nurse paused, then Sister Stella stepped forward.

"That means I'm in charge of the patient, Captain."

Bullock studied her, then the Doctor then pointed at himself. "You mean me?"

"You can be responsible for stationing a sentry outside the entrance," she said pointing to the tent opening. "But the only ones allowed in here until the operation is over and the patient has had a chance to rest will be medical staff."

"How long will he need to recuperate?" Captain Bullock asked as Sister Stella shooed him away.

The Doctor stopped as he approached the bedside. "A week at least, maybe more."

"Shoo!" Sister Stella said forcefully as Bullock stepped outside and looked around, confused. A couple of USVC soldiers walked by and he stopped them.

"You two," he said. "You're in charge of Colonel Roosevelt's tent. They're going to be operating on him."

The two men straightened and beamed with pride and gave a salute.

"How will we know who is allowed in, sir?" asked the corporal.

"The Sister will make sure you know," Captain Bullock said with a smirk and walked off.

# INTERLUDE 83
March 30, 1917, 9:33 am
Mochogueachi Valley

E rnie awoke asleep under the same oak tree. A blanket
appeared over him in the night. *God, my leg hurts!*

The Apache camp stretched out for a hundred yards in any
direction he looked. In the small valley with few trees, they were
surrounded by cliffs so high Ernie found himself unable to raise
his head enough to see the tops of them. Dozens of tents covered
in animal skin stretched in a half-circle in front of him. Several
dome-shaped huts were arranged in the center of camp.

In a grassy area beyond the tents, several children played,
both boys and girls. They had a large buckskin ball about the
size of a soccer ball and they were kicking and throwing it.

*It's so warm.* Ernie threw the blanket off and tried to stand.
The pain shooting through his body made him collapse face-
down to the ground with a loud cry. He lay there for several minutes, his head spinning so severely he couldn't even lift his chin.

After some time, Chief Bronco came up and turned Ernie
over. He took a look at the wound on his leg and spoke to one of
the women.

The chief bent down close to Ernie as he struggled to focus
through tears of pain.

"The Ndee not trust," Chief Bronco said softly. "You come
from sky. They fear chindi. I bring covering. Bring food." Bronco

paused to see if Ernie understood. Ernie nodded, breathing heavily, and the Chief smiled. "Ndee friends. Bring shaman."

Then Ernie passed out.

When he awoke, a lean-to tent stood over him and he lay covered in blankets. *Now I'm freezing.*

His hand went to the wound on his leg. The Indians covered it with broad leaves and sticky sap and wrapped with a bright bandana.

An elderly man sat nearby, burning something in a wooden bowl and chanting softly. Ernie sat up and the man produced another bowl and a couple of apple-like fruits he had seen on cactus when he wandered near Shakespeare. *Must be a medicine man.*

The shaman crushed up the small fruit and handed out a bowl.

"Hoosh," the Apache said, nodding and pushing the bowl forward.

Ernie tentatively tasted the crushed fruit. *I'm hungry.*

He dipped his fingers into the bowl and pushed the mixture into his mouth. That's when he noticed all the activity in the camp. Ornate headdresses on the women and men were wearing beaded buckskins. Several blankets were covered with meats and a wide variety of fruits and vegetables. *Rabbits, deer, squirrel.*

He sniffed at a pot of meat smoking over a fire. *Bear.* Ernie watched as several members of a family built a tipi in the center of the village, started a fire pit, and began cooking.

Then the medicine man got up and made a sand painting in the ground in front of Ernie's lean-to.

*It looks like a snake.*

The shaman shook a cows tail over Ernie and pollen spread all over him. He sneezed. Another Indian came up with two dishes.

"Hi. Wow. Well, that's really hot," he said looking at the dish with a hot coal from the fire. The other bowl held a ground meal mixture.

"That looks like corn flour," Ernie said. He dipped his fingers in and touched it to his lips. "Yep," He looked up at the Indian, who smiled. "What do I do?"

The Indian dropped the coal into the cornflour and placed the bowl in front of him. The smoke rose up and he started to cough.

The medicine man made the motion for Ernie to breathe it in. So he did. And he coughed again.

Ernie sat back, took another couple of deep breaths, and looked around. He smiled at the medicine man.

The medicine man simply nodded, saying nothing. He then offered a long pipe.

Ernie stared at it, then back at the elder. The medicine man urged the pipe towards him, so Ernie took a draw on the pipe, exhaled a cloud of smoke and coughed again. *I feel pretty good. I just love everybody, and my leg doesn't seem to hurt.*

Then the medicine man drew another animal shape in the sand of a big fox or a bear.

Ernie noticed a group of men painted with oblique white stripes on their bodies. Women chose their men to dance with. Some of the men had their hair sculpted in the shape of horns. Everybody ate and laughed and sat around enjoying life.

Ernie smiled, farted, and passed out before his head hit the ground.

# INTERLUDE 84
March 31, 1917, 12:52 pm
The Flagship Cornelius Agrippa

Victor Frankenstein stood in the lower hold of the port vessel, staring at the line of beds with his dead and damaged soldiers lying on them. Doctor Kowalski and several other doctors and nurses were tending to the men. Many were not even conscious, but several sat up and saluted.

The Prince placed his fist over his heart in return and walked over to Kowalski. "Doctor, how quickly will you have the men restored?"

"The new serum is working much more quickly, my Prince." The doctor handed several syringes to a nurse. "The advances made by the results of the two subjects are showing remarkable rapidity in the wounded. Soldiers with prolonged death exposure have seen a complete neural recovery." He shook his head, smiling. "In some cases, memories are better than before. And the skeletal and muscular regenerations are breathtaking, my Prince. By morning four-fifths of your soldiers will be back to full mental and physical capacity." He tilted his head towards several bodies covered in sheets. "The rest will need reprogramming, and what little rehabilitation is absolutely necessary."

One of the bodies moved under the sheet, sitting up. A small green crystal sunk in silver glimmered from a hole in the man's chest. He had tubes running into both arms. He didn't look

232

around, only moaned through a mangled nose and upper jaw. As the blanket fell from his body it became clear the soldier had also lost a right leg.

Two nurses ran over and gently laid the living-dead soldier on his back and applied restraints.

"It's working better than we had hoped, Doctor." Frankenstein beamed proudly. "A procedure that used to take weeks takes hours! The restorative memory enhancement and genetic muscular improvements are all working as I predicted. Years of testing is finally bearing fruit!"

Doctor Kowalski nodded. "Indeed, my Prince."

"And the new implants?"

"Better than we could have hoped!" Gesturing, he led Victor through to the back of the medical area and through a door. In the next room, dozens of hexagonal green crystals shone brightly, lined up on the far shelf. In the center of the room, on a table, sat a complex green garnet the size of a hatbox. It had complex carvings of an indecipherable script and intricate shapes carved into the rock. Four metal plates were positioned equidistant around the rock at the edge of the table. A heavy set of lamps from above bathed the table in light. Wiring ran from the back of the metal plates and under the table.

The multifaceted crystal didn't just glow, it pulsed. As they watched, a section at the top of the crystal grew another geometrical shape from its form about the size of a pocket watch. The doctor went over, produced a pair of forceps from his pocket, placed them around the new piece and snapped it off.

"The Vim grows at the same continual pace." The doctor walked over to another table where a cluster of shiny silver ingots sat and placed the crystal next to them. "But when we embed the power source into the processed ore, the reaction is magnitudes greater than anything we have seen!"

"The silver catalysis?" Victor asked excitedly.

"The organic transformation to bioconjugation is nearly instantaneous. The nucleic acids and proteins form multicomponent conjugates in the cells and behave as your own blood does my Prince. In fact, the planarian stem cells are ninety percent intact." The doctor beamed with pride.

"Only ninety percent?" Victor growled.

Flustered, the doctor tried to keep from being defensive. "My Prince, with that ninety percent a recently dead hero of Silesia can be given the formula and live a normal, full life!"

"So you can't stop the aging process," Victor said flatly.

The doctor shook his head but remained emphatic. "But this means that no Silesian soldier ever needs to die on the battlefield again—unless he is simply too damaged, of course."

Victor looked over at the glowing rune stone with the odd carvings on the sides. He approached it slowly, then leaned in and studied it. "Any change in the monitors?"

The doctor shook his head. "We can detect energy fluctuations, but we know the crystal is in an inert state. We have learned to harness power by emitting magnetic fields at the right times."

Victor smiled for the first time that day, a green glow over his features. "We can keep the vacuum open, but we have no idea how to truly use the energy. We can project it, we can protect our ships with it. We can make them fly with it." Frankenstein stared at the doctor. "But it's only true worth as a weapon is... when it fails."

Doctor Kowalski shuddered. "The zero point barrier is extremely dangerous, my Prince. Only when the field is shattered is the aether released."

Frankenstein wheeled on the doctor, enraged. "I have seen cities leveled by this energy! This energy has moved islands and changed the very face of our planet. The Vim is the greatest gift bestowed on a mortal in a thousand years!" He pounded the wall with his fist. "And all I have been able to do with it is a few parlor tricks. Flying boats and walking mutants," he scoffed.

Frankenstein turned and stormed out. He walked past the wounded soldiers and did not pause to salute them as he left. He took the main stairwell to his cabin level and entered.

The young boy ran into his arms. "Tata!"

"Peter!" Victor said with warmth and affection.

"I want to go fishing, Tata. But Mummy says no," the boy pouted.

"Really?" Frankenstein held the boy in his hands and carried him across the study and through to the rear of the cabin. When his eyes fell on Aleffra he paused and ruffled the little boy's hair.

"Well, I am sure we can talk to Mummy. There must be something we can do."

"Oh, you're going to take him fishing are you?" Aleffra said, dripping sarcasm.

Victor put the boy down and pointed him towards the desk in the center of the room.

"There are some cards in the top drawer. Go play with them."

"What about fishing?"

"Fishing later, I promise."

Attention drawn with a new distraction, the boy ran off. Frankenstein turned.

"When I fire the Vim energy into the earth's crust, the resulting blast will impact the major tectonic plates of north and south America. The Cocos plate will shift, splitting from the North American plate. The rippling effects will drop the southern half of Mexico a hundred feet below sea level."

Aleffra cocked her head. "And then what? They're going to let you in?"

"Our mutual friend promised an audience if we made it impossible to ignore us."

"Victor, if you end up trapped for eternity like me, it would be fitting." Aleffra looked away and sipped her water.

"You can hate me all you want for giving you life. Soon I will change the world forever."

She smiled without glancing at him. "One thing for sure, I'll be around to watch."

# INTERLUDE 85
April 1, 1917, 6:52 am
Cavalry Camp Columbus

*My dear Kermit, I am much obliged for your present and your letter which had a great deal of good news in it. Wherever did you find a bottle of Dalmore Cigar Malt in Mesopotamia? Things are amiss at the Mexican border, son. But no events should so trouble you knowing your father is getting on very well.*

*I am sorry to say that at the moment there has been a big hitch in our southern excursion. The White House asks us to operate with one eye blind and one hand behind our backs. We had an encounter with the bandits and I am laid up with a black eye. But no matter. General Pershing and I will have it all sorted out shortly.*

*I am no longer given to believe I will receive the long-awaited cable from Washington. It has been made clear to me that when going abroad, not only do I not represent the wishes of the government at home but when, as a matter of fact, that government is delighted to take some action to thwart my intentions and make them seem inconsistent with fact. I am pretty well disgusted with our government and with the way our people acquiesce.*

*But enough of that. I write to you about a matter of very real importance in which I wish you to bestir yourself actively, and I know you will be glad to do so. Your brother Quentin is embarking on a quest to join in combat. He has abandoned Harvard and is learning to fly. Your mother hasn't been told and I fear her response at having both boys off to war. I also feel it highly impolitic and undesirable that he should be asked to return home.*

*I want you to write the strongest letter you know how; say you speak for all the educated and cultivated men, and all the believers in service to their country. Make her understand every man would take it as the greatest blow if he were to be turned out.*

*There is another point. Could you send out for me the three-pint felt-covered aluminum water-bottle and small shoulder-bag with two compartments we looked at?*

*Sincerely Yours,*
*Father*

# INTERLUDE 86
April 1, 1917, 8:52 am
Mochogueachi Valley

Ernie turned over on the hard ground and opened his eyes. He rolled outside of his lean-to and drew back the blanket. *How bad is it?*

His leg had nearly healed. *How many days has it been? So hungry.*

Food sat out on a blanket near the main gathering area. One Indian came over to Ernie and held up two plates of meat. There were cooked pieces of some kind of animal, slices of sunbaked bread, and small chunks of familiar bloody meat.

*I know what bear looks like. God, I'm hungry.* He reached for the chunks of bear meat. *Wonder if it'll taste like juniper berries.*

He chewed several pieces, leaving his face and fingers glossy with bear fat. *Rank and stringy, but satisfying.*

The Indians watching laughed and came over and clapped Ernie on the back as he chewed hungrily. After a few minutes, the Indians all went back to preparing the meal, laying food out for the camp around the fire pit, and baking more bread. Kids came and went, some played that dodge-the-ball game again.

Chief Bronco came over after Ernie had swallowed the last and clapped him on the back too.

"Is good," the huge man said, smiling. "You ate like Ndee."

Ernie looked at Bronco, confused. Then he watched the other Indians. Several were smiling at him, but a couple of them watched him warily, tucking away their knives and hatchets.

"What do you mean?"

"Eat bread first, or cooked meat first, warriors would have tortured." Bronco smiled. "You are Ndee."

The realization of how close he had gotten to dying a horrible death came over Ernie. *Don't vomit.* Everything started to spin. *Don't you lose it, man.*

The thought of being tortured for the weakness of vomiting kept it down.

As Ernie watched the Indians though, many made signs that he had pleased them. *So they were going to kill me if I ate like a white man. What else would they kill me for?*

One of the women came over and gave him a large jug and pointed toward the river on the other side of the trees.

*They want me to fill the water jug. Is this another test?*

He slowly stood up and found he could actually remain upright. With a pronounced limp, he made his way across the camp towards the river to fill the jug. As he walked, some kids broke away from their play and followed him.

*They're not sending me out here to kill me and drop me in the river?*

Ernie glanced over his shoulder and saw Chief Bronco smile and nod at him.

*Seems like I'm doing fine.*

They showed him how to fill the jug. But it became so heavy when full that, when he tried to stand up with his weak leg, Ernie fell under the water.

The children laughed and helped him up and just when he had stood up, they let go of the jug and he fell under the water again. *Very funny. Just steady yourself, man.*

This happened several times until Ernie became so tangled in the hemp rope around the jug that he could neither stand without the jug nor stay above the water with the jug. All the while, the children laughed and giggled riotously. *Don't get upset. If they are smiling, you aren't dying. Just breathe.*

He spat out water and hacked loudly several times. *I hope someone hears me.*

At last, Chief Bronco came through the trees. Whether to investigate the squeals of the children or to find out why he had not returned, he could not tell. But upon seeing Ernie stuck in the water he said something harshly to the children who quickly ran off. The big man waded into the water and lifted him and the jug out of the river, carrying him to shore.

When Ernie finally got back to camp, he found several older women waiting for him there. They smiled and laughed and dragged him gently behind a row of tents. There the Indians had dug a large pit and filled it with water for bathing. The Indian mothers began to strip his clothes off.

"What is going on?" The Apache women would just shake their heads, or nod, and continue. They pushed him into the water and began scrubbing him with rocks wrapped in rough leaves.

"Look, you don't have to do that," Ernie said, waving his hands. One of the women started scrubbing the lower part of his body.

"Hey!" he yelled. But the women just laughed and kept on. *They don't understand a word I'm saying. This is some ritual.*

So Ernie started reciting the first thing that came to mind. A prayer his mother had taught him in the little protestant church near their home. *Lord, give me the grace to hold righteousness in all things that I may lead a clean and blessed life and prudently flee evil and that I may understand the treacherous and deceitful falseness of the devil. Make me mild, peaceable, courteous, and temperate. And make me steadfast and strong. Also, Lord, give Thou to me that I am quiet in words and that I speak what is appropriate. Amen.*

When they finished bathing him, they tossed his rags of clothes, except for his jeans which fascinated them, into the fire and handed him a buckskin coat and mocassins.

Dressed like an Apache he stumbled back into the clearing where he found the children again waiting for him, nearly bouncing up and down with anticipation. This time they had fishing poles. Ernie enthusiastically set out with the kids to do some fishing. They moved up and down the river for a couple of hours, catching fish and playing games.

*The mind conjures the ideals of savage customs. But I struggle to draw from the broad range of my language how it feels to be among savages who raid and steal and terrorize. Watching them laugh and play, catching turtles and trout, tossing rocks, I almost feel normal.*

Several warriors came charging through the trees and grabbed Ernie.

*No, no, no. We were having fun!* He tried to fight them and the Apache clubbed him until he collapsed. The children all backed away as the hunters bound his hands and legs and carried him back to the camp. *What now? I'm dead, mother. You'll never know what happened. They'll scalp me and abandon my body in the forest to be devoured by wild beasts.*

Tied up, they tossed him to the ground and moved several feet away. Standing in a circle they talked fiercely among themselves. Several of the warriors had their weapons out and were gesturing with them. Every now and again one of them would run towards him, swinging his drawn hatchet and threatening to brain him.

*I am deprived of everything that is near or dear to me but life. But I must not absorb myself in melancholy. Fortitude is my friend.*

After about an hour one of the Taramahura from the other night ran into camp. Right behind him came Chief Bronco on his horse with several of his hunting party. He came down off his horse and, seeing Ernie on the ground tied up, spoke with authority to the group. They spoke in harsh tones to the Chief, pointing at him.

*The Indian has slaughtered entire families: men women and children since the French Indian Wars. Dear God, let death be quick.*

One of the Indians held up his rucksack. Chief Bronco took Ernie's satchel, opened it and looked inside. Whatever he had seen scared him because the Chief closed the bag quickly. He glanced at Ernie, speaking in low serious tones to the other Indians. Several were unhappy and made more gestures with their weapons. But Charlie shook his head and the warriors moved away.

*Am I not to be killed, dismembered, my torso burnt to a crisp and parts scattered? I have heard that it is the custom of the Indian that if a family member is killed, the tribe replaces the loved one with a prisoner. Maybe they're arguing over adoption.*

Chief Bronco carried Ernie's bag over to him and set it on the ground next to him. He cut his ropes and helped him sit up. Sullen fierceness mingled with the quiet of the savage arrested the attention to this huge man. Chief Bronco opened the bag and revealed the green medallion from Black Mountain.

Bronco watched him with deadly seriousness. "Devil."

Ernie sighed, eyes closed, smiling at the Apache Chief. "Good story."

# INTERLUDE 87
April 1, 1917, 1:36 pm
Cavalry Camp Columbus

With a somber look on his face, General Pershing entered the ex-president's tent.

Colonel Roosevelt, piqued at the General's mood, set his notebook aside. "What are the bastards in Washington up to now, General?"

"I have been proceeding as if I am going to be in charge of a division in France, Mr. President. But the Secretary of War has called to tell me, unofficially, that I am to be considered for the Commander of the Armed Forces in the European theater. However, that news went out before the deaths in Chihuahua. The White House and the General Staff have no inclination to allow us a second opportunity."

The ex-president threw the covers off his bed and stood up.

General Pershing held up a hand. "As we speak, the news is being broadcast that U.S. forces looking for remnants of the Villaistas encountered federal Mexican forces in Chihuahua. Both Zapata and Carranza are taking responsibility to make themselves look good and said they chased forces of the other out of northern Chihuahua."

"They can't let it stand, John. We have to tell them what's going on!"

"Tell them what, Theodore? And exactly what are they going to do about it? The General Staff isn't properly organized. Most of the senior officers have no understanding of their duties."

"They've got to send reinforcements!"

"There aren't any. I have been given the task of organizing the artillery and infantry regiments to form the divisions. The War Department has indicated the available soldiers are already here." General Pershing turned to the open canvas flap and indicated the movement of soldiers that could be seen beyond the threshold. "We're staring at them."

"But...are we that unprepared?"

"The Secretary indicated the announcement won't be for another month, officially. Soldiers are being trained for Divisions that will follow the first troops to Europe by summer."

"Well, certainly congratulations are in order, General."

General Pershing closed his eyes and gritted his teeth. "Why? I've been put in charge of a theoretical army that doesn't exist yet. It has to be constituted, equipped, trained and sent overseas by a bunch of bureaucrats who have no idea how an army really works. The Selective Service Act has been recommended to Congress by the President but won't go into effect until May 18th even if it's passed tomorrow."

The ex-president sat back down on his bed. "Yes, I see your point."

"When I asked them what transportation and tonnage they were making available for the supply and movement of the army, the General Staff responded 'Whatever we have.'" General Pershing shook his head.

"General, you've seen the reports. Flying boats. Automatic machine guns. You've seen the metal monsters, the Thing machines."

"Mr. President, I agree with you," General Pershing nodded. "But the current occupant in the Oval Office is on the verge of declaring war on Germany and Austro-Hungary. We have polling places ready around the country, local support has been building for the creation of the armies necessary to fight the war. What happens if he declares war and then says, oh sorry, we have to send armies into Mexico to fight rotters?"

The ex-president said nothing.

"The country's local support for the Selective Service would be devastated. They would all close up shop. Not a single mother would want to send their sons to battle against rotters. And hey, who would be in charge of sending them? The moment the newspapers get the story about rotters in Mexico, support for the current administration and the war in Europe would collapse. Their ability to conduct any type of governing would be thrown into total chaos."

T.R. paused, then said, "What about volunteers?"

"You've seen what they did to you when you tried to raise volunteer forces. They are so afraid that your volunteers would consider themselves a special class and expect priorities for supplies and assignments that they had to squash your efforts. Anything that would materially affect the enforcement of the Draft Law, or create special groups of soldiers has to be stopped. Not to mention the numbers of experienced officers that would join such an effort at a time when the military needs everyone."

"What if I went to talk to them?"

General Pershing shook his head sadly. "Mr. President, if I went to Washington and told them what happened here, you'd never hear from me again. They would appoint another Armed Forces Commander, lock me in a dark hole, forget all about me and move on. Nothing, but nothing, is going to interfere with the Selective Service Act, a Declaration of War, the raising of three million new soldiers to serve overseas, and the distribution and transportation lines that will get them there."

"What do we have then, General?" T.R. asked, quite somber now.

"Major Harbord has been on his way from Camp McArthur for the last three days. He is bringing a large shipment of weapons from Texas. The quartermaster signals from Texas indicate it is twelve railcars of weapons and munitions."

245

# INTERLUDE 88
April 1, 1917, 3:12 pm
Mochogueachi Valley


The small band of Apache, including Chief Bronco and Ernie, proceeded through the canyon.

*We've been walking for miles now*, Ernie thought. *Where are they taking me?*

Here and there they would encounter a rock overhang with a shelter or series of shelters built under its protection. Each time an Indian family, or a group of families, would emerge and watch the hiking party pass. Unlike the Apache, they wore brilliantly patterned blankets and cloth, and only simply sandals. They also had animals around their homes. Ernie saw chickens and ducks and sheep roaming everywhere nearby, even going in and out of the dwellings.

*The Apache prefers to hunt and never domesticate anything long enough to breed.*

The watchful Indians would never speak and the Apache would never approach. The great white Chief would only wave and keep walking.

"Tarahumara," said Chief Bronco, glancing at Ernie. "Their people here five hundred years." They continued walking across the desert landscape, up one ravine and down into another. After another hour, they passed through a series of vertical rock formations and onto a rockier path.

They came to a place where the trail split in two. One path went uphill, one headed downhill. Chief Bronco held the green medallion wrapped in a colored headscarf and gave it to a warrior. As the young man ran off downward, Ernie and the rest of them proceeded up. This took them to the edge of a cliff.

Ernie looked down into a small ravine and saw a pit dug out of the earth. He watched as the Indian warrior went in and placed the green medallion carefully in the center of the carved out rock. Two warriors appeared in a cleft of the mountain, rolling a boulder into place above a slope carved from millennia of snowpack.

Chief Bronco indicated that Ernie should get down on his stomach and watch over the edge. He gestured down. "Chindi."

With a nod from Bronco, the two warriors released the boulder and stepped back from the edge. The smooth rock rolled down the crevice, slid off the edge, and plunged right into the center of the rock pit.

Instantly Ernie felt the heat rise from the floor of the ravine and a bright green light burst out. It came out about thirty feet and he felt as if he were staring into a void before the light collapsed and a thunderclap of noise reverberated the very ground. Trees shook. Rocks tumbled.

Ernie stared into the pit blinking. The hole in the ground had grown twice as deep as before. The rock formation hadn't blown out, or blown apart. No dust or debris. It had simply vanished.

Chief Bronco sat back. "Devil medicine very bad."

# INTERLUDE 89
April 2, 1917, 8:34 am
the Royal Yacht Johannes Trithemius

The royal yacht detached from the Cornelius Agrippa and slowly descended into the crescent valley. Victor Frankenstein, wearing a bespoke woolen suit and a ceremonial sash of black and yellow, stood on the deck of his personal vessel, studying the magnificent beauty of the canyon, the waterfall, and the lush vegetation. He breathed in deeply. *Magnificent. Too bad.*

As the yacht grew closer to the ground, a small clearing on the mountainside became apparent. A large tunnel, twelve feet tall and twice as wide, bored into the base of the canyon. The boat slowed, then settled with a slight shudder.

Frankenstein stepped off and directly into the tunnel, without any retainer or guard. Black-clad Silesian soldiers stood at attention in the tunnel every ten yards on either side as he walked for several minutes, at his brisk pace, down the slightly grading shaft until he came to a massive iron door. He stood within a foot of the door, staring the signet ring on the index finger of his right hand. Then he placed the ring squarely against a small medallion on the door's surface.

As the portal swung outward, a low rumbling hum emanated from beyond the threshold and a wall of freezing air hit Frankenstein in the face. Bright lights illuminated the interior of the mountain cavern. A massive chrome and bronze steam machine came into view. Twice as tall as a man, it had a long cylindrical boiler with a pipe leading from the top feeding back into the fire again. Set around the circumference of the boiler were massive magnetic flywheels eight feet tall, generating tremendous amounts of energy that rippled off of them in bursts and bright arcs.

Against the walls of the cavern were huge air cooling units which drew in freezing water through pipes that snaked up the walls and disappeared into the rock. The machines then pumped frigid air into the vast space. Ice covered everything the first few dozen feet and here the Silesian guards wore freezer suits.

A soldier gave the Roman salute and handed Victor an oxygen mask with a visor. Frankenstein pulled it on and waited for the frost from his breathing to adjust as the mask temperature regulated itself. As he stepped across the threshold, a sign hung above that read "Exposed Skin Will Freeze". Frost covered gangways crisscrossed the air above the steam engine and several men wearing black freezer suits, goggles, and breathing apparatus worked at different stations, reading meters and adjusting valves.

As the giant door shut behind him with a shudder, Frankenstein made his way to the center of the chamber. The closer one got to the massive turbine, the less ice persisted on every surface. Victor climbed the main staircase and approached a man in a yellow freezer suit near the center. Despite being the only one dressed in normal clothing, Victor did not appear in discomfort.

When the man saw Frankenstein approaching he became animated. "My Prince! It is exciting. Tremendous! We have created observable vacuum energy!" His voice by a speaking device in the helmet.

Victor's features or demeanor did not change behind the mask and he spoke flatly. "Really, Doctor Exner? Tell me I didn't waste my time coming into the cold. Show me."

The two men moved across the walkway toward the center of the chamber and peered down into the middle of the accelerator.

The turbine sat around a hollow cylindrical device built of concentric metal rings of varying rainbow hues that ran deep into the ground. A familiar greenish hue emanated from deep below, throwing shadows across the multiple colors in the shaft.

"We have achieved supersymmetry. We believe the device is ready to test, my Prince."

Victor studied dials and gauges in front of him. "If these numbers hold, it won't be a test, Doctor." Victor looked back at the instruments, then into the deep round chasm. "And then America will have a crisis at its southern border it cannot ignore. All right, let us proceed."

He pressed a button and a series of arc lights came on across the ceiling. The men in freezer suits all moved into positions on the ground at various points around the machine.

Frankenstein opened the panel with a key on a chain around his neck. Beneath the opaque panel sat a single keyhole and a flat dull green button. The Prince of Silesia inserted the key and turned it counter-clockwise. The button slowly raised about a half-inch and now glowed a familiar green.

Frankenstein looked around once. Noting everyone in their proper positions, he pressed the button.

The cylindrical rings vibrated, then slowly rotated. The steam boiler hum grew louder.

As Victor watched, the green glow got brighter and brighter.

The ground shook. First came simple rumbles and quivers. A jolt came on that shifted the massive steam engine several inches and the metal cylinder quivered and shifted position.

"It's working!" Victor shouted over the growing noise.

Rock fell from the ceiling as the quakes increased, first small, then larger. Rubble fell on one of the scientists. He collapsed and didn't move again. The roar of the turbine, the oscillation of the rings and the humming of the magnets grew so loud Victor couldn't hear anything else. Looking a mile straight into the earth's crust, he watched it disintegrating under the power of the Vim. Frankenstein shouted with joy but couldn't hear his own voice. The scientists were all watching him, and no one moved.

He adjusted several gauges and levers and the vibrations subsided for a moment. One of the spherical rings broke loose, rattled in the hot core and shot into the ceiling. It embedded itself in the rock. Then the steam pipe burst. More rocks fell from the ceiling and Victor noticed that parts of the steam engine were melting even in the freezing temperature. He waved at his men and they moved away.

A clanging alarm went off throughout the cave and the giant door swung open. Frankenstein watched as the refrigeration units in the corners and the ceiling shook. Pulses of energy from the device were now not simply being directed down into the earth's crust, but bouncing back.

As the wave of power filled the cavern, the cooling units blew circuits and a blast of freezing air churned and pushed through the opening and into the tunnel. Three black-clad soldiers, without masks or protective gear, rushed in at the sound of the alarm and froze in mid-stride.

The first quake jolts struck and the floor began a violent rolling motion. Frankenstein staggered in front of the console, gripping the guardrail for support. He reached out, his outstretched hand wavered a moment before slamming down the green button next to the key slot. The steam engine immediately stopped churning, the magnetic motors slowed, and the vibration of the Vim accelerator ebbed.

# INTERLUDE 90
April 2, 1917, 11:07 am
Ten Miles West of El Paso

The passengers had ridden for over two days, boarding the 4-4-2 Santa Fe Deluxe in Chicago. They would travel for sixty-three hours to get to California. The three dozen men, women and children just had a one hour stop in El Paso to stretch their legs before the train moved west.

The young man in a tweed suit looked out over the New Mexico landscape with expectation and excitement. He watched the dejected young woman in the pink dress sitting across from him and spoke with encouragement. "You know, Norma. It took the Pullman company a year to design the cars on this train. There's a drawing-room just back here," he said, nodding over his shoulder. "And you still haven't been to the dining car." His eyes widened as he spoke. "It has air conditioning."

Norma rolled her eyes. "Robert, I don't care."

Robert looked sullen. "I don't know what you're so upset about. So we get to spend the summer in San Francisco." He sat forward. "What's so bad about that?"

Norma scoffed and blinked back tears. "I hate the ocean. I enrolled in beauty school. I had friends. I had a boyfriend. I didn't want to leave."

"It's just for the summer, Mother and Father didn't ship us off."

"We're moving, Robert." Norma waved her hands with exasperation. "They want us out of the way. Papa has dried goods he is going to start moving from San Francisco."

Robert looked nervous. "That won't happen. I told Debbie we were just leaving for the summer. She's coming to visit and then I am supposed to take her home. I planned to..." He shook his head. "No, you'll see. It's just for the summer." Robert went silent and looked at the floor.

Norma said nothing and turned to look out the window. The desert passed by, mile after empty mile.

After a long silence, Robert's face brightened and he looked up. "When we get to California, they give the woman a bouquet of flowers and a basket of oranges. You'll love it there."

Norma sat up and her face went pale. She squirmed in her seat, moving away from the window, making a strangling noise. A moment later, Norma, let out a scream of terror as Robert turned to see what had so terrified his sister.

A ghastly form blotted out the windows of their section. It slammed into the side of the railcar and cracked the window. A giant metal arm clamped on to the roof, buckling the metal. The monstrous scarred face snarled, ropes of thick metal snaking from its neck and chest.

The railcar rocked as a half dozen Thing machines slammed into it.

The engineer pulled the emergency threw the air compressor switch as a swarm of figures rushed the train tracks. The brakes squealed and the locomotive slowed. The driver only had a moment to stare in horror as rotters crawled over the water tank and into the cab windows.

Robert and Norma scrambled to the opposite side of the luxury car during the initial melee, along with a half dozen other passengers in the luxury car. But when the second pounding came, Robert lost Norma's hand as a couch slid against him and he blacked out.

The second passenger car behind the engine fell on its side with a tremendous bang and the entire train ground to a halt

253

Moments later, ax-wielding rotters climbed on top of the crippled car, smashing windows and scrambling inside. Screams followed briefly before they stopped.

The Thing Machines assaulted the locomotive, crippling its two main axles, then ripping holes in its water tank. Slowly, the engine died.

Robert awoke with his head in Norma's lap, a trickle of blood from his nose, and Norma crying. When she saw his eyes flutter open she whispered, "Thank God," and just kept rubbing his forehead.

The young man sat up. "What's happened?"

Norma moved back against the wall. "It's a nightmare."

Slowly Robert got to his feet and looked through the window. Outside, in the afternoon sun, Aztec rotters and grotesque metal monstrosities stood watching...and waiting.

# INTERLUDE 91
April 2, 1917, 1:15 pm
Cavalry Camp Columbus

General Pershing stepped to the platform as the U.S. Army 101 Line with the 2-8-0 pulling four freight cars arrived at the Columbus station. Major James Harbord stepped off the forward stairwell before the train had come to a complete halt. A tall, broad-shouldered man with a square chin and a long aristocratic nose saluted General Pershing solemnly.

Pershing returned the salute. "Major, good of you to make it. I understand they're finally going to make you a Lieutenant Colonel."

Major Harbord raised an eyebrow. "Only because they couldn't find anyone else who wanted to be your chief of staff, General."

Both men broke into grins and shook hands.

"What do we have, Major? I understood we were expecting twelve railcars of munitions. I only see four." Pershing asked as the two walked the platform.

"Last year, Congress appropriated twelve million dollars for the production of machine guns." Major Harbord stopped. "However, they have not yet decided which model they prefer to manufacture."

"So, what have you brought us then?"

Harbord rapped on the side of the first railcar. It slid open two feet, revealing two U.S. soldiers operating the door on the

255

inside. They pushed the freight door all the way open, revealing the wooden crates. Harbord nodded at the two soldiers and they stepped back and pulled the lid off one of the wooden crates to reveal a gleaming chrome ten barrel monster inside..

"The Gatling Gun, General. Manufactured during the Spanish American War. Ten twenty-six inch barrels, firing two hundred rounds per minute. I took the War Department's entire allotment. Sitting in a warehouse gathering dust. No one wanted them. One hundred guns," Two railcars slid open their freight doors. "and five million rounds of ammunition."

Pershing eyed the final car. "What's in the last one?"

"Enough ammunition for nine hours at the ordinary rate used to lay down a barrage in an infantry attack." The Major cleared his throat. "Given the limited number of weapons on hand."

"Dammit, Major. What are they thinking? I've got sixty-five officers and a thousand men in the Air Service Section, of which about thirty-five can actually fly. And with the exception of five or six of them, none of them could meet the requirements for battlefield conditions. And one of those has gone missing! They have no technical experience with aircraft guns, bombs or bombing. I've got fifty-five training planes, fifty-one of which are obsolete. And I'm already hearing requests from the French and the British to provide aircraft for 300 squadrons when I can't field one!"

"General, I wish I had an answer for you. Neither the War Department nor the Governor's office had any response to my requests for supplies."

A Signal Corp Private ran up to General Pershing with a telegram. "It's an attack, General!"

# INTERLUDE 92
April 2, 1917, 4:48 pm
Ten Miles West of El Paso

Robert stared with fury at the motionless horrors standing in the desert surrounding the crippled train. "What the hell do you want," he shouted at the top of his lungs. Immediately everyone else in the car hushed him.

"You trying to get us killed, son?" asked a gray haired gentleman in a bowler holding a shaken woman who looked old enough to be his mother.

"Look, we have to try to get out of here," Robert said hysterically.

The elderly man pointed to the rear of the car. Through the open door into the vestibule to the adjoining car lay the bloody body of the train conductor. "That's what happens when you try to leave. Now why don't you just sit down and shut up. The telegraph follows the rails. And when the train passes certain points, it sends a signal to the station ahead. They know something is wrong. Help is coming."

Norma placed a hand on Robert's shoulder and nudged him down into his seat. At the same moment, an explosion outside rocked the car and Robert shot back up to his feet and screamed.

Elements of the Seventh Cavalry regiment charged over the dunes, and two Curtis R2's soared past. Another explosion from the mounted Vickers Rocket Gun scattered parts of three Aztec undead into the air and the Thing machines opened fire into the sky.

The U.S.Cavalry charged into the ranks with unwavering bravery, bringing their gunfire to bear on the more vulnerable axe-wielding rotters. About two dozen soldiers dropped from their horses and engaged the rotters hand to hand.

Two minutes of melee brought down most of the axe-wielding undead, but the rest of the regiment had focused on the monstrous Thing machines and they weren't so lucky. As soon as the R2's had soared out of gunfire range, the monstrosities turned their arm cannons on the Americans.

The rapid gunfire tore into the cavalry ranks, ripping horse flesh and soldier bodies apart. The entire front line of cavalry toppled over or finally staggered to their deaths in the first minute.

The Thing machines paused and the Curtis fighters returned. They poured hot lead into the sky and one fighter burst into flames and exploded in mid-air. Pieces rained down on top of and around the train car and people screamed as a body hit the ground outside.

The other elements of the cavalry, over their momentary shock at the decimation of their comrades, charged in guns blazing on the Thing machines. One staggered and fell over but the other half dozen levelled their gunfire and brought down the rest of the regiment in short order.

The passengers in the railcars watched as several rider- less horses tried to flee and were ripped apart with gunfire. The metal monsters surveyed the damage for several minutes before finally striding off.

# INTERLUDE 93
April 2, 1917, 6:09 pm
Mochogueachi Valley

*Dear Family*

*Scuse the use of your letter and the scrawl, but I don't have the typer with me. In fact, you may never read this. I've been gone for nearly a week now. I fell in with Indians after the plane crashed in Mexico. I hope this is the last letter you get from me before you see me. If I get home I will be an advocate for moonlight swims and fishing for rainbow off the point. The Indians have had me running and hunting all day, without a break. They haven't fed me today, but watch me with expectant pride. They are waiting for something.*

*I don't want to commit some fatal conceit and grow Philipic and misspell some word like abominable in a charming or ingenious way. So I won't misspell it. What's the stuff about conceit. Am I really so conceited?*

*I know that getting this letter one day will take on a tremendous significance so I hope someday I can be forgiven.*

259

*I am sorry about the numerous diatribes I might have written agin any of you whilst in a very remote and unreal seeming period profoundly irritated by you.*

*I am very sorry if any ever discover the secrets of my dretful past. Especially Mom.*
*I hope you never lose your sense of humor, any of you. People lose their sense of humor so very completely when they fall in love. Or become a christian scientist.*

*Write something good about me, all of you. Or if for some bad or bitter reason anyone is off of me til death doth come, write me a fine dramatic, cold and haughty letter about why you never want to hear from me again. I always liked a fine dramatic situation like that. Just something about it.*

*So mote it be.*

*So mote it be.*

*I hope this gloomy letter helps you all appreciate what a fine time you are all having.*

*Wish you were here to cheer me up.*

# INTERLUDE 94
### April 3, 1917, 4:17 am
### Mochogueachi Valley

Ernie awoke when Chief Bronco shook his shoulder. The sun had not begun to rise. The big man had him put on his white cotton tunic, and marched across the camp. There, in the center, stood a large tent. Before the tent stood one of the Tarahumara runners getting drunk the other evening.

*I'm starving*, Ernie thought.

The Indian smiled at him. "There are things you will need to collect. Thirty-one logs must be gathered. Forty-eight rocks must be found. An equal number from the riverbank, from the cliff, from the forest and from the water itself. You will bring these here."

The Tarahumara smiled, then Chief Bronco said something, and the Indian nodded. "The Ndee prefers existence in simplest terms. Life is danger, but is happier than white man world. Virtue is physical excellence. Strength is beauty. Ndee is always prepared to volunteer at any cost. Generous to last mouthful of food, fearless of hunger, suffering, death." When the Tarahumara finished, he walked away.

Chief Bronco stepped in front of Ernie, leaned forward and whispered, "We believe in 'to be'. Not 'to have'. Now—thirty-one logs."

An hour later, Ernie sat inside the tent, cross-legged like the other men, glowing hot rocks stacked in the center. Across from him sat the Tarahumara translator, Chief Bronco and the sha-man. A portrait of Geronimo painted on buffalo hide hung on the wall behind them.

"Eagle Soldier," said the translator, indicating the elder. "Geronimo's brother."

The shaman began to chant.

The Tarahumara passed sage and sweetgrass amongst the participants to toss into the heat.

*I'm already dripping with sweat,* Ernie thought.

A final flap fell across the dim doorway and darkness came.

"If too much," the Tarahumara said in the blackness, "just say *'mitakuye oyas'in'* and door will open."

"This not endurance test," stressed the Tarahumara. "Is spiri-tual experience. Humble."

Someone poured water on the hot stones and steam filled the tent.

"Water first medicine to Ndee," Chief Bronco's words emerged from the dark.

*My mouth tastes like dirt brought up from the steam. But it feels good.*

Soon the old shaman told the Apache story of creation.

# INTERLUDE 95
April 3, 1917, 5:45 am
Mochogueachi Valley

After what felt like an eternity, the flap opened and Ernie blinked at the sunlight. *Feels like I've got a weight on my chest. And my legs are asleep.* He had trouble sitting upright and cross-legged for this long, but none of the other three appeared to be fazed.

The shaman chanted again as cool air rolled in, then fell silent.

"You may share intentions," said the Tarahumara.

Ernie looked puzzled. "Intentions?"

"What you wish?" asked Chief Bronco. "Who you suffer for?" Whispers between Chief Bronco and the Tarahumara.

"What want from life?" asked the Tarahumara.

*Jesus. What do I want out of life? A good woman and a good rifle, for starters.* "I want to experience life. I want to live as a man. I want to hunt. I want to run with the bulls."

"Run...with bulls?" asked Chief Bronco.

The Tarahumara and the Chief whispered again. A strange look came over the bearded giant's face and he grinned. "Sound like fun."

"What do you wish?" asked the Tarahumara.

"I want to be a writer. I want to write about life, about living, about being a man."

The shaman began to chant again.

The Tarahumara pointed east. "To the east, comes the sun and life." His hand moved. "To the west, the thunder approaches

263

which decides when we die." He pointed west. "To the north is transformation." As he pointed north the shaman held the pipe out over the hot pit.

Ernie watched Chief Bronco, who indicated he should take it. *I feel this intense need to smile with contentment.* He smoked from the long pipe and the door flap brought darkness and stifling heat again. Eagle Soldier stopped chanting.

"This is the time for cleansing," said the Tarahumara in the darkness. "For forgiving, for embracing."

After another thirty minutes in the torturous environment, Ernie laughed, then nearly passed out from exhaustion. Eagle Soldier said something, but it sounded distant.

*I've lost feeling in my hands and feet.*

"Manifest healing for yourself and others," said the Tarahumara.

Ernie found himself crying.

"Take control of life," said Chief Bronco from the darkness.

*Is this what dying from heat exposure is like?*

"What is the fear you have embraced?" asked the Tarahumara.

"I stood up to a bear. He came into my camp and I yelled at him to leave and he did. And when he came back again, I shot him."

The door opened for the last time and Ernie crawled out. He stood up slowly and breathed in the cool mountain air, swaying back and forth, sweat still beading on his brow.

Behind him, Chief Bronco, Eagle Soldier and the Tarahumara emerged. The tall Indian walked past and out of sight, but Chief Bronco just stood there. Slowly, Ernie's eyes focused, and he pulled himself up and looked at the tall Chief.

The yellow bearded giant held up a necklace of bear teeth.

"Thank Creator," Chief Bronco said, smiling. "You are Ndee. Your name is Haadi'a tsét'soyé."

Eagle Soldier nodded and smiled.

"Ha-di-ya Set-so-yay," Ernie repeated.

Chief Bronco nodded. "Singing Bear."

Ernie smiled broadly.

# INTERLUDE 96
April 3, 1917, 3:12 pm
Hachita, New Mexico

A young white boy sat in the dirt of the hardscrabble desert, dragging a stick though a colony of fire ants. He pushed it around in the parched soil, trying to crush as many fire ants as possible. He poked at a hard object in the ground and, as some of the dirt fell away, a smooth shiny blue stone peeked out.

The young boy yelped and jumped back as a fire ant bit him. He dropped the stick, shook his hand, then lunged in and grabbed the blue rock. He shook his hand again and rubbed it against his shorts. "Ouch," he said.

He looked down at the azure stone. He rubbed at the dirt caked to it. As more of it feel away, its shape became clearer. The boy's eyes widened and he took off running.

The tall, thin man in the tan farmers' shirt and high water pants he kept up around him with a rope tossed rock from the wheelbarrow into the ore crusher one small boulder at a time. The machine rattled and hummed, and the belt squealed as it turned, conveying the rock into the crusher to be pulverized into sand. The man next to him bent and retrieved a ladle of water from a nearby bucket. He took a deep drink, dipped again, and poured the water over his head.

"Damn, it's hot," said Earl.

265

"Eh?" Jim Booker looked up. "You say somethin, Earl?" he shouted over the din of the machine.

"I said, it's damn hot, Jim!"

Jim rolled his eyes. "At least we ain't down in the damn Hornet mine, Earl. Ol' Steve passed out yesterday down there and hasn't woke yet. His wife is fit to be tied."

Earl nodded and bent to pick up another piece of ore when the young boy ran up.

"Poppa, look!" The young boy held the stone in his hand like a trophy.

Jim turned to the boy and held up a hand for him to stop. "Stay back, Tom. If the ore grinder kicks out shrapnel in your direction, you'll be mighty sorry."

The boy, disappointed, waited about ten feet away, holding up his object with urgency, bouncing on his toes. His father took off his gloves, turned off the machine, and came over to his son. Earl took the moment to have another ladle of water.

"Let me see that," Jim said. He took the shiny piece and looked it over, brushing more dirt caked to it. "Well, that's quite a find, son."

"What is it, Poppa? Is it treasure?"

"Yes, it is. See, the Indians who lived here a long time ago mined these mountains for gold and silver. And for something even more valuable." He glanced at Earl. "Turquoise. Now, gold and silver they traded with each other. But turquoise had such value that if an Indian found it, he kept it for himself. Whoever found this made a hatchet out of it."

"A hatchet?" The little boy's eyes bugged out.

"That's right. Now, you go home and show your mother. She'll help you clean it up and tonight we'll polish it up nicely." He handed the souvenir back to the boy who took it and ran off.

When Jim returned to the ore grinder and turned the machine back on.

"You know that's why they call this place Hachita. They find those hatchet heads all over the place," Earl said.

"Course I know it, Earl. But the boy needs to feel like he's doin something. If I can't find enough gold to get us to El Paso, what kind of life has he got to look forward to?"

The young boy ran up the main street of town, about thirty buildings, past two men on horseback, leading a small group of steer through town.

Walter Williams, aka Bronco Billy, had a scowl on his face and his right hand rested on the six-gun on his hip. "Burt, all I wants to do is get these cattle back to Wagon Mound."

Burt Mossman, the former Arizona Ranger in charge of the Double-A Cattle operations in New Mexico, nodded his head. "After they found those Mormons dead up at Corner Ranch nobody's sleeping well around here."

Williams spat. "I heard they found 'em missin' arms and legs, mutilated all to hell."

"Strange days," Burt said, and the men went silent. They passed the saloon without a glance.

Lieutenant Colonel J.C. Waterman, standing on the porch across the street from the saloon, where his small detachment in town bunked, saw the uneasy look in the two men as they rode by. Can't blame 'em. *Town's got a dead feeling to it.*

A young Lieutenant Davis came out and watched the herd and the two wranglers bringing up the rear.

Davis chewed on a toothpick as he spoke. "One of the Apache scouts, Fred Barefoot, says there's strange activity on the other side of the border. He's never seen so many deer and bear."

"What the hell does that even mean, Lieutenant?" Waterman glared at Davis with consternation.

267

The next moment, the saloon across the street exploded.

Waterman and Davis awoke on the ground a moment later, thrown against the wall of their barracks. They couldn't see across the street, for the smoke and debris that filled the air. But they didn't need to. Three Thing machines came marching down the middle of the street, spraying gunfire into buildings. One of the mechanized horrors pitched flames from its mechanical arm and set the small feed and grain store next to the saloon on fire.

As Waterman struggled to get to his feet, a terror emerged from the smoke. A yellowish figure wearing ancient Aztec garments wielded an ax over his head. The commander of Camp Shannon stood dumbstruck at the impossible sight swung the ax and struck Davis in the chest. The young man barely had time to let out a cry of anguish before he died.

Waterman raised his gun and put six bullets into the rotter in front of him. He put two into the things head before it could pull the ax from the poor soldier's chest.

As he stood there, three more Aztecs strode down the town's sole street, and a moment later the Livery Stable a hundred feet away exploded. Twenty feet overhead, a fishing boat sailed by.

*God help us*, thought Waterman.

Bronco Billy and Burt Mossman followed the stampede of cattle past the barracks. They were riding like mad and firing their pistols into the air wildly. At what, Waterman couldn't see, as another explosion drove him back through the door of his barracks.

Tom and his mother were hiding under a Honey Locust and flinched at the explosion nearby. A fog of dirt and dust drifted across the hillside where they were hiding and muffled the screams and cries from the town. When they could no longer see anything flying in the sky, Tom's mother took his hand and they ran for their shelter.

"What are they momma, what's goin on?" The young boy kept stopping and glancing up to see.

"Keep going, Tommy!" His mother urged, pulling him along.

Jim Booker had heard the first explosions and immediately ran for his family.

He had run up behind Main Street on the small hill that led to their cabin. The homestead came into view a hundred yards away. Jim searched for his wife and child as he ran, finally seeing them coming up the hill behind the burning Feed and Grain. His wife had Tom by the hand as they ran into their shack.

A moment later the home exploded, but Mr. Booker couldn't hear anything but his own screaming.

# INTERLUDE 97
April 4, 1917, 6:23 am
Mochogueachi Valley

E rnie awoke to find his buckskin coat returned along with a
pair of high moccasin boots. In front of his tent, someone
had prepared a breakfast of fruit and cornmeal. He sat alone,
watching the camp, eating, as the men of the camp began to
move.

One of the Apache scouts motioned. "Haadi'a tsét'soyé."

Ernie made sure he had his canteen and penknife and followed them through the soft light of the grey cloudy sky.

The group went to the far end of camp where the horses were
tied. Chief Bronco sat on his horse, the Harpy eagle on his shoulder, the Tarahumara riding beside him. Two young Apache warriors had the reins of a gray pony between them. They looked
identical and smiled at him.

*This is what an invitation looks like.*

"Haadi'a tsét'soyé," the two young men said in unison.

Ernie jumped up and straddled the horse, grabbing the coarse
rope to hold fast. The young Apache to his left held out a red
scarf and indicated he should put it on. He tucked his cap in his
shirt and tied the bandana around his head as the others wore
theirs.

Chief Bronco moved forward, followed by the rest of the
dozen warriors on horseback. The young Apache to his right held

on to a tether on Ernie's horse and pulled him along. The horse took up the trot without instruction and maintained the pace.

Ernie just had to hold on. The young Indian on his left nudged his shoulder and he turned to find the Apache smiling at him.

"Haadi'a tsét'soyé," said the young warrior, holding out a small calfskin bag.

Ernie looked in, sniffed. *Ground cornmeal. What am I supposed to do with this? I've seen the hunting parties take bags of this along on long trips. I've seen women take bags of this with them when they go and gather fruits and nuts among the trees.*

He looked at the Apache who had handed him the bag. The warrior saw the confused look on his face and made a motion of putting food into his mouth. *Must be food for the ride.*

The group moved along for more than an hour before they came to a cave sealed up with mud and rocks. Ernie and all the Indians, except Chief Bronco, got off their horses and proceeded to tear out the concealment. It took very little time before the contents were revealed. Arrows with finely tipped points, one type made of mountain willow, the other of cane. And there were bows made of mountain willow some of the men worked on when sitting around camp.

After packing the weapons they rode through the valley for the rest of the morning, through seemingly endless fields of hemp, then winding through dense forest, guiding the horses over rocks and ruts.

Ernie kept watching the two young Apache riding next to him for some clue. *Where are we going? This feels like a war party.* But any gestures were returned with signals he didn't understand. The group continued along a dirt road carved into the side of the canyon for another couple of miles. The winding trail took them down to a stream and a series of deep turquoise-colored pools, into the very deepest parts of Copper Canyon. The Indians all dismounted and dipped their feet in steaming waters.

*Hot springs. This place might not be so bad after all.* He pulled off his moccasins and sank his tired feet into the warm water. *Things might just turn out.*

271

# INTERLUDE 98
April 4, 1917, 9:17 am
Hachita, New Mexico

Waterman peered out from the second floor of the barracks, watching two of the machine monstrosities pace up and down the center of town, in opposite directions. The saloon and the grain and feed had stopped burning but still smouldered. The bodies of men and women lay strewn on the streets.

A second-story window of a boarding house three buildings away opened and a rifle stuck out.

"No, you idiots," he said to himself.

The rifle fired, and the shot struck one of the machine monstrosities in the neck. It roared, turning its mechanical arm on the building. The automatic fire shattered the windows and tore the front visage of the second floor apart. In a minute, the outer wall crumbled and there were three more bodies to count.

Lieutenant Brown appeared in the doorway and crawled towards his superior officer.

"For some reason, they haven't cut the lines. It took us all night but we managed to break through walls to the telegraph station about fifteen minutes ago without being seen, sir."

"Good job, Lieutenant."

"Camp Columbus is sending reinforcements, sir."

Screams outside drew Waterman back to the window. Two dozen ghastly men in Aztec garments were going into homes and businesses, smashing windows and breaking apart doors with their jade axes. Waterman grew angry and aghast, then puzzled, as the nightmares emerged, dragging dead bodies. They were dragging them into the street and out of town.

From the hotel diagonal to the barracks, Waterman saw very distressed and frightened people staring out from the windows as two rotters dragged a dead man and woman away. The Aztec rotters grabbed those who had died in the street, threw them over their shoulders, and lumbered off slowly.

*What are they going to do with those people? Are they cannibals? Lord, help us.*

Waterman heard footsteps below and opened the door to peer down. An Aztec with yellowish skin and pale milky eyes dragged poor Davis from the porch and glanced up at him. Without a hint of interest, the hideous thing just went about its business.

Waterman spotted men moving around on the roof of the Dry Goods store near the end of town. One of the flying boats sailed overhead, throwing its shadow down on Main Street, heading toward the Dry Goods store. As it neared, the men on the roof opened fire.

The air around the boat shimmered and it looked as if the bullets ricocheted away before they ever reached their target.

Waterman watched projectiles spewing from the flying boat and ripping the roof and the men to shreds. *No! Please God, no more dying!*

# INTERLUDE 99
April 4, 1917, 10:24 am
Cerro Mohinora

At one point the brilliant blue sky broke through a patch of forest as the party mounted an overlook of a ridge that gave a view of the canyon for miles. They were looking at a valley bound on either side by towering rock bluffs, with pine trees sprinkled across their ridges and outcroppings.

Chief Bronco dropped back and rode next to Ernie for a moment, and nodded to the two young Apache leading his horse.

"Singing Bear, this Owl," the Chief said, pointing to the warrior on the left. "Hawk," he said, pointing to the right. The Chief clapped Singing Bear on the back. "Haadi'a tsét'soyé!"

Everybody nodded and smiled and the huge warrior Chief moved back to the front of the party. He had thought of asking the Chief what had happened to the eagle but decided against it.

*Owl has a scar across his cheek, otherwise, they look like twins.*

The look of the valley had begun to change. Outcroppings of dark igneous rock and many different trees like hackberry, maple, and walnut dotted the canyon walls.

"Haadi'a tsét'soyé," Owl tapped Ernie on the shoulder and pointed up the side of the cliff.

Ernie turned to see a large bobcat perched on a ledge.

"Ndołkah," said Owl.

274

The large cat watched them with intense interest. Then came a loud screech and the bobcat scattered as the Harpy eagle swooped down at it. The cat snarled in irritation once and disappeared.

As the morning grew to midday, the blazing light withdrew and the party reached its first impasse. Huge gleaming white boulders that had washed in from the last flood or fell from the canyon were stacked high upon one another, the whole width of the valley, blocking the way. At this point, all the Indians dismounted and began a steep climb to the summit of the largest boulder.

"This place *Tse tigai dah sidil*," Chief Bronco said.

"What does that mean?" Ernie asked.

"White rocks above," the Tarahumara responded matter-of-factly.

Ernie stared up at the stacked white boulders as he started to climb. "Makes sense."

Once on top, Hawk opened a large leather bag he had hauled up. The young Apache produced a pair of bolas that each held several equal sized stones bound dozens of times in thick hemp rope.

Chief Bronco pointed to a cliff on the opposite side of the canyon dozens of yards away and simply said, "There." The ridge behind them stood a good fifty feet higher than the face before them.

*I don't see how we get there.*

Owl produced his own bag of coils of thick rope. The young Indian tied one line to the first bola, and Hawk whipped the bag around his head half a dozen times and sent it up the side of the canyon behind the party. It whipped around a maple jutting from the edge of the cliff. In another moment, Owl scampered up the braiding hand over hand.

Once Owl got to the tree, he tied the line several times. Hawk tied the other end of the line to his second bola, whipped it around his head a dozen times and sent it whipping across the canyon. It landed on the top of the cliff in front of them. After a couple of tugs, the bag wedged itself in a crevice.

Owl pulled up the slack across the canyon until the line held tight, and proceeded across the canyon to the far side, hand over hand, a second line tied around his waist.

Hawk followed Owl's path up the rock face.

Ernie watched Owl cross the canyon, pull out the bola and tie both lines of hemp around a huge boulder. As he lashed it down, Hawk whistled. Two Indians that had wanted to kill him earlier walked towards him smiling. Gently, they led him over to the cliff and tied the rope around his waist. "I don't think I can climb like that."

The Indians just kept nodding and saying his name. "Haadi'a tsét'soyé."

Hawk free repelled from the maple tree and all of a sudden Ernie lifted up. He sailed twenty feet in the air, legs dangling before he had a chance to get some purchase on the cliffside.

"Whoa!" Ernie said as he grabbed some branches and steadied himself. In a short time, he had scrambled up the side, onto the tree and now stood staring down at the rest of the party. He threw down his line and Hawk climbed back up the rope. Next, he went over to the double line crossing the canyon. Hawk produced a six-foot length of corn silk rope, tied it around Ernie's waist, then looped the bowline around the top hemp line across the canyon.

Hawk whistled again and both Indians started pulling on separate lines. Legs flailing, Ernie dangled over the canyon, hanging on for dear life, as the two Indians quickly pulled him across. When he reached the far side, he didn't get up right away. He laid on his stomach for several minutes, his face pressed to the igneous rock, eyes closed. *I might just lay here awhile.*

Ernie didn't start to move until the second Indian behind him had crossed the valley. He stood, brushed himself off, and smiled at the grinning Apache. He observed as another Apache made the crossing. Soon five warriors were across, then ten, then Chief Bronco crossed last. Once across, the party proceeded on foot. There were potholes and crevices everywhere. He nearly stumbled into one but Owl grabbed his arm.

"Thank you," Ernie said.

The young man just grinned. "Haadi'a tsét'soyé."

The cliffs and the ground got darker as Chief Bronco's footsteps slowed.

*Lava rock.*

Finally, they reached the end of the mesa which stretched for miles in all directions. And as Ernie stepped to the edge, expecting to see a river rippling its way through the gorge, he saw a sight that staggered him. Two massive Galleons hovered in the air in the center of the canyon, connected with ropes, walkways, and arches. The small flying boats he had seen from Black Mountain buzzed around beneath it and Thing machines patrolled the main deck.

# INTERLUDE 100
April 4, 1917, 1:07 pm
Cavalry Camp Columbus

T he ex-president half-limped and half-marched into the command tent while General Pershing spoke with several of his
senior advisors. General Pershing stood with his back to the
door as the other men sat, reading the documents.

"It comes from our friends in Paris," General Pershing
explained as he paced. "We are to build forty-five hundred airplanes, training personnel and provide material for the French
front in 1918. We will need five thousand pilots and fifty thousand mechanics."

Colonel Owen P. Ransom threw his hat to the ground. "It can't
be done!"

"That's two thousand airplanes and four thousand engines
every month," Pershing said flatly.

The four men sitting around the table said nothing, staring at
the table and the papers.

"The deeper we get into this, the more overwhelming the
work ahead of us appears. We are being called upon to make
up in a few months for the neglect of years." General Pershing
shook his head sadly.

"General, may I have a moment of your time." T.R. finally
spoke.

"What is it, Colonel Roosevelt?" Pershing turned with surprise

"I would like to take the remnants of my Volunteer regiments back into the Sierra Madres."

Pershing sighed, then grabbed a folder and waved it at the ex-president "Do you understand what's going on here, Colonel? The War Department is constructing sixteen new training camps in the coming weeks, one for each new division we are building."

He watched the four men, then back at his former commander-in-chief. "Even if I gave every soldier in Camp Columbus a non-commission promotion for war-time experience, I wouldn't have enough NCO's to staff the camps."

"Let me be blunt General. I'm not asking for permission. Washington has not seen fit to utilize the Volunteer Regiments. I offered to die on the field of battle and if I didn't I would never return and still that lily-livered skunk in the Oval Office refused me! At least allow me the courtesy of getting out of your way. I will take my men into the New Mexico desert and you will never have to hear of us again. Just provision us and we are a memory."

Pershing stood silent for several moments then looked directly at the ex-president somberly. "As of seven o'clock this morning, every Volunteer of drafting age is officially enlisted in the Regular Army. You have about two dozen men left who, according to the War Department, are too old to be any good in battle." Pershing turned back to the table. "You may take them and what provisions you need."

At that moment, Sister Stella threw back the tent flap and marched into the tent.

"Colonel Roosevelt! I will not have you running about in your condition."

T.R. turned to her with a smile, patient. "Madam, now look…"

"Don't you madam me," she nearly shouted.

"Excuse me, nurse. I think everything is—" Pershing began, but the Nurse cut him off.

"Now see here," Sister Stella eyed all of the officers in the room, including those at the table. "The President of the United States needs to rehabilitate that leg of his. Nobody runs the hospital but me. No Generals," she glanced at Pershing "and certainly no stubborn patients." She put a large hand on each shoulder and guided the ex-president out of the tent.

"But...but...." the former commander-in-chief stammered helplessly. He looked for help but they were all looking at the floor.

"There, there," Sister Stella said softly. "You're going to be just fine."

Turning back to the table, Pershing said over his shoulder, "May God be with you, Mister President."

# INTERLUDE 101
April 4, 1917, 2:31 pm
Cerro Mohinora

Ernie lay near the edge of the precipice, raising his head occasionally catching a glimpse of the impossible craft.

*Fore and aft castles. Two enormous galleons. Each one's got to be a hundred and fifty feet long. Just hovering there. It's impossible, but there you are.*

He dropped his head, resting his cheek on the cold stone and waited for the courage to look again. He saw the Indians moving and slid back from the edge.

Carefully, silently, as if a cough or a kicked rock could bring a storm of undead—or worse—they clambered down into a narrow crevice at the center of the lava plateau.

But the crevice opened up once through the first narrows, expanded some more before ending at a hole large enough for a man to crawl into. Owl came out on his hands and knees holding a lit torch, a huge smile on his face. The young Apache gestured, beckoning the others inside, then vanished back into the hole. Hawk followed without hesitation, and three other warriors also went in without glancing back.

Ernie studied Chief Bronco. The huge man with the yellow beard looked back, then at the entrance, then back at him and pointed into the hole. "Haadi'a tsét'soyé."

281

Ernie shrugged and followed. *I can feel a draft. I think that's a good sign. Got to be coming from somewhere on the other end.*

After a short crawl through the narrow tunnel, the passage opened to a series of large boulders blocking the path. With some grunts, effort, and some pushing and pulling, the party made it over a series of obstacles and continued on.

The tunnel grew less like normal rock formations and more subterranean. The walls became covered with sharp white bumps. At one point in a narrow spot, Ernie brushed against the protrusions and his shoulder started to bleed. The ten men bunched up, stopped around a large pit, about six feet in diameter. A pile of wooden support beams sat in a pile along the wall. Hawk lit a second torch from Owl's and tossed it in. It landed about ten feet down.

*Not a bottomless pit.* Ernie laughed at himself, earning some strange glances.

One of the Apache produced some hemp rope and Hawk descended. At the bottom, he dropped to his hands and knees, looked up at the others and gestured for them to follow before disappearing. Owl nearly leapt into the hole to follow and shimmied down the rope.

Ernie went next, reached the bottom, and shuffled forward on his hands and knees. "Damn!" he muttered softly. *The floor is covered in soft dirt but it masks the bed of flakes and shards everywhere.*

As he continued on all fours, everything that touched the surface bled.

Mercifully, the crawling ended in about a hundred yards and they moved forward with enough room to stand. When a winding route ended in a dead-end, they would backtrack, take another path, then try again. One path led to a pool of water and the Apache stopped.

*The caves back in Illinois often had routes through water that led to other tunnels.*

The group backtracked from the water and were rewarded with a passage so low they had to scoot along on their bellies.

That torture didn't last more than a few minutes before it opened up where everyone could stand again. That's when Ernie noticed the passage becoming brighter. A green glow masked everything as they moved on. Soon Owl and Hawk had extinguished their torches with enough ambient green to show the way.

Then the humming began and grew louder as they moved forward. Finally, they came to an arched opening. The passage opened up ten feet in every direction and had a flat floor easy to walk on. At the far wall there appeared to be an indentation, maybe three feet deep, with a hole at the far end.

Ernie sat down, exhausted. *I smell dust, sweat, and guano. What I wouldn't give for some fresh air. Is today Sunday? I never go to church on Sunday. Too busy. If I get out of this I might start.*

As they all looked around, the room appeared to be just another dead end. That is until Owl scooted over towards the hole. He turned, wide-eyed, and made a clicking noise, like a cricket or a cave mouse.

The group moved over towards Owl, realizing what he had found. The floor took an upward slant that had remained hidden in the light. They could all see it now. The floor angled up then dropped away, creating an opening about two feet wide. Owl scooted into the crevice, came out the other side and peeked in through the hole, making that clicking again. One by one, they all scooted under the overhang to the other side.

They were standing on about twelve inches rock ledge running along the wall, a hundred feet in the air. And below them, a massive machine hummed and roiled on the cavern floor beneath their feet. The huge machine gave off the eerie green glow and emitted a powerful, deep sound.

*I can feel the vibration in my bones.*

Figures in thick suits worked around the machine, and men in black uniforms with guns moved around the edges. Hawk kept shuffling to his left, trying to get a look at something, when a bit of the ledge gave away. Owl reached out to keep him from falling, but the debris clattered down the wall, broke into little pieces and scattered across the floor.

Ernie froze as a half dozen heads turned to the sound. The heads turned to the floor, then slowly moved up the side of the wall until all eyes were pinned on them. Gunfire erupted and they ran.

# INTERLUDE 102
April 4, 1917, 4:07 pm
Cerro Mohinora

E rnie hit the ground at full speed and slid several feet on his stomach beneath the low hanging passage and crab-walked as quickly as he could. Behind him, he could hear more gunfire. Owl and Hawk were behind him, pushing him on. He emerged from the low tunnel with his jacket in tatters, ripped and torn apart and his arms a bloody mess. But he didn't stop to examine the wounds.

One of the Apache had picked up the torch and, now that they were beyond the area where the green ambient glow lit their way, used a flint to light one again. The hemp cloth began burning immediately and the Indian motioned Ernie to take it. He did so, waiting for the others to catch up.

Within a minute, Owl and Hawk appeared. One of them grabbed the torch and led the way. The other three warriors brought up the rear. After a few minutes of twists and turns the men slowed down a little. Owl and Hawk exchanged glances and snickered at each other.

*Did we escape?* Ernie asked himself.

With a clamor of dust and rock, the ceiling of the tunnel behind them collapsed as a Thing machine crashed through the hole. The mutant creature machine lay there a moment, then turned its body to look up from the ground. The Indians all ran as it slowly started to rise.

Ernie took one look back and saw that, as the first monstrosity moved forward, another one leaped down into the hole behind it. He stopped turning to look back.

They wound through tunnels, tracing their steps back without running into a dead end.

Another burst of gunfire and the Thing machines were behind them again. They kept running. Owl slipped, fell against the wall of jagged cuts and went to his knees. Hawk stopped and helped him up.

They were on all fours again, and that meant the pit opening loomed ahead. Ernie dragged his hands and knees along the jagged ground, emerged into the hole and climbed as fast as he could. As he made it out of the pit he saw the three Indians over at the pile of timber supports.

Owl and Hawk exploded out of the hole simultaneously, screaming their heads off. No sooner were they out than a huge mutated arm with metal plates and tubing emerged from the darkness.

As the Thing machine rose up, its eyes shifted to Ernie and its gun arm swung in his direction. He closed his eyes and waited for the gunfire. *Sorry, mother.*

But it never came. Two of the Apache had picked up one of the huge support timbers and they drove it through the Thing machine's back and out its chest. The half-man half-machine creature let out a short plaintive howl. The massive wooden joist spanned several feet on either side of the hole, leaving it suspended over darkness.

Ernie looked down at his feet and saw a familiar green crystal embedded in a silver casing, with some metal framing around it. *The heart of the beast.* He picked it up and they all kept running. They scrambled over the large boulders, then were on their hands on knees again. They studied one another. Quiet but for their shallow, desperate breathing. *So close now.*

Then, finally, sunlight. Owl had gotten in front and made the final curve. Ernie could see light but Owl had scrambled out of sight. He rounded the bend, and the light blinded him as he tumbled through the hole. He could make out only legs and feet. Everything else became a blur as he rolled to his side.

Hawk made the final turn, squinting from the light, crawling the last ten feet of the tunnel. A Thing machine appeared behind him, moving unbelievably fast. The monstrosity's arm grabbed Hawk by the leg and jerked him back so ferociously that he slammed against the wall of the tunnel and left a smear of blood as he sagged. The Thing moved back around the first turn, still holding Hawk by the leg, and dragged him away.

Owl screamed and tried to go back in after his brother. But Chief Bronco held him back. The young man kicked and roared in fury but Chief Broncos huge arms held him. One of the other Apache punched Owl and knocked him out. Bronco threw the young warrior over his shoulder and they quickly made their way out of the crevice and ran across the lava rock mesa.

At one point, they should have made a different turn and veered off to the left to get back to their ponies. But Chief Bronco, still carrying Owl, headed to the right. They headed down some cliff trails that were definitely steeper than they had come up. Ernie slipped a couple of times on the moss-covered rocks. They also jumped down from some outcropping to another ledge eight or sometimes ten feet down. Bronco made the jump with Owl on his shoulder, and no one slowed.

Finally, the huge man slowed. He turned and pointed ahead. The waters of one of the rivers of Copper Canyon rushed by.

At the edge, expecting to find another drop to another outcropping, Ernie found a straight drop into the gorge. "You want us to jump?"

Chief Bronco nodded. The other Apache shuffled anxiously.

"That's got to be a hundred feet!"

Chief Bronco's massive arms picking him up and throwing him over the edge became the last thing Ernie saw before he hit the water.

# INTERLUDE 103
April 5, 1917, 6:44 am
Hachita, New Mexico

L ieutenant Colonel Waterman awoke with his head on the windowsill, sucked in a lungful of air and aimed his rifle around the empty room. Blinking, he looked out the open window onto the quiet street below, pulling back as a sleek bi-plane roared overhead.

The hotel next to the smoldering, collapsed saloon directly across the street came alive with gunfire. Two mechanical monstrosities screamed with fury and let loose with automatic gunfire into the air at the first plane. Two sparkling arcs came from behind Lieutenant Colonel Waterman's view and slammed into the hotel rooftop. The center of the building collapsed and the two nightmarish visages disappeared as a second Curtis R2 sailed past.

*Thank God for the American military!* Waterman said to himself.

The street came alive with Aztec rotters clambering from every doorway and alley, their jade axes raised. They were not disappointed. The sound of thirty-seven-millimeter gunfire erupted and two armored vehicles, each with a dead rotter tied to its hood, came racing down Main Street.

The vehicles barrelled into the walking corpses at top speed. Rotters were pushed aside or fell under the thick desert wheels of the assault cars. As Waterman watched, one freak with an animal headdress swung a jade ax through an open window and the vehicle snapped the rotter's arm clean off as it went by.

Over the hill behind the burning saloon, the Lieutenant Colonel watched a half dozen of the hulking metal men lumber towards town. He saw some townsfolk fleeing into nearby hills. The striding monstrosities saw them run but didn't shoot.

Then, down the street, coming from the same direction as the armored vehicles Waterman saw the first movement of actual American soldiers.

*Oh shit.*

The men were progressing slowly, moving from building to building, clearing each one as they went. When the rotters would get close enough on the street, the soldiers didn't fire wildly. These men took careful aim and put a bullet into the head of each horror. There were more than a dozen Thing machines visible now.

*They are walking into a trap!*

"Lieutenant Brown," Waterman rasped into the hallway. Immediately the young soldier appeared.

"Yes, sir?"

"Do we have any heavy armaments?"

The Lieutenant shook his head.

Lieutenant Colonel Waterman turned back to the street. The American soldiers were a hundred yards from the remnants of the saloon. He could hear the hiss-thump of the monstrous footsteps of the Thing machines.

*How can they not hear that noise?*

At that moment, the soldiers on the street froze. The lead monstrosity stepped into the rubble of the saloon from the rear when gunfire erupted over the hill.

Two Harleys with armored sidecars burst over the hill, the heavy cannon placements spewing hot lead. The first burst shattered two Thing machines from behind.

Waterman shouted and pounded on the sill. "Get em, boys!"

Four arm cannons fired simultaneously. The bullets slammed into the armor plating of the lead sidecar, then tore apart the cycle and the driver. The loose sidecar veered wildly and slammed into a tree.

The lead Thing machine pushed through the cinders of the saloon and emerged onto the street, firing its arm cannon. Soldiers ducked into alleys and doorways and fired back.

As the Thing machine poured bullets into structures and ripped bodies apart, two soldiers had gotten behind the monstrosity. They were holding grenades. The two infantrymen moved close, pulled the pins, and shoved them into the Thing machine's body.

The moment it happened the Thing machine turned and cut the men down. The bullets tore into their backs and they fell dead in the street. The next instant, the grenades went off.

First, the shrapnel devices went off, creating a tremendous bang. Less than thirty yards away and one floor up, Lieutenant Colonel Waterman covered his ears but didn't look away. He would have never believed what happened next.

A bright green flare erupted from the spot where the Thing machine had stood, and a vortex swirled in the spot. Tremendous heat flared out and Waterman watched paint peel off the hotel next door. Then an area about twenty feet in diameter and ten feet deep vanished beyond the event horizon of the vortex before another shuddering explosion rocked the street. Remnants of the burned-out saloon, the front corner of the hotel, the dead Americans, and ten feet of the soil of the very street itself just vanished.

Three more armored Harleys opened fire into the other Thing machines. Four monstrosities had their chests ripped open or their heads were blown off and fell before the others moved away from the town. In the street, the soldiers were moving house to house again, taking out the rotter horde. The armored cars were rolling slowly from the other end, catching stragglers. Soon there were no rotters left.

A humming noise overcame everything as two flying boats came in and settled on the hill. A Curtis R2 made a pass and fired a couple of its Vickers Rocket guns. They slammed into the earth next to one of the ships and the air became full of projectiles. The four-pounders slammed into the R2 and it broke apart in the sky.

Waterman and Brown watched the monstrosities as they boarded the hovering vessels under fire from the armored motorcycles. The craft slowly lifted off and disappeared over the hill.

From the town, the company of soldiers holding the town gave a hurrah of triumph.

Lieutenant Colonel J.C. Waterman looked out at the burned-out buildings, the dead bodies of the small town of Hachita, the aftermath of what he had seen, and did not cheer.

# INTERLUDE 104
April 6, 1917, 7:01 am
Cavalry Camp Columbus


The ex-president stood in the center of the tent and looked at what remained of his Volunteer Regiment. He had a small bandage around his leg, but he no longer limped. Sixteen officers were either former Rough Riders with the ex-president in the Spanish American war or former military officers who had signed up to help him form the Volunteers. They were all over thirty. The retinue included Captains Bullock and Groome, Frederick Burnham, John Parker, Henry Stimson, John Greenway, Raymond Robbins, R.H. Channing, David Goodrich, Richard Derby, William Donovan, Sloan Simpson, D.C. Collier, W.E. Darne, James Garfield—the son of ex-President Garfield, and cousin George Roosevelt. These were all the men that remained.

"Men, as good Americans we all loyally obey the orders and wishes of our Commander-in-Chief. You men who have volunteered can now consider yourselves to be absolved of such obligations. Our sole aim has been to help in every way the successful prosecution of the war. We rejoice that a division comprised of our fine soldiers under the command of General Pershing are going abroad."

The Volunteers shifted uncomfortably.

T.R. continued. "The compromise is that France gets soldiers, but Teddy will not be leading them. If this does not serve as an explanation for the matter, I gladly say we are all unselfishly pleased to have served this purpose." He cleared his throat. "Naturally, we regret not getting the opportunity to have been allowed ourselves to render active service."

Bullock stepped forward. "Dammit, Colonel Roosevelt. You deserve better."

The ex-president held up a hand. "The President believes our proffered service would be of use—politically, but would not contribute to the success of the war. More specifically, the opinion in Washington is that I will not contribute to the success of the war. So this old Moose will hunt no more."

"What are you going to do? We'll follow you," came a voice from the back.

"I will watch the anticipated success of the war effort. Nothing in this world is worth having without effort, pain or difficulty. If I have to watch from afar, it will be painful and it will be difficult, but I shall endure."

Sergeant McBryar, now dressed in the U.S. Infantry uniform, stepped into the tent. "Colonel Roosevelt, there's someone here to see you."

"Not now, son. I'm addressing my men."

"Sir, General Pershing requested I accompany them directly to you. They're...." The Sergeant looked confused. "They're Indians, sir. They're right outside."

The ex-president turned, strode to the tent entrance, and pulled the main fold back. There stood two tall Tarahumara Indians, in running sandals and cotton tunics.

"You speak English?" T.R. asked.

The two men nodded. They looked haggard.

"Where are you from?" asked the ex-president.

"Chihuahua," said one of the men. The Indian sat down on a chair and quickly toppled over, dazed. Two Volunteers picked him up and moved him to a bed.

T.R. looked noticeably shocked. "How did you get here?"

"Run," said the other man.

Several of the Volunteers scoffed. "That's over five hundred miles," exclaimed Captain Groome.

"Yes," T.R. said, without taking his eyes off the tall Indian. He motioned to the Volunteers. "Water."

Immediately, several canteens of water were pushed towards the Indian standing, while two men provided water to his companion. The Indians drank heavily for several minutes.

At last, T.R. asked, "What do you have to tell me?"

The standing Tarahumara ran the back of his hand across his parched lips. "Singing Bear."

# INTERLUDE 105
April 7, 1917, 10:23 am
Cerro Mohinora

Victor Frankenstein stood at the railing, looking down into the cylindrical rings that glowed and hummed with power. On the console in front of him sat a series of black dials. As he turned the first dial, the machine started to turn. The steam engine began to churn and the temperature in the room dropped as the air condensers compensated for the rise in heat.

Frankenstein turned the second dial. The steam engine vibrated, the glowing rings cycled and the magnetic flywheels encircling the machine started to turn. Victor nodded at the group of scientists working at a wall panel near the sealed door. They were all manning different gauges for the air compressors. The men in suits all moved switches that required two hands simultaneously and liquid nitrogen pumped into the cylindrical hole that ran deep into the earth's crust.

Victor turned the third dial and the roiling giant steam engine glowed. The air compressors were pumping out so much freezing air that Victor's breath crystallized in front of his face, but the metal floor plates around the Vim machine were starting to buckle from the heat. The familiar green glow emanated from the hole in the earth. Frankenstein held his hand over the fourth and final switch but stopped, then pulled his hand back.

The machine kept working, the rings kept rotating, the steam engine kept pumping, and the magnets were at full capacity. Then a mighty crack came from deep inside the hole in the earth and a low rumbling shook the cavern. Frankenstein steadied himself and hit the power button on the machine to turn it off. He stood there for a minute, breathing heavy with exhilaration.

Dr. Exner, wearing a thick protective suit, ran over and removed his shielded helmet.

"My Prince! The seismographs indicate a massive earthquake has struck Guatemala!"

A sneering grin crossed Frankenstein's face. "How strong?"

The scientist said slowly, "Five point six. That's enough to crack homes and streets. We may have destroyed some cities."

"It's not enough."

Dr. Exner stiffened. "Sire, it's only the first step. Your magnificence and brilliance will see this project through!"

"I want nine points. Ten. I want tsunamis. I want thousands of square miles underwater."

"And it shall happen, my Prince. The addition of liquid nitrogen made all the difference! It kept the coils stable under immense pressure."

Frankenstein stared down into the abyss for several long moments. "What do we know about the intruders? How many did we hunt down?"

The scientist relaxed. "Sire, they were aborigines. We killed one and brought it back. They are stone-age people. There are so many tunnels in these mountains, its impossible to block them all."

"Increase patrols in all the tunnels. Have the crusaders blocking every cavern, hole, and external route. We don't want any surprises."

"Yes, my Prince," Dr. Exner said stoically, nodding. The scientist bowed slightly and ran off, happy to be away.

# INTERLUDE 106
April 7, 1917, 12:11 pm
Creel, Chihuahua, Mexico

The sun beat down hard on the men in two vehicles. The ex-president drove the Packard while Captain Bullock drove a Liberty truck behind him. One Tarahumara Indian sat in the passenger seat and four of the remaining Volunteers were seated in the back, each holding their weapons, with a knapsack and mess kit tied in a bundle on their laps.

A small building on the outskirts of a tiny village marked the name of the town, CREEL.

T.R. stopped the vehicle behind the building, got out and stretched. "End of the line, gentlemen. From here we proceed on foot."

Fred Burnham stood up with a groan and John Parker awoke with a snort and a start.

James Garfield climbed down from the back of the Liberty, carrying his supplies and SMLE, and studied the shack and the rail tracks. "We could have taken a train up here?"

The ex-president shook his head. "The train to Creel only runs once a month. The provisional government set up this settlement and transplanted a Mexican population into the area with the Raramuri in order to try to bring the native Indians into the fold." He frowned. "Intermarriage."

All the USVC veterans were out of the vehicles now.

The Tarahumara turned to T.R. "No more roads." He pointed into the high mountains, beyond where the dirt road ended.

"Smell the dew-soaked creosote, men?" the ex-president said, sniffing deeply and a huge flock of quail took flight. He looked at his men, nodded, lifted his own sack and mess kit and moved ahead with long strides.

The simple town consisted of adobe shacks, a central plaza and a towering church in the center. Porches were lined with wooden plates and bowls, woven baskets and clay pots. The party moved up through the town with towering cliffs beyond beckoning them. Despite the town appearing as if it held a couple of hundred people and stayed well-kept, it sat silent and empty.

"Where is everyone?" asked Captain Groome, pausing to peer through a window.

"Tesguino," said the Tarahumara.

"What is that?" asked Captain Bullock.

"Corn beer festival." replied the Indian.

"Now that I could certainly be interested in!" said John Greenway. A tall muscular man who had earned a Silver Star with the T.R. at the Battle of San Juan Hill.

"Explain to me again why we don't have animals for hauling our supplies?" Garfield asked, irritably as he steadied himself with his pack on his back.

The ex-president stopped and glanced at the middle-aged stockbroker turned soldier. "Because where we are climbing, the animals will do us no good. We'd have to leave them behind at any rate."

Captain Bullock slapped Garfield on the back. "Maybe you can get Bill Donovan to help you. He can row three men to victory by himself and he's got shoulders like an ox."

Donovan, a huge athletic aristocrat, playfully sneered at Bullock. "Screw you, Deadwood."

"The mountains cut against the sky like tombstones," said George Roosevelt, staring up.

From high in the cliffs came a strange, low animal sound. *Rrrrrrhhh, rrrhhh, rrrhh.*

"The jaguar!" TR exclaimed, taking off his hat and straining to look up the cliffs.

They climbed all afternoon. Mesquite and Spanish bayonet covered the high chaparral, and the tilted masses of rocks seemed to overhang the men wherever they walked.

"You know, when I finished Law School a quarter of a century ago I came out to the Chihuahua. And I remember thinking how everything in the Sierra Madres looked so green. The popular conception of the Sierra Madres is of a dry, arid, brown land." said Henry Stimson.

They came to a spot where the path diverged and the Indian guide climbed rather than continue on the path.

Stimson stopped. "You know, that looks kind of steep. Maybe we should go this way." Stimson pointed toward the winding path with less of a grade.

Garfield started up the hillside and looked back with a grin. "Hey Stimson didn't you just lose the election for Governor of New York?"

Stimson sputtered without saying anything, then nodded, staring up the mountain.

"Then maybe you should just keep your mouth shut," Greenway finished.

After a hundred feet or so, T.R. stopped at an extended ledge and gave a review of their route. "In case anyone missed it, we passed a Tarahumara village about twenty minutes ago," he said, "It's good we were all too busy watching our asses and making sure no one fell that we didn't notice. Families don't like visitors and they won't be of any help." The ex-president dug into his pack and brought out a small empty bag. "But we are going to be passing some wild figs in a few minutes. I spotted them from the last switchback."

299

Several of the men peered ahead as if to make out the fig orchard. As they did so, T.R. looked across the canyon. There, on a boulder, watching the men, stood a spotted jaguar. *A beautiful two hundred pound specimen.*

R.H. Channing turned to see what had captured the Colonel's attention, spotted the animal and raised his rifle. T.R. put a hand on the barrel, gently nudging it down. He said nothing to Channing for a beat, then glanced at the other men. "Our Indian guide says there is a grove of Spanish oranges up ahead so we'll pause to grab some. They were planted by local Tarahumara families but they moved to another part of the valley."

The USVC soldiers filled every empty space in their packs with the large ripe oranges before climbing another series of outcroppings. At the next pause, the Tarahumara stopped to fill his flask.

James Garfield found a separate stream through the rocks and started to fill his military canteen, then stopped. "The water looks funny," he announced. All the men paused.

"It has a slightly whitish appearance, probably from minerals deep in the earth," T.R. said. "The Indians call it *Agua Blanca* and consider it the best water they have. It's a great honor to be offered to drink from the spring of *Agua Blanca*."

Every man filled up, especially Garfield, who drank several times before he stopped, sated. More climbing followed until at last they came to the Urique plateau, and the men stopped in awe.

"Helianthus…" T.R. whispered.

A forest of sunflower trees confronted them. Twelve to fifteen-foot high sunflowers covered the mesa ahead of them, with blooms as large around as a cowboy hat. On the outskirts of this no-man's land, the Tarahumara sat.

The soldiers glanced at each other in bewilderment, then the ex-president spoke. "I believe the Indian is giving us a hiatus gentlemen. He ran all the way to Camp Furlong and I do not expect he needs or desires a rest. But as long as he is accommodating. I feel we should oblige."

"I'm gonna have me some oranges," Seth Bullock announced as he sat down.

From somewhere up ahead, the cry of the jaguar filled the afternoon air. The men glanced at T.R. but the Colonel didn't even look up from his oranges.

# INTERLUDE 107
April 7, 1917, 4:16 pm
Cavalry Camp Columbus

General Pershing and Major Harbord entered the former commander-in-chief's tent and immediately stopped short. The General's mouth gaped and the young nurse in the tent nearly dropped her medicine kit at her surprise of the two men. Where the ex-president had lain for several days recovering from surgery to his wounded leg there now lay a tall, emaciated Indian in ragged clothes and sandals.

"Who are you?" General Pershing demanded to the Indian, stepping forward.

The nurse stammered, but General Pershing waved his hand and she went silent. As Pershing approached the bed, the Indian raised his head.

"Daniel," the Tarahumara said softly. Then closed his eyes and lay back.

"Where is President Roosevelt?" General Pershing waited a moment, but the Indian did not stir. He looked at the nurse who shook her head.

"Haadi'a tsét'soyé," the Indian croaked, opening his eyes.

General Pershing cocked his head. "What?"

The Tarahumara breathed in softly and whispered his next word. "Hemingway."

302

"Hemingway? The journalist they found on Black Mountain? What happened?"

The Indian lifted his head and spoke with urgency. "We found Chindi." Then he closed his eyes and settled back.

"Found what?" Pershing leaned closer.

"The Valley of the Monks." Then the Indian lapsed into unconsciousness.

General Pershing straightened up and looked at Major Harbord and the Nurse with exasperation. "What the hell does that mean?"

An explosion rocked the tent. One entire side collapsed and Major Harbord shoved General Pershing out the far side. They could hear rallying cries from the south end of the camp. Smoke and debris filled the air leaving them coughing and hacking, and they stumbled over a dead soldier.

Absolute pandemonium broke out. Half-dressed soldiers ran to and fro. When a flying boat soared overhead and shot down into the Camp, pack animals broke free of their tethers and headed for open country.

As Pershing and Harbord made their way across the camp, one young soldier went running past them, rifle in hand.

He stopped and turned to them. "Do you need an escort, General?" The corporal had a dazed look with his hair mussed, but other than that he looked fine except for the fact that he no longer had a left arm. A badly burnt stump protruded from a ragged and bloody sleeve.

Both General Pershing and Major Harbord stared at the corporal, then each other.

"No, son. I'll be fine." General Pershing said hoarsely.

The corporal slung the rifle over his right shoulder, saluted and ran toward the front.

General Pershing and Major Harbord followed, amidst the chaos and tumult another flying boat soared by and soldiers fired uselessly into the air. The two men got within a hundred yards of the main defense line when they saw the figures in the distance, kicking up a dust storm as they approached.

The Winged Hussars lined up across the horizon and charged. First at a slow trot, then they picked up the pace with a canter.

When they broke out into a full gallop, Lieutenant George Patton stepped to the front and raised his sword. "Sabers, men!" Patton shouted.

Dozens of soldiers stood up, pulled blades from their sheaths and moved to the front. Patton marched forward in long strides, his sword up in front of him.

Two hundred yards away, the Winged Hussars doubled their gallop speed and lowered their twenty-foot lances. Their wings rattled and howled and filled the valley with an eerie sound.

*"En garde!"* Patton shouted as he ran forward, and the soldiers moved to stay with him, keeping the line.

A flying ship sailed overhead, parallel with the line and the ground exploded around them. But the swordsmen did not break rank.

"Do not seek the blade of your adversary!" Patton shouted, still running. "Aim for the man!"

The Hussars charged as if the hounds of hell nipped at their heels now, crossing a hundred yards away, then in the next moment fifty yards.

General Pershing held his breath as the Winged Hussars clashed with the Americans. The swordsmen waited until the point of the Hussar lances came within the furthest reach of their swords, then lunged. This forced the Hussar lances to the outside, as the blade slid up the length of the shaft, exposing the riders, and the next instant brought half the Hussar regiment down.

As soon as Patton's blade struck a Hussar and pierced his chest, Patton withdrew the blade, turned on his heel and shouted, "Charge saber!"

Every able-bodied swordsman responded to Patton's call, and assumed a position of the lunge to the right, twisting the sword wrist and bringing the weapon to eye level.

The Winged Hussars scattered, finding their ranks open and broken. Many turned and charged back into the line of swordsmen. Others simply broke ranks and tried to retreat, and got picked off with rifles. Some lancers continued towards the front line, thinking the men would scatter as before. But the American line held.

When the Hussar cavalry charged back through the swordsman line, this time hardly a single American fell. Riderless Hussar horses took off across the desert by the dozens and the Americans let out a cheer.

# INTERLUDE 108
April 8, 1917, 9:22 am
Mochogueachi Valley

The soldiers had already walked since the sun came up and now found themselves in the lower part of the canyon. Only a trickle of a stream and a few standing pools marked the bed of the arroyo.

"They having a drought?" Bullock asked T.R. as they rode side by side in the baking heat.

The ex-president shook his head. "The whole stream is still here. It's just underground."

Raymond Robbins ran up next to the two. "What do you mean, it's underground?"

"In the dry months, the water in many areas shifts to underground flows, where it cools." T.R. pointed to the pools. "If you put your canteen there, you'll find cool, clean water, filtered through the rocks."

Several USVC broke from the column to replenish their water.

"Mark these spots and return at high water. It's the best fishing in the world where the trout hide all year long. The Indians call them *Ojos*, the eyes. You'll find a different species of rainbow trout for every river here." T.R. pointed to a waterspout emerging from a slice in rocks formed over thousands of years. The water came down in a perfectly formed jet, splashing and disappearing into the ground.

Robbins ran over and stuck his hands under the stream. It knocked his hands apart and he stood back, surprised. "It's freezing. And it felt heavy. Dense even." He stuck his face into the stream and his head came back soaked. "That's wonderful," he exclaimed.

The caravan paused as the men one by one filed by the spout, soaked their sunned faces, and filled their canteens. Even Colonel Roosevelt Bullock grabbed handfuls of water and slicked their hair back.

The Volunteers continued for another mile as the canyon narrowed, and the day grew hotter. The Tarahumara took a trail that led them up to a ridge covered in yellow pine. The path led the men through the dense foliage and out into the open.

The sun bore down and the soldiers were shading their eyes with their hands to see any distance ahead. Then they were hiking down again, through another pine grove with junipers.

Just as they descended below the tree line T.R. looked east and tapped Bullock on the shoulder. "Look at that," he said, pointing.

In the distance, a series of magnificent black rock spires jutted up from the landscape, towering over the hills and treetops, cutting a line across the horizon like a mighty fortress wall.

"You are in Valley of Monks now," Tarahumara said softly.

They could see they were in a narrow arroyo with cliffs so high the stream cutting the gorge would appear as nothing more than a shady line from above. The uppermost canyon walls faded into shadow, but the light reflecting off the sycamores jutting out from the cliffs in patches lit everything brilliantly.

"The temperature's dropped," Bullock remarked.

"Yes. You won't be able to find a spot on the map that'll have any live water in May. But I'll wager the water trickles up from the ground and runs along here and keeps this little valley green and lush all year long."

Then the group emerged from the pine grove and there, incredibly, an Apache village spread out before them. Dozens of tipis framed from long poles and covered with hides formed at the far end of the small canyon. Several more permanent structures with domed roofs stood in the town center. Beyond that, the valley narrowed such that a man could touch both cliff faces with his hands.

"Oh, my God," Bullock whispered. The Volunteers all stood still as the Indians slowly made their way toward the newcomers.

The Tarahumara glanced at the ex-president. "I will tell them you are the leader of your people." He held out his arms and called out to the people. "Chu huí tangwaci mohora belú!"

"No one reaches for their weapons. Remember, we need their help," T.R. said.

Two figures emerged from one of the wigwams. One of them appeared to be a young white man with jeans, only he wore a breechcloth and had a leather headband. The man who emerged behind him stood well over six-and-a-half feet tall and had a long mane of blonde hair and a braided beard. Singing Bear smiled and waved.

# INTERLUDE 109
### April 8, 1917, 10:57 am
### White Rocks Above, Cerro Mohinora

"I woke up after the plane crashed and wandered around until I found water," Ernie said, as he rode alongside his favorite President. He looked around at the Apache braves carrying bows and arrows, riding amongst the Volunteer soldiers with their British SMLE's slung over their shoulders. "They saved me. Took care of me." He had a huge grin, but lowered his voice, "There were times I figured momma would mourn a missing son."

"And now we're going…" T.R. let the sentence trail off.

"The hunters are going to take us back to the Devil's Valley." Ernie glanced at the young Indian riding in silence beside him. Owl still had not gotten over the death of his brother.

"The Devil's Valley?" repeated Colonel Bullock as he and the ex-president glanced at each other.

"That's what the Ndee call it. It's where the rotters are from."

Henry Stimson riding behind them spoke up. "Pardon me Colonel, but we shouldn't we let Camp Columbus know?"

T.R. shook his head. "They are engaged in the effort towards war in Europe gentlemen. If they were distracted it might prove detrimental. This is why we are here, to make sure they are not."

"Do we have enough men for this?" R.H. Channing asked.

"Do what you can, with what you have, where you are," T.R. said, ending the discussion.

They rode in silence for a few minutes before T.R. spoke again and nodded towards Chief Bronco. "Who's the big man?"

Ernie broke into a huge grin again. "That's Chief Bronco. The Apache killed his family and took him prisoner as a young boy and made him a member of the tribe. Now he leads the last of the free people." He leaned over, grinning. "They made me a member of the tribe. First, I thought they were going to kill me. Then they helped me get better after I hurt my leg in the crash." Hemingway's eyes widened. "Then they were going to kill me again because I had one of the evil stones in my bag!"

"Evil stones?" Bullock asked.

Ernie nodded. "It came from one of the Thing machines. I think it's what gives them their power. I brought it with me." He shook his head. "It scared them. Scared me after they showed me what it can do!"

T.R. and Bullock glanced at one another.

"How do you communicate with them?" George Roosevelt asked from behind.

"Chief Bronco speaks a little English," Ernie said, glancing over his shoulder. "But the Tarahumara have helped. I guess they went and got you."

"Yes they did, young Hemingway," George nodded.

"We are going to White Rocks Above. I've never seen anything like it. It's amazing, Mr. President. The massive white boulders are stacked higher than any building I've ever seen. They shine in the sunlight like starlight. And these two Indians crossed the canyon with ropes a hundred feet in the air and—" Ernie stopped himself and glanced at Owl. The young Indian paid no attention. "They were the best. Zip, zip, quick as you please."

"What else have you seen?" T.R. asked.

"Well, I'll tell you, sir. I've never been on a plane before and I've never been in a crash before. But we didn't crash because the engine quit or a drunken pilot!" He sat tall in the saddle and nodded. "Something reached out and knocked us down." He waved his arms. "No, it grabbed us and threw us around."

The party reached a narrow part of the valley. Owl dropped

down, pulled out the lengths of rope he carried, and scaled the rocks in an all-too-familiar pattern. But this time, another Apache joined him and no one laughed or let out whoops of excitement. The young man's mourning fell over all the Indian riders.

T.R. looked at the Indians, then Ernie. "What's the matter with them? They're suddenly quite solemn."

Ernie lifted his chin toward Owl. "His twin brother got killed by one of the Thing machines."

# INTERLUDE 110
April 8, 1917, 12:03 pm
Cerro Mohinora

On the far side of the canyon, the ex-president stood watching as John Parker and Frederick Burnham crossed hand over hand on the pulley line last and admired the ingenious mechanism.

"Remarkable," he said softly.

Then they were up and crossing the top of the mesa. T.R. noticed that many of the Apache that had crossed with them were no longer in sight and paused in his stride.

"Where did the other Apache go?" he asked the Tarahumara.

"To get prepared," the Indian said softly.

The remaining Indians all paused at a high point on the plateau, still far from the rim of the hidden valley. They just sat and listened. William Donovan groaned and his knees popped as the sat down. Several Apache glared at him, then went back to listening.

Ernie crawled next to Captain Bullock and the ex-president and leaned in, near enough to whisper. "We're close. Everything's covered with lava rock from here on."

"What are they waiting for?" Bullock asked hoarsely.

Very softly, there came a small shudder across the petrous plateau. Everyone held their breath and crouched a little lower. The hiss-thump footsteps of the monstrosity got louder.

"For that," Ernie said, eyes wide with horror.

The men watched between rock crevices as the Thing machine came into sight from behind a rock outcropping and stepped onto the lava rock clearing. The Indians and the Volunteers had only fifty feet of rock behind them to the cliff with a hundred yards of open space ahead of them.

"Our backs are up against it, boys," T.R. muttered and readied himself.

The Tarahumara put a hand on the ex-president's shoulder gently. The Thing machine took four more steps, standing in the center of the mesa, and paused. Two coils of rope descended around the monstrosity and it looked up.

On the rocks above them, the group could see two Apache, Owl and another young Indian. They each had the rope tied around their waists and they jumped from the high cliff. Before it could bring its weapon arm up or shout alarm, the Thing machine slammed to the ground, dragged over the rocks past the Indians and Volunteers and disappeared over the edge. A second later they heard a tremendous crash as the monstrosity hit. Several of them ran to the edge to see the two Apache dangling halfway down the cliff from another set of ropes and cutting the ties to the inhuman thing lying in pieces.

Owl waved, but his grim visage never changed.

Quickly the group moved towards the far edge of the mesa, crouched low and peering carefully over the edge. The twin-Galleon mother-ship hung ominously in the air, soldiers in black uniforms patrolling its decks.

From where he lay, T.R. could see nearly the entire top of the crescent canyon the huge ship occupied. Slightly to his right, he caught movement. The spotted jaguar bounded from one precipice to another. The ex-president turned to Seth Bullock with a huge grin and gritted teeth. "Battle!"

Chief Bronco waved to his warriors. Each took out their bows and a single bone arrow pulled back and released. In seconds, every Silesian soldier lay dead on the deck of the ship or the floor of the canyon below.

313

James Garfield and R.H. Channing opened their satchels and pulled out several grouped sticks of dynamite. Parker set his satchel down as Channing pulled out two bundles.

"All American Football," R.H. said with a grin. James Garfield struck a match, lit two fuses and ran to the edge. He reached back, hurled the bundle fifty yards like a perfect spiral, and watched as the first landed perfectly on the deck of the nearest Galleon. The former quarterback paused, and every man watching held their breath.

Then the dynamite exploded. The concussion put a massive hole in the main deck and collapsed one of the main masts. It toppled over the side, pulling cables and a few wandering rotters with it.

Channing leaned back, Garfield lit the next bundle and it shot out in another perfect spiral and went right into the gaping hole. The second explosion cracked the wounded Galleon in half. It hung loosely, connected with beams and rope to the second Galleon, burning slowly.

The Indians and Volunteers let out a triumphant cheer.

Channing shouted "Give me more! Give me more!"

Garfield ran over to his bag and opened it, then look confused. "What the hell?"

T.R. came over. "What's wrong, man?"

"The dynamite's gone!"

Captains Bullock and Groome studied the rest of the men and the Apache with irritation.

"Who took the damn dynamite?" Groome asked.

Everyone remained very still, glancing at one another, the imminent danger overwhelming.

Then softly, Chief Bronco asked, "Where is Owl?"

The men all fanned out across the black rock mesa.

Ernie went back towards the tunnel. He dropped into the crevice and caught a glimpse of a moving figure. Following for a few yards he came, once again, to the opening at the base of the wall. He knelt down and looked in. At the end of the short tunnel, Owl looked back, sitting on his feet, without emotion. He carried the dynamite, the green crystal they had recovered from the chest of the monstrosity in the tunnel, and a torch.

"Owl, no." Ernie held his arms out, imploring his friend to turn back.

A moment later, Bullock and Groome were standing at the opening, peering in.

"Oh hell," Captain Groome said.

At last, Owl smiled before he disappeared.

Captains Bullock and Groom glanced at one another.

"Run!" Ernie whispered as he leaped to his feet.

# INTERLUDE 111
April 8, 1917, 2:14 pm
Cerro Mohinora

Grinning from ear to ear, Victor Frankenstein peered down into the vibrating machine boring onto the center of the earth. The humming nearly overwhelmed the senses. When AN explosion outside the cave occurred, Frankenstein paid no heed. A few swaying lights and some annoying rubble on the platform caused barely a glance. He crossed the main testing ground, within feet of the magnetic wheels, exulting in the thrumming and the vibrations of the powerful machines as they coursed through his body. *The power*, he told himself.

As Silesian troops began running for the blast door, and more came from inside the facility, Frankenstein stopped and moved down the stairwell. *Now, what the hell is going on?*

Through the outer tunnel, he could see his men standing on the platform beyond the entrance, looking up. Ten feet from the tunnel entrance he saw the first fiery pieces fall into the valley.

He looked up and saw his flagship Cornelius Agrippa, crippled and listing. Half the ship had been broken in half. Masts and debris were coming down all over the place.

*No!* He ran for his Royal Yacht parked on the platform, boarded and immediately engaged the Vim for lift. So quickly did he take off that a Crusader moving to follow only got half-way up the stairs before the ship raised. It carried the half-man

316

for a hundred feet or so before the creature either lost its grip or decided immortality had proved worthless. It tumbled into the rocks below, smashed into several pieces and likely welcomed the hereafter, whatever the cause for its fall.

Owl reached the end of the tunnel, went under the secret ledge and stood on the rim of the cavern for only a moment. Then he scrambled down. He had the pack around his shoulders storing the dynamite and the crystal, and a torch in one hand. With the other hand, he descended the side of the wall, catching a small outcropping or a small crevice. Ten feet from the ground his footing slipped.

The monstrosity hiss-thumped toward the strange noises and falling rocks, it's gun arm moving around in anticipation of finding a target. It nearly stepped on the small form lying in a fetal position before it. The Thing machine leaned over to look closer and pulled the small figure into the air.

Owl dangled in front of the hideous Thing machine, holding the roll of dynamite and the green Vim crystal. The fuse had been lit. He glanced down, then into the monstrosity's mangled features, and smiled.

The scientists and the soldiers all had only a moment to scream before the dynamite exploded, ripping apart the steam engine and the Vim machine. In another moment, everything vanished beyond the event horizon.

# INTERLUDE 112
April 8, 1917, 2:27 pm
Cerro Mohinora

E rnie ran, following Chief Bronco and the other Apache as they crossed back over the lava rock mesa, and veered once again to the right. The ground shook under them and most of them fell to the ground. Cracks appeared in the very mountain itself and a blinding beam of green energy broke off the top of the mountain and shot into the sky. Dust and debris landed all around. Every man covered his head and waited for the rock storm to end, watching in awe. Beyond the crest of the mountain, the valley where they had seen the flying ship, everything glowed green.

The ground continued to shift as the mountain began collapsing in on itself. When the shaking subsided, they moved down the same familiar cliff trails until they were, once again, at the same precipice.

"I don't want to do that again," Ernie said, shaking his head and stepping back from the edge.

T.R. stepped up next to him, peered down at the hundred-foot drop into the river, and looked at Chief Bronco. "I'm an old man. I'm adventurous, but that's insanity."

Chief Bronco smiled and waved them over. On the far side of the cliff, the first section covered in bushes, a set of steps had been carved out of the rock and led down to the ground. It looked narrow and dangerous, but they were stairs.

"Stairs," Ernie said flatly. "Why didn't you tell me there were stairs?"

Chief Bronco and the other Apache grinned and giggled. "More fun," the yellow bearded giant said.

The mountain shuddered and the group went silent and descended quietly in a single file. Themen stepped carefully down the winding staircase hugging the face of the sheer cliff. They were about halfway down when they heard the pounding.

The ex-president held his hand to the cliff face and looked at Captain Bullock. "Something's coming. I can feel it!"

A moment later, a thunderous impact above made the men glance up. Fifty feet above and a dozen feet out, huge chunks of the mountain were punched away, creating a large hole.

The air filled with rock and debris as a Thing machine came charging out of the breach. The half-man half-machine monstrosity roared with fury or pain, flailing its arms.

*It's glowing green,* Ernie thought.

It sailed past the men, on its way to smashing to pieces on the canyon floor below.

The party started down the staircase. Chief Bronco led the way and moved faster now, urgently.

Another roar from above and another Thing machine came through the hole, glowing that same awful green. It pounded around the edges of the hole, first bringing one arm through, then another.

*That's weird. It's like its bigger than the last one. It can't fit through the hole. But that's...*

The monstrosity finally brought the remainder of its body through, its head smashed another two feet of rock out. It looked down at the fleeing men and roared with fury.

Ernie moved quickly to keep the descent going. *That's definitely bigger than anything I've seen.* The Thing machine toppled out of the hole, firing its arm gun wildly as it screamed in madness or pain and sailed past them to crash on the rocks below.

When they reached the bottom, the Apache and the Volunteers dashed across the open area, heading for a game trail into the forest. David Goodrich and Richard Derby, who were the last down the mountain, were the first to hear the noise. The sound of a large object hitting the ground caused them to turn.

David Goodrich looked up, thinking the rotters might be throwing axes or boulders. The son of the rubber magnate looked up just in time to see a green-glowing Aztec rotter hurling itself off the cliff above. As it struck the ground, Goodrich saw the first impact had been made by another rotter. Neither of the undead tried to move. Apparently, a hundred-foot drop proved too much even for the recently resurrected.

Richard Derby decided he couldn't take the chance and put a three-round burst into each rotter's head with his SMLE.

"Hurry men!" Captain Groome shouted, waving the men on as the rest of the group disappeared into the heavy brush. Without a second look, the two men broke into a sprint to catch up as another Aztec body struck the ground.

The Apache and the Volunteers kept running. A fourth rotter body struck the ground as the third one started to rise to its knees. A fifth and sixth body struck the ground in the next moment.

When the trail reached the river, the group crossed a small hanging bridge. Goodrich and Derby were again bringing up the rear, right behind George Roosevelt The three men were halfway across the river when the first rotter appeared. It came out of the brush thirty feet down, glowing green.

"Something's really wrong," Bullock said aloud. The others turned to see what he meant. The fall had smashed the Aztec rotter's face in and the chest looked mangled. But the body gave off the green glow and, as it came closer, they could feel quite a bit of heat emanating from its body.

The ex-president stared at the undead thing, and blinked, not believing his eyes.

"Its arms and legs are pulsing, I think it's growing."

As the growling, howling rotter reached the hanging bridge, everyone could see. The creature stood well over seven feet tall, literally ripping out of the quilted cotton armor and its sandals that were too small for its huge frame.

Captain Groome shouted to the three men. "Move it!" Captain Bullock raised his SMLE and as the rotter took the first step forward, he put three bullets into its head. It shattered the eagle mask and snapped the thing's head back.

Bullock smiled. "Take that you sonofabitch."

The rotter staggered back two steps before it stopped, lifted its head, and moved forward again.

Chief Bronco came up next to Bullock, wielding a huge knife, and sliced through both support ropes for the bridge in one cut. The bridge fell into the Sinaloa along with the rotter and the flotsam disappeared downstream.

# INTERLUDE 113
April 8, 1917, 2:45 pm
Cavalry Camp Columbus

G eneral Pershing responded to the pedal gongs going off all across the southern end of camp. As soon as they started, men began running for positions. General Pershing stepped out of his tent about a hundred yards from the southern border and bent slightly as a flying boat passed overhead. Its four-pounders rained down and explosions erupted around him.

"They make their attack at dusk when the light favors them." He gritted his teeth as Major Harbord ran up. "They won't be trying a lance charge again. Man the tanks."

Harbord nodded, saluted, and barked orders to the tank drivers. "Man the FT-17s!"

Two more flying ships came in low over the far side of Camp, near the rail depot, tore up part of the camp, gained height and circled around for another pass.

General Pershing strode towards the southern perimeter when he jerked to a stop and waited. A stack of pots and pans outside the small mess nearby toppled over the same moment General Pershing's eyes widened. He ran. Small arms fire broke out up and down the two-mile line as he reached the outer perimeter. In the distance, a dust storm approached.

*Am I wrong?* Are they trying another lancer charge? As the first hulking giants appeared in the dusty haze, General Pershing drew a breath. *Thing machines.*

Figures dressed in ancient garb, adorned in paint and feathers, wearing animal head-dress, appeared alongside them, waving their jade axes aloft. Then there were sharply dressed, normal soldiers, waving sabers and adorned in grey double-breasted jackets, riding beautiful black Arabian stallions. Someone amongst them carried a banner with a double-headed eagle crest and an F emblazoned in the center. In the sky, flying ships followed the front line in. *It's an all-out assault.*

Four of the SPAD XIII met the flying boats in the air and one of the SPAD exploded. The other three fired their rocket guns. One of the shots hit a flying boat and it listed hard to port.

"Hold!" Pershing shouted as he came up behind the main barricade. They had stacked a series of crates on top of anything they could move in camp and were shooting over them and around them, using them for cover. Pershing watched as the enemy charged. *Five hundred yards.* He winced as a flying boat blew up a section nearby. *Four hundred yards.* "Now!" General Pershing yelled.

Soldiers clicked latches on the crates and their sides fell, each revealing a gleaming Gatling gun with a box of ammo within, already loaded with a belt of shiny 30 caliber bullets.

As the Gatling guns opened up at four hundred rounds per minute, eight Curtiss R-2's came in from behind the flying ships. Each long-range aircraft had been refitted. The co-pilot seat now had an elevated rocket gun on a tripod set behind the pilot, but high enough for plenty of clearance over the wings and propellor. The co-pilot/gunner now stood in the seat, strapped in with six different belts to keep him in place.

The Curtiss firepower tore into the flying boats before they had a chance to maneuver or fire back and four of the eight craft were ripped apart. Two exploded in a bright flash in mid-air, disappearing behind an event horizon, and the other two spun wildly and crashed into the desert.

As General Pershing watched, the Gatling guns Major Harbord had delivered did their job. They ripped apart the oncoming mass of rotter, man/metal and cavalry. As fast as a belt would run out of bullets two men were there to feed more into the monsters. The killing frenzy went on for at least five minutes before the soldiers realized they had nothing left to shoot at. Two of the flying boats were left, but when the troops lined their Gatlings into the air, one vessel exploded and took the other with it in a bright green burst.

# INTERLUDE 114

April 8, 1917, 3:45 pm
White Rocks Above, Cerro Mohinora

The Volunteers and the Apache scrambled down the cliff-side, keeping in close formation two and three at a time. Their horses were tethered to trees in an overhang just a couple of hundred feet below. Ernie huffed and puffed with T.R. beside him keeping pace. Every few feet a couple of the Apache in the lead would peel off from the group to the left or right, sometimes vanishing around a corner or peeking out from a perch, and more Apache would leapfrog forward to take their place.

Ernie looked back for a moment and saw Chief Bronco pause, then fade into the underbrush. *Got to keep moving.* Ernie stumbled and had to grab the side of the hill to keep from falling. When he glanced back again, Chief Bronco had disappeared. Then he heard the throbbing, humming noise and knew what that meant. In the following moments, all the Apache vanished from sight.

"Get down!" T.R. barked as two flying boats came around the corner, wobbling and drifting. A Thing machine on the forward craft opened fire with its arm cannon but it went by too fast to get a good shot. Gunfire from the flying boat blew up dust and rock shards and ricocheted harmlessly. A couple of Apache arrows bounced off its hull shot from somewhere in the rocks above.

A half dozen rotters leaped from the decks of the crafts as they passed. They glowed green and had grotesquely misshapen figures. They wielded their jade axes high, growled and plummeted, nowhere near close enough to reach the fleeing party.

Ernie watched as the rotters bashed themselves on the rocks or pinwheeled down the cliff as the flying boats slowed and then clumsily ran into each other turning around. *It's like they're drunk or delirious.* Then he watched as the rotters that had smashed to the ground slowly rose again. Their bodies pulsed like they were still growing.

A whirring sound came from high to his right and Ernie looked up to see two Apache standing on a tall outcropping, swinging bolas. The bolas were released and sailed across the narrow valley, landing and securing within rocky crevices on the other side. Ernie watched as the Apache let out dozens of feet of slack so the thick hemp rope didn't hang high across.

The two flying boats had reorganized themselves and were coming back. They hovered about a hundred feet off the ground, trying to line up with the Americans and the Apache as they continued their descent. Gunfire erupted from the nearest craft. The Volunteers fired back with their SMLE's. Two more rotters leaped from the boat and then a hemp rope went taught. It caught the lead craft just above the deck line. The line swept the Thing machine and the last three rotters off, then ripped off the mast and sent the craft wobbling in an upward trajectory where it wandered out of sight.

The rotters on the ground were started to ascend towards them now. Ernie started picking up boulders as large as he could muster and hurling them down. One of the projectiles caught a stumbling rotter square on the head, crushing its skull. It collapsed and did not rise.

As gunfire went off all around him Ernie bent to pick up another rock, but T.R. stopped him and held out his personal .45 revolver. He held the ex-president's gun in his hand, astonished. Snapping back to reality a moment later, he took aim at a rotter climbing towards him. But before he could pull the trigger two

Apache arrows struck the creature; one through the neck, the other through the eye. It tumbled backward down the mountain.

The remaining flying boat slowed and the Thing machine onboard roared in fury. As it screamed, it let loose a furious barrage from its arm cannon, sending Ernie, T.R. and the Volunteers scrambling for cover. Ernie aimed and took a shot but couldn't tell if it went high or wide. A blur of movement made him pause and look upwards.

Rappelling from above, Chief Bronco used the second hemp line to push out from the side of the cliff. He swung out about twenty feet above the flying boat, and let go. The giant Apache landed solidly on the deck of the flying boat, pulled a huge hunting knife and plunged it into the skull of the nearest rotter as it swung its jade ax at him. The mutant rotter stood several inches taller than the yellow-haired Apache but it went down all the same. Two more Apache landed on the boat behind Chief Bronco and engaged three more rotters on the aft deck. The flying boat cruised forward slowly.

Bronco picked up the jade ax from the fallen rotter and moved toward the Thing machine. The inhuman mech turned toward the Apache chief, swinging its arm cannon and growling. Chief Bronco wielded the jade ax, took two powerful strides towards the monster and planted the ax deep in the Thing machine's chest. The creature staggered and Bronco shoved—hard. The Thing machine toppled over backward, arms flailing.

Ernie watched as the two other Apache struck down two of the rotters and tossed the third over the side. Chief Bronco jerked the jade ax from the Thing machine as it started to rise. It thrashed its arms, crushing the taffrail as it worked to right itself. The inhuman mech pounded its metal legs trying to get up and plunged them through the wooden deck. The Thing machine rose halfway up when Chief Bronco swung the ax again. The flying boat continued to cruise forward, slowly.

The two other Apache leaped from the boat, catching the dangling hemp line moving out of reach and clambered up. A cry from the cliff made Chief Bronco turn as he lifted the jade ax

327

for a third strike. He made the final blow, sending the jade blade through the top of the Thing machine's skull. It sat there, in an awkward sitting position, as an Apache hemp line rose up.

The line caught the flying boat in the aft third of the craft and it tilted upward in the rear. Chief Bronco made an enormous leap from the shifting deck and found purchase against the rocky cliff. The wounded Thing machine looked about, dazed, as the rear of the craft tilted up and up until the boat flipped on its own momentum and the mechanized freak toppled out and smashed on the rocks below.

Ernie watched as the capsized craft wobbled and drifted toward the far cliffside. When it struck the rocks, it began a wild spinning action and drifted downward. It spun and drifted down. There were a couple of rotters still trying to get up who couldn't make their broken limbs work nearby when the flying boat crashed into the ground and exploded.

*The horses*, Ernie thought, as a great wall of heat passed over him. He fell to the ground as a green glow enveloped everything around him, then the air around him vanished for several moments.

Half a minute passed before Ernie could breathe again and he sat up. At the bottom of the mountain where there had been a cliff overhang, a dozen Apache horses and evil rotters, only a smoking crater remained. *Well, now we're screwed.*

# INTERLUDE 115
April 8, 1917, 5:22 pm
Mochogueachi Valley

Moving at a steady jog through the Pine and Juniper, the Volunteers were exhausted. The Apache had kept up a strong pace since crossing the river.

The ex-president huffed and wheezed and paused, though he did not lean or sit.

Captain Bullock did the same. "Christ, how long is he going to keep this up," the Dakota lawman gasped, sucking in lungfuls of air.

T.R. pointed ahead. Bullock squinted through the sweat in his eyes. "We're there."

The black rock spires of the Valley of the Monks jutted up above the tree line.

Sloan Simpson and D.C. Collier were bringing up the rear, sweating and gasping.

"Sloan, I don't recall you being this slow on our coyote trip!" T.R. barked.

"Mr. President, I haven't run that far since Harvard."

A shot rang out and Sloan cried out and collapsed, clutching his leg.

The ex-president and Bullock spun around to see the black-clad soldiers coming over the far hill. The next moment D.C. Collier clutched at his shoulder and fell also.

329

"I didn't hear anything!" Bullock squawked, pulling his side-arm reflexively.

T.R. watched the Silesian soldiers approach. "I've heard of some rifles the Austrians deploy in battle. They don't use gun-powder. They propel their bullets with compressed air."

"Holy shit! They can hit us?" Bullock asked, grabbing the ex-president's arm and dragging him lower.

"I would say we are at the far end of their range. The wounds don't look severe. Let's get them up and moving." They helped Collier and Simpson into a thicket of juniper and followed their fellows.

In the brush, they ran into Ernie wearing the ex-president's slouch hat. T.R. smiled at the young man, patted him on the shoulder, and took his hat back.

Bullock pointed towards the river. "We've got company!" he shouted through the trees.

All seventeen Volunteers huddled in a tall thicket, surrounded by felled pine trees. The bullets fired from silent guns whizzed by occasionally. The Volunteer had their SMLE's and shot at that anything moved, or even might move.

T.R. nodded at Captain Bullock. "We can't let them pick off the stragglers. We have to keep moving. We've got to get back to the valley."

"Where did the Apache go?" shouted James Garfield as he fired a round into a scrub brush and a descent of woodpeckers erupted into the sky.

"They know these woods well. They are probably circling behind our enemy," T.R said as he took aim at a black-clad soldier emerging through the trees and fired. The Silesian soldier cried out and staggered back. A moment later, the man reappeared, a hole rending the center of his tunic. Beneath the shredded silk, he glimpsed tight links of chainmail. *Bulletproof tunics.*

The ex-president raised his rifle to fire but not before the soldier got a shot off. Captain Groome behind him went down. He hesitated a split second before taking the shot but the soldier vanished. T.R. bent over to see Groome groaning on the ground, but snapped back up a second later upon hearing shouts. Four Silesian soldiers came charging out of the wood, bayonets out, as they fired a volley.

Garfield and Goodrich ducked the onslaught, but that left the ex-president standing there alone as four men charged straight at him. In four steps the men were going to be on him. Even if the other soldiers were to turn they might not get a shot off in time.

*This could be it,* T.R. thought.

Four screeching phantoms came in out of the sky and slammed into the soldiers. T.R. couldn't believe his eyes. Harpy eagles had just attacked the Silesian soldiers. They were grunting and waving their bayonets, but the birds of prey had their talons dug into the men's faces and necks.

The ex-president raised his rifle and fired three bolt action shots center mass into the nearest soldier. The first burst apart the vest and the second and third shots brought a spurt of blood from the fighter's mouth.

Garfield and Goodrich had raised back up by that time and fired several times, taking down two more. The fourth soldier turned to run and a shot came over T.R.'s shoulder. The bullet hit the soldier in the back of the head and he tumbled forward and didn't try to get up.

The ex-president turned and smiled at Captain Bullock holstering his pistol. He looked up to see the Harpy Eagles soaring up the cliff face before landing on a small outcropping where four Apache warriors were kneeling. The birds each landed on a warrior's shoulder. More gunfire broke out but not in their direction. Both T.R. and Bullock roused the men to move. They would make their last stand in the Indian village.

# INTERLUDE 116
April 8, 1917, 5:53 pm
Mochogueachi Valley

Chief Bronco came jogging into the Apache valley with Ernie and half a dozen of his warriors behind him. The women and children were being led through the narrow passage at the far end by Inda Jani. The Indian runner nodded and followed the last woman and child to safety, disappearing through the

An explosion rocked the little valley as T.R., Bullock and the Volunteers appeared in the midst of the smoke and gunfire. The soldiers were turning and firing back into the trees blindly as they sought cover amongst the tipis and boulders by the river.

"They're throwing grenades!" the ex-president shouted.

Chief Bronco looked a little confused until he saw a small object sail out of the woods and land in the shallows. When it exploded a moment later, he understood and yelled up into the cliffs. "Tú Ndee ...Táági!"

The other Apache offered to help him up the last part of the climb, but Ernie waved it away.

*I didn't get to go huntin. I didn't get to pick a wife, and there were a couple eyeing me real nice. Instead, here I am showing the rest of the tribe I can climb as good as them.*

He pulled himself over the edge. Four other warriors were crouched under an overhang about halfway up the cliff. They were bunched together because a large boulder, about twice the size of a man, sat perched just back from the edge. The Apache had wrapped it a dozen times with thick cords of hemp rope and two lines extended out across the cavern.

Ernie looked across and saw four Apache sitting in a nearly identical overhang on the other side. While not directly across it had a boulder too, and the second line stretched from it back to the overhang.

*What are they gonna do with those?*

The gunfire increased below. Soldiers in black uniforms were appearing out of the pine forest at the far end of the valley. They were firing guns, but they made no sound.

*That is really strange. Silent guns?*

The Americans, towards the narrow edge of the valley, were getting hit hard. Soldiers were getting cut down while others took cover. T.R. lay next to Captain Bullock on the riverbank, crouched in the fading light. Ricochets were going every which way. A Volunteer stood up to shoot back and he staggered and fell, clutching his leg.

*It's definitely gunfire.*

Then more of the black uniforms appeared and charged with fixed bayonets across the open grass towards the village. The Americans were fighting back ferociously. Black-clad soldiers were going down two and three at a time.

The Apache started to move. Four of them crowded around behind the boulder while one stayed to watch. First, the watcher made one hand motion and the other Apache pushed. Then Ernie joined in. When the rock moved slightly, they paused. All eyes on the watcher only lasted a few seconds as he made another hand movement and they all pushed one final time.

"We're going to be out of ammunition in a few minutes," Bullock shouted as he shot twice more.

The ex-president nodded. "It'll be hand to hand." A grenade landed in the shallows a dozen yards from them and showered them with rocks and spray. *The predator is coming. We have to be ready to corner him.*

T.R. gasped as a huge boulder, twice the size of a man, swung down from the cliff. It picked two Silesian soldiers off the ground and smashed them against the far escarpment. The bodies left red smears as they fell and didn't move. The other soldiers paused and fired in the opposite direction, across the face, up into the craggy outcroppings. Then another slab came from down, picked up two more soldiers and smashed them against the nearest face. The broken bodies fell into the village.

The black-clad soldiers began firing wildly in all directions. Nearly a hundred of them were now in the clearing and more were coming through the woods.

Captain Bullock stayed low behind a large boulder, next to T.R., and checked his pistol. "Not many bullets left," the lawman muttered.

"It is hard to fail, but it is worse never to have tried," the ex-president muttered somberly, lying on his back as bullets zinged just over his head.

"Maybe it's not over yet," Bullock spoke with an edge.

T.R. glanced at his friend to find him staring up at the cliffs above the narrows at the end of the valley. He smiled. There on the ridge stood Lieutenant Patton and several soldiers.

Patton had a Vickers Rocket Gun on his shoulder. So did four of the other men. He gave a nod and fired.

As the armaments streaked over their heads the ex-president and Bullock turned to see the 1.59-inch trench-clearing ordnance explode amidst the enemy. Black-clad bodies flew into the air and blew apart like rag dolls.

Gunfire turned the Volunteers back toward the narrow entrance as American soldiers began streaming through, firing their Springfields. Patton and his crew of Rocket Gunners fired another round, just past the treeline, and more Silesian bodies were thrown into the air.

At the same time, the Apache rained their bone arrows down on the soldiers. The shafts pierced stomachs, arms, legs, and heads, staggering Frankenstein's disciplined troops. As good as they were, they could not effectively fight an enemy on the high ground from three sides. A third boulder swung from high on the cliffs, struck two more enemy soldiers, and crushed them against the wall. A triumphant Apache cry went out.

T.R. looked up as two Curtis R-2's came in over the narrow end of the gorge and fired their Rocket Guns on the heels of the soldiers. More black-clad soldiers were tossed in the air and ripped apart and the Silesians pulled back. A moment later, one of the R-2's literally stopped in mid-air. A green glow reached across the sky and gripped the plane, stopping its momentum completely. Then the craft made a three-sixty yaw pitch and dropped into the ravine on the far side of the narrows. A plume of smoke followed a muffled explosion.

The ex-president looked back and could see a large flying boat coming towards them, at the far end of the valley. Larger than the other flying boats, it hovered high above the tree line, coming towards the black rock spires that marked the entrance to the Valley of the Monks. The green beam of energy pulsed out from the flying vessel. The second Curtiss banked sharply and disappeared over the mountain, away from danger.

A volley of four-pounders from the steam cannons slammed into the narrow end of the gorge. U.S. Soldiers were battered, torn apart and sent running from the onslaught. Still, the Americans kept coming through, firing back at the Silesian soldiers who were still holding to the tree line.

# INTERLUDE 117
April 8, 1917, 6:17 pm
the Royal Yacht Johannes Trithemius

Victor Frankenstein stood on the flying bridge, shaking with anger, teeth clenched.

*My crack soldiers and cavalry are failing. The Cornelius Agrippa is crippled. The Vim accelerator is destroyed. Dozens of my Crusaders have been obliterated. I can create more but I cannot allow this nuisance to continue. I need more time.*

"Full stop," he barked to the drivers seated in front of him. The Royal Gunboat slowed and hovered, with the black stone spires a dozen yards ahead.

He watched as his bow gunners aimed the Thunder of Archimedes into the small valley and tore everything apart. *Movement along the canyon walls. Two guns is too slow. The enemy has much of the high ground.*

He glanced at Commander Aders standing next to him. "How many Needlefish do we have?"

Aders studied Frankenstein and swallowed. "Three craft, my Prince."

The muscles in the Prince of Silesia's face visibly clenched. "Send them in." Then added, "Direct them to clear the cliffs and bluffs where the enemy is hiding."

Commander Aders gave the Roman salute, turned and nodded emphatically to the senior signalman, who had been watching both men. A bead of sweat had broken out on his forehead. The Silesian spoke into his microphone, giving Aders a Roman salute.

"They are moving now, my Prince," Aders confirmed.

The three Needlefish gunboats crossed over the Johannes Trithemius in the waning daylight, their shadows casting across the flying bridge. The moment they were beyond the bow, their steam cannons opened up into the cliffsides. The four-pounders tore into the formations and rocks, boulders and Apache flew off the canyon walls.

"Continue the barrage along the far end of the valley," Frankenstein said coldly. He watched with ferocious satisfaction as the American soldiers were torn apart, with little room to hide.

"Die, Yankee," he muttered. Then the look of pleasure turned to astonishment.

As the first Needlefish crossed over the towering black spires, something went wrong. The green glow that emanated from the center of the flying craft's deck flickered. The boat rocked side to side and lost altitude. As the other two Needlefish crossed over the spires, the same thing happened. The green glow on the first vessel went out and it dropped out of the sky, smashing into the forest below. The other two, recognizing the danger, tried to turn. Their green energy evaporated and they collided with one another as they dropped out of the sky. This time, when they hit the ground, one of them exploded and a fifty-foot area of the forest vanished.

"No!" Frankenstein screamed.

The Royal Yacht shuddered.

"My Prince, we're losing power," one of the drivers sitting in front of him said.

"Perhaps we should withdraw, sire," Aders said, a tick in his cheek.

Frankenstein's sword came out and crossed in a wide arc, making barely a ripple in the air. The whole move finished in half a second, and the Prince of Silesia's arm came to his side before Commander Ader's head rolled off his shoulders.

"Forward," Frankenstein growled. He glanced at his signal-man and screamed, "Fire!"

The helmsmen went rigid, stared straight ahead, and pushed the Royal Yacht forward.

The Thunder of Archimedes opened up from the bow placements and ripped up the valley again. The Royal Yacht passed over the black spires and the men on the deck held their collective breaths.

"Cowards," Frankenstein muttered, glancing around. The lights flickered for a moment, then returned as the ship moved ten, then twenty yards beyond.

# INTERLUDE 118
April 8, 1917, 6:35 pm
Mochogueachi Valley

The Volunteers shouted with triumph as the three needlefish crashed at the entrance to the valley. The explosion and the loss of their air power caused the Silesians to pause their attack. T.R. and Bullock and several of the Volunteers who still had ammunition continued to fire, holding the black-clad enemy to the tree line.

Lieutenant Patton appeared next to Colonel Roosevelt, a Vickers Rocket Gun in his hand.

"Mr. President, glad to see you are alive and well." Patton rose, placed the Vickers on his shoulder and fired. The hit took out a section of woods and several Silesian soldiers.

T.R., lying on his side, glanced up the canyon wall. As the flash of battle illuminated the cliffs. he caught sight of the spotted jaguar, peering from a narrow breach in the rocks. Another explosion made him blink and then the animal vanished. *Had it really been there?*

Steam cannons fired from the deck of the large flying vessel coming at them. Two soldiers came alongside Patton, each carrying a Rocket Gun. They both fired at the flying ship. The rockets streaked through the sky, exploding against an invisible shield that shimmered green with each impact.

Then the tremendous impact of four-pounders stopped. All eyes were on the flying vessel as it staggered in the air. The lights flickered on board. Patton and the other two stood and reloaded their Vickers.

"Hit it again!" Patton roared.

Three rockets streaked out and slammed into the bow of the flying boat. Smoke billowed and the craft dipped nose-first. The pilots struggled to right the ship but lost the vain effort. It crashed into the river and settled on its back in the shallow water.

T.R. stood and raised his pistol, leading the American charge against the Silesians as two shapes appeared in the starry sky. Two B-type American airships, each more than a hundred and fifty feet long and carrying a gondola to hold dozens of men, dropped low into the valley and hovered over the forest area. Silesian air rifles shot up the airships and, in response, the blimps each released two aerial bombs into the forest.

After the aerial bombs exploded, the Americans waited for signs of more hostility. Slowly, black-clad soldiers began walking out of the woods with their hands in the air.

A scream from behind them made T.R. and his men turn. An American soldier who had been investigating the crashed ship sank to his knees, toppling over into the water. The upside-down door kicked open and Victor Frankenstein stepped out, holding his sword.

"Who is a man of honor?" The Prince of Silesia barked, a trickle of blood running from a cut on the side of his head. He stood poised and calm and raised his sword.

T.R. started to move but a hand landed on his shoulder, pausing him. He turned to find Lieutenant Patton beside him. Patton looked at T.R., nodded, then dropped his rifle to the ground and drew his saber as he stepped forward.

Frankenstein stepped downstream, past the stern of his crashed gunboat, and Patton came at him. As the Lieutenant grew parallel to the main section of the boat there came a deafening roar and a Thing machine burst from the innards of the craft, firing its mechanical arm towards the village and reaching out for Patton.

Patton deflected the first grab, slamming his saber against the inside of the arm and causing it to miss. The creature roared with anger and swung the gun arm towards the Lieutenant. Then the creature stopped, its roar of fury dying in its throat. Its mouth remained open, its eyes blazing with anger. It staggered a moment, then rocked forward and fell face-first into the river, its back stitched with bone arrows from the Apache on the cliff above.

Patton pulled his gaze from the unreal sight just as Frankenstein charged, his sword held high.

The Master of The Sword did not back up and did not hold his weapon defensively. Instead, Patton pointed the saber of his own design at the rushing Silesian Prince. Here he comes. Patton held his sword out in a stance to keep him at bay. *Steady.*

The moment before he came within reach of Patton's sword, Frankenstein thrust with the maximum force possible. Patton parried sharply and slapped his blade aside. The Prince of Silesia frowned.

Patton smiled and stepped sideways, feinted, and twisted his body slightly to the left making a riposte counterattack. The blade just scratched the vest of the Silesian, and he withdrew quickly, making a mock salute.

Frankenstein glared at the American with disbelief, his feet firmly planted, left foot forward. Then slowly drew his second sword, holding them over his head.

"Ichi-ryu," Patton said with admiration.

"I shall not kill you quickly out of respect," Frankenstein sneered and brought his right sword down, holding his left in defense, then alternated with the left sword in attack and his right sword in defense.

*He doesn't feel the need to move his feet. Mistake,* Patton thought. Recognizing the Silesian's longer reach, he extended his body so that he bent forward, his arm lifted parallel to the height of his eyes, carried his left shoulder forcibly behind him, and thrust his saber out underneath Frankenstein's counter-strike.

Frankenstein flicked the thrust away with ease and smiled as Patton lifted his right foot off the floor. *The fool is going to make another thrust.* He cut down fiercely slightly to his left where he expected the American's body to be. His sword passed through open space.

*Lift the foot as a head fake and move,* Patton thought as he spun, his body making a complete rotation. The whole action moved his body eighteen inches away from Frankenstein's cut. The energy created by his body's motion created a strong thrust almost ninety degrees away from where Frankenstein has expected him to be. The blade went deep into the Prince's chest, and upward. Patton rotated his wrist and withdrew the blade quickly.

Frankenstein looked at Patton with total shock and coughed up blood. *The little bastard,* he thought. With bloody phlegm smearing his lips he sneered and swung again, moving forward. The American made a beat on his blade and Frankenstein thrust, seeing Patton's blade slightly off-target for the moment. *I'm going to crush him.* He used his whole body and took three steps to close the gap, bringing his advantage of weight and reach to bear.

*Taunted you into charging,* Patton thought. He stepped to the right as Frankenstein came forward, his saber catching the outside of the Prince's left sword and forcing it to miss him. But the Prince's right sword came down in a slicing arc and caught Patton on the right thigh. He cried out.

As Frankenstein moved past him, Patton did not turn, gritting his teeth in pain. Looking back and down at his foe's feet, Patton held his breath and lowered his sword.

Frankenstein turned and, seeing Patton wounded with his back to him, went for the kill. *Eliminate the fool,* Frankenstein thought. He moved into a bind motion with his left blade to block an upper thrust and made a hacking motion with the right. *He's going to try to strike upwards. It won't save him.*

*He's expecting a low blow,* Patton thought. Instead, he moved his forearm to the horizontal and without turning around extended the blade forcibly to the rear as he bent his body backward from the hips up. The body motion once again provided the most thrust possible.

At the same time Frankenstein's sword came down across Patton's left shoulder, the American's saber passed completely through Frankenstein's heart and out his back. Grunting with pain and gushing blood across his chest, Patton turned. He held onto his blade embedded in Frankenstein's chest as the Silesian prince slumped to his knees.

The mighty and nearly-immortal Prince of Silesia looked up into Patton's face. "A worthy opponent," he rasped. He coughed and hacked, dropping his sword.

"There is so much more to the Vim." Frankenstein smiled. "The Adept is going to bring them home. And then the Masters will rule. The time of Man is short. You have stopped nothing."

Patton withdrew his sword and the Prince of Silesia's heart convulsed and stopped. He groaned, fell over and sank into the shallow stream.

# INTERLUDE 119
April 9, 1917, 7:22 am
Over The Sierra Madres

The ex-president and Ernie stood next to one another and the pilot, watching Copper Canyon grow distant as they gained altitude. Already, the flat land of the Chihuahuan desert could be seen in the far distance in the light of the rising sun.

"I'm going home," Ernie said. *See you soon, mother.* Beneath them, the Apache and Chief Bronco watched them go, their faces fading in the dim light as the ship rose into the sky.

*They wanted me to stay. Made me Ndee. But Charlie understood. I have to go back. I have an intention for my life.*

"Where do you think they'll go?" he asked.

"I don't know, son. I think they probably feel pretty safe where they are. I'd like to know what made those flying vessels crash."

"Chief Bronco said the Devil couldn't fly in the sacred valley."

Both of them looked down at the towering black rock spires that formed a sort of barrier against the rest of Copper Canyon, then they were above the clouds and they faded from view.

The ex-president laid a hand on Ernie's shoulder. "So tell me, son, what are you planning on doing when you get back?"

"First, I'm gonna go home and kiss my mother. Then tell my father he should be proud of me. Then I'm going to wire the editor of the Kansas City Star and tell him I'm going to Europe." Ernie smiled. "I want to write about the war."

"Well, you know son, I came looking for one last war to fight and I forgot my most important rule: the hunt is not always about the kill. I wanted one last battle to ride into history, and it came where I didn't expect it. I think maybe I'll ring up your editor and make sure he knows what a fine war correspondent you would make. You know, maybe I'll even write with you!"

"Oh, I don't know if I want to be a reporter. I want to be in the war. I saw myself, what I would become. I'm going to do what I can to help in the war, and then I'm going to be a really great writer."

"Saw yourself?"

"Yes sir," Ernie said, staring out at the sky. "They call it a sweat lodge ceremony. I saw my future if I want it. The Apache has a simple and practical view of life. You become your intentions."

The ex-president smiled and nodded. "Yes, you do."

# EPILOGUE
September 23, 1919, 9:31 pm
Tianjin, Austro-Hungarian Colony, China

The Old Concession, founded in 1860 under the Treaty of Nanking, sat between the Jingshan Railway in the East, and the Haihe River in the West, effectively encompassing several dozen square miles. In the hands of the Europeans for more than half a century, the vast majority of structures were imposing deco hotels, corporate office buildings, and even castles. The area had been divided among the major European powers but now, with the close of World War One, and the collapse of one of the governments, the property in Tianjin would be redistributed.

The property in question this evening, within a week of the dissolution of the Austro-Hungarian Empire, sat overlooking Hangzhou Bay. The magnificent four-story Tudor Revival mansion sat on more than twelve pristine acres of well-tended woodlands, with twin elongated red brick chimneys at each end. It had been built with brickwork on the ground floor and half-timbering on the remaining floors, with small square windows.

The Americans who crashed the gate, led by the young Sergeant Barnes, didn't care about its steeply pitched roof and prominent cross gables. Nor did the soldiers care about the rich interior, the marble and hardwood entry hall nor the carefully crafted wood-paneling of the staircase.

Sergeant Barnes ordered the men up the stairs, arresting every servant, cook, and maid. No one put up a fight. They progressed all the way to the fourth floor, at the end of a very long and luxurious hallway, filled with famous works of art. The soldiers were growing tired of searching. They fired shots into the Tudor style ceiling which showcased molded plasterwork in delicate, geometric patterns, and Sergeant Barnes barked at them to stop.

When they got to the end of the hall, they did not find the massive arched oak door locked. Sergeant Barnes opened the door slowly and stepped in, his gun confidently at his side. The room glowed an eerie green, throwing a strange shadow over everything. Only a single bulb glowed at the back of the room.

A young woman sat on an ornate couch ten feet in front of them with a blanket over her legs. She had on a beautiful nightgown that did not hide her endowed figure. Several of the soldiers snickered.

"Get up, " Sergeant Barnes barked, motioning with his rifle.

The woman did not move as sounds came from the blanket.

Three soldiers raised their rifles threateningly.

"Take off the blanket," the Sergeant said. "And get up. I won't tell you again."

With a French accent, the woman purred. "But Sergeant, the young man is so very sick." She pulled the blanket back to reveal the quivering body of an adolescent boy, his back to them, curled in a fetal position in her lap.

"You are prisoners of war of the United States government. The Austro-Hungarian Concession is to be divided among the U.S., the British and the French. We'll decide what to do with you later." The Sergeant motioned with the rifle. "Let's go."

Allefra sighed. "Very well then, if you please, turn on the lights."

The Sergeant opened his mouth with a sneer but one soldier flipped a switch next to the door before he could get a word out. The green light disappeared and the chandelier above came to

347

life, bathing the room in normal incandescent light. Allefra stood up, but the boy on the couch screamed in pain.

"What's wrong with him?" The Sergeant asked. He shouted over his shoulder, "Medic!"

"I told you, he's very sick." She stepped away from the couch. "It's a full moon, you see."

A medic ran over and knelt beside the crying figure. As he got near, the figure turned and lashed out, biting the Medic on the throat. The soldier went to the ground with a gurgle, spraying blood. The other soldiers raised their rifles as the figure rose with a chunk of the Medic's neck in its mouth.

The Sergeant tried to yell for his men to fire, but the woman standing next to him had her hand on his throat. No, not quite right. *Her hand is holding a long blade, and she has stuck it in my throat.* The woman became a horrible rotter with sunken eyes and ghastly teeth—and rotten breath that he smelled as he died.

The young man stood up on the couch, raised his hairy snout and deadly claws into the air and howled. Then both horrors descended on the soldiers. Screaming, crying, agony and lots of blood followed.

# AFTERWORD

**Theodore Roosevelt**, the 26th President of the United States, would go on to write *The Foes of Our Own Household*, an indictment of Woodrow Wilson and the Great War. A work which is largely attributed to the Democrats regaining control of Congress in 1918. Quentin Roosevelt would be shot down over Europe at the age of 20, something T.R. never recovered from.

On the morning of January 6th, 1919, Theodore Roosevelt died in his sleep. The sitting Vice-President put out the following statement: "Death had to take Roosevelt sleeping, for if he had been awake, there would have been a fight."

Roosevelt dictated his final article to the Kansas City Star on January 3rd, 1919, writing alongside Ernest Hemingway until his death.

**Ernest Hemingway** would go on to Europe and serve as an ambulance driver. From his war experience over the next decade, Hemingway would write a number of books about war. Among them, The Sun Also Rises. It explored the themes of love and death, the revivifying power of nature, and the concept of masculinity. In 1954, he would be awarded the Nobel Prize for Literature for his collective works.

**Seth Bullock** became the first person to erect a monument to Theodore Roosevelt on his death. He erected a Friendship Tower on a high hill just outside Deadwood. Today it is called

Mt. Roosevelt. Seth Bullock would die of colon cancer the September after Roosevelt's death.

Many of the Volunteers who served with Roosevelt or helped raise troops for the effort went on to serve in corporations and government. William Donovan would found American Intelligence, known as the OSS.

**Sadie Orchard** would die after giving everything away, with just enough money for Mr. Ying to bury her in Truth or Consequences.

**Kermit Roosevelt** would serve in both World War One and World War Two. He committed suicide in 1943.

**George S. Patton** would command the Third Army in France following D-Day and died December 21, 1945, under mysterious circumstances following a long and distinguished career.

**General John Pershing** would command the U.S. forces in World War One and would become the only officer promoted to *General of the Armies* rank in his lifetime.

Some people believe that the giant blonde chief of the Apache, **Charley McComas**, died in a bar fight in 1940. Many are certain that no free Apache wander the wilds of Copper Canyon in the modern age. Still, others point to reports of missing hikers, missing cattle, and places where even the drug smugglers and the marijuana growers won't go. In 1958, Jason Betzinez, a Chiricahua who had been with Geronimo, wrote in his autobiography that, as of that date, the Broncos and their descendants were still out in the mountains, and free.

Terry Mark is a former presidential campaign advisor and webmaster in the NHL. He currently works for a marketing company in northern Colorado, ranked one of the best places to work according to GlassDoor.

He lives with his very patient wife and adorable dog.

*Book One of*
# THE VIM HOOD CHRONICLES
## AVAILABLE ON AMAZON IN PAPERBACK AND KINDLE!

*KILL THE NIGHT* is an adventure stretching from Paris to New York, through the 1893 Chicago World's Fair, to the Old West.

Nikola Tesla and Thomas Edison are in a race to see who will be the first to light an entire city. But the night holds tightly to its dark corners. A mysterious gunslinger is watching and waiting for the opportunity to turn back history. He will chase Tesla, Edison, and journalist Ida Tarbell across the Kansas plains to the mountains of Colorado.

Believing their electricity will end everything he loves, the gunslinger has one objective—stop the inventors and destroy their inventions. He must not let them *KILL THE NIGHT*.

Made in the USA
Columbia, SC
08 September 2022

66535746R00217